"The future cannot be prevented now," The Prophet told Buffy. "Already the clockwork grinds on. But I can show you my vision, so you may see what is coming and perhaps better prepare for it."

Reeling, Buffy glanced at Willow and Oz, then at Xander and Anya. They all seemed as stricken by the specter's words as she was. *Prediction*, Buffy told herself quickly. *It isn't fact yet. We don't know it's true.*

But it felt true. The words of The Prophet were heavy with finality. With doom.

Buffy swallowed, then looked at the oily silhouette again. "Show me."

"I must only touch you, and you may see."

"Do it," Buffy instructed her.

The Prophet's slick, shimmering form slithered forward. The tear in the fabric of the world extended toward her, fingers like tendrils reached for her.

"Buffy," Willow said cautiously, a tiny bit of fear tinging her voice. "Maybe this isn't such a good—"

The Prophet touched her

Invaded her.

Buffy screamed.

Buffy the Vampire Slayer™

Buffy the Vampire Slayer
  (movie tie-in)
The Harvest
Halloween Rain
Coyote Moon
Night of the Living Rerun
Blooded
Visitors
Unnatural Selection
The Power of Persuasion
Deep Water
Here Be Monsters
Ghoul Trouble
Doomsday Deck
Sweet Sixteen
Crossings
Little Things

The Angel Chronicles, Vol. 1
The Angel Chronicles, Vol. 2
The Angel Chronicles, Vol. 3
The Xander Years, Vol. 1
The Xander Years, Vol. 2
The Willow Files, Vol. 1
The Willow Files, Vol. 2
How I Survived My Summer Vacation,
  Vol. 1
The Faith Trials, Vol. 1
Tales of the Slayer, Vol. 1
Tales of the Slayer, Vol. 2
The Journals of Rupert Giles, Vol. 1
The Cordelia Collection, Vol. 1
The Lost Slayer serial novel
    Part 1: Prophecies
    Part 2: Dark Times
    Part 3: King of the Dead
    Part 4: Original Sins

Child of the Hunt
Return to Chaos
The Gatekeeper Trilogy
  Book 1: Out of the Madhouse
  Book 2: Ghost Roads
  Book 3: Sons of Entropy
Obsidian Fate
Immortal
Sins of the Father
Resurrecting Ravana
Prime Evil
The Evil That Men Do
Paleo

Spike and Dru: Pretty Maids
  All in a Row
Revenant
The Book of Fours
The Unseen Trilogy (Buffy/Angel)
    Book 1: The Burning
    Book 2: Door to Alternity
    Book 3: Long Way Home
Tempted Champions
Oz: Into the Wild
The Wisdom of War
These Our Actors

The Watcher's Guide, Vol. 1: The Official Companion to the Hit Show
The Watcher's Guide, Vol. 2: The Official Companion to the Hit Show
The Postcards
The Essential Angel Posterbook
The Sunnydale High Yearbook
Pop Quiz: Buffy the Vampire Slayer
The Monster Book
The Script Book, Season One, Vol. 1
The Script Book, Season One, Vol. 2
The Script Book, Season Two, Vol. 1
The Script Book, Season Two, Vol. 2
The Script Book, Season Two, Vol. 3
The Musical Script Book: Once More, With Feeling

Available from SIMON PULSE

The Lost Slayer
Omnibus Edition

by Christopher Golden

Based on the hit TV series created
by Joss Whedon

SIMON PULSE

NEW YORK LONDON TORONTO SYDNEY SINGAPORE

Historian's Note:
This serial story takes place at the beginning of
Buffy's fourth season.

First Simon Pulse omnibus edition January 2003

Prophecies™ and © 2001 Twentieth Century Fox Film
Corporation. All rights reserved.
Dark Times™ and © 2001 Twentieth Century Fox Film
Corporation. All rights reserved.
King of the Dead™ and © 2001 Twentieth Century Fox Film
Corporation. All rights reserved.
Original Sins™ and © 2001 Twentieth Century Fox Film
Corporation. All rights reserved.

SIMON PULSE
An imprint of Simon & Schuster
Children's Publishing Division
1230 Avenue of the Americas
New York, NY 10020

The text of this book was set in Times.
Printed in the United States of America.
2 4 6 8 10 9 7 5 3 1
Library of Congress Control Number 2002112878
ISBN 0-7434-1226-5

These titles were previously published individually by
Pocket Pulse

Contents

Part One:

PROPHECIES

CHAPTER 1

All dressed up and no one to slay.

A chill wind blew off the Pacific Ocean. Buffy Summers zipped her navy blue sweatshirt up to her throat and shivered, just a little. All right, it was November, but still, Southern California in November was not usually quite so brisk. She was tempted to pull her hood up but there was something just a little too gangbanger about that look for Buffy's tastes.

As Buffy walked along the waterfront, she stuffed her hands into the pockets of her sweatshirt and grumbled softly to herself. Her gaze darted around the wharf and the canneries and the large shipping vessels out on the water. Sunnydale had its share of gorgeous California beaches, but this wasn't one. This was Docktown, the part of town the Chamber of

3

Commerce desperately tried to divert tourists from. In a way it was surprising these streets were still on the map.

Patrol had been completely uneventful thus far, and it was growing late. Midnight had come and gone and by all rights Buffy should have long since returned to her dorm. She had class at ten minutes to nine the next morning and she was determined not to oversleep. Now that college had started, she was turning over a new leaf. The Watchers Council held as conventional wisdom that a Slayer could not carry on a personal life and be effective in the war against the forces of darkness.

Come hell or high water, Buffy intended to prove them wrong. She would be the most efficient, most effective Slayer who ever lived. But she would also immerse herself in the college experience, both socially and academically. In high school, she'd failed to balance the two, had really made a mess of things a few times. But college was going to be different. Maybe she'd never be normal, but with the enhanced physical capacity that came with being the Slayer, she believed she could juggle it all.

If she managed to get to class in time in the morning.

What the hell am I doing all the way out here? she thought.

The answer came back quickly, and what a simple one it was: *the job.*

She was doing exactly what she was supposed to be doing. Buffy was the Slayer, the Chosen One, the one girl in all the world with the power to combat the forces of darkness.

Tonight, though, things had been quiet. Patrolling Sunnydale was a vital part of her work as the Slayer. But when patrol was slow, that was when a bit of doubt might creep in; doubt that she would actually be able to pull off the balancing act she was attempting with school, her mom, her friends, and slaying.

What she needed now were action, adrenaline, and a nice, juicy monster or two. See Buffy. See monster. See Buffy kick monster's ass. It was what she needed to keep her focus.

A scream rent the night air with the blunt brutality of a gunshot. A quick and violent instant that caused Buffy to flinch even as its echo died above the waves.

Despite the ominous quality of that scream and what it might mean, she could not hold back the ghost of a smile that flickered across her face. Heart pounding in her chest, Buffy sprinted along the wharf. Her legs pumped as she ran past the harbormaster's quarters on one side and a long, ugly concrete building that housed several shipping companies' offices. She waited for another scream but none came. At Dock Street she instinctively turned toward town and ran alongside a liquor store and half a dozen run-down multifamily homes mostly utilized as boardinghouses, renting rooms to fishermen and merchant sailors.

Halfway along the next short block she saw the

cracked and flickering neon sign that hung in front of The Fish Tank. Experience told her that was her destination. There was no activity out front so Buffy stopped short at the entrance to the stinking alley beside the bar, a place so sleazy calling it a dive would be an insult to dives everywhere.

No scuffle in the alley.

Buffy frowned. Her instincts could have been wrong. She looked around, alert for any sign that might lead her to the screamer. Patrol had taken her here before; The Fish Tank was just the kind of place that bottom-feeding vamps afraid to draw the attention of the Slayer liked to hunt, thinking it beneath Buffy's notice. It wasn't.

A muffled laugh came from farther along the alley, deeper in the shadows.

Something was going on there in the darkness, where things let out small giggles weighed down with sinister intent and gleeful perversity. It was amazing all the evil a laugh could contain.

Buffy ran the length of that darkened alley between buildings, then paused just at the corner of a building, her back to the brick wall. To her left there was a small paved area behind The Fish Tank lit by a single bulb above the back door. In its sickly yellow glow she could see an open Dumpster filled to overflowing with shattered beer bottles and the remains of what the place mockingly called food.

It was a narrow drive that ran behind a number of the small businesses on the block, and Buffy was amazed that somehow a garbage truck fit itself back there at least once a week.

It stank, sure. But more important, it was remote and dangerous, with the buildings on one side and a chain link fence on the other. It wasn't a place anyone would go by choice.

Yet somehow they'd gotten the woman back there—a woman all by herself.

Vampires.

Three of them crowded around the woman, who had screamed once and then had been unable to scream again. They were locked onto her as though they were entranced, one with his mouth on her throat, fangs piercing the soft flesh and a small rivulet of blood dribbling down to stain the collar of her Aerosmith T-shirt, and the other two at her arms, also suckling her blood but not quite as sloppily as the first. On their exposed skin Buffy could see markings, unfamiliar symbols she could only assume had some arcane meaning. The rest of their bodies was covered in leather.

The woman was maybe forty and had no business in the Aerosmith T-shirt and cutoff denim shorts she wore—unless she was a regular at The Fish Tank, where head-banging rock and hard drinking were the order of the day and a woman could be twenty-four and look forty, and still the guys would get all crazy around her.

What a life. Buffy didn't understand places like The Fish Tank or the people who went into them.

But she didn't have to understand to care. To act. To

take vengeance. Given that there were three vamps feeding off her, and the way she hung in their arms, completely limp, eyes without any spark, Buffy knew the woman was beyond her help.

Too late, Buffy thought bitterly.

From a sheath at the small of her back she withdrew a long stake with a smooth grip and a sharp, tapered end. She liked to feel its weight in her hand. With a single breath Buffy stepped out of the alley and into the dimly illuminated drive in front of the huge blue Dumpster.

The vampire whose fangs were buried in the woman's neck grunted and looked up at her. He had a black tattoo across his face, a bat with its wings spread, eyes peering out from inside each wing. A gnarled symbol shaped like a bonsai tree was carved into his face at the jawline. Bonsai's eyes narrowed.

At first Buffy thought it was just a trick of the jaundiced light, but then she realized it was no illusion. The vampire's eyes glowed a faint orange; a kind of energy seemed almost to radiate from him, to crackle around his entire body.

This wasn't like any other vampire she'd ever seen.

For a moment it threw her off. Then she chuckled and shook her head as she thought about how badly she had been itching for a fight. *Careful what you wish for,* she thought.

"I can't decide," the Slayer declared, her voice sharp and clear in the brisk night air. "Could be you're in a gang. Sunnydale Flying Rodents. Something like that,"

Buffy said, ticking off possibilities on the fingers of her left hand while still clutching the stake. "Could be you got lost on your way to some comic book convention. Or, possibly, you've just gone all freaky-geek over *The Matrix* and now have no life outside the film."

The vampires let the woman's lifeless form slump to the filthy pavement and she saw that the eyes of the others also sparked with that unnerving orange glow and exuded an aura of energy so different from other vampires she had fought. All three of them, it turned out, had bat tattoos across their faces, around their eyes. The overall effect was profoundly disturbing. They moved slowly toward Buffy, forming a half-circle around her, as if to prevent her from running away. Of course, she had no intention of running.

"Then there's always *D*," she said idly. "All of the above."

All three of the vampires snarled at her, their fangs glistening in the dim light, eyes blazing. When they moved it was as one, a savage onslaught that would have made her think them barbarically stupid if not for the air of dark intelligence each of them had. Yet they were silent.

Buffy didn't like them silent. The ones who were cocky and boastful were easy kills. The silent ones were usually more dangerous.

With a single hiss they lunged for her. Buffy backed herself up against the metal Dumpster as if they had her cornered. Her lip curled with disgust from the stench and from the company.

She waded into them. The one on her right was inches ahead. She ducked past him, under his reach, then came up fast with her elbow and rammed it into the back of his head, cracking his skull between her bone and the Dumpster without ever looking at him.

Bonsai reached her more quickly than she had anticipated. Even as she turned to thrust her stake at him, he was on her. Powerful hands wrapped around her throat and he lifted her off her feet with a strength that surprised her. All vampires were strong, but this was something more. The creature thrust her against the Dumpster hard and her head clanged on the metal. Had she been a normal human, it likely would have been over for her then.

But she was not a normal human being. She was the Slayer.

Fireworks went off in her head and black circles appeared before her eyes. The beast choked her harder, and Buffy could not get even a single breath of air. Her eyelids fluttered for a moment and she felt a kind of terrible exhaustion, a dark fatigue, sweep over her. Though she beat at his face and chest with her hands, pulled at his fingers, she could not break his grip. She wondered if it was the vampire's somehow draining her of energy, or just the lack of air.

Not that it mattered which. The key was breaking Bonsai's grip on her throat. Over his shoulder she saw the other two, the one recovered now, just hanging back and waiting with hyena grins.

Those grins pissed her off.

From a primal place deep within her she summoned all the strength of the Slayer. With the Dumpster at her back, she hauled up her legs, planted her feet on his chest, and shoved him away. Her hands thrust up and her fingers clung to the top of the Dumpster. The other two ran at her and she swung her feet up and kicked them both away, then dropped to the pavement in a crouch.

While trying to break free, she had dropped her stake. Now she snatched it up as the trio ran at her again. Bonsai was in the lead. He came at her, barely defending himself, as though confident her escape was merely a fluke, that his power was superior. She thrust her stake into his chest and its tip punched through his heart. The vampire's eyes went comically wide, outlined by the black bat tattooed across his face, and then he exploded into cinder and ash with a muffled thud.

The Slayer was determined not to be surprised by them again, and not to let any of them get their hands on her. Whatever had supercharged them, whatever made their eyes burn with that dark orange glow, she thought it might also allow them to leech energy from a person the same way their fangs could leech blood.

The other two came at her fast. Buffy landed a high, spinning kick that knocked one away, but the other, whose body was the most heavily tattooed with arcane symbols, kicked the stake out of Buffy's hand. It went skittering along the pavement into the shadows. The vampire grabbed her by the hair and she felt some of it give way, her scalp beginning to bleed, as he hauled her backward to expose her throat. The face of the beast stared down at her, those orange, blazing eyes almost mesmerizing, and the vampire dipped his fangs toward her neck.

Buffy frowned deeply. *Can't let him weaken me any more.* She slammed her head up into his face, splintering his nose and causing him to stagger backward.

"What, are you kidding? You go up against me, you go for the kill, moron. That Nosferatu intimidation crap doesn't work on me."

Even as she spoke she moved in, fists flying. He tried to defend himself but the vampire had no hope. He had lost the upper hand and would not be allowed to get it back. Buffy spun and kicked him, bones in his chest cracking as he flew backward and slammed against the chain link fence that ran along the back of the narrow drive.

Buffy found the stake.

The two vampires rushed her again, and it occurred to her that these monsters were not only somehow enhanced, but also a savage but regimented breed. The tattoos showed organization, and organization among vampires was not only rare, it was a very bad sign.

Buffy snapped a side kick at the one on her right, then spun and shattered the other's jaw with another swift kick. He went down. She dropped down with him, stake in her hand, and then he was dust. The breeze off the ocean swept him away with the stink of rotting fish and stale beer.

On his knees, the survivor moaned.

Buffy kicked him over. He slammed into the Dumpster again. She grabbed him firmly by the throat and held the stake to his chest, just above his heart.

"The tattoos. What are they?" she demanded.

The vampire grinned, licked his own blood off his lips and red-stained teeth. The skin on his forehead was split, a wound in the image of the bat.

"I don't like that you guys are all marked the same. I don't like that you're so quiet. I don't like that someone's embellished the vampire formula here. I want answers. You can tell me what I want to know and die easy, or I'll stake you out buck naked on the roof of one of those concrete bunkers that pass for offices down the street and you'll burn inch by inch as the sun comes up. New and improved model or not, I have a feeling you'll still torch."

The vampire flinched, the thick ridges of its monstrous brow deepening, and a growl built low in his chest.

Buffy pressed the point of the stake hard enough so that it punctured the skin, put all the weight of her body on the injured vampire, and returned the same snarl the creature had been giving her. She kept an eye on his hands, just in case he tried to sap her strength as Bonsai had.

"This kind of marking, the way you guys move together. There are more than three of you. How many? Who's in charge? Where can I find them?"

"You won't need to find him," the thing growled,

his voice raspy and thick with an accent Buffy did not recognize. "Camazotz will find you. And his followers are legion."

"Where?" she demanded.

He laughed at her, a throaty, knowing, evil sound. Buffy stood up, kicked the vampire in the chest, then hauled him to his feet and slammed him against the Dumpster again.

"Here comes the sun," she said with forced levity. "You're toast."

In the distance sirens began to wail. Buffy glanced over at the back door of The Fish Tank and saw eyes—human eyes—watching from within. The door was open four or five inches, but when she looked over it was slammed shut.

The sirens grew closer.

The last thing she wanted was to have to answer questions. There was no time to haul the vampire down the street and hoist him on to a roof. Buffy felt a dark anger rising inside her, but she shook it off. Nothing to be done about it. Plus it wasn't like she could baby-sit the thing all night and still make it to class in the morning.

"Last chance," she told the vampire. "Final Jeopardy. Can't ya just hear that theme in the background?"

His orange, feral eyes sparkled with cold fire, unafraid.

Buffy dusted him.

"So much for saving Giles some research," she muttered.

The corpse of the vampires' victim was sprawled against the back of The Fish Tank with her Aerosmith T-shirt rucked up under her arms. Buffy knew she was dead but she knelt down beside her and felt for a pulse. She couldn't walk away without checking. But there was nothing, of course.

The sirens screamed closer.

Buffy got up and began to sprint away from the scene, along the backs of the buildings where other trash bins awaited pickup. At the end of the block she paused and glanced back. Blue lights swirled in the drive. Police cars roared up the narrow way usually reserved for garbage trucks. Buffy rounded the corner and the lights disappeared behind her.

She slipped her stake back into its sheath. Earlier she had been cold, but now she was too warm, so she unzipped her sweatshirt and tied it around her waist. A bell rang on a buoy out on the ocean and the salt air felt good, invigorating.

When Buffy at last lay her head upon her pillow, sleep would not come. Every time she closed her eyes she could see those burning orange eyes and feel powerful hands upon her throat, the drain of the life force within her. Her mind whirled as she thought about this new breed of vampires. Their tattoos and attributes unified them. They were a single unit, not a group of individual scavengers. She would have to talk to Giles the next day, get to work on figuring out what she was up against.

At last, exhausted, Buffy drifted off to sleep, and she dreamed.

She dreamed she was back in Docktown. . . .

Orange eyes blazed in the shadow of every alley. Buoy bells echoed up from the wharf, where the surf rattled wooden timbers and crashed against the sea wall. A chill breeze whistled through cracked windows in a darkened storefront off to her left and whipped bits of trash along the street. An empty beer bottle rolled along the pavement with a tinkling of glass like mournful wind chimes.

Buffy quickened her pace. They were not attacking, the beasts in the shadows, but she did not like their eyes upon her. They made her feel weak, skittish, like an animal about to bolt into traffic. . . .

When she looked up, her path was blocked by a ghost.

Buffy recoiled, prepared to defend herself, her heart beating wildly. But in a single eyeblink, she relaxed again. It was a ghost in front of her, that much was true. But this particular phantom bore her no ill will. In fact, the dead woman whose spirit drifted intangible and translucent before her had been a Slayer herself centuries before.

"Lucy?" Buffy stared at her, stunned.

The spirit of Lucy Hanover now walked the ghost roads, the pathways between the world of the flesh and the hereafter, helping lost souls find their way to their ultimate destinations. She had aided Buffy sev-

eral times, but usually appeared to Willow, apparently somehow in tune with Willow's magick.

"I come with a warning, Buffy Summers," the ghost said, her voice a wisp, like dry leaves rustling in the breeze. "In my journeys I have come upon the soul of an ancient seer. The Prophet tells of horrible events about to take place."

Through the ghost's shimmering form Buffy could see the street beyond, a Dodge up on blocks, a dog on a rusted chain that ran toward the street and began to bark. At the dog's alarm, Buffy glanced around, hoping the police would not hear and come to investigate.

But she knew there would be no police. She knew this was a dream. With the Slayer, however, a dream was rarely just a dream. Though it took place upon the dreamscape, Lucy's visitation was all too real.

The sound of the surf crashing beneath the docks nearby almost drowned out Lucy's words, so soft were they.

"It will be your fault," the ghost said.

"What's that mean?" Buffy asked. "What will be?"

"I cannot be more specific as yet. I will search for The Prophet again and see if her vision has grown clearer. Until then, I can only say be wary of all that you do and of all the dark forces gathering around you."

The ghostly Slayer shimmered again and then dissipated altogether, first into what looked like static on a television or spatters of rain on the windshield, and then Lucy was simply gone.

Buffy stared at the space where she'd been. The dog kept barking.

Her eyes fluttered open, but only for a moment. An abiding sense of dread had been planted within her, and it lingered in the back of her mind even as she fell back to sleep.

"Great. Thanks," she muttered as she drifted off again. "That was very helpful."

Yet it was not the last dream she would have that night.

Nor the worst.

CHAPTER 2

"Buffy."

In the dream, she slept in Angel's arms, by a blaze he had set to burn in the enormous stone fireplace at the mansion. Though she knew that his embrace was all of him that she might ever hope to enjoy, still his strong arms around her gave her a deep and abiding sense of contentment. Of peace. It was a peace that her waking hours never afforded her, particularly not of late.

Bliss.

Yet bliss quickly gave way to a kind of dark suspicion. Her sleeping face creased with a frown. There was a malignant presence attempting to worm its way into her mind, to draw her from Angel's tender caress into a world of chaos and horror and sadness.

"Buffy!"

It reached for her, icy grip on her bare shoulder, the warmth from the fire leeched away in an instant. Buffy shook her head, tried to deny the creature's power. She glanced at Angel, but he slept on unaware that she was being attacked, that she was being taken from him.

"No!" she cried, and flinched away from the thing's frozen touch. The Slayer lashed out with a powerful backhand. . . .

"No!" Buffy snapped, as she sat upright in bed, eyes barely open, vision fogged by the remnants of dream. Thoughts slipped slowly back into place in her mind, as though tearing away cobwebs that had been spun there while she slept.

Once, twice, Buffy blinked. Her knuckles stung with the echo of a blow she had landed only a moment ago. She glanced down at her hand and then, horror mounting in her chest, turned to her right, where her best friend and roommate, Willow Rosenberg, sat holding a hand over a growing welt on her face. Willow's eyes were wide with shock, her mouth open in a little "o" that would have been comical under other circumstances.

"Oh God, Will," Buffy muttered groggily. "Oh . . . I was . . . I was dreaming. I'm sorry."

Willow frowned and rubbed her cheek. "That's the last time I try waking you up." With a frustrated sigh she grabbed a light sweater off the back of her desk chair and began to slip it on.

"Are you okay?" Buffy asked. She climbed out of bed and pushed her sleep-wild hair away from her face. "I just . . . I don't know what happened. I was having this dream and I guess you waking me was part of it, but in the dream you were this horrible monster that wanted to . . ."

While Buffy had been talking Willow had gone to the mirror in their room and begun gingerly to touch the still-growing red welt on her left cheek. Willow winced when she poked at it a bit too hard. When Buffy, horrified by what she had done, stopped speaking to watch, Willow turned to face her.

"Your alarm went off a bunch of times. You hit the snooze. Then you turned it off. That was half an hour ago. Since you have class in, like"—she glanced at her watch—"seven minutes, I figured I'd better wake you up. You said you couldn't afford to miss it."

Buffy's mouth opened, but no words came out. She shook her head and let out a long breath. "I really am sorry, Will. I was out really late on patrol last night. Guess I just got carried away with the sleep thing. Can I make it up to you?" she asked brightly. "Mochaccinos on me?"

For a moment longer Willow's grumpy expression remained. Not that Buffy blamed her for it. Then, suddenly, it dissipated as if it had never been there, though the welt remained. Willow offered her patented shy, half-smile and rolled her eyes slightly.

"After last class this afternoon. I want lots of whipped cream. I'm so weak." She sighed. "I've got to have more practice at staying mad."

Buffy offered a sympathetic nod. "It's not your

fault. I didn't play fair. The mochaccinos are like Willow-kryptonite."

"They do drain my resolve," Willow agreed. "That's the problem with fighting with your friends. Devastating knowledge of your vulnerabilities."

"Exactly why we shouldn't do it. Nobody wins."

Willow flashed a sunny grin at that, then winced with the pain it caused, a hiss escaping through her lips.

"Oh, Will," Buffy said quickly, moving toward her. "It hurts that bad? I hope I didn't crack your cheekbone or something. Let's have a look."

They moved together to a half-open window where Buffy could get a good look at Willow's face in the sunlight. Already the swelling had gone down just a tiny bit, but the redness was quickly being replaced by a dark purplish bruise that was certain to draw attention Willow would likely rather do without.

A cool breeze slipped through the window and Buffy shuddered a little.

"It looks pretty bad. Sure you don't want to cover it up? I've got a pretty heavy base you could use."

Willow shook her head sadly. "No time. Besides, that'd kinda make it look even more like the battered-spouse special, don't you think? I don't want anyone thinking I have something to hide. That'd look pretty sad for me, and even worse for Oz."

"Oz," Buffy repeated, and cringed. "He's gonna kill me."

"You marked his girl," Willow told her with grave resignation. Then she nodded firmly. "I'll talk to him.

See if I can keep him from putting that hit out on you. Anyway, a sparkly new glamour oughta cover it up, I just need some time to do it. Meaning after class. Speaking of which, hello, class? You're a brand-new Buffy, remember? Supergirl. You should get going."

Panic swept through Buffy. The next couple of days were going to be a true test of her resolve about juggling her life. Not only did she have a history exam tomorrow, but a research paper due for soc class on Monday. Now on top of that, and keeping up with her classes, a new crew of nasties were in town to complicate things.

Sometimes she felt like Jekyll and Hyde, Buffy and the Slayer, with one persona taking over and pretty much screwing things up for the other. Accidentally slugging her best friend was a perfect example. But Buffy knew if she worked at it hard enough, she could maintain the balance.

"I'm gonna be a little late," she said. "Professor Blaylock will be annoyed, but I've got to call Giles. There's new talent in town, and I want to figure out what I'm up against."

Willow nodded, concerned. "We'll go over there after mochaccinos this afternoon. Research mode is just a flick of a switch away."

"I got it, really," Buffy said quickly. "You've got other things to worry about."

"So do you," Willow reminded her. Then she shrugged. "I'm here when you need me."

"Thanks. Just give me a second."

She called Giles's number, then grimaced with frustration as the machine picked up. "Giles," she said, "it's me. Patrol was kinda crazy last night. We should talk. I'll try again later."

With a sigh, she put down the phone. Willow watched her impatiently. Quickly as she could, Buffy pulled on a heavy wool jersey and blue jeans. Frantic, she poked around her bureau until she found an elastic to tie back her hair.

"Y'know, after Kathy, kinda wondering if maybe you're not cut out for the whole roommate thing," Willow suggested, one eyebrow arched mischievously.

She was joking. That much was clear. The roommate Buffy had been stuck with at the beginning of freshman year had been as aggravating as they came, a total spoiled brat with bad taste in music and zero social skills. She'd also been a demon, but that was another story.

"You're a riot, Will. Thanks a lot," she said dryly. A smirk touched the corners of her mouth as she sat on the bed to put her shoes on. "Okay, I'm in and out at all hours, but I think I'm a pretty good roommate. And you're not exactly perfect yourself. Wet towels on the rug, CDs all over the place, and never mind the studying. You're up so late cracking the books all the time that I'm getting a total inferiority complex. I mean, Kathy had the whole demon excuse. What's yours?"

When Willow didn't respond, Buffy looked up to find her best friend staring at her with a hurt expression on her face. Hurt that gave way to a deep, angry frown.

"I never said I was perfect."

"Hey. I was just teasing," Buffy said. But suddenly she was not certain of that. A part of her had been very serious about the things she said. They had only come out because she was tired and on edge, but now she couldn't take them back.

She went to Willow and placed a hand on the other girl's shoulder. "Really," she promised.

Willow nodded. "I know. We're both sleep deprived, which brings on the crankies, and trying to figure out the wacky world of college. I feel all sitcom couple-y, but maybe you should try to leave the stress of work at the office. We've got heapin' helpings here already."

Buffy sighed with relief. "Deal. Let me just brush my teeth, then we can take off."

"If it's okay with you, I'm going to go on ahead," Willow replied, heading for the door. "I don't want to be late for class."

"Oh," Buffy said softly. "Okay."

Willow went out without another word and closed the door behind her. Buffy stared at the door for a long moment, playing back the scene in her head. Willow had brushed it off, but Buffy knew the things she had said must have hurt. A punch in the face she could forgive, but half-serious comments about her behavior as a roommate had gotten under her skin. Buffy didn't understand it. She just hoped that over the course of the day Willow would forget about it.

They were best friends. In it together, no matter what.

Meanwhile, the clock was ticking and she was already three minutes late for class.

Professor Blaylock's sociology class was held in the Bibeau Social Science Building, in an auditorium with seating for more than two hundred. It was a popular class, and he was a popular teacher. Fortunately for Buffy, that meant that it was usually possible, when late, to sneak in through the back door of the auditorium, wait for Blaylock to turn toward one of the large blackboards on the wall, and then slip into a seat before he noticed.

She had been late a lot the first couple of weeks, but Blaylock had only caught her once.

Buffy slipped in through the door and went halfway up the short stairway that led up to the back of the auditorium. A thick-necked guy with a crewcut and a nose that looked as though it had been broken at least once glanced down at her and smiled conspiratorially. A football player, she thought. It was not the first time she had noticed him, but they had never spoken.

The guy held up a finger to caution her, his eyes on the front of the auditorium. Buffy could hear Professor Blaylock talking about "the epidemic of depression in America," which she thought might well be his favorite subject. He veered off into manic-depression and the sound of his voice changed as though he had turned away. Buffy glanced expectantly at the football player, who looked over and nodded with a grin.

As surreptitiously as possible, Buffy went up the last few steps and jostled her way past three people, headed for the nearest seat in the last row, right next to Mr. Football.

"Well, well, hello there!"

Buffy froze.

The voice belonged to Professor Blaylock.

Embarrassed, she turned to regard him, all the way down at the front of the auditorium. He had his hands on his hips and he was smiling amiably.

"Sorry," Buffy said sheepishly. She shrugged, then gestured toward her seat. "I'll just—"

"No, no, remain standing, please."

Buffy blinked, surprised, then just stood there awkwardly as every student in the auditorium stared at her, most of them with smirks on their faces.

"Your name, please? I'm sorry I can't keep track of all of you."

"Buffy," she said quickly.

"I'm sorry, speak up, please." He was still smiling, but she realized now that there was no humor in it.

"Buffy Summers," she said, a bit snippily now, as anger replaced embarrassment.

"Ah, yes, Miss Summers. Might I presume that your tardiness is due to a last minute's bit of diligence on your research paper?"

A deep frown creased Buffy's forehead. "Well, yeah. I mean, I'm still working on it."

Professor Blaylock's smile disappeared completely. "Still working on it? Which I take it means that you're not prepared to hand it in at this time?"

Buffy blanched. Her mouth went dry. They were all still staring at her, but some of the smiles were gone. Now their expressions were more like the pitiful glances people gave accident victims as they drove by a crash site.

"The paper's not due until Monday. I . . . I wrote it down."

"Then you wrote it down wrong," Blaylock replied coldly.

For the first time she saw the three large multicolored piles of plastic folders on the lecture table at the front of the hall. In the first row, she saw the professor's two teaching assistants turn to look at her with sympathy. Ironically, that made her feel worse.

"I guess I must have," she said so quietly that she was not sure if he heard her. Not that it mattered.

"I guess you must have," Blaylock repeated, not quite mocking her. "You know, Miss Summers, if you had been on time to class today, it might not bother me so much that you don't have your paper. But I find myself disinclined to believe that this was a simple error on your part."

That made her angry again. "It was a mistake, Professor."

"Perhaps. Or maybe you think deadlines don't

really apply to you. Either way, you don't have your paper, do you? So here's what we're going to do. You take all the time you need, Miss Summers. Until the end of the semester, if you like."

Buffy blinked, even shook her head a bit. "I'm sorry?"

"You should be," Blaylock told her. "But, let's move on, shall we? You may deliver the paper whenever you like, Buffy. But for each weekday that passes, you will lose ten points. The weekend you may have off. As of midnight tonight, Wednesday, you will begin with a ninety. Midnight tomorrow, an eighty, and Monday, a seventy. If you should decide to surrender, take your lumps, and simply never deliver the paper, I guarantee you will fail this course.

Buffy could only stare at him.

"Now you may sit."

Mochaccinos with Buffy had been a huge disappointment for Willow. After her last class of the day let out that afternoon, Willow had walked with her to the Espresso Pump and did her best to keep things relaxed and fun. It was supposed to be a best friend thing, a just-girls thing. But Buffy had been so ticked off by her soc professor's humiliating her, and so frustrated with herself, that it had been a tense, awkward hour together.

Willow had tried to tell her that it was an honest mistake, that anyone might have made it. But Buffy was being so hard on herself lately, holding herself to such an impossible standard, that nothing Willow said seemed to make her feel any better.

It killed Willow not to be able to help.

If she's so set on doing everything herself, what does she need me for? Willow thought sadly.

But it wasn't only sadness that she felt. As she walked across campus to the house Oz shared with some other students, she was frustrated and angry as well. Somebody had to have a talk with Buffy. She was pretty sure that somebody was going to have to be her. But unless she could make Buffy listen, it would do no good. And the truth was, nobody could really *make* Buffy do anything.

With a wince of pain, she touched the bone-deep bruise on her cheek and sighed.

Troubled, she rapped on the front door of the house where Oz lived. It was opened by a silent, towering guy with whom Willow had never exchanged a word and who bore the peculiar name of Moon. Not that, as a girl dating a guy named Oz who also happened to be a werewolf, she had any real problem with peculiar, but she kinda thought a housemate named Moon was more than a little ironic, all things considered.

"Hey," she said, by way of greeting and thank you.

Moon raised his eyebrows and shook a finger at her, though whether in welcome or disapproval she did not know. Then he walked off, leaving Willow to find her way upstairs on her own. In his room Oz sat on the floor with a fat-bellied acoustic guitar on his lap, working a complicated series of chords that were proof that he was a more talented musician than he would ever admit.

"Hey," Willow said softly as she entered the room.

Oz glanced up and grunted in surprise. His normally impassive face twitched enough that Willow could almost have said he had made an expression. Not that he *never* made expressions—she'd made him smile often enough—it was simply that they were rare.

"Nice shiner." Oz kept strumming but he missed a note as he said it.

"Woke Buffy up this morning. She was having a nightmare, I guess. Not something I'm all aching to do again. And, okay, best friend and all, so I forgave her, right? Kinda part of the gig. But then later she was just so . . . I don't know. Off?"

Oz studied her with great concern.

Willow went and sat on the floor next to him. Oz watched her and began to strum something soft and sweet, a blues riff she'd heard him play before. Just keeping his fingers busy. *He probably doesn't even know he's playing,* Willow thought.

"I mean, I know all this adjusting is hard for her. But, hello? She's not the only one here. Okay, not exactly out on patrol myself every night, or doomed to die in combat with the forces of darkness, so Buffy does get extra credit. That still doesn't mean she has to be so tense."

Willow paused and looked over at Oz, who had

stopped playing. A tiny smile lifted the corners of his mouth.

"You're her best friend," he said.

"I know," Willow replied with a frown. "But it's not that simple."

"Why not?"

Her mouth opened, but no words came out. Grumpily, Willow narrowed her gaze and stared at him. Then she sighed.

"I know, I know. That means I have to be the cutter of much slack. Which I do! Often! And . . . in this case, maybe not so much. Yes, I'm kinda irked. And not just about the bruise. But I'm also worried. She's putting too much pressure on herself. Superman's got the whole superhero/Clark Kent thing pretty much down, but, hello, comic book character!"

"Next you'll tell me Santa's not real."

"You mock," Willow said grimly, "but I'm serious. I'm guessing this whole Martha Stewart perfection kick is backlash after high school. It must be freaking her out that she has so little control over her life. Even this morning, she's got something cooking . . . 'cause I can always smell something Slayerish cooking . . . but she doesn't want to let anyone in. She has to handle it all herself. Part of the brand-new Buffy mantra. She must feel so alone."

Oz's features were deeply serious now. "But she's not alone," he said.

"No," Willow agreed. "She's not. Which, granted,

is a warm and fuzzy thought, but how do I prove that to her?"

"Maybe you can't," Oz suggested. "Maybe it's something she has to learn on her own."

In the narrow cubbyhole that the woman who had rented him his apartment had deemed a kitchen, but which he had thought looked more like the galley compartment of an airplane, Rupert Giles opened the oven to peek in at the meal he was cooking. The air in the apartment was thick with the rich scents of dinner, and he smiled to himself and hummed a snatch of The Who's "Going Mobile."

Giles opened the refrigerator and reached in to touch the two bottles of Piesporter he had chilling, and was pleased to find them suitably cold. He fished about within and retrieved a block of brie, then pulled a box of crackers down from a cabinet. As he was arranging them on a plate, the doorbell buzzed.

"Hmm?" Giles muttered. He blinked and glanced at the clock on the stove. It was barely half past five, and it was quite unlike his guest to be early.

Curious, he crossed the living room and opened the door. Buffy stood on the welcome mat, the dark canvas bag she carried weapons in slung over one shoulder, and a bemused expression on her face.

"Good evening, Buffy," he said pleasantly. "What exactly do you find amusing?"

She shook her head slowly, her grin widening. "The clothes *do* make the man."

Giles glanced down at himself. He'd dressed casually but with style, as always. *What does she find so . . .*

He blushed slightly. The apron that hung around his neck and was tied behind his back bore a full color image of an enraged Daffy Duck, above which were printed the words "You Want Dinner When?"

"Looks like you're expecting company," Buffy went on. "Is that why you haven't called me back?"

Giles blinked. "Sorry? You called?"

"Five times."

Troubled, he glanced across the apartment at a small corner table in the living room. An old black phone sat by an answering machine that was practically an antique. He had placed a potted plant on the table as well, and the phone and machine were partially obscured.

"I'm terribly sorry," he said as he strode across the room toward the phone. "I was out at the store early this morning, and I've been a bit distracted today. But I'm not deaf. Five times is a bit of an exaggeration, yes?"

Even as he spoke, he slid the potted plant aside and saw the red light blinking on the machine, right next to the number 5.

"Five times," Buffy repeated.

With a muttered apology, Giles turned toward her and shrugged. "Either your timing was pitiful, or I'm even more distracted than I thought."

"Maybe both," Buffy suggested, smiling softly. Then her smile disappeared. "What time's your company arriving?"

Even as she spoke, Giles detected a hint of something in her voice.

"Not for a little while yet," he assured her. "Olivia's coming in for a few days and I've got dinner on, but I'm perfectly capable of talking and cooking simultaneously."

Buffy hesitated. "Don't want to cramp your style."

"By all means, cramp away," he told her as he stood aside and let her enter. "That didn't come out quite right."

"I get it," Buffy said, her tone quite droll. She walked into the living room and slid into the most comfortable chair. "So what are you cooking for your sweetie?"

Giles blinked. "Well, I'm not sure she quite qualifies as my 'sweetie,' but I've made a chicken cobbler she particularly likes."

Buffy stared at him.

"It's . . . well, it's a bit chilly out, and Olivia's never been shy about her appetite, so I thought—"

With a sigh, Giles folded his arms and sat on one arm of the sofa. He regarded her coolly, though quite aware that his cool was somewhat mitigated by the infuriated cartoon duck emblazoned on his chest.

"Now then. We've got trouble, I assume?"

Buffy's expression changed, darkened, as she considered the question. "With a capital 'T,' " she admitted. "I don't know if it's anything really major. Nothing that screams apocalypse or anything. Just kinda weird and I thought, y'know, that you could do some research."

Giles listened carefully to her recounting of her adventure of the previous evening, including the dream visit from Lucy Hanover. When Buffy was still taking orders from the Watchers Council, he had been her Watcher. They had both long since severed ties with the Council, Giles by their choice, Buffy by her own. Yet though she was no longer officially his responsibility, Buffy had come to mean a great deal to him. He might not be her Watcher any longer, but he still considered himself her mentor as well as her friend. She rarely needed him to provide physical backup for her any longer, but the Slayer still needed counsel, and information.

"These vampires are interesting."

"Meaning creepy and a little upsetting?" Buffy prodded.

"Hmm? Oh, yes, precisely that. It's not like anything I'm familiar with. If they hadn't drained that poor woman I'd be wondering if they were truly vampires at all. The energy sap you felt, and the burning eyes, sound a lot more like a demon than a vampire. I'll begin my research with those attributes, and also concentrate on their tattoos. Perhaps they belong to an order or brotherhood that requires it. It may even be the mark of their master, this Camazotz they mentioned.

"The dream you had about Lucy Hanover may or may not be connected. Either way, her coming to you like that is unusual. I imagine she must have had a powerful reason for doing so, and yet her message seems so oblique, so—"

"Annoyingly vague?" Buffy offered.

"Yes, actually," Giles admitted. "You should be extra wary in the coming days. We all should. Perhaps these vampires you met last night are the threat the ghost warned you about. This Camazotz—"

"I got a feeling there were more of them," Buffy interrupted. She shuddered a bit at the memory of the bat-faces. "A lot more."

"I won't doubt your intuition," Giles told her. He thought for a moment. "Camazotz. That does sound familiar, though I can't fathom where I've heard it before. And I really don't understand these tattoos you mentioned. Popular culture links bats to vampires, but as you well know that is only myth."

"Maybe they've seen too many movies," Buffy suggested.

Giles nodded slowly. "Anything is possible."

"I was joking," Buffy said gravely.

He raised an eyebrow, about to chide her, when the odor of burning pastry reached his nostrils.

"Oh Lord, the cobbler!"

In his frenzied rush to the kitchen, Giles rapped his knee on the coffee table and barked in pain. When he whipped open the oven and reached in, the pot holder slipped slightly in his hand and his thumb touched the baking dish. He hissed and put the dish down on the counter, where it promptly began to burn the Formica.

Giles cursed loudly as he slipped a pair of pot holders under the cobbler, too late to save the counter or his poor thumb. He ran it under lukewarm water, then stuck it into his mouth and began to suck on it. Then he remembered Buffy.

He looked up to see her watching him with an alarmed expression.

"How bad is it?" she asked.

Embarrassed, Giles plucked his thumb from his mouth. "Stings, but I'll be all right."

"I meant dinner. Is it salvageable?"

He studied the brown crust on top of the cobbler, then used a fork to break it open. "I think I'll be able to manage, yes. If I can just get some of this burnt part off the top before Olivia—"

The doorbell buzzed.

Giles closed his eyes and sighed.

"Know what?" Buffy said brightly. "I'm gonna go. Patrol. City that never sleeps, and all that? Maybe I'll find some more bat-face guys and I can, I don't know, take a picture or something for you. And . . . so . . . you'll look into this Camazotz guy?"

"Yes. Get the door, would you?"

"No rush or anything," Buffy told him.

"I'll take care of it. I'll call when I've got something."

Buffy had reached the door. She opened it to find a surprised-looking Olivia on the other side. Giles mustered the best smile he could manage, then remembered the apron and quickly tore it off and tossed it across a chair.

"Olivia, hey," Buffy said. "Just leaving. You guys

have a nice night." She smiled at Giles. "Have fun, you two."

Then she was gone, pulling the door shut behind her. Giles looked at Olivia. She had just come off a plane from London, and yet she seemed perfectly put together as always, in dark pants and an ivory top that seemed to make her cocoa skin even more lustrous. Her sweet smile warmed him, and he let out a long sigh.

"You're a sight for sore eyes," he told her.

"You're not so bad yourself," Olivia replied with a mischievous grin. She went to him and slipped her arms behind his back, lifting her mouth to be kissed.

He obliged.

"I'm afraid I've made a bit of a mess of dinner," Giles confessed.

Olivia's eyes sparkled. "Dinner can wait, Rupert."

Xander didn't hear the knock at first. He was sprawled on the floor in front of the television with his fist stuffed into a tub of Planters Cheese Curls. The tape in the VCR was a bootleg Hong Kong action movie called *God of Gamblers,* with the too-cool-for-the-room Chow Yun-Fat in the title role. His mind was occupied with the task of reading the English subtitles that ran in yellow print across the bottom of the screen, so his visitor had to knock a few times before it caught his attention.

With a frown, he glanced up at the door, then back to the television, and he tried to pretend the knock had been in his imagination. Then it came again and he was forced to push himself up from the floor and amble to the door with his hand still stuffed into the Cheese Curls.

"Don't wanna sign up for your new religion," he muttered at whoever stood on the other side of the door. "Don't want to buy steak knives or encyclopedias."

Of course, since the door in question was around the back of the house and led into the apartment he'd set up in his parents' basement after high school graduation, he knew that whoever was out there wasn't some door-to-door salesman. Which saddened him in a way, as he had for an instant secretly prayed that he would open the door and find Girl Scouts out there.

For the cookies, of course. *'Cause, okay, Girl Scouts, pretty much jailbait,* he thought.

Cheese Curls clutched to his chest, Xander pulled open the door. There was nobody out there.

"Hello?"

He stepped out onto the cement stoop and glanced around just in time to see Buffy heading back toward the front of the house. She turned at the sound of his voice and smiled when she saw him.

"Hey, Xand."

"Buffy, hey. To what do I owe the ecstasy?"

"Just hadn't seen my bud in a while and thought I'd come by, see if you wanna do bump-in-the-night patrol with me tonight."

Xander blinked and stared at her. Back in high school, he and Willow and Buffy had been inseparable, formed the core of what he'd playfully dubbed "The

Scooby Gang." They hung around at the Bronze, they hung around in the school library, they hung around in cemeteries. But with college, things had changed. Xander had come out decidedly against anything resembling more school, even though Willow, Buffy, and Oz had gone on to U.C. Sunnydale. The Scooby Gang still existed, particularly in a crisis, but they did a whole heck of a lot less hanging around than they used to. Buffy just dropping by for a one-on-one visit, and asking him to go on patrol, was a bit out of the ordinary.

"Xander?" Buffy prodded, a frown creasing her forehead.

"Sorry," he replied with a shake of his head. "Brain not able to multitask, and I'm having a hard time not making sexual innuendos surrounding the phrase bump-in-the-night."

"Got it." She bounced a bit on the balls of her feet, crackling with what Xander thought of as good old let's-kill-something Slayer energy. "So, patrol?"

Still curious, but happy to be asked, he rubbed his chin in a way he hoped would imply actual contemplation. "Hmm, let me see. Eat tasty snacks in front of beautifully orchestrated Hong Kong action, or get a little exercise, witness it firsthand, and put my life in mortal jeopardy." He shrugged. "Don't ever quote me, but for some reason only my therapist would understand, I think I'll take mortal jeopardy for a hundred, Alex."

Buffy seemed puzzled. "No mention of Anya."

"Out spending money on girl fashions. She said it

was a gender imperative. Whatever that is." He nodded back toward his apartment. "Let me just grab a jacket."

Nearly two hours had passed without any sign of supernatural presence. Buffy had begun to grow discouraged, but she was still more than a little curious about the bat-faced vampires from the night before. The last thing she wanted was to go home empty-handed, particularly since Giles wasn't exactly on fire with the research at the moment. Of course, she could have asked Willow to get started on it—was actually feeling kind of guilty about not doing so—but when they'd met for mochaccinos earlier, Buffy had felt a bit of tension between them. A kind of distance. She didn't like that at all.

Willow was her best friend. She ought to be able to speak her mind if something was bothering her. But, then again, Buffy hadn't exactly spoken up earlier. Both of them had sort of just let the tension drift until Buffy had taken off for Giles's, worried that he still was not answering his phone.

As soon as she got back to the dorm that night, Buffy vowed to talk to Willow, dispel the weirdness that had been between them since that morning. Meanwhile, she deeply regretted having invited Xander to come on patrol with her.

What the hell was I thinking?

But she knew the real reason she had asked Xander along. With Giles occupied by Olivia, and with the awkwardness she felt with Willow at the moment,

Buffy needed someone around to reassure her that she wasn't just the Slayer.

Though she and Xander had patrolled around the Bronze and through the major cemeteries, Buffy had rushed through it and drifted west toward the ocean. There were some very nice neighborhoods near the beach, but they were not her target. She certainly did not expect to find the tattooed vampires back at The Fish Tank again, but once the major hunting grounds turned up empty she decided to sweep the wharf area again. Xander complained about his feet and about the distance, but not very much. It seemed to Buffy that half the time he only brought it up to give them something to talk about, to remind her that he was there.

If it had been earlier, she probably would have pretended to bail on patrol and walked him home, then come back out by herself. He made her laugh, of course. Xander was always good for that. Made her feel like herself, just another nineteen-year-old girl. But that was only on the surface. Underneath, she worried for him, and felt guilty for having dragged him along just to mark "hanging out with friends" off the checklist in her head.

But it would be okay, she told herself. That pressure was part of balancing her life.

She refused to let Professor Blaylock's humiliating her, or the research paper that still hung over her head, or even the exam she had in the morning, shatter her focus.

Focus. That was what it was all about.

The temperature had dropped considerably in the hours after dusk, and she shuddered despite the heavy wool jersey she wore over her shirt. Xander turned up the collar of his jacket. Buffy rotated her head and a muscle in her neck popped, releasing some of the tension she felt. The canvas bag over her shoulder was a minor annoyance, but worth it for the crossbow she carried inside it. Xander had a couple of stakes she had given him stuck in the pockets of his dark brown jacket. Together they walked down a deserted sidewalk in a block of run-down apartments that ended with a gas station on the corner.

Across the street from the gas station was a dingy-looking Italian place called Maria's that Buffy suspected might be Mafia-owned. Next to that was a tattoo parlor, and on the other side of that, the Kat Skratch Club. It was an ugly-looking place with a lot of neon in the window and on the sign, but a layer of grime seemed to sit over the whole thing. A blinking string of letters in the window promised "Live Girls," which Buffy appreciated, considering the not-so-unrealistic alternative was dead ones. The Kat Skratch had topless dancers 365 days a year, according to a hand-painted sign in one window that they spotted as they crossed the street toward it.

"Maybe we should stop in, rest our feet, grab a . . . mineral water or something?" Xander suggested.

Buffy shot him a doubtful glance and Xander put on his wide-eyed-innocence face and shrugged in return.

"Why'd you bring me?" he asked suddenly.

Buffy was surprised by the earnest expression on his face. She would have asked what he meant by the question, but she didn't want to play coy woman with him. Just wouldn't be fair.

"I'm not allowed to miss you?" she asked.

"You're not allowed, you're required," he told her archly. "But there's more going on. You could've asked Willow. Or Giles. Not that I'm anything less than battle-ready at all times. Xander Harris and his fists of fury await the call of combat. But . . . there's a but. You can feel it in the air. A but. So what's the but?"

Buffy nodded slowly and sighed. Then she shot him a hard look. "I do miss you, though."

"Understood."

"I kind of had a fight with Willow. And, y'know, I'm all about the learning now. Got an exam in the morning and I'm pretty much ready. How often can I say that? But I blew a major deadline in my soc class today and I don't even know how it happened. I mean, I'm totally on top of things. Except, apparently, this."

Xander smiled. "You've got a jam-packed life, Buffy. It's gonna get messy sometimes."

Buffy stared. "I can't afford to have it get messy anymore, Xander. Sometimes I feel like Buffy's going to disappear and then there'll just be the Slayer left."

"Not as long as I'm around. That's what your friends are for." Xander's smile disappeared after a moment and he studied her with great seriousness. "Speaking of, what's up with Willow?"

For a moment Buffy tried to find the words to explain not only her argument with Willow, but her feelings about it. Then she glanced over at the front door of the Kat Skratch Club and saw three men and a woman shoving and laughing as they spilled out onto the sidewalk.

All four of them had bats tattooed across their eyes.

Buffy reached into her bag.

"Hold that thought."

Chapter 3

"Wow, you let girls in the club, too? I wish you'd told me, so I could get a goofy tattoo on *my* face."

The four bat-faces glared at Buffy. As they did, their eyes began to flare with orange sparks. The female, cinched and draped in black leather like the others, took a step forward and tilted her head with curiosity, eyeing the Slayer up and down. Buffy had dropped the bag in front of the pawn shop and now held the crossbow in both hands, primed and ready. It was an old-fashioned Chinese model, a repeater, able to shoot six bolts with only a couple of seconds between them.

"What are you supposed to be?" the female asked, an expression of amusement on her face. Her forehead and the corners of her mouth crinkled and Buffy saw that she had caked white makeup on her face, ap-

47

parently to make a more striking contrast with the black ink of the bat.

Buffy returned her smirk. "Me? Look in a mirror lately?"

One of the males, a broad-shouldered goon with a face like a bulldog and a chain that ran from his right ear to his nostril, snorted with derisive laughter. His electric eyes blazed brighter.

"You don't know how funny that is," he rumbled in the same weird accent she had heard the night before. Seemed they all had it.

"Actually, I do."

That gave them pause. All four of the vampires regarded her a bit more closely. A dog began to howl down along the block and several took up the cry in response.

It was chilling. Buffy shivered, but she smiled to cover it. She had faced evils older than man, demons whose depravity would make the bravest soldier weep, and had come out on top. Four wannabes with face paint weren't about to rattle her.

Yet in some way, they did. That bat tattoo was part of it. It spoke on an instinctive level to some primal part of her, and a frisson of fear ran through her that she could not blame on howling dogs. But more so, their eyes bothered her, for with that burning energy came her memory of the way the one the night before had sapped her strength. If she had not broken away when she did, she would have been powerless.

Powerless. Nothing frightened her more.

Xander had approached them with her, a good six feet back and over her left shoulder, just where she wanted him. Now she sensed him shifting slightly, perhaps unnerved by the dogs.

"Not sure I like the math here, Buff," he whispered.

The vampires glanced quickly at him, as one, almost like a pack of dogs. One, whose bat tattoo spread its wings almost all the way around his bald head, licked his lips. Then they grinned and turned their attention back to Buffy, and their faces shifted all at once, their fangs protruding from their mouths, their brows growing thicker and more bestial.

"Nobody likes math, Xander," she said, almost under her breath. "But we do it. For instance . . . subtraction."

Buffy lunged.

The vampires rushed her.

"Don't let them touch you!" she snapped at Xander.

With a grunt deep in her chest, right hand holding the crossbow out to one side, Buffy used her left arm to grab the nearest bat-face around the neck and choke him. With her weight on him, she launched a snap-kick high and hard, and the side of her foot caught the bulldog with the nose chain under his jaw. Bulldog crashed backward into the clown-faced girl and they both went down. When she came down, she was still choking the first one that had attacked her. Buffy twisted him around and flipped him onto the pavement. It was a throw her first Watcher, Merrick, had taught her when she was fifteen years old. That was one of the earliest lessons she'd learned as the Slayer. Go with what works.

"Xander!" she shouted.

Even as she turned to defend herself against the bald one, she caught a glimpse of Xander falling upon the one she'd flipped and dusting him with a stake.

Suddenly, Buffy felt a little better. These guys were faster and stronger than other vamps she'd fought, and they seemed to surge with that weird, phosphorescent energy . . . but if Xander could dust one, how tough could they be?

Bulldog was furious at having been knocked on his butt. He had just extricated himself from the clown-faced girl, or was trying to. She bumped into him, cost him a half a second. The bald one rushed Buffy then.

Crossbow held firmly in both hands, she fired a bolt into the vampire's heart, which exploded into dust. The next bolt snapped up into position and she swung the crossbow at Clownface and Bulldog, who froze for just a moment before rabbiting back toward the club. Buffy fired two more bolts before they slammed through the front door of the Kat Skratch, and both of them thunked into Bulldog's back with a wet, tearing noise. He didn't even slow down.

"Happens every time," Xander said as he stepped up beside her. "They see me, they cower in terror and then flee."

"You're a pretty imposing presence," Buffy confirmed. "Really. I think it's the bowling shirt."

Scandalized, Xander glanced down at the blue and

brown shirt he wore beneath his jacket. "Hey, this is very much in style. And, okay, a bit pungent, but Mom's a little behind on the laundry, okay?"

"Your mother stopped doing your laundry when you moved into the basement."

Xander raised an eyebrow. "That explains a lot."

"So," Buffy went on. "Four minus two."

"Equals two. Call me the math whiz. What next?"

Buffy looked at the door to the club. "We keep subtracting."

"Never thought I'd be happy to hear that, but live girls await. Lead on!"

The inside of the Kat Skratch Club was awash with multicolored lights and roiling with music so loud and jarringly discordant that Buffy doubted it could still be called rock 'n' roll. For a place dedicated to the consumption of alcohol and the ogling of half-naked women, nobody seemed to be having a very good time. Bikers and fishermen and dockworkers made up most of the male population of the place . . . which pretty much made up the population of the place. There were very few women there who weren't either onstage or waiting on tables, and Buffy figured most of them were either prostitutes or girls who worked hard at looking like prostitutes.

When she and Xander walked in the bouncer had his back to them, his gaze locked on a girl onstage who wore the remnants of a Catholic-school uniform several sizes too small for her. The bar ran down the entire left wall, and two stages jutted out from the wall on the right. In between there were plenty of tables. Buffy narrowed her gaze against the strobing lights and concentrated enough to cut out most of the music. There was no sign of the vampires, nor any sign that anyone had even noticed them come rushing through.

"Suddenly bump-in-the-night patrol has a whole new meaning," Xander said, voice tinged with awe.

The bouncer heard him. The burly, bearded guy turned to glare at them and his eyes ticked to the crossbow in Buffy's hands, then back to her face. "Only way you're getting in here, girlie, is up on that stage."

"Not that the idea doesn't hold some appeal," Xander told the man, "but you *so* should not have said that."

With a violent twinkle in his eye, the bouncer scoffed and moved toward Xander. "Yeah, weasel? And why not?"

At his most charming, Xander grinned. "Mainly 'cause I'm guessing Lloyd's of London? Not holding an insurance policy on your teeth?"

Just as the burly guy reached for Xander's throat Buffy grabbed the bouncer by the wrist. He winced in pain, stared at her in surprise, then tried to pull away. Buffy held on. He could not break her grip.

"You're not going to touch my friend or me. We're not here to drink. We'll be in and out before you know it. You shouldn't have tried to hurt him."

"You arrogant little—" the bouncer growled, cutting himself off as he threw a punch with his free hand.

Buffy stopped the punch with the stock of her crossbow, then shoved him back, hard. He went down onto the beer-sticky wooden floor without so much as a grunt.

"Five minutes. Then we're gone like we were never here."

The bouncer swallowed once and rubbed his wrist. Then he nodded slowly and began to rise, turning back toward the door to the club. A ripple of angry mutterings went through the club, and onstage two of the girls stopped dancing to stare. A couple of bikers got up from a nearby table and loomed menacingly toward them.

"Sit," Buffy said impassively, as she raised the crossbow to chest level. She would never have shot them with it, of course, but they didn't know that.

They both glanced at the bouncer, then sat down.

"Come on," she said, and then she started weaving through tables, past glaring, thick-necked laborers. Xander muttered something as he followed her, but Buffy paid no attention. They had taken too much time at the door. The vampires were nowhere in sight. That meant either the rest rooms or some other room in the rear. Buffy figured they'd head for a back door, if there was one. She headed for the heavy wooden door at the far end of the bar. None of the lights reached that far, so most of the patrons wouldn't even have noticed the door.

The music kept pummeling the room, the girls started dancing again, and before Buffy and Xander had even reached the door, everyone's attention was back on the girls or their drinks. Buffy held the crossbow at the ready and set herself in a fighting stance, muscles tensed.

"Xander, get the door."

All seriousness now, no trace of amusement on his face, Xander edged up beside her, reached down to turn the knob and shove the door open, then dropped back. Buffy surged forward into what appeared to be a dingy dressing room for the dancers. Lockers and mirrors abounded, but the room was poorly lit. Not so dark, however, that she could not see them.

Bulldog. Clownface. Four . . . no, five others.

Buffy froze just inside the door, blocking Xander's entrance.

"What is it?" he asked anxiously.

"More math." She reached back and handed Xander a stake. He took it. Then Buffy grabbed the door and slammed it shut behind her, leaving him out in the club. Xander shouted her name and she called back to him to stay put.

If there were other vamps out in the club, she doubted they would reveal themselves. But if they did, Xander had the stake. Meanwhile, she had room to work.

The vampires moved in almost total silence across the room, seeming to uncoil from the darkness like serpents. Clownface and Bulldog hung back while the others moved closer. In the near darkness, the orange fire of their jack-o'-lantern eyes set into the black inks of the tattoos that were etched across their faces was unsettling.

They began to chant something, all at once and all together, in a language Buffy did not recognize. It was in a kind of deep undervoice almost as though they were whispering it to themselves. The chanting slipped under her skin immediately, eerie fingers trailing along her spine and raising goosebumps on her arms. Buffy felt her eyes flutter and the lids grow heavy.

With a surge of anger and adrenaline, she shook it off.

"You think I'm that easy?" she asked dismissively.

Xander called her name again and pushed open the door behind her. In a single motion, Buffy spun and slammed it shut, knocking him back out into the barroom, then turned to face the vampires, just as they swarmed her.

Her finger tightened on the trigger of the crossbow. A bolt flew, punched through the heart of the vampire closest to her, and he exploded in a blast of hot ash. Another bolt ratcheted into place but another vampire, a thin white scar slicing through the markings on his face, lunged for her throat, his long tongue slaking out over his fangs. Talons reached for her. She knew she could not let them get a grip on her. With a backhand, Buffy slammed her left fist up under his jaw and caught the vampire's tongue between his teeth.

He screamed in pain and staggered back, clearing Buffy enough room to aim at a third and fire again. The vamp's eyes went wide as the bolt slammed into his ribcage and then through his heart. A second later he was dusted.

"Too quiet," Buffy chided the remaining bloodsuckers. "Vampire mimes, is that it? Let's have heaps of arrogant swagger. You guys love arrogant swagger."

They said nothing. There were still five of them, but Buffy saw Clownface grab Bulldog's arm and hold him back as the other three came for her again, trying to corner her. Buffy had one last bolt in the repeating crossbow. She swung the weapon up just as they all attacked. This time she was not fast enough. The crossbow was batted from her hand with a blow hard enough to make her right hand numb. It clattered to the floor and Buffy heard the wood crack.

"Hey!" she snapped.

One of the vampires pushed the others out of the way, greedy to get at her, and wrapped his talons around her throat, choking off her words and her air. The thing slammed her into a mirror and a rain of shattered glass cascaded across the floor.

Buffy pushed her feet against the wall for leverage and then head-butted the vampire as hard as she could. Her aim was a little off and her skull crushed his nose with a splintering of bone and a spray of blood.

"That bow," she snarled, "was an antique. Giles is not going to be happy. He might even swear."

One of the others came at her from the left. Buffy ducked the blow, leaned back and snapped a kick at the vampire's chest that staggered him.

Another bat-face reached for her, but Buffy was too fast. She reached behind her and withdrew the stake from its sheath at the small of her back, then spun and punched it through his chest. The scarred one with the broken, mashed nose lunged at her through the cloud of his comrade's dust. Buffy swung her right fist in a blow that came up from her gut and he went down hard on the floor.

After that she moved in a single fluid motion. A spinning kick to the face of her remaining attacker was followed by a thrust of the stake, and more dust blew around the room. She dropped to the floor, stake above the scarred one's heart, nose to nose with the vampire. His breath was wretched, the stench of old blood.

Buffy dusted him.

Instantly she was up, turning, body tense and ready for more, wanting combat and, with some luck, answers. She had figured to interrogate the last one alive. But she had not expected them to run away. The last of them, the two she had come to think of as Clownface and Bulldog, were gone, a distant rear door to the club hanging open to the night.

Half a dozen wisecracks came to mind, but none made it as far as her lips. Vampires ran from her all the time, but this was different. There was no doubt in her mind that the two escapees had not run out of cowardice, but as some form of strategic retreat. The idea disturbed her profoundly. The vampire breed was a contentious one and they rarely got along well enough to form alliances, never mind packs or families. Only the most charismatic and powerful like the Master were able to gather followers in that way.

Whoever this Camazotz was, he had trained his acolytes well.

With those dark thoughts in mind, she pulled open the door to the club. Xander leaned against the wall to her left, staring at the two girls on the stage closest to them. It took him nearly ten seconds to notice Buffy standing there watching him.

"Hey. Just on the job. Making sure you're not disturbed," he said nervously.

"My hero." Buffy raised an eyebrow.

Xander balked. "You pushed me out of there. Closed the door in my face not once but twice. Kinda figured that meant I'd just be cannon fodder if I forced my way in. If you needed backup I thought you woulda yelled for me."

"I would have," Buffy agreed. Then she smirked. "Whether or not you would have heard me is another question entirely."

"What?" Xander asked. His eyes strayed to the stage. "Oh, that? Barely noticed them. Just backing you up, Buffy. You will tell Anya it was you who dragged me in here, right?"

Buffy made her way around tables and toward the front door of the Kat Skratch Club amidst clouds of cigarette smoke. None of the patrons even gave her a second glance.

Xander trailed after her. "Buffy? You'll tell her, right?"

CHAPTER 4

The dentist's-drill buzz of the alarm clock woke Buffy at just after seven o'clock the following morning. One eye flickered open and she glared at it with as much hatred as she had ever felt for more corporeal demons. Just looking at the thing would not make it shut off, however, so she was forced to sit up, eyes slitted open, and click it off.

"I hate Mondays," she grumbled under her breath. Of course, it wasn't Monday. But it felt like one.

With a frown, Buffy looked around the room. Willow's bed was still made, unrumpled. Her roommate had not come home the night before. It wasn't unheard of for Willow to spend the night at Oz's, but Buffy could not help but wonder if the brief argument they'd had the day before had anything to do with it.

She was tempted to call Oz, but it was too early. Willow would likely be up already, but you could never tell with Oz. One day he might make all of his classes and the next he might sleep until after lunch.

"No," she told herself sternly. "No grumpy thoughts."

Determined to make a fresh start of the day, she got up and peered out the window. The sky was gray, overcast, but it was almost guaranteed to burn off. It was fall, sure, but it was also Southern California. Bad weather happened, but it was rare enough that nobody believed it until it did some damage, then afterward they pretended it had never been there. Almost exactly the same way the people of Sunnydale dealt with the supernatural.

"No grumpy thoughts," she said again.

Humming a snatch of some tune the Dingoes always played at the Bronze, she got her things together and went down the hall to take a shower.

Fifteen minutes later she was back in her room. Her mind drifted to the run-in at the Kat Skratch Club the night before. The tattoos, the vampires' eerie chanting, their eyes, and their arrogance; much as she hated to admit it, even to herself, they creeped her out.

Giles had promised to do research on Camazotz, and she knew he would get it done as soon as possible. But having Olivia around would complicate things. After the chaos of last night Buffy had been tempted to go back to his apartment and check in, but the idea of interrupting their romantic evening stopped her cold. The last thing she wanted to do was disturb Giles's love life, never mind walk in on it.

Shudder. That thought was creepier than bat-faced vampires.

Buffy glanced at her enemy, the alarm clock. It was a little after seven-thirty, still plenty of time before class, and the desire to call Willow and square things if they needed to be squared lingered with her.

Oz answered. "Yeah?" he rasped.

"Hey, Oz. Sorry to call so early. Is Willow up?"

"Hang on."

A muffled exchange on the other end, then Willow came on.

"Hey."

"Hey. Sorry to bother you guys."

"No bother," Willow said brightly. "At least, not me. But I'm not a cranky old bear in the morning like certain boyfriends. What's up?"

Buffy paused. It would sound silly if she brought up their argument, or just said she was checking in.

"Buffy? You okay?"

"Good," Buffy replied quickly. "No grumpy mornings over here. Listen, there's some interesting new talent in town and I was going to head over to Giles's this afternoon, see what we could dig up. Want to come with?"

"Mmm," Willow replied, sounding a bit distracted. Buffy tried not to be envious that her best friend had a guy who loved her to be distracting. "Why don't we meet you there?"

"Deal. Gotta go, though. Time to make with the book learnin'. Got my history exam this morning. Then I've got to work on that paper for Professor Blaylock. As of today, I'm starting with a ninety."

"Knock 'em dead," Willow said. "Only, y'know, not literally."

They said their good-byes and hung up, and when Buffy left the dorm room she had a broad smile on her face. Willow meant the world to her and Buffy had no idea what she would do if there ever came a day when Willow did not feel the same.

Oz sat cross-legged on the floor of Giles's apartment, excavating ancient treasures from the man's vinyl record collection. Olivia, a woman Willow had only met a time or two before, but who clearly meant a great deal to Giles, sat on a cushioned chair by Oz and exclaimed over a number of the records he pulled out, many of which spurred her to regale them with embarrassing stories of Giles in his younger days.

She was certainly a beautiful woman, and her British accent gave her an added allure. Willow felt badly for having interrupted their time together.

"Are you sure this is okay?" she said, keeping her voice low.

Giles sat beside her at the dining room table as the two of them pored through a stack of arcane texts. A couple of them were even older than the most antique volumes she had previously seen in his collection, and most were in Spanish.

"Giles?" Willow prodded.

He blinked several times, then looked up at her as though he'd just been snapped awake by a hypnotist. "I'm sorry, Willow, what was that? Have you found something?"

"Not yet, no. I just . . . I know you and Olivia don't get to see each other very often. She's not in from London for very long. Are you sure you want to be doing this today?"

Giles removed his glasses and offered her a gentle smile. "It's very sweet of you to be concerned. The answer, of course, is no. I don't want to be doing this at all. But I also realize that lives may be in jeopardy from these new arrivals, and a bit of research is the least I can do to help Buffy in her effort to combat them. She may have decided that she's going to be invincible, but unless someone goes 'round and gets the rest of the world to agree, we must back her up."

He glanced over his shoulder as Olivia laughed about a particular record. Oz said something under his breath. Something ironic, Willow was sure, because he was Oz, after all.

"Oz seems to have Olivia quite well entertained at the moment," Giles reassured Willow. "Though how he manages to do that and maintain his usual twelve-word-an-hour rule is a mystery to me."

"He's a good listener," Willow said, a lopsided smile on her face as she watched her guy. When she smiled, the bruise Buffy had given her the previous morning made her wince. The glamour she'd used could hide it, but not make the pain go away.

"So anything?" she asked Giles.

"Quite a bit, actually." He separated out two of the books from his pile. "I just thought I'd hold off until Buffy arrived to avoid having to explain it more than once."

Troubled, Willow wondered where Buffy had gotten off to. That morning she had asked that they all meet at Giles's after classes were over. Willow knew for a fact that Buffy's last class of the day was out before three o'clock. Now it was going on four and still no Buffy.

"I expected her long before now," Giles added.

It only made Willow more concerned. "I hope she's all—"

She was interrupted by a knock at the door. Willow leaped up from the table to get it. Giles reached for a book he had set aside. Engrossed in the record collection, Oz and Olivia were about to put on an early Rolling Stones album, but they paused to look up.

Willow opened the door to find Buffy standing on the stoop.

"Hey!" Willow said. "You're okay."

"Sorry I'm late. It's just, this paper for Professor Blaylock. I thought I had a lot of this stuff down, but I feel like I'm starting from square one. No way am I going to finish before Monday, which is when it was due in the first place. I'll be starting from a seventy. It'll have to be perfect for me to pass. Then, this afternoon, I run into Aaron Levine, who's in my history class? We got to talking about the exam this morning, which I thought I'd done all right on. Turns out, not so much. I mixed up a couple of royal families, so one of the big essays is written in the language of gibberish. I just don't know what's wrong with me."

Willow frowned, then forced a smile. "Tell you what? You've got the stress. Maybe you'd feel better if you went back and worked on that paper. Let us deal with the mystery for a while. Then, when you feel like you've got a better handle on things—"

"I've got a handle on things now," Buffy snapped.

Surprised by her anger, Willow took a step back. She glanced around the room and saw that everyone was staring at Buffy.

"Except, perhaps, your temper," Giles chided her.

Buffy began to form some sort of retort, but then her features softened. She gazed apologetically at Willow.

"Sorry, Will. Maybe I am wound a little tight right now, with all this. Thanks for worrying about me, but I really can handle it. I *will* handle it."

"Preferably without the crankiness," Willow replied, still a bit hurt.

Buffy put a hand on her shoulder. Willow saw the regret and the stress in her eyes, and wished she could do more to help.

"Hey. Are *we* okay?" Buffy asked.

"Peachy," Willow said with a firm nod. "Without the pit, even."

"We're in a place with fruit," Buffy replied happily. "Gotta like it. As long as we go nowhere near lemons. There's a whole sour element there."

"No lemons," Willow promised.

Giles rose from the table as Buffy approached.

"Sorry for the lustus interruptus," she said, casting a meaningful glance at Olivia, who smiled and waved without the faintest trace of embarrassment.

And why should she be embarrassed, Willow thought. *It's her boyfriend's apartment, they're consenting adults, and we're the intruders here.* On the other hand, with their positions reversed Willow knew that she'd be blushing scarlet and barely able to speak beyond a babble.

"Yes, well, ritual mass murder does tend to take priority over almost anything else," Giles told her.

Buffy cast a sidelong glance at Willow. "See, it's the 'mass' in there that always gets me. I hate vampires with ambition. Why can't they be ambition free?"

In the corner, as he placed the needle on vinyl, Oz spoke without looking up from the antique record player. "Everyone's gotta have a dream."

Giles cleared his throat. "Yes, well, your timing is impeccable as usual, Buffy. I believe we've found what we're looking for."

"We were just waiting for you to get here," Willow said helpfully. "Giles didn't want to repeat himself."

"Sorry I held you guys up."

Giles held up a hand to wave away her apology. "No matter. Let's get down to business, shall we?"

Willow and Buffy sat together on the sofa. Oz left

the Rolling Stones on with the volume low and wandered over. Olivia gazed at them for a moment, then rolled her eyes good-naturedly and went up the stairs into the loft.

Giles gave them all a sheepish glance and shrugged. "Olivia's a skeptic," he told them in a stage whisper. "Thinks we're all a bit mad, I suspect."

"She should spend more time in Sunnydale," Buffy replied. "It'd make a believer out of her."

Oz settled deeply into an old chair. Giles stood before them, leaning only a little against the dining room table, cracked leather book in his right hand.

"According to all the legends I've been able to find, Camazotz was not a vampire, but a god," Giles began.

"Ooh, pagan deities. Have we slain any of those yet?" Willow asked excitedly.

Oz smiled down at her, touched the side of her face. "None of the big ones."

"Camazotz is not exactly a household name," Buffy put in. "I'm guessing he's not one of the big ones, either."

"On the contrary," Giles countered. He opened the book in his hand and flipped to a page toward the end. The paper crackled as he turned the pages. When he held it up for them, Willow saw immediately what he meant for them to see. A drawing in the lower left corner of the page showed a hideous creature like a giant humanoid bat, with prickly fur and pointed ears, long tapered talons and leathery, veined wings. It had a dozen smaller limbs with their own talons protruding from its chest and a thick ratlike tail with what appeared to be a sharp spike at the end.

"According to the ancient Mayans," Giles continued, "Camazotz was the god of bats. He was wed to the dark goddess Zotzilaha Chimalman, and purportedly dwelt in an ancient, tomblike cave that led to a realm of darkness and death. Translated, the name of his lair was simply the House of Bats."

Buffy shifted on the couch. "So we're thinking demon. Tunnel to realms of death sounds like a Hellmouth to me."

"Or," Willow put in quickly, "at least a Hell-nostril."

Everyone looked at her oddly.

"Bad metaphor," she muttered to herself. "Bad, icky metaphor."

Giles turned to slide the tattered old book onto the dining room table. Then he picked up another, smaller volume that was obviously much more recent, though still quite old. When he opened it Willow could see that the text inside had been written by hand and she knew it must be one of the journals kept by the Watchers over the ages.

"The Council let you keep those?" she asked, before she could stop herself.

"Hmm?" Giles glanced up at her and frowned.

Willow wished she had not brought it up. Giles had been fired from the Council because they had felt his relationship with Buffy had become too emotional, that he cared too much for her to be an effective Watcher. He had been angry with them and seemed more than content to cut off all contact, but Willow suspected it was still a sore spot. Still, she had brought it up.

"The journal," she said. "Kinda thought with, y'know, the divorce, that the Council would have asked for those back."

"Ah, yes. Well, Wesley did confiscate most of the handwritten ones I had. I was allowed to keep those that were not originals and this single volume. It was written by my grandmother, who was quite a story-teller, actually. She cataloged many of the odd vampire myths and legends she came across. I thought I remembered something about Mayans in here. If the stories she was told are true, Camazotz was the spawn of a union between a true demon, one of the first to walk the Earth, and a god. What 'god' means in these terms is really anyone's guess, since no one has ever really been able to catalog a meeting with one, to my knowledge.

"Suffice to say, Camazotz is a very ancient creature. Decidedly not a vampire, you understand, but my grandmother notes one particular theory that Camazotz was the demon responsible for the *creation* of vampires."

Buffy slid to the edge of the couch and stared at him. "Can that be true?"

"We have no way of knowing," Giles replied. "Nor have I been able to ascertain, thus far, why his vampire followers should have powers greater than their brethren."

"The god of bats. So the markings on their faces are what, his personal logo?"

"It probably comes from that cave," Willow suggested. "Okay, assuming dark and nasty lair really existed, not much of a stretch to think lots of bats there." She nodded sagely. "I'm thinking maybe he believes his own hype. God of bats. Tattoos the lackeys."

"Or a brand," Buffy said. "Like on cattle. To mark them as his."

Giles seemed to contemplate that for a moment, then held up his grandmother's journal. "The one thing in the journal that reflects the Mayan legends is the idea that Camazotz was the prince of the Mayan legions of darkness, a leader among the creatures of the night. He is a formidable foe."

"That's all we've got? Nothing on the lackeys?" Buffy asked, resignation in her voice. "Sparkly eyes, life-force sucking? Nothing?"

"For the moment I'm afraid that's it," Giles said. "It's possible the draining effect was the sorcery of that particular vampire, but time will tell. Buffy, why don't you—"

"I'll patrol again tonight. See if I can't finally hold on to one of these guys. With the brands on their faces, they're hard to miss. I might swing by Willy's and see if he's got any information for us."

Buffy stood up, tossed her jacket over her shoulder again, and started for the door. While they'd been talking, she'd been relaxed and even joking around.

But Willow saw the change come over her. Suddenly she was all business again, doing it all on her own.

"Will, can you call Xander, ask him and Anya to come by. Giles can brief them. If Anya has any contacts among the demon set that she's still willing to talk to, maybe she can make a few calls. Otherwise you guys should just be checking the paper, airline records, shipping manifests, trying to figure out how they got here and where they could all be staying. That's a lotta new vampires at once. Bigger than a breadbox. My guess is Camazotz will have a Sunnydale version of his House of Bats somewhere. That's something else to check. Where would we find bats around here?"

As Buffy spoke, Willow's eyes widened with alarm and awkwardness. "Um," she countered. "Maybe Oz and I can just go by Xander's. Giles has sort of done his part for the moment."

Buffy glanced up into the loft where Olivia had gone. "Right!" she said quickly. "Absolutely. All done with Giles, at least until the morning. We'll do just fine. Really. We'll check in tomorrow."

Giles busied himself with reorganizing the books on the table as Willow and Oz quickly followed Buffy out.

In front of Giles's apartment, they turned to face each other.

"Sure you don't need any backup on patrol?" Willow asked.

Buffy shook her head. "I've got it. Besides, I'm just going to sweep the regular circuit and swing past the areas where I've seen them before, then I'm going to head back to the dorm early, try to work on that paper and not think about how badly I messed up my history exam."

Willow wanted to reach out to her, to help in some way, but Buffy had been like one big frayed nerve the last few days. Still, she had to try.

"Hey. I know you're hell-bent on handling everything yourself, but everybody needs help sometimes, right? Are you sure you don't want us to round up a posse, go out and pinch-hit for you tonight so you can get that paper in? You could save yourself a whole letter grade. It isn't like we haven't done it before."

Buffy sighed with frustration. "I know that, all right? And it isn't that I don't appreciate it. But you shouldn't have to. It isn't your responsibility, it's mine. I can't keep leaning on you or anyone else. If I'm going to have a life beyond being the Slayer, I've got to do it myself, I've got to know that I can handle it."

Oz said nothing, only watched the two girls. Willow gazed imploringly at Buffy.

"Your friends are part of this life you're talking about having, Buffy."

Buffy's mouth twitched and a grimace of hurt washed across her features. Then she sighed and her expression hardened.

"You don't understand, Will. But that's okay, really. How can anyone?"

With that, she turned and walked away. Willow stared after her best friend as she disappeared into the darkness, hoping Buffy would turn around, hoping she would see that she could not do it alone.

Willow was about to call after her when Oz put a hand on her arm.

"Let it go."

She gazed at him, not understanding.

"It's hard for her, trying to make it all work," he said.

Willow glanced down, trying and failing to hide her hurt. "It's hard for all of us. Can't she see that it isn't just her? That nobody can deal with everything life throws them if they're all alone?"

"Give it some time. She'll come around," he promised. Then he slipped an arm around her and walked her to his van.

As they drove over to Xander's house, Willow stayed silent, holding her hurt close.

CHAPTER 5

"We got nothing."

With a frown, Giles looked up from the map of Sunnydale that was spread across his dining room table. Xander and Anya sat on the floor in the middle of his apartment with the previous week's local newspapers arranged around them so expansively it appeared as though Giles had bought a puppy that was not yet housebroken.

"Surely there must be something," Giles said, disheartened at Xander's declaration. "A downed plane. Strange stories from the border patrol. Violence at airport customs in Los Angeles. Something to give us just an inkling of where they might have made their lair locally."

Anya gestured with a hand to indicate the newspapers. "Nothing. The new mayor has issued more lies disguised as promises, as expected of the more talented politicians. The Coast Guard is fighting charges they didn't act fast enough to clean up that oil spill last week. Nothing. Last night was boring and pointless. So is today."

"We've got bubkes," Xander added.

Anya, a former demon herself, and Xander's girl-friend, glanced at him uncertainly. "Bubkes?"

"Nada," Xander told her. "Zilch. Zip. Zero. Squat. Diddly." He shrugged. "Bubkes."

"Odd," Anya told him. She shook her head ever so slightly, an expression of frustration with the confusing world around her that was almost as common as the disparaging tone she took with most everyone. "It sounds almost like a sexual act."

"Oh, for God's sake," Giles muttered under his breath. The two of them did go on a bit about the more carnal aspects of their relationship.

"You're right," Xander said thoughtfully. "I think it's our job to invent that. Bubkes. We'll be the first."

"Do you two mind?" Giles snapped. "What we're dealing with here is quite serious. An infestation of new vampires led by an ancient demon-god. Lucy Hanover visits Buffy in a dream to warn her that something terrible is on the horizon just as she runs across this new group? I'm certain there's a connection. I suggest you get serious about working with me to figure out where these new arrivals are secreting themselves, or simply take your . . . distractions with you and go elsewhere."

Anya grinned, an amiable expression on her face. "Excellent," she said, climbing to her feet. "Let's go, Xander. We've only made it halfway through the *Kamasutra* and there are dozens of—"

Xander had the good sense to be somewhat embarrassed. "Um, Anya? That was sarcasm. Hard to tell with Giles, I know. But he needs help and was kidding about wanting us to leave." Then Xander frowned and glanced at Giles. "Right?"

"Not terribly certain of that myself," Giles replied dryly. "But, yes, I could use all the help I can get. I don't know why Buffy and Willow have not yet called me back."

"The Buffster's got nothing or she would have called you this morning, don't you think?" Xander said. "She went down to Willy's Alibi Room, intimidated Willy. If she'd gotten anything from him she would have called."

Giles glanced across the room at his phone, then glared down at the map on the table as if it were purposely withholding information from him. In a way, he almost felt as though it were.

"I suppose," he allowed. "And if anything had happened to her, Willow would have informed us this morning."

"Or she might have, if she wasn't so ticked off at Buffy," Anya interjected.

Both Xander and Giles looked at her with identical expressions of confusion.

Anya only rolled her eyes. *"Men.* You never pay attention. I'd bet someone's soul—not my own, of course—that Willow stayed at Oz's last night and hasn't spoken to Buffy at all today."

"Right," Giles snapped. He pushed back his chair and gathered the map up in his hands. "Let's head over there straightaway. If this Camazotz identified her as the Slayer, it's quite possible that—"

The phone rang.

Giles hurried to pick it up. "Keep looking," he told Xander and Anya. He interrupted the second ring.

"Hello?"

"Hey, it's me," Buffy said. "Sorry I haven't gotten back to you yet. I had classes and then library time."

"Yes, well, I admire your dedication to your classwork, Buffy, but Lucy Hanover's warning was a bit ominous, wouldn't you say? This situation with Camazotz requires our full focus."

"I'm on it," she said coldly. "I will save the world, as usual, all right? But there's also this thing called college that I have to do. Look, I know by now I'm not getting this paper done before Monday, so I won't hit any more classes today. But give me some breathing room, Giles. I wasn't the one with my girlfriend in town."

Startled as he was by her obvious anger and frustration, Giles hesitated. He wanted to defend himself, to argue that he had not shirked his duties at all while Olivia had been visiting, and in fact it had soured their visit somewhat. But he worried that, stressed as she was, Buffy might see that as an accusation.

"Are you all right?" he asked, as gently as he could.

"Peachy," she replied, but her voice was cold.

"Funny, you don't sound at all peachy. Buffy, one of the first lessons taught to any Slayer is that in order to survive you must learn to adapt, to improvise, to react to any situation fluidly and quickly. In your admirable attempt to create an orderly life for yourself, I fear you may have forgotten that."

"That's what I'm doing, Giles. Reacting. So I'm trying to create order out of the chaos that's been my life since the day I found out I was the Slayer. Is that wrong?"

He sighed. "You live your life in chaos, I'm afraid. In order to combat it, you immerse yourself in it. It's one of the sacrifices you make in exchange for the gifts of the Slayer, the power to keep the rest of the world safe from that very same chaos."

There was a long pause before Buffy spoke again. "I don't know if I can live like that anymore. If I give up trying to make sense out of things . . ."

"Buffy, you know you have my full support in that effort. It's simply that there are times—"

"I know," she replied sadly. "It's fine. I'll work it out. Moving on, now. I left my hand print on Willy's throat last night, but he's got nothing. Heard about the bat-faced vamps, but no word on who they are, why they're here, and where they're hanging their hats."

"Bubkes," Giles muttered.

On the other end of the line, Buffy paused. "You've

been watching old reruns of *Hill Street Blues* again, haven't you?"

"You were moving on?" he reminded her.

"I did a short patrol downtown, cemetery sweep, went by the Bronze. Fashion crimes notwithstanding, not a peep from anything soulless. Did a run through Docktown. Lot of tattoos, none of them bats."

As Giles listened to Buffy rattle off her actions of the night before, he stared at the map on the table and mentally traced the path of her patrol. It ended at Docktown, the section of Sunnydale used as a shipping port for a century. The Fish Tank, where she'd first run into the minions of Camazotz, was on the north side of Docktown, closest to the wharfs where vessels would be moored. The Kat Skratch Club was farther south and another block or two inland.

Both were far from the center of town, which was usually teeming with young life, and almost always ended up the primary target of vampires in Sunnydale. It was also much closer to the Hellmouth, which he believed drew them with almost magnetic power. Supernatural creatures in town did not generally stray far beyond its influence.

Docktown. And to the west, nothing but Pacific Ocean.

"Buffy," Giles said, his voice laden with regret. "I'm an absolute fool."

"You tell me this now, after I've been taking your advice all this time?"

"It's got to be a ship," he said. "The new House of

Bats, the lair of Camazotz." Giles glanced up at Xander and Anya, who had risen from the floor to come stand by the table and study the map with him. "It has to be a ship. Somehow they managed not to attract undue attention from customs and the harbormaster, even though they all have that brand on their faces."

"Makes sense," Xander admitted. "But they've got to have someone with a human face doing their nasty bidding. You can't make a whole ship invisible. There's gotta be a record of it somewhere."

On the phone, Buffy echoed his words. "That would explain why I haven't seen any of them in town. Yet. And even if you're wrong, we're no worse off than we have been. But how do we pinpoint them exactly? Breaking into every ship moored off Sunnydale is gonna be risky from the getting-arrested perspective, and really time-consuming."

"It might be possible to find what we need through a computer search. Otherwise, I think I may have an idea for a magickal solution. Either way, you should call Willow."

"Why don't I go down and talk to the harbormaster?" Buffy offered.

"You could try that," Giles admitted. "But he'd have no real reason to cooperate, and it would be inadvisable to try to intimidate anyone connected to the local authorities. We need to be prepared to search for them electronically, and mystically. For that, we need Willow."

* * *

After Buffy hung up the phone, she stared at it for almost a full minute without moving. Giles wanted her to call Willow. There was no question in Buffy's mind that Willow *could* help, but she disagreed with Giles that it was necessary. Even if it meant a little intimidation of the harbormaster, or the ship-to-ship search she knew she didn't have time for, Buffy thought those would be better. Or, at least, a part of her did. The other part recognized that Willow and Giles were probably right. But she feared that possibility. If that were true, a little voice whispered in the back of her mind, then the day might come when she would have to choose between her life as Buffy Summers, and her obligations as the Slayer.

Making that choice would tear her apart.

Buffy wished that she had been more insistent with Giles, that she had told him that they should all just stay there and continue their research. Instead, she knew, she would have to do her best to keep them all safe, yet another responsibility on her shoulders. But she would handle it.

She would.

Reluctantly, she dialed Oz's number.

He picked up on the third ring. "Hey."

"It's Buffy. Is Willow around?"

"She went to pick up pizza."

A surprisingly powerful wave of relief swept through Buffy. Giles thought they needed Willow. Having her around would certainly make things easier. But being the Slayer wasn't about making things easy.

If Willow wasn't around, maybe she would be able to send Giles home—tell him they would just try in the morning.

Then she could look into it herself, in her own way. The hard way.

"Buffy? Something going on?" Oz asked.

"Could you ask her to do something for me?" she began. Then she explained to him about the computer search, the little bit of illegal hacking that Giles wanted her to do. It couldn't hurt to have her do that, at least. Sitting at the keyboard was safe.

"I'll try to call later, see if she's got anything."

"I'll let her know," Oz replied. "She'll be glad."

His words carried more meaning, as always, but Buffy did not ask him to elaborate.

Darkness had fallen by the time Buffy made it to Docktown. When she reached The Fish Tank she stood in the shadows of a crumbling apartment house a block or so away and scanned the street. Across from the sleazy bar, she spotted Giles's ancient Citroën parked and dormant. Without the engine running, the thing looked almost abandoned. Though around here it wouldn't have been abandoned for long without being stripped.

Buffy knew better.

As she approached the car she passed a narrow alley where a homeless man had built a lean-to against a brick wall out of weathered wood he'd probably torn off the poorly kept docks just down the street, or picked up from the rocky shore beneath them. He noticed her noticing him, and then hissed at something in the shadows behind him. A chill ran through Buffy as she wondered whether he communicated with a creature of real darkness, or something from his fevered imagination. She found that the latter possibility unnerved her more.

Though she continued to move mostly in the shadows of buildings, Buffy picked up her pace. A moment later she stood behind the Citroën. Inside, in the dim light thrown from the guttering neon of The Fish Tank across the street, she could see Giles behind the wheel. He had a greasy brown paper sack of fried clams, French fries, and a can of soda. Not his usual cuisine, but she figured he had to pick something up in a rush. She couldn't blame him. It took her a moment to realize she'd eaten nothing since breakfast, but even now she did not feel like eating. Her stomach felt small and tight as a fist, like it couldn't have fit a single bite.

Later, when it was over. Then she would eat.

Buffy crouched down beside the car and rapped on Giles's window. He started, dropped a fried clam, then cursed about the tartar sauce he'd gotten on his sweater.

He motioned for her to come around the other side. Buffy slid into the passenger seat beside him while Giles tried to clean off his sweater. When he looked up, he was clearly mystified.

"You're by yourself? What happened to Willow?"

Buffy stiffened slightly. "I called Oz's, but she was out. I explained to him about the computer search, but I'm thinking we're going to have to postpone the magick until morning."

"Did you impress upon Oz the urgency of our situation?"

She shrugged. "Willow wasn't around, Giles. Oz isn't a witch. I guess we can call and see if she's come back, now, but is another twelve hours going to make that much difference? If she does her Internet magic, we may not even need the witchy stuff."

Buffy raised an eyebrow as she regarded him.

Giles cleared his throat and shot her a withering glance. "Twelve hours could make an enormous difference, Buffy. Another night could cost any number of lives."

Buffy glanced out the window at the dingy street. "I'll stick around, patrol all night if I have to. As you know, tomorrow's Saturday. So I'll sleep in. Maybe I'll even do some sleuthing in Docktown, come up with something. You guys can keep researching the burning eyes thing, right?"

"Xander and Anya are doing precisely that. I've begun to believe this isn't a separate, undiscovered breed of vampire, merely vampires who have somehow been enhanced by Camazotz. They are following that line of research. However, regrettable as Willow's absence is, we should exhaust all avenues presently available to us in our efforts to locate their lair."

Giles started up the car and put it in gear.

"Hey!" Buffy said, startled. "Look, Giles, I'm serious. You can be of more help with the books. When it comes to patrolling, maybe handing out some bloody noses to get the information we need, that's Slayer business, right? I'll start with the harbormaster and go from there. Xander and Anya are probably canoodling back at your place. We're not going to figure out what we're up against with them hitting the books. I stay, make with the fisticuffs. It's what I do. You go, make with the cross-referencicuffs. It's what *you* do."

Giles shot her a brief, sidelong glance, one eyebrow arched curiously. "Buffy, I have been on patrol with you dozens, perhaps hundreds of times. Why are you so insistent upon excluding me? After all this time you cannot possibly be worried about my safety."

"I'm not," Buffy said dismissively.

"Well, that's a comfort, I suppose."

Buffy glanced away, then up at him again. "I'm worried about mine. You've told me yourself, Giles, that traditionally Slayers operated alone. They didn't have friends around like I do, people they could rely on. They also didn't have lives outside being a Slayer. Well, I do, or at least I'm trying to. If I'm going to lead two lives, I've got to work twice as hard at both. For the Slayer, that means I take the responsibility of being the Chosen One, of my duties, on myself. I was Chosen, no one else. Sometimes it sucks, but I have to learn not to rely on anyone else but me. One girl in all the world, remember? That's what you told me when we first met. Not 'one girl in all the world and her Watcher and her best friends and their boyfriends and girlfriends and whoever else we happen to pick up along the way.'

"It's on me, Giles. You go. I stay."

"Everyone needs help sometimes, Buffy. That's why Slayers have Watchers in the first place," Giles argued, gazing at her with obvious concern.

"But The Powers That Be don't choose Watchers. Just Slayers."

Giles removed his glasses and let them dangle from his fingers as he considered her words. At length he looked over at her again.

"Now is probably not the time to argue the point, Buffy. But have you forgotten what I said about threatening the harbormaster? I tend to think that, particularly if he's not involved, the local authorities might be a bit agitated. We'll drive over there, and I'll speak to him first. If he seems suspicious, then perhaps you can have a go at him."

Buffy started to argue, but Giles was obviously determined. She also had to admit to herself that it would be better if he approached the harbormaster first. Not that she was happy about it. But there was little she could do except go along with him.

For the moment.

There was still a light burning in the harbormaster's office. Buffy had argued the point again, but Giles had insisted she wait in the car. Contrary to what she was trying to prove, Buffy could not do everything. Case in point, he was certain that the harbormaster would be much more likely to have a conversation about his work with an adult than a teenage girl.

He parked the Citroën a block and a half away and walked down to the office. It was a small building, not more than two or three rooms, overlooking the ocean, appropriately enough. The hours were posted on the door and it was long past official closing time, but Giles took the light on inside as a good sign.

There was no bell, so he rapped lightly on the door. Just when he would have rapped again, the doorknob rattled and then the big oak door was hauled open.

"What the hell do you want?" growled a bearded, gray-haired man with a cigar jutting from between his clenched jaws.

Giles stared at him. The man was almost a caricature of what he imagined a harbormaster ought to look like. He tore his eyes away, though. The last thing he wanted was to offend the man with such improprieties.

"You're the harbormaster, I take it?"

"Do you see the time?" the man demanded.

"Indeed I did, sir. But if I might have a moment. I'm an . . . investigative journalist and I had a few questions about recent goings-on here in Docktown. Gang presence, to be precise."

The harbormaster narrowed his eyes and puffed on his cigar, regarding Giles with great suspicion and likely more than a touch of xenophobia.

"You're British," the man said.

"Yes."

"What the hell does a Brit want with poking around Docktown asking questions? What business is it of yours what goes on down here?"

Giles hesitated. He had been afraid that this would not work, but it was not as if the man would have believed him a police officer, or answered questions if he had told the truth.

"As I said, sir, I'm an investigative journalist working for the *L. A. Times* and I'm looking into recent gang activity here," he insisted. With nothing to lose, he pressed on. "Apparently there has been a spate of violence by a group of ruffians with a very distinguishing mark. They all have a bat tattooed on their faces."

"Hrrrm," the old man grunted. He scratched his beard and puffed on his cigar. Then he let out a blast of smoke that swirled around Giles's face and nearly made him retch. "What'd you say your name was?"

"Robert Travers."

After another moment's thought, the harbormaster rolled the cigar around between his teeth and then nodded. "Might be I've heard something about that. Might be one of the dock rats I know's even seen something. You payin' for information?"

Giles smiled. "Of course."

The old man's eyes narrowed. "You just stay right there while I make a call."

"Absolutely. I'm at your service."

The old man closed the door.

Gulls cawed overhead in the darkness. The sky was a bit overcast, with very few visible stars. A car horn beeped far off and it drew Giles's attention to the road. So few cars down here this time of night, though he could hear a truck rumbling nearby. Metal clanked as the rise and fall of the ocean rocked the floating docks just down from the harbormaster's office.

Time went by.

Eventually, with a frown, he glanced at his watch and pressed the button to illuminate it. Nine-seventeen. He hadn't checked the time before, but he had the impression it had been at least five minutes, perhaps closer to ten, that he'd been left standing out here on the stoop. He wondered if the old man had simply been pulling his leg, making a fool of him.

Giles stepped away from the door and glanced up the street at his car. It was dark inside, though, and he could not see Buffy. With a sigh he went back to his post and tapped his foot as he waited.

At nine twenty-two, he rapped on the door again, more loudly than the first time.

It took longer for the harbormaster to open the door this time. When he did, he wore a cruel smile.

"You're a persistent one, ain'tcha?" the old man grumbled.

"It's my job," Giles replied.

"You do yours," the harbormaster said, chewing his cigar and hitching up his ragged blue jeans, "and I'll do mine."

With that, his hands flashed out with inhuman quickness and latched around Giles's throat. The old man spat out his cigar as he hauled Giles inside the office and tossed him across the room.

Giles crashed into the harbormaster's desk, shouting as his back struck its edge, then went down on the dirty wooden floor.

The harbormaster hissed at him. Even under the scraggly gray beard, Giles could see the fangs.

CHAPTER 6

This is taking too long, Buffy thought. She leaned over the dashboard and peered through the windshield.

Giles stood just outside the door to the harbormaster's office. As Buffy studied him, he glanced at his watch. *So I'm not the only one who thinks this is taking too long,* she thought.

A moment later Oz's van pulled up behind her. Buffy grimaced. This was complicating things even further, and she did not want that. With a glance up at the harbormaster's office to check on Giles and to make sure no one was looking out the window, Buffy climbed out of the car and went back to the van.

Willow was in the passenger seat. Buffy was simultaneously annoyed and pleased with her arrival.

Above and beyond the call of duty. The window was down.

"Hey," Willow began.

Buffy shushed her. "Open the back."

The back door popped open and Buffy went around and climbed in, only to find herself face to face with Xander.

"Hey," he said. "What's Giles doing, just standing there?"

Buffy narrowed her gaze, worried. "I don't know, exactly. Waiting for the harbormaster. The guy came to the door once, then shut it, and now Giles is just waiting. What are you guys doing here, anyway?"

Oz kept his eyes on Giles, but Willow turned around in her seat to face Buffy and Xander in the back.

"We thought we should back you up," Willow said. "When Oz told me you called, I tried calling back. Obviously you're not there, so I called Giles's. Xander told me what was going on. We picked him up and came here. Just in case. Figured Anya could handle the research for a little while."

"Thanks." Buffy smiled. "But we've got it covered, I think. You guys should get back. Research. Pizza. No worries."

"Already ate the pizza," Willow explained. "Or Xander did."

"Hey!" Xander protested. "Research makes me hungry."

"What doesn't?" Buffy asked.

"You didn't mention a spell," Willow said.

Buffy looked at her. "What?"

"When you talked to Oz. You didn't mention anything about a spell but Xander said Giles wanted me to get some stuff, do a locator spell or something. I could have gotten the ingredients together."

"You weren't around, Will. I thought we could just do the spell tomorrow. Besides, Giles wanted to talk to the harbormaster, see if he knows anything," Buffy replied.

There was a sort of tension in the van, but Buffy pretended not to notice and hoped Willow would just let it go. As if the conversation were over, she leaned forward slightly and looked past Willow through the windshield, to see that Giles still stood impatiently at the front door of the office.

"You think something's up?" Xander asked.

Buffy thought about that, let it roll around in her mind a little. This part of Docktown was deserted late at night. Just a short walk would take them to The Fish Tank, where there would at least be a few people stumbling in or out of the place. But down here . . . nothing. Too much of nothing, in fact.

Through Willow's open window, she heard a siren wail somewhere far off. Out on the sea, the bell of a buoy tolled on and on as if it were forever midnight.

Buffy studied the doors and windows of the buildings around them. In several, the silver gray flickering of television sets cast eerie shadows. Most were dark, though. A horrible, queasy feeling roiled in her belly and the fine, downy hairs on her arms and the back of her neck prickled as though an electrical storm were about to sweep down upon them. Her heart beat a little faster.

"This isn't right," she said.

Willow and Xander also seemed spooked. They were staring out from the van as though at any moment the shadows themselves might come alive.

"You feel it too?" she asked.

Xander shrugged. "I don't know. I always feel a little bit like this when we're on monster duty."

But Willow met Buffy's gaze directly. "Something. You're right. I don't know exactly what it is, but . . . something."

"So you've got spider-sense, too?" Xander asked her.

"There's nothing supernatural about it," Willow told him. "Maybe we're all just paranoid. It is a bit freaky down here. But I'm with Buffy."

"I never should have let him go up there. Look, you should all go home," Buffy said as she rifled through her bag, pulled out the crossbow and handed it to Xander. "You're riding shotgun. I just want to be prepared if anything—"

"Buffy!" Xander interrupted. He pointed past her head, out the windshield.

The Slayer turned around just in time to see the old man haul Giles inside the harbormaster's office with inhuman strength. The door crashed shut behind them.

"Back me up, but don't get out of the van unless I tell you to."

As she leaped out of the van, Buffy's heart felt like stone in her chest. A feeling of profound dread, bone-deep, welled up within her. Though she sprinted down the street toward the harbormaster's office, it felt to her as though the world had slowed around her, as though the small shack was miles, rather than feet, away.

"Giles," she muttered under her breath, her friends almost completely forgotten in the car behind her. She heard the engine rattle to life and knew they would be following her in a moment.

But Giles might not have a moment.

Her legs pumped, the soles of her shoes slapped the cracked pavement, and her face felt suddenly cold, despite the exertion. The rest of the world disappeared and the only sound Buffy could hear was her own breathing. Everything else was muffled, as though she were underwater.

Buffy sprinted up to the door of the harbormaster's office, whipped a stake out from its sheath, and kicked the door in with such force that the frame splintered and was torn off its hinges. The place was trashed. Paperwork was strewn about the huge oak desk in the far corner. A lamp lay broken on the floor next to a phone that was off the hook. Both had been knocked off the desk. An old framed painting of a schooner about to crash onto the shore by a lighthouse hung nearly sideways on its hook. A shelf of books had been knocked over. Two other lights still burned in the room, dim, but plenty of illumination to allow Buffy to see the horror that was unfolding before her.

In a narrow doorway that led into another part of the office, Giles lay half in one room and half in the other. His pants leg was torn and blood had begun to seep through the cloth. He tried to sit up, eyes glazed over as he shook his head, blinking rapidly. His face was already bruised and cut, blood dripping down his chin from some unknown wound inside his mouth.

The vampire was hunched over him. In his sharp-clawed fist he held Giles by the front of his shirt. With his other hand, the gray-bearded vampire gripped Giles's throat. When Buffy crashed through the door, the vampire looked up at her and snarled. His appearance was startling to her. Rarely did she see vampires who looked *old.* Existing vampires usually bred only with the strongest and most attractive humans, which was why most of them looked so young and vibrant. Then it clicked in her mind; Camazotz's followers had made this man a vampire because he was the harbormaster. With his aid, their entry into the U.S. would be that much simpler.

The harbormaster hissed at her, bared his fangs. His brow was ridged and hideous, his eyes alive and feral, yet not burning like the others. Another mystery.

"Let him go," Buffy demanded.

The vampire laughed, a deep, throaty, gurgling sound. "Or what? You'll kill me? And if I free him, what then? You'll let me go? We're not all that stupid, you know."

With a grunt, the creature hauled Giles up and spun him around, holding him as hostage, as shield.

"Buffy . . . you must . . . go." Giles croaked.

The vampire rammed his head forward into the back of Giles's skull. The impact was loud, and sounded perilously fragile, as though something had broken. Buffy cringed and felt as though she might throw up. Giles's eyes rolled up to white and he went limp in the vampire's powerful hands.

Fury kindled within her like a furnace. She gripped the stake in her right hand even more tightly.

"Maybe you don't know who you're dealing with, moron," she snapped. "Or maybe you're just too stupid to know better. I'm Buffy Summers. I'm—"

"The Slayer."

The voice came from behind her. Buffy spun, put her back to the wall so that she could see both the doorway and the harbormaster. Amidst the shattered remains of the door stood a creature whose appearance made her breath catch in her throat. Naked from the waist up, the tall, hideous thing was hunched over and a pair of skeletal wings jutted up from his back. They looked as though they had been torn apart, or ravaged by fire. On his chest was an enormous scar, and at the center of the scar an open wound that seemed partially healed, as though it might never close completely.

His hair was black and thickly matted, as was his long beard. He had a short, ugly snout with wet slits for nostrils, and his chalky, green-white skin was pockmarked all over. Upon his forehead were ridges that resembled those of a vampire. From his mouth jutted rows of teeth like icicles, and his fingers were inhumanly long and thin, white enough to have been little more than bones.

But what struck her most deeply were his eyes. Blazing orange fire, just like its vampire followers.

"Camazotz," Buffy whispered, hating herself immediately for the horror and awe she heard in her own voice.

"I'm touched you know me."

The monster grinned.

"No wonder you live in a cave," Buffy sniffed dismissively. "Who'd go out, looking like that?"

Out of the corner of her eye she watched the harbormaster, just in case her taunting of the vampire's master would cause him to do something rash—like snap her mentor's neck. But the creature remained impassive. For his part, where many others would have raged at the insult, Camazotz merely grunted with amusement.

"The man means something to you," the demon-god said. "Your Watcher?"

His voice was wet and thick, something trapped in quicksand and desperate to be free. There was an accent there as well, but nothing Buffy recognized, much like that of the bat-faces she had fought before.

Her gaze ticked toward Giles, still unconscious, and back to Camazotz. There was no percentage in lying. He was obviously far from stupid. But that didn't mean she had to tell the freak her life story.

"Not my Watcher. A friend," she admitted. She

hefted the stake in her right hand, turned its point toward him. "So you're the god of bats, huh? Considering the job description, those are pretty pitiful wings."

Camazotz actually flinched. While he had not responded at all to Buffy's previous taunt, this seemed to have gotten under his skin. Curious, Buffy gazed at him again, took in the bony things that jutted up from his hunchback.

"Sore spot, huh?" She gestured with the stake at his back. "Someone gave you a good mangling. Can you even fly with those?"

Camazotz lost all of the cool reserve he'd shown, and a primitive snarl split his features. His eyes flared and sparked.

"I knew I would have to destroy you to reach the Hellmouth, cow. I am prepared. My Kakchiquels are bred and raised by me. They do not fear you, girl, because they have never *heard* of you. They will face you without hesitation, down to the last of them, because they do not know what a Slayer is."

"They will," she promised, returning his snarl as she relaxed and tightened the grip on her stake. "I've killed bigger and badder and uglier than you. You want me? Come and get me." She stared at him, letting the moment of silence charge the air between them with crackling energy. Then she smiled.

"Let's get it on, stumpy."

The flesh of the ancient creature seemed almost to ripple with his rage. He shuddered, nostrils flaring, long needle teeth bared, and he rose up to his full height, about to lunge at her.

Then Camazotz smiled.

Buffy swore silently, her hopes dashed, her heart aching.

"You want to antagonize me into direct combat, believing you can destroy me and still save your . . . friend," Camazotz said, slippery voice tinged with wonder. "And maybe you would at that, Slayer. Maybe you would. But I have walked upon this Earth since before the human virus infected it, and I have grown cautious in that time."

Camazotz gestured to the harbormaster. "If she does not obey me instantly, kill him. *Drink* him."

Tongue flicking out over his teeth, Camazotz glared at her. All trace of humor was gone from his horrid countenance. "Throw the stake down. On your knees and crawl to me."

Her heart raced and Buffy tried not to let Camazotz see the effect of his words. For all her bluster, she knew he had her. But her mind raced along all the possible avenues of the stalemate in an instant, and she knew there was only one possible choice. If she did as he commanded, they were both dead. If she attacked, Giles would be savaged, possibly murdered, before she could reach him. She had to bank on Camazotz's keeping Giles alive to use as a lure to try to destroy her.

One choice. He might still die, but it's my only choice.

With a final glance at Giles and a burning in her eyes that might have been tears if she dared allow herself to feel the pain in her heart, Buffy turned away from both of them and ran at the harbormaster's desk. Camazotz screamed behind her, but Buffy did not slow. She leaped up onto the desk and dropped her shoulder as she crashed through the window and onto the street beyond, around the side of the building from the main road. She hit the pavement in a shower of shattered glass, sharp edges slicing her skin.

Hating herself, filled with fear for Giles, she rolled and then jumped to her feet. It had been her only choice. Now she had to get to Willow and the guys and get—

Buffy rounded the front of the building and froze, mouth open in horror. The Kakchiquels were there, arrayed in the street like an army. Perhaps two dozen, maybe even more, and each of them wore Camazotz's brand tattooed across his face. Or her face. Lots of hers.

But they did not even notice Buffy. Their attention was on the van.

Oz's van was parked in the midst of this sea of monsters, this swarm of silent vampires. Through the windshield, Buffy could see Oz and Willow, frozen as though they were afraid that any motion would set off the vampires. They dared not attack as long as they were not attacked, so pitiful were the odds.

Then the Kakchiquels began their chant. It rose in volume but lowered in pitch, until it shook the ground beneath her feet and thundered against her like the distant thump of fireworks on the Fourth of July.

It was a moment. A single moment.

Camazotz emerged from the harbormaster's office, blazing orange eyes upon her. The demon-god dragged Giles along by the throat as though he were a rag doll. For a moment, Buffy worried that he was already dead. His glasses were long gone and the blood on his face had begun to dry. His eyes were glazed and dull. A corpse. That's what came into her mind. He was a corpse.

But he still breathed.

That was enough to break her paralysis, to splinter the frozen moment like a thin layer of ice across a pond.

"Oz!" she screamed. "Drive!"

Camazotz screamed something in a language Buffy did not recognize. It was as though a switch had been thrown, for the Kakchiquels surged to horrible, vicious life. They shattered the windshield of the van before Oz could even put it in gear. A startlingly tall female with rings piercing her face in painful adornment used both fists to smash the passenger window just as the van's engine roared and it shot forward a few yards, battering four vampires back and off their feet, and crushing one beneath the tires. The broken leech shrieked his pain, but he would not die. Could not die. It would be in agony for ages.

Good, Buffy thought.

She waded into the swarm with no grace or elegance at all. *Odds like this,* she thought, *it's all or nothing.* Vampires were all around her, clustering like insects as they tried to find an opening in her defenses. Buffy cracked a backhand across the bridge of a nose, snapped a high kick off that shattered a ribcage, stamped hard enough to break a leg . . . too many to focus on killing them. She had to cripple them instead.

But after the first few seconds, a rhythm did work its way into her bones, into her muscles. As if it were merely a closed-fisted blow, she punched the stake through one heart, then a second, parried a fist, dodged a kick, then dusted a third. Ash and cinder blew in a cloud around her, stealing the salt smell of the ocean from the air and replacing it with the smell of moldering tombs and unfiltered cigarettes.

Someone shouted, grunted, barked a war cry, and she knew it was her own voice. Sweat ran down her face and she knew she had descended inside herself, to a place where only the warrior remained. In the heat of battle, Buffy went away, leaving only the hunter. The Slayer.

Bat-faces lunged at her but she didn't even see them anymore. All she saw was that spot on their chests where the stake should go, and the tender places on their bodies she could break.

Then, lost in that place of blood and perfect fury, she heard her name tear the night, slicing through her battle fever. Buffy glanced up at the sound and saw the same bat-face woman, tall as an Amazon, pierced all over, dragging Willow out through the windshield even as Oz tried to gun the engine and run her over. But half a dozen Kakchiquels had lifted the rear of the van so it could not move. The rear window shattered, and Xander popped the crossbow out the window, shot one through the heart. He dusted, but another was there to take his place instantly.

"Damn it, no!" Buffy screamed.

With a leap, she spun and kicked the bat-face in front of her hard enough to break his neck. Buffy landed and ran for the van. Vampires blocked her way but she leaped up and over them and onto the roof just in time to stake the vampire who was trying to drag Willow out of the van. She exploded in a cloud of dust and Willow dropped back through the windshield, bleeding from several long scrapes on her arms and belly.

"Get out of here!" Buffy snapped as she leaped down to the pavement.

Through the shattered windshield, she could see Xander notching another crossbow bolt in the back of the van. Oz watched Willow expectantly, revving the engine. Willow stared at Buffy.

"But Giles—" Willow began.

"We can't help him if we're dead," Buffy interrupted. Then she leaped up on top of the van again, jumped off the back and drop-kicked two of the vamps holding up the car. She dusted a third.

"Now!" she cried, turning back to see Xander firing another bolt from the crossbow through the back window.

Oz floored it. Willow stared at Buffy through the open rear window, face etched with despair. More vampires grabbed onto the van as it went, but Oz ran over several of them and in seconds was dragging two down the street.

As Buffy fought, she tried to watch as they made their way to safety. They were almost out of sight, away from the Kakchiquels, but one final leech still clung to the roof of the van. As Buffy glanced over again, Xander stuck his upper body through the broken rear window. The vampire rose up, about to lunge at him, and Xander fired a bolt into his chest.

Dusted.

The van rolled out of sight.

Safe, Buffy thought. *Now Giles.*

She turned to seek out Camazotz and her unconscious former Watcher. At least a dozen Kakchiquels were dead by her count, but there seemed so many more. Slayer or not, Buffy was growing tired. A spinning kick, a hard elbow, a thrust of the stake and for just a moment her path was clear. Camazotz still stood in front of the harbormaster's office. Buffy stared at him.

Their eyes met.

Gazes locked together, their contact was intimate with the knowledge that Buffy could not win.

Camazotz lifted Giles up with one hand. The man's head lolled to the side but his eyes were open and it looked as though he might be waking, finally. Then the ancient demon, the god of bats, drew one long talon along Giles's throat and blood began to flow.

Amongst the surviving vampires arrayed near their master, two came forward. Clownface and Bulldog.

"Giles, no!" Buffy cried, frozen, paralyzed by the flicker of fire in Camazotz's eyes, and the inescapable truth that she had lost.

Then she screamed his name again and rushed toward the vampires. Camazotz began to laugh.

As if awakened by her cries, Giles began to fight back. He roared his outrage as he gazed around at the vampires surrounding him, filling the street. Buffy tried desperately to reach him, staked one vampire, kicked another in the jaw so hard it nearly tore his head off. Then, through the crush of Camazotz's minions, Giles saw Buffy, and his screaming stopped.

Their eyes met.

"Get out of here!" he snapped at her. "You can't defeat him alone. Get Angel. Get—"

"Shut him up!" Camazotz snapped.

Bulldog held Giles, and Clownface struck him with a single, hard blow to the skull. The Watcher was dazed and fell limp once more, and the two vampires handed him over to the others of their brood.

"Choose, Slayer," the god of bats instructed her.

Buffy wanted to scream her hatred at him, but the words would not come. Only anguish. She released it in a shriek that seemed to tear from her lungs and scrape her throat raw, and she ran at Camazotz.

There were vampires in between.

Off guard, driven only by her fear for Giles, Buffy did not see the baseball bat cutting through the air, nor did she hear it split the wind. It cracked against her head and the wooden bat broke in two as she went down hard on the pavement.

Blinking back the pain, brushing away the blood in her eyes, she looked up. The ghost-white vampire woman she thought of as Clownface stood above her, grinning like an idiot. A heartbeat later, Bulldog came up beside her.

Then they started kicking Buffy.

A rib broke, maybe two.

A foot hit her in the face and a tooth rattled loose. Her mouth was bleeding.

She rolled over and took a kick in the spine that shot pain to every nerve ending. Her eyes flashed open and she saw, thirty yards away, the end of the road. The docks thrust out from the land and the ocean beyond was black as the abyss.

Clownface swung a kick at her eyes. Buffy grabbed her ankle, twisted it enough to throw her off balance. Then she whipped her own feet around and dropped Bulldog's legs out from under him.

Two more came at her but they could not stop her. Buffy cut them down with a flurry of quick blows and ran on. The chanting had stopped during the brawl but it picked up again now and Camazotz roared something unintelligible. Buffy bit her lip and prayed to whatever powers were on her side that he would keep Giles alive as a hostage. For insurance.

Then, brutalized and bleeding, clutching her chest where her cracked ribs blazed with pain, she reached the dock, ran its length, and dove into the churning waves.

At least two vampires came after her. Underwater she heard the disturbance as they dove in.

And they don't need to breathe, she thought. Hope seemed to be seeping from her along with blood.

Buffy swam deeper, farther, kicking and pulling the water past her, moving into the murky depths of the Pacific and praying that they would not find her before morning.

Yet morning was so far away.

And she was running out of air.

She had drowned before, of course. But this time, there was no one around to bring her back. Her eyes were stung by the salt water but Buffy kept them open, peering into the blackness. Her lungs burned. The darkness in her eyes was not merely the shadows under water, but an encroaching dimming of vision.

Her limbs slowed.

Her mouth opened and she choked back her first gulp of sea water.

She stopped swimming.

"Buffy."

She squeezes her eyes shut, tight against the blazing heat that beats down upon her. Copper blood tangy in her mouth, she chokes on something and hacks and spits it out, rolling her face on the ground.

"Buffy."

Eyes snap open, wincing from the sun. Chest heav-

ing, throat ragged, too painful to speak, almost too agonizing to breathe.

"Buffy."

Moist sand beneath her bruised cheek and water washes up over her legs and lower torso. Eyes slitted, she peers up to see who speaks her name so urgently.

A ghost. And oh so appropriate, for she feels as though she must be dead. Lucy Hanover lingers in the air, a phantom through which she can see the trees swaying farther up the beach. A specter whose grim features speak of horrible things, whose eyes are like ghosts themselves, a ghost of a ghost, Lucy haunting herself with what she sees and what she knows.

She has no legs.

Instead, there is only a kind of mist, like the low fog that sometimes creeps across the ocean in the early morning. Perhaps that's what it is, after all.

She floats.

"Buffy."

"Lucy." Her own voice is little more than the rasp of a crab scuttling across sand.

"Catastrophe—"

"Is coming," Buffy chokes. "Kinda got it."

"No."

Lucy hovers closer, places her hands over Buffy's eyes. The heat of the sun that had seared them disappears, replaced by a soothing coolness that seeps through her body. Relaxing.

But . . .

"No?"

"Camazotz is not the threat I warned you of. At least, not entirely. The Prophet says there is more. A plague of vampirism is coming. A plague that will blot the sun from the sky above the Hellmouth."

"Not Camazotz?"

"Not entirely. I only communicate what little she has seen."

"My fault?"

Lucy weeps the ghosts of tears. "Yes. I'm sorry."

Buffy has no tears. "I don't care."

"What do you mean?"

"Giles," the Slayer says. "The only thing that matters. I left him."

Sad understanding illuminates Lucy's face. Blue sky and clouds behind her, through her. "You lived. Your other choice was death."

"Not dead?" Buffy feels the shock of it rushing through her, filling her up even as waves wash over her again.

"Not yet."

"Buffy?"

The dream shattered and blew away. Her eyes flickered open and she cringed from the harsh sun, tasted wet sand in her mouth and felt the damp squelch of it beneath her. The surf washed in, tiny waves almost touching her. The beach. She had made it to the beach.

A pair of familiar silhouettes made shadows across her body.

"Are you all right?"

It was Willow. Her eyes brimmed with tears. Oz stood beside her, his normally impassive face taut with concern.

"Will," Buffy rasped. The pain in her throat was excruciating. "I think I almost drowned," she whispered, and that didn't hurt quite as much. "I feel like hell."

"Looks like you've been there," Oz told her.

"God, Buffy, we've been out all morning looking for you. I thought you were dead."

So did I, Buffy thought.

Willow hugged her gently, careful not to touch anywhere that was bruised. Buffy's heart nearly broke, so grateful was she for the simple warmth of her best friend's touch, for the bond between them, and the strength that Willow gave her in that moment.

Then she remembered.

"Willow," Buffy said, stricken, almost unable to breathe. "They got Giles. Camazotz did. I don't know if he's still . . . I don't know . . ."

Lips pressed together, determined, hiding her own anxiety and grief, Willow nodded. "We'll find him. I swear we will."

CHAPTER 7

"I should've stayed."

Buffy felt numb all over, and cold. Though her cuts and bruises had begun to heal, even to fade, she felt completely drained, as though her life force had been siphoned away from her by her fight with Camazotz. And, in a way, it had.

Willow laid a hand upon hers and Buffy grasped her friend's fingers as though they were the only thing keeping her from drowning. Drowning. Though they sat, now, in the dormitory room they shared, Buffy felt as though she had never washed up on the sand, as though she still rolled beneath the waves with the ebb and flow of the tide.

Oz leaned against the back of the door. Anya sat on the edge of Willow's bed, with Xander stretched out on it behind her. Like Willow, he had scratched his whole body on the broken glass in the van. A line of black stitches was sewn tightly into the left side of his forehead. Apparently he had stitches on his back as well, but Buffy hadn't asked to see them.

Xander was unusually silent. And in pain.

"God, I can't believe this," Buffy muttered, and shook her head.

"Hey," Willow said softly. "You did the only thing you could do."

Eyes searching, Buffy gazed about the room at her friends, then out the window, and finally, at Willow. "Will . . . I *ran*. Giles could be dead. I *ran!*"

"No. You escaped with your life. Buffy, there's a difference. You said yourself that if you'd stayed you'd both be dead now. It was your only possible choice. Now we have a chance."

"If they haven't . . ." Buffy could not finish the thought.

Xander winced as he sat up to look at her. "They haven't," he said flatly. His eyes lacked their usual sparkle, but there was an intensity in them Buffy had never seen there before. A sharp edge, a glint of light as if off a finely honed blade. Pain and rage could do that. Buffy knew almost better than anyone.

"Xand . . ."

He cut her off with the wave of a hand. "It wasn't a trap, Buffy," he told her. "But it might as well have been. Camazotz knew you'd come looking, and he was ready. Giles poked around, got the vampy harbormaster suspicious enough to call his boss, the bat-god. He didn't kill Giles then, and he could've. Easy. Camazotz didn't kill him either. He's their insurance policy. You know that's true. Instinctively you knew it then, or you wouldn't have gone for that swim."

Still numb, Buffy glanced around at the others. Oz had a grim expression on his face, eyebrows knit together. Anya was watching her expectantly. Willow's eyes were filled with both love and sorrow, and she cradled her arms as though to hide her own injuries from Buffy. But it was Xander's bruised, scraped face that drew her gaze the most. He stared at her intently, saying nothing more for what seemed too long.

"Two more things, Buff," he added. "Then I'm going to pass out, if nobody minds. First, Willow, Oz, and I'd be dead if not for you. I feel like I've been hazed into the vampire fraternity, but that's better than being a corpse. Second thing, I think Giles is still alive. Nothing else makes sense. Now, not to be Mr. Pushy Guy or anything, but kinda thinking maybe we ought to get up a posse, go and get him out of there."

All the weight of it, the responsibility for what had gone before and whatever was to come, felt impossibly heavy on Buffy's shoulders. With their eyes upon her she gazed down at the floor. Her nostrils flared and her teeth ground together, and the numbness began to leave her. She realized, suddenly, that it had been her own doing, that numbness, a way to keep the despair and anger and her fear for Giles at bay.

For a time, she had been lost.

No more.

"Buffy?" Willow ventured.

She placed her hand over Willow's, nodded once and stood up. Grim-faced, she paced the room once, mind awhirl not only with the events of the previous night, but with the ominous dream words of Lucy Hanover, the dire predictions of some distant spectral Prophet. While washed up on the beach, half-drowned and barely conscious, she had been visited by Lucy again. The ghostly Slayer had told her that Camazotz was not the danger she had previously been warned about. That troubled Buffy almost more than anything else. With Giles's life hanging in the balance and a threat as significant as Camazotz in town, she could not afford to be blindsided by something else.

"This is because of me," she whispered. "I got so carried away with trying to handle everything on my own that I . . ."

Buffy closed her eyes. The numbness threatened to sweep through her again but she shook it off. "Willow," she said quickly. "You can prepare the same spell Giles wanted to use. Let's assume you can locate their ship. Anything you can do, magickally, to hide us from them when we invade their lair? A glamour, something to make us invisible to them, give us the element of surprise?"

Willow frowned, deep in thought. "I don't know. Giles might . . ." She looked up guiltily. "Let me do some research. Maybe a cloaking glamour. A spell like that's serious magick, but—"

"Don't try it if there's any danger. I can't afford anything happening to you. To any of you." Buffy glanced around at her friends. "Here's the plan. Anya, you're with Willow. Research and magick preparation right-hand girl. Centuries of demonic hijinks have to be worth something, right? Oz, you're with me. Weapons gathering and recon."

"Hello?" Xander said, waggling the fingers of his right hand from his prone position on Willow's bed. "What's my mission: impossible?"

"I need you here," Buffy told him. "You have to wait for Angel."

That got their attention. Willow and Anya spoke in unison.

"Angel?"

Buffy nodded gravely. "As soon as we're done here I'm going to call him, tell him what's going on. I don't know if he'll come—"

"He'll come," Willow said sadly. "You know he'll come."

"I hope you're right," Buffy replied. "We can use all the help we can get. I didn't want to have to . . . but with what Lucy Hanover told me, we don't even know what else might be out there."

She turned to Willow. "We need to find out. We need to know more. That means summoning Lucy and trying to get a direct line of communication with this mystery-ghost Prophet. See if we can get her to say something more specific than 'you're doomed.' "

* * *

For once it was sunny outside . . . just when a little gloom would have been appropriate. Inside Buffy and Willow's room, the shades were pulled down so that only the thinnest glimmer edge of sunlight streamed through on either side. White candles were placed in a rough circle around the room and the white-orange flames that flickered from each of them seemed to sway in a breeze that came from nowhere.

Buffy and Willow sat opposite each other in the wooden chairs from their desks, which they had dragged over between their beds. With Xander and Anya on one bed and Oz on the other, the five of them formed a rough circle. From previous experience, Buffy knew that what they had thrown together was a sloppy séance, or summoning, or whatever the official name for it was. But they did not have time to worry about the niceties of such things. No time at all.

"Clear your minds," Willow instructed.

Her voice seemed somehow different to Buffy, deeper, more confident. It was as though at times like this, the teenage shell that surrounded Willow was stripped away to reveal the triumphant woman she would become in time. The hesitation, the tacit apology, that so often lingered in her voice and mannerisms had disappeared entirely. Radiant with this power, head tilted back and eyes closed, Willow seemed to flow with the candlelight, then merge with the energy in the room. Buffy thought she had never been more beautiful.

Willow's eyes snapped open, fixed directly on Buffy. "I said clear your minds."

"Oh," Buffy said sheepishly. "Sorry."

Eyes now closed, Buffy took a long, deep breath, let it linger within her for a moment, and then let it out as though it were her very last. It was a cleansing, meditative technique Giles had taught her way back during sophomore year of high school. It worked.

Giles.

Buffy cleared her mind as best she could, but thoughts of Giles lingered like prisoners in the deepest dungeons of her mind.

"With hope and light and compassion, we open our hearts to all those walkers between worlds who might hear my plea and come to aid us in this dark hour," Willow began, intoning the words slowly.

Buffy felt Xander's hand grip hers on one side, and Oz's do the same on the other. It was as though the innate power within Willow, the peace and mystic qualities within her heart and soul that made her so naturally attuned to the energies of the supernatural, had created a kind of electrical charge that ran through them all. A circuit of benevolent magick, a beacon to the souls to whom Willow now spoke.

Does she hear them when she closes her eyes? Buffy wondered. *Can she see them in her mind?* They had never talked about it, and for some reason, Buffy doubted she would ever ask. It seemed somehow too intimate, like asking the details of a passionate romance.

"Spirits of the ether, bear my voice along the paths of the dead, whisper my message to every lost soul and wanderer," Willow continued, voice lowering in timbre, becoming not unlike a kind of chant. "I seek the counsel of Lucy Hanover, she who was once a Slayer. She who holds high the lantern to light your path on the journey between worlds."

Giles.

Buffy frowned to herself as a sliver of sadness pushed past the defenses she had erected in her mind. Giles was alive. She would not believe anything else. But she knew what his fate might be, had seen how badly he had been beaten, seen the harbormaster's fangs in his flesh, the blood that flowed when Camazotz slashed his neck.

Reluctantly, she recalled the last time they had called upon Lucy Hanover's aid, and what Giles had said. *I want to be on record as having opposed this. Calling on the spirits of the dead is a tricky business.*

Undoubtedly, he was right. It had once been his job to know such things. But the hard truth was that at the moment, they had no choice. Without him, there seemed no other way to discover what they were truly up against, and what part, if any, Camazotz was to play in it. More than that, what part Buffy herself was to play in the danger ahead.

After half a minute's silence, Willow spoke again, this time her voice barely rose above a whisper. "Lucy, do the lost ones bring my voice to you?"

The answer was immediate.

"They do."

Buffy opened her eyes. The others were all looking as well. Lucy Hanover was there in the center of the circle they had created. The flickering candles and the slices of sunlight that leaked around the shades made a dim gray illumination that washed out the room, washed out the ghost herself, so that she seemed less a thing of mist and spirit than an antique sepia photograph somehow projected onto the air.

"Greetings, friend Willow," Lucy said, her voice sounding hollow and distant. Then the ghost turned her dark eyes upon Buffy. "We meet again, Slayer. I am sorry for what has happened, Buffy. The ghost roads are ripe with gossip and dire news."

Ice spread across Buffy's heart. "Giles?" she asked, almost too afraid to speak his name. "He's not . . ."

Lucy's eyes were kind, then. "No. He is not yet among us. There is time for you, yet, to go to him."

Though she had felt almost suffocated by her concern for him, it was not until Buffy heard those words that she truly understood how afraid she had been. A tiny voice in the back of her mind had been taunting her all along with the thought that it was already too late, that he was dead.

Buffy nodded. "I'll get him back."

"Lucy," Willow interrupted, "Buffy has shared with us the things you told her in her dreams. About this Prophet. Your warnings have been so vague and with all that is happening, with Giles captured and the dangers we all face, we need to know all we can. There must be more to this prophecy."

Lucy shook her head sadly. Her image seemed to shudder, to flicker like the candlelight, and the swirl of mist that obscured her lower half extended, as though she had somehow stood taller.

"I am no seer, Willow. I cannot promise that what this Prophet has scried will come to pass, for I know her only by what the lost souls have whispered. They say that she can see the future, that the mists of time are clear for her. I have only informed the Slayer of her predictions so that you might all be wary."

Willow glanced over at Buffy with deep concern, seemingly at a loss for how to continue.

Buffy did not hesitate. "Can we talk to her?"

"If she will speak with you," Lucy replied in that hollow voice. "I will seek her."

Then, as if she had never been there at all, she was simply gone.

Oz was the first to break the circuit. He let go of Buffy's hand and then Buffy released her grip on Xander's, and they all exhaled loudly, blinking and looking at one another in silence.

Anya examined Xander as though she thought the exertion might have drained him. Buffy thought it was both sweet and creepy, like a coroner autopsying the corpse of a loved one. Willow seemed to have shrunk a bit, and she looked slightly lost as she glanced around the room, obviously uncertain what to do next.

Oz broke the silence. "Well," he said. "That was bracing."

"What now?" Xander gazed at Buffy, sort of nodding his head to prod her to answer the question. His eyebrows went up as further punctuation. "Buff?"

"We wait."

"How long do we wait?" Anya pressed. "I need to pee. Though some think it erotic, I have always found the process rather revolting and would rather it remain a private thing."

Buffy wondered if her facial expression was enough to convey her horror and disgust. "With you on the revolting . . . revulsion. Please. Be my guest."

Anya rose and strode toward the door.

A gust of wind nearly knocked her off her feet. It cut through the room fast and hard enough to scour the walls. In her rat cage, Amy squealed and ran in circles. The windows were closed tight, but the wind tugged at all of them. Impossibly, though the flames guttered with the gusts, the candles still burned.

Then, in a single moment, as though they were atop a birthday cake, every candle in the room was snuffed.

Somehow, even the slices of daylight that had filtered in around the shades were gone.

The wind swirled tighter and tighter until it no longer touched them, instead creating a miniature tornado in the center of the room. Then the wind itself seemed to bleed an oily black, the oil to spread and flow and take form. The wind slowed.

It *became* something.

"She has agreed to speak with you."

Buffy glanced quickly toward the window and saw the ghost of Lucy Hanover hovering there, watchful. Wary.

When she looked back, the wind had died and the flowing black core of it had coalesced into a figure, the silhouette of a woman. The Prophet had no face that Buffy could see, nor flesh, not even the diaphanous mist that gave Lucy shape. Instead, The Prophet was like a female-shaped hole in the center of the room, a black pit that lingered in the air like soot from a smokestack.

But it spoke. *She* spoke.

"Slayer. You summoned me. How may I be of service?"

Her voice was like the whisper of a lifelong smoker whose throat had been ravaged by cancer. Pained and ragged and knowing, in on the perversity of the joke.

Buffy spoke quickly. The sooner The Prophet was gone from the room, the happier she'd be.

"Lucy told me you'd seen something bad coming. Apocalypse-size evil, or at least the giant economy size. She also told me you thought it was going to be my fault. I need your help. Isn't there any way I can cut this thing off at the pass? Not make this mistake? And if there's no way to do that, then I need to know more about what this evil will be, what form it will take, and how I can combat it. There's a demon in town, an ancient, powerful—"

The Prophet laughed. Her obsidian form shimmered where it hung in the room, a wound between worlds. It was sickening to look at, though Buffy could not have said why.

"Not seeing the funny," Xander said abruptly.

Anya shushed him, and Buffy did not blame her. Dealing with beings like this, none of them should be inviting attention. But Buffy had no choice.

"You won't help, then?"

"Not won't. Cannot." The swirling shadow moved just the tiniest bit closer to Buffy then. *"The thing you fear has already been set in motion. The die is cast. Your mistake, Slayer, has already been made."*

"What?" Buffy asked, horrified. Her mouth dropped open. Her lungs refused to work. For a moment, even her heart seemed to refuse to beat. Then, shaking her head, she gasped a tiny, plaintive cry. "But I haven't done anything. How can that be? And nothing's changed."

"But it will," the Prophet told her. *"The future cannot be prevented now. Already the clockwork grinds on. But I can show you my vision, share with you the sight, so you may see what is coming and perhaps better prepare for it."*

Reeling, Buffy glanced at Willow and Oz, then at Xander and Anya. They all seemed as stricken by the specter's words as she was. By the window, Lucy Hanover reached out both hands toward Buffy as though she wished to help, to somehow hold Buffy up so that she would not collapse under the weight of this news.

Prediction, Buffy told herself quickly. *It isn't fact yet. We don't know it's true.*

But it felt true. The words of The Prophet were heavy with finality. With doom.

Buffy swallowed, then looked at the oily silhouette again. "Show me."

"I must only touch you, and you may see."

"Do it," Buffy instructed her.

The Prophet's slick, shimmering form slithered forward. The tear in the fabric of the world extended toward her; fingers like tendrils reached for her.

"Buffy," Willow said cautiously, a tiny bit of fear tinging her voice. "Maybe this isn't such a good—"

The Prophet touched her.

Invaded her.

Buffy screamed.

Torn away.

Buffy hurtled forward, not propelled from behind but tugged, dragged, hauled, painfully and suddenly into a black and red abyss. It felt as though only her face had been torn away, pulled on farther and farther into the chasm of infinite black before her, but the rest of her left behind, all the weight that flesh and blood and bone added to the image she had of herself. What was she? Mind and heart and soul. Face. Eyes and ears and mouth. Words.

Red whirlpools punctured the endless velvet shadow around her, flashing past as she was dragged by. As if the universe itself were wounded and bleeding.

Vaguely, in the fog that seemed to comprise her mind, a dark certainty overwhelmed her.

This was not a vision. Somehow, her spirit had been torn from her body and was now on a journey. Traveling. Hurtling out of control toward some unfathomable point in the distance.

Buffy felt her mind slipping away from her, felt herself shutting down as she was drawn through the void . . . and drawn . . . and drawn. Lulled into a kind of hibernation, aware and yet unresponsive to her surroundings.

Then, suddenly, some sense that the void was not endless, the abyss not infinite. Somewhere ahead was a barrier, a wall, and she was hurtling toward it, bound for collision. She peered into the darkness ahead but all had become black now, as though she were blind. But blind or not, she could feel it, sense its proximity as she was whipped along a course toward inevitable impact.

Collision.

Cold water splashed her face.

Shocked, Buffy stared at her fingers, splayed before her. At the grimy, cracked porcelain of the sink and the water running from the faucet. Instinctively she looked up for a mirror over the sink but there wasn't one.

Of course there isn't one. They took it away the first day, she thought. She flashed back to that time, five years before, when Clownface and Bulldog had thrown her, beaten, bloody and barely conscious, into this cell for the first time. *They didn't want you to cut your wrists.*

Like a cornered animal Buffy spun and her eyes darted around the room. The cell. Bars on the two high windows barely allowed the tiniest bit of light from the outside. Ten-foot stone walls all around. A steel door with rivets driven through it and neither handle nor knob nor even keyhole on this side.

Built for me. This was built for me.

Her hands went to the sides of her head and she squeezed her eyes closed. Then she opened them wide and gazed around the room, hugging herself tightly. Buffy knew things. She did not know how, but she *knew.*

Impossible.

But inescapably true.

She had been here, in this cell, for a very long time. Reluctantly, afraid of what she would find, she looked at her hands again. Rough, hard hands, with lines that had never been there before. She stretched, felt her body, *looked* at herself.

No thinner than before. But harder. Tighter. Rippled with muscles she remembered seeing in magazines and on television whenever they showed women who were Olympians, whose very life was exercise, exertion, sport.

But there was nothing sporting about this.

Buffy's body was taut and dangerous. She felt it, even in the way she moved. She felt like a weapon.

Gathering dust.

This cell. Endless days and nights alone, with only these four walls and the ruthless way she forged her body into this steel thing. Vampires with tattooed faces and orange flames in their eyes; they fed her, kept her alive, but nothing more. No talking, not even threats or taunts. Only the toning of her body kept her sane, that focus on the day she would escape.

And in time, even that focus blurred and there was only the routine of exercise. Hope dimmed.

These aren't my memories. Can't be my memories. I remember yesterday. They took Giles. Camazotz is preying on Sunnydale. Lucy Hanover came in my dreams and Willow summoned her and . . .

Buffy stared down at her hands again. And they *were* her hands. Just as the memories of this room—month after month becoming intimate with these four walls, eating the awful slop they fed her, and waiting for an opening—just as those recollections were hers.

Lines on her hands.

Five years since she had been put into this room.

"No," she whispered. *It's impossible.*

"No!" she screamed.

With a roar of fury and hatred surging up from her chest, Buffy ran full tilt at the door. Though her body still felt foreign to her, she loved the way it moved. Fluid and powerful and deadly. She launched a drop kick at the steel door, slammed into it hard enough to rattle her jaw, then fell to the ground and banged her head hard on the stone floor. Adrenaline screamed in her, and she pushed the pain away. With a flip, she was up on her feet, and she kicked and punched at the door with only the echo of her own grunts in the room to accompany her.

Several minutes passed. She slowed, breathing heavily.

The adrenaline subsided. The ache in her skull and the pain in her bloody, ravaged knuckles was real. The skin on her fists was scraped raw. Buffy reached up to touch the back of her head, where she'd struck the floor, and her fingers came back streaked with blood.

She would heal quickly. After all, she was the Slayer. But the wounds were real. This was real.

Even as her mind recoiled in horror at these thoughts, even as she examined her body and her surroundings, she felt her memory of the battle with Camazotz begin to dim. Desperate to save Giles, they had summoned Lucy Hanover. Lucy had called upon an entity known only as The Prophet, who promised Buffy a vision of the future, a vision that might help her prevent it and save Giles's life.

The Prophet had touched her.

But this was no vision.

Whatever The Prophet had done, somehow she was not nineteen anymore. Buffy Summers was twenty-four, at least. Maybe twenty-five. Somehow, the entity had torn her spirit from her body that day, years ago, and thrust it into the future, into this body.

Her memories of that day faded, now. Though she knew in her heart that in some way it had happened only moments before, she remembered it as though years had passed. But there was a blank spot there as well . . . a period of days she did not remember at all . . . the time during which she had been captured. A gap in her memory existed between The Prophet touching her and the day when Clownface and Bulldog threw her into her cell.

For more than five years, she had wondered what had happened in that dead space in her memory, that blackout.

No. It isn't me. I haven't been here. It never happened, she reminded herself. And yet there was no longer any doubt that this was real. She could feel every muscle, every scratch, every sensation. This was her own body, her own life, and yet somehow her nineteen-year-old mind had been fast-forwarded into an older body, a dark, horrible future.

And all she could do was pace the cell. Work her body. Train for the day the vampires let their guard down.

Days passed. She trained and slept and washed and trained. They brought food before dawn and after dusk, always armed, always in groups of three or more. Made her stand in the far corner, afraid to have her come too close, as though she were a wild animal.

It made her smile.

* * *

Perhaps two weeks later, they brought the girl.

It was dark when they threw her into the cell, bruised and bloody but conscious. Alive. The girl was a brunette, dark and exotic. Italian, maybe, Buffy thought. Tall, but young. Even through the blood, when she looked up with her defiant, crazy eyes, Buffy could see that she was just a kid. Not more than sixteen, maybe less.

For a moment Buffy only stood there staring at her, five years without human contact having built up a callus on her heart and soul. She was two people in one, two Buffys at one time, the hardened prisoner and the young warrior. Then suddenly it was as though the part of her mind that was still nineteen simply woke up. It was as though she had been frozen in this body from the moment she had realized what had happened to her.

Now she thawed.

Ice melted away from her true self.

Buffy went to the girl, reached down for her. "Are you all right?"

The girl's eyes changed then. She blinked and her mouth opened with an expression of absolute astonishment.

"Oh my God," the girl whispered, voice cracking. "You're . . . you're her, aren't you?"

"I'm not tracking."

The girl backed away, stood up slowly, painfully, and stared at her. "You're Buffy Summers. I've seen pictures."

"Yeah? How do I look?"

Beaten, bleeding, the girl actually laughed. A discordant sound, but a welcome one just the same. "Like hell," she said. "You look like hell."

"Who are you?" Buffy asked.

But she thought she already knew the answer.

"I'm August."

Buffy frowned. "You're a month?"

"It's my name," the girl said, annoyed. She wiped blood from under her nose but it was still bleeding. "I'm the Slayer now."

Buffy closed her eyes. Shook her head to clear her mind. She felt a little unsteady on her feet. So many questions. But if this girl was a Slayer, what did that mean for—

"Faith?"

August nodded. "Six months ago. They tried for years to catch her, the way they . . . the way they did you. If it weren't for her they'd have the whole West Coast by now, maybe more. At least that's what my Watcher says. They caught her outside of L.A., I heard."

Wary, maybe even a little afraid, the girl gave Buffy a cautious look. "Have you been here all along? All this time?"

No. I just got here. A couple of weeks ago. I'm not supposed to be here. Those were the first thoughts in her head, but even as they flickered through her mind she knew they weren't really true.

"All this time," Buffy told her. She turned her back

on the girl and began to pace the room. "And now I've got company."

"But haven't you tried to—"

Buffy spun to face her, nearly growling. "Every day. What the hell do you think I am? I'm the Slayer."

"You're *a* Slayer," August corrected. "Not even the main one anymore. Not for a long time. The Council, they just call you the Lost Slayer now. Not even your name."

Buffy took that in. In her mind she reached back to the moment she knew was truly hers, where her mind belonged. Her soul . . . where her soul had been pushed away, into the here and now, and her body left behind. Hijacked.

What had happened between then and now? Where were they all? What had happened to Giles?

"How much territory do they control? Camazotz and the vampires?" she asked.

August seemed deeply troubled. She stared at the steel door, then turned back to look at Buffy, sizing her up.

"Well?" Buffy prodded.

"Sunnydale. A few other towns. Maybe a thirty mile radius around."

"And nobody knows?"

"Nobody believes," August told her. "Nobody wants to believe. That's how they win. Spin control. Marketing the illusion that everything's normal. Plenty of humans willing to help for a piece of the power."

"God," Buffy rasped.

"So there's no way out of here?" August asked, her voice taking on a kind of quiet desperation, as if she had surrendered a part of herself. "You've tried everything?"

"Five years is a long time," Buffy told her. "Maybe with two of us now it'd be different, but I figure they'll just send more guards now to bring the meals."

"Then I guess we don't have any choice," August said softly. Her eyes filled with moisture and she wiped at them bitterly. Then she took a breath and steadied herself, a grim expression on her face.

"Again, not tracking," Buffy told her.

August stared at her as though she were stupid. "They captured you because they finally got smart. If you don't kill the Slayer, there won't be another one. Keep you in here . . ." She whirled around, threw her arms up in near hysteria. "Keep us in here, and there'll never be another Slayer."

Buffy stared at her. "You have a gift for stating the obvious."

"You're just going to let them? There's nothing to stop them from spreading even further now." August bit her lip, shook her head and hugged herself as though attempting to deny the thoughts that were filling her head.

"It sucks. It truly does," Buffy said, hearing the pain in her own voice. The despair. "But until they get stupid, or let down their guard, there's nothing we can do."

August pushed a lock of her short, black hair behind her ears. She would not turn her iron-gray eyes up to look at Buffy.

"There's something I can do," she said softly.

One eyebrow raised, Buffy studied her. "What's that? What can you do?"

Finally, August met her gaze. Her soft eyes had hardened again. Crazy, defiant eyes. Eyes cold and decisive.

"I can kill you."

To Be Continued . . .

Part Two:

DARK TIMES

CHAPTER 1

I *can kill you.*

The stone walls of the cell echoed back the words, and then silence descended. No noise came from the corridor beyond the steel door. The only thing Buffy Summers could hear was her own gentle breathing, and that of the sixteen-year-old girl standing across from her. The one who had spoken those impossible words.

Buffy tensed, taut muscles bunched, and she rose on the balls of her feet. Five years she had been in this fifteen-foot square, a chamber of rock and metal constructed with the express purpose of keeping her within. Five years she had honed her body until it was a coiled spring, a scalpel, a bullwhip . . . all of that and more. When the vampires came to bring food or clothing or bedding, they came in force, with stun guns, and they used them. In all the times she had tried to escape and failed, all the dreams she had had of combat, never had she imagined that the next threat she would face would come from another Slayer.

The girl, August, sensed the alarm in Buffy, and her stance altered slightly, subtly. Though younger, the dark-haired girl was taller than Buffy, and likely thought that an advantage.

"You're not thinking clearly," Buffy said, a rasp in her voice. She had used it so little in recent years.

August seemed to quiver, almost humming with energy like a high-tension wire. Her tongue snaked out and wetted her lips. "My thinking is perfectly clear, Summers. It's your head that's not screwed on straight here. Look around. You're a zoo animal. They've kept you like a tiger in a cage, and you've *let* them."

Again, her words echoed off cold stone. The two young women began, slowly, to move, to circle, eyeing one another, looking for vulnerabilities. In the back of her mind, a voice shouted for Buffy to stop this madness, not to let it happen. It was the voice of her younger self, somehow implanted within this twenty-four-year-old body. But the two minds were both *her*, and so they had begun to merge. The two were one. Despite the reluctance she felt, Buffy knew that only a fool would leave herself open to attack.

It was simple caution for her to be wary of August's threat. The girl, the young Slayer, had a desperation in her eyes that said she might do anything.

"For more than three years, I tried to escape every time the door was opened," Buffy said. "They took to stunning me on principle. After a while I decided to study them instead, try to figure out the psychology of my jailers. Within six months I knew them all, their vulnerabilities, what would work to distract them. Just from listening and watching. Two days before I planned to make my escape, they were all replaced. Someone knew. Someone understood what I was doing."

"Exactly my point," August said grimly. She shook her hands out as she glared at Buffy. "You're a pet. Your master knows you too well."

Buffy froze. "I don't have a master."

"Look around. They might as well have one of those little hamster wheels in here. Or a Habitrail."

Buffy stepped slightly back from August and kept the girl in her peripheral vision, then did indeed look around. Though the room was cold stone, there were several throw rugs on the floor. A plastic rack upon which were piled the blue jeans, white tanks, and sweatshirts they supplied her with; all U.C. Sunnydale sweatshirts, which were all the vampires would give her. Some kind of joke, she was sure. There was her metal-framed bed—all welded to keep her from using part of it as a weapon, and a steel table bolted to the floor. Nothing wood, of course, for wood could splinter, and splintered wood could kill her captors.

"I don't see what you see. They need me alive," Buffy said. "Food and water, clothing."

August shook her head. The expression on her face might have been called a sneer if not for the sadness in it.

"All this time, though. If you realized that you couldn't escape, you could have found a way to force them to kill you. Could have killed yourself, if that didn't work. Shatter that porcelain sink, use it to slash your wrists, bleed out here on the floor. But you didn't. Why didn't you?"

Buffy shook her head. *"That's* your solution? What's the Council teaching you? I'm the Slayer. Once I get out, there'll be hell to pay."

Though she had been on guard, the absurdity of August's rantings had caused Buffy to pause for a moment in surprise.

August moved. With a single, fluid motion, so fast Buffy barely had time to react, she stepped into the space between them and lashed out with a savage backhand. The blow struck Buffy's cheek hard, but she rolled with it, turned in an instant and readied herself for another attack.

None came.

Instead, August only stood and stared at her, face reddened with rage. Tears began to stream down her face.

"How can you be so arrogant?" August demanded. A lock of her hair had fallen across her eyes but she did not move it. "You're *a* Slayer, not *the* Slayer. You're not what's important. The only thing that matters is that there be someone out there to fight them.

Once you get out, there'll be hell to pay? That's what you said. It's *already* hell out there, Summers. Can you help them?"

A chill seemed to weave frozen tendrils all through Buffy's body. Though the idea horrified her—everything August was suggesting did—there was a kind of blunt, primitive truth to it as well. Was it arrogant of her to think she was more valuable alive than dead? Simply by staying alive, she had given her captors what they wanted. Yet the idea of doing anything else . . .

She shook her head. "No. Listen. Now that we're both in here, we'll find a way. Before they figure out what it takes to contain us both."

August laughed bitterly and wiped away a tear. "You've been here five years! We can't get out, Buffy. The only way for there to be a new Slayer, out there, fighting the darkness, is for one of us to die. If you're not willing to do what has to be done . . . I will."

The dry shuffle of their feet upon the stone floor was an eerie whisper. The two Slayers began to circle again, and though she rejected the very idea of what was happening, Buffy could not deny it. It was a dark, vicious irony, a nightmare made real. Her throat was dry, but she felt the power in her body, tendons and muscles moving with grace and precision.

"I won't kill you, August. But I'm not going to let you kill me, either."

The girl's face darkened further. Fresh tears sprang to her cheeks. The teenager beneath the Slayer's façade was revealed.

"Damn you!" August cried, the words heavy with the weight of her pain and grief. "Do you think I want this? I've got people I love out there. Dying every day, trying to keep the vampires from spreading. Someone's got to protect them."

"We'll find a way. It may take a little time—"

But the conversation was over. August glared at her coldly, now, and wiped the last tear from her red-rimmed eyes. Her lips were pressed together in anguish, and she shuddered once, then was still. The girl dropped into a battle stance that Buffy was all too familiar with. It had been the first one Giles had taught her when he took over as her Watcher.

"August—"

"Quiet," the girl snapped.

August leaped at her in a spinning kick aimed directly at her head. Though Buffy saw it coming, had been prepared for it, it was only instinct that saved her from the blow. She darted her head to the side, dodged the kick by a scant half-inch. With her right hand, she caught August's ankle and reversed the direction of the kick, spinning the girl onto the floor. August's shoulder struck the stone hard, but even as Buffy moved in on her, the girl rolled, swung her foot out and swept Buffy's legs out from under her.

Even as she fell, Buffy spun and threw her body forward. She ducked her head, went into a roll that took her across the room, then leaped to her feet only inches shy of her bed.

August was already there. As Buffy came up, the

younger Slayer snapped a side kick at her chest. Buffy could not avoid it. Something in her chest cracked and all the breath went from her lungs. She crashed into the plastic shelving holding her clothes and it splintered and broke apart beneath her.

Her rib cage grated painfully as she moved, but Buffy rolled up against the wall, amidst the wreckage of the shelves. A shard of plastic pierced her side, but she ignored the lancing pain, so superficial compared to the burning in her chest when she breathed.

Mouth still set in that grim line, eyes red with tears fallen and unfallen, August went for a simple kick. Buffy had counted on her believing that her chest injury had caused her to cower against the wall to make herself less vulnerable. August was young. She bought it.

With an open hand, she stopped the kick mid-swing and shoved August backward. Braced against the wall, Buffy had enough support to knock her off her feet. With the enhanced strength of the Slayer, she pushed the younger Slayer with such force that August flailed at the air, unable to spin out of the fall. Her head struck the edge of the steel table as she went down.

Though she pushed herself up on her hands and knees, August was too slow, too vulnerable.

Buffy was up, frustrated, searching for some way to stop this fight before it ended the way August wanted it to.

She was stronger than this girl. Probably faster as well. August had been Slayer for six months, maybe trained for a year or two before that. Buffy had been the Slayer more than three years before she was captured and had worked her body mercilessly in the interim, not merely with exercise, but with shadow-boxing and a martial arts *kata* she had devised from the various disciplines she had studied before.

But she was trying to reason with a girl on the brink of madness, a Slayer driven past rationality by the world she lived in. It disturbed Buffy deeply to think how desperate things must be to drive August to this.

Not that it mattered, now.

The girl wanted to kill her. In order to prevent that, to reason with her, she would have to incapacitate the younger Slayer, at the very least.

She watched August warily, her eyes wide, imploring. "It shouldn't be like this."

August shook off the blow to her head. She would not raise her eyes to look at Buffy, only crouched there for a moment on hands and knees.

"No. It shouldn't," she agreed. "But it is."

Silent, lightning fast, August shot up from the floor and barreled into Buffy. It was a brute's move, with no finesse, no precision, but it worked. August used her greater height and weight to ram Buffy up against the stone wall. The impact drove the air from Buffy's lungs again, and the fire of pain in her chest from her cracked ribs flared even more brightly.

August snapped her open hand forward in a palm strike that drove into Buffy's shoulder quite precisely, dislocating it with a loud pop and an agonizing tear. Black spots clouded Buffy's vision, but she knew that was just the pain.

Pain was an old and familiar friend, by now.

It woke her up.

It pissed her off.

But before she could react, August gave her a quick shot to the face. Her nose broke and blood began to flow.

The next blow never touched her. Buffy dodged and August's fist hit the stone wall. Something in her hand broke with an audible snap, but August only grunted softly.

"That's it. You don't get any more free shots," Buffy snarled.

The copper tang of blood touched her lips, her dislocated arm hung loosely at her side, but Buffy popped August with a head-butt. Stunned, August staggered back. She cradled her right fist, then tried to spin up into a high kick.

Buffy ducked in, slammed her palm into August's upper chest, and knocked her down. The gash in her side did not slow her, nor did her dislocated shoulder or her broken nose.

"Get up," Buffy told her. "Stop this. If I have to, I'll break both your arms, but I don't want to have to feed you for the next few months."

August glared at her, beyond reason. The crazed girl leaped up again, back into a battle stance, despite her shattered fist.

"Damn you," Buffy whispered.

With a cry of anguish, August launched a blow with her good hand. Buffy dodged, but the girl followed through, stepped into her blow, past Buffy, then brought her arm back and shot an elbow at the back of Buffy's head.

Furious, Buffy stumbled forward and then turned to see August lunging at her again. The steel table was behind her. Buffy hopped up on top of it, avoiding August's attack. Then she kicked out at the girl's damaged hand and August shrieked with pain and staggered back.

Tears sprang to August's face again. She stood for a moment, panting, glaring at Buffy. "They need us, don't you get it?"

"Not like this," Buffy said softly. "Not like this."

"I won't stop," August vowed. "One of us is going to die."

Buffy only shook her head in denial and clutched her dislocated arm against her body.

August rushed the table. Buffy dove into the air, executed a somersault over the girl's head and landed on both feet. In one fluid motion, she shot a hard kick up at the younger Slayer's head. August tried to dodge. She was a scant heartbeat too slow.

There was no time for Buffy to even try to abort the attack. The kick caught the other girl in the side of the neck, just where her jaw met her neck. With a wet snap, her spinal column broke right at the top, and her corpse tumbled backward with the force of the kick and rolled in a heap across the stone floor.

August did not move, not even a twitch. Buffy knew she was dead.

"Oh God, no," Buffy whispered.

Hot tears came into her eyes, but her grief was quickly overcome by anger. "Dammit, no!" she shouted. "No! No! No!"

With her good hand she covered her eyes, spun around in a small circle. It *was* a nightmare. It *had* to be. But the raging pain in her shoulder and the copper taste of her own blood on her lips, was real.

The girl in front of her, August, a Slayer, was dead. That was real.

"How?" she whispered. "It wasn't supposed to be like this. Stupid girl . . ."

But she was not sure if that last part was meant to be addressed to August or to herself. It was cruel, without doubt. All this time alone, then finally contact with not just another human being, but a person who was part of the same mission. And now this.

Her tears felt cold on her cheeks compared to the heat of her blood. Buffy knelt by August and pushed a lock of her hair away from her fine, Italian features, and just studied her for a moment. She wondered if she herself had ever looked so young.

New hatred welled up within her, bearing a razor edge sharper than anything she had felt in years. They had taken Giles from her, Camazotz and his vampire hordes. They had imprisoned her. But they had never been able to take even a sliver of her hope and her faith.

Until now.

Teeth gritted together, a violent surge of adrenaline making Buffy bounce slightly on her feet. She used her good hand to drag August around near the front of the cell, only inches from the door. It would hit her when it opened.

Where August's corpse had lain, she knelt, took a breath, and whacked her broken nose with an open hand. She let the cry of pain come, and sagged a bit. Then she bent over and let blood flow onto the floor. After a couple of minutes, she rolled up the back of her shirt and felt for the puncture wound left in her side by the broken plastic that had impaled her. The wound had already begun to heal.

Buffy used her fingernail to dig it open.

Again, she bled.

But the loss of blood did not weaken her. For it was not her own lifeblood that drove her now, but hatred for her enemy, like nothing she had ever felt before. Her world had been gray for so long that she could remember almost nothing else. Gray and numb and lifeless.

It had color again. The world was crimson as her blood, and black as a vampire's heart.

She allowed herself only one more minute to recover, to breathe slowly. Then she stood and went to the sink, still cradling her dislocated arm. She sat on the floor. With some difficulty, she managed to wrap both hands around the pipe that came down from beneath the sink. Strong hand over the weak one, holding it in place, she planted her feet against the wall under the sink, took a breath, and pushed out as hard as she could.

An awkward angle, but there was enough force behind it to snap the shoulder back into the joint. It felt as though someone were trying to separate the bones with a jagged knife. Buffy could have stopped the scream by biting through her lip. She did not.

Her mouth opened and she shrieked loud and long, releasing all the pain and misery she had been holding inside. Somehow she managed to find her feet and stumbled to the shattered plastic shelving. She snatched up a splintered piece, brought it to her flesh, and sliced a long, clean, horizontal cut across her throat.

Buffy hissed air in through her clenched teeth, for the cut stung, but it was superficial. Nothing vital was hit. After her shoulder, it was almost nothing.

Quivering from the pain and her emotional turmoil, she staggered to the place where she had made herself bleed. A small pool of her blood was there on the stone. Not enough, to her eyes, but it would have to do.

She dropped the plastic dagger to the floor a foot away, then lay down on her side, right cheek already sticky where it touched the edge of the puddle of her blood.

Maddox stormed down the corridor with a cigarette clenched firmly in his lips and a two foot stunprod gripped in his right hand. One of the guards—a rookie named Theo who was practically a newborn—followed behind him like a puppy.

"Whaddaya think's goin' on, Maddox?" Theo cooed excitedly. "There were screams and everything.

Sounded pretty nasty. Got a serious Slayer catfight, I think. Woulda loved to've seen that."

"We'll see."

They rounded a corner and Maddox saw four other guards up ahead, the two who were supposed to be on the door, and two others who had likely come down from the upper level when the commotion began.

"What the hell's going on?" Maddox demanded.

"Told you, Maddox," Theo said, grinning. "They're tearing each other apart in there. When you said put the new girl in there, that's the last thing I expected."

With a grunt, Maddox froze. He turned to stare at Theo. "Who sired you?"

Theo blinked. "Um, Harmony did."

Maddox sighed. "Of course she did."

Then he tapped Theo's chest lightly with the stun-prod. The vampire jerked and shuddered as electricity surged through him. His eyes were wide, white against the black tattoo Maddox thought he brought shame to. Theo slumped to the ground, jerking a bit. He opened his mouth and a tiny bit of bloody drool spilled out with the tip of his tongue, which he had bitten off.

With a sigh, Maddox turned to the four guards. They were proper vampires, eyes crackling orange, grim-faced, not at all perturbed by what they had seen. Or, at least, not revealing it if they were.

"Remind me to kill Harmony," he said.

The others all nodded, once, silently.

"You're ready?"

Each of them unsnapped a prod similar to the one Maddox held, only smaller and more portable. Maddox could smell the blood inside the room, the scent seeping beneath the steel door. It worried him. He was responsible for what happened within that cell.

Anxious, he gestured to the guards. "Open the door."

The one in front, Brossi, glanced once at Maddox. Other than Maddox, he was the only one who had been there from the beginning. The two of them had been part of the group that had captured Buffy Summers in the first place. They knew what she was capable of.

The door itself was testament to that. There were three locks, equidistant from one another. Each controlled an inch-thick iron deadbolt that, when engaged, locked into a metal casing that itself was plugged into the center of the three-foot-thick stone wall that framed the door. There were two more deadbolts each at the top and bottom of the door, though these had no locks.

It took Brossi a few seconds to unlock the door, then disengage the three main bolts. He hesitated for a moment, turned to glance at Maddox, and then his face changed, forehead erupting into the brutal guise of the vampire. His fangs lengthened and he ran his tongue over them.

Maddox had more control than that, but he did not blame Brossi for feeling threatened. Every time they opened that door, twice a day, they had to be prepared for a fight. Just when they thought Summers was beaten into submission, that was when she was most likely to attack again. When he had been instructed to put the new girl into the same cell, Maddox had balked. It was just asking for trouble. No question it was going to make feeding time even more difficult.

But this was the last thing he had expected.

"Careful," Maddox told the guards.

Brossi slammed back the bolts on the top and bottom of the door, sliding them abruptly out of their metal casings. There was no way to do it quietly, so he opted to do it quickly. The other guards with their stun-prods gathered behind him, tattooed faces expressionless, only the glittering fire of their eyes giving away their anxiety. Maddox stepped up behind them, but at a respectful distance. It was not that he was a coward. Quite the opposite, in fact. If this was some sham and the two Slayers killed them all, it would fall to him to stop them.

"Go!" Maddox ordered.

Brossi shoved the door open with his shoulder, tensed for an attack. The steel door swung eight or nine inches, then hit an obstruction with a dull thump. The vampire guard took a half-step back and prepared to defend himself. Nothing happened, and after a moment, he pushed at the door again, put his weight behind it, and it opened slowly as the obstruction slid out of the way.

"What the hell is that?" Maddox asked, trying to see over the shoulders of the guards.

Half inside the door, Brossi glanced back quickly. "The new girl. She's down."

Cursing loudly, Maddox shoved the others aside and moved up behind Brossi. It was his job not just to keep the Slayers prisoner, but to keep them alive. Maddox peered over Brossi's shoulder, trying to see deeper into the room to make certain Summers wasn't lying in wait. Then he turned and glared at the guards around him.

"Stay back. Either one of them makes it to the door, take her. Break something, burn something, whatever, but I don't have to tell you what will happen if any of you kill one of them."

He gave Brossi a nudge. "Stun her."

Maddox's gaze ticked down to the still form of the teenaged Slayer on the floor, then back at the room. The door was still only partially open, and he could not see Summers anywhere.

She's there, though. A frisson of fear went through him. There was something about the woman that had always given him the creeps a little bit. She was warm and soft, like all humans, and yet there was something almost haunting about her, almost mystical. There was a promise in her eyes every time she looked at him; a promise of payback.

Brossi extended his arm through the open door, stun-prod in hand. Maddox stood back a little, just in case the door should be slammed shut suddenly, his own electrical prod held up at the ready.

As Maddox watched, Brossi tagged the downed Slayer with the prod. Electricity sizzled through her with a crackle and the smell of sizzling hair. The girl did not so much as twitch. There were none of the muscle spasms that electrocution brought.

"Dammit," Maddox whispered. *I'm screwed.*

The girl looked badly beaten. There had been a knock-down, drag-out brawl inside that cell. One Slayer was dead. But what of the other one?

"I'm coming in, Summers. Keep away from the door!" he called into the cell.

Then he motioned Brossi out of the way and kicked the door with all the strength he could muster. Something broke in the corpse on the floor when the door collided with it, but it slid open another half-foot.

Just enough for Maddox to see Buffy Summers lying in a pool of her own blood, bruised and beaten, throat slit, eyes wide and cold and staring right at him.

"No!" Maddox screamed. He struck out at the air, then rammed a fist against the door with a clang and did not even feel the pain. "Dammit, no!"

Furious, and filled with terror as he began to wonder what fate awaited him now, Maddox strode into the room. His stun-prod hung at his side. Astonished, he stared around at the shattered plastic shelving, the clothes strewn about. From a distance, he examined the splintered piece of plastic that had obviously been used to slash Buffy's throat.

"Maddox, how . . .?" Brossi began to ask.

His words trailed off when Maddox glared at him. "New girl cut Summers's throat. Summers broke her neck before she died."

"I don't know," Brossi said slowly. "Better keep back from her. Give her a few volts before you get too close."

Maddox hesitated. Then he studied the Slayer's eyes, the haunting eyes that had promised him death so many times. There was nothing there now. Like tarnished marbles, they were.

The way she lay, mouth partially open, the blood from the wound in her throat had pooled up against her lips. That was the thing that convinced Maddox. That whole side of her face, her hair, her nose, lay in blood, and with her mouth open like that, if she were alive, well . . . she would have been able to taste it. Her own blood. Like a vampire.

Her chest did not move. Her eyes were dead ice fragments. But it was that one detail that convinced him.

Still, Maddox was cautious as he reached out with the stun-prod. The eyes still gave him a chill. The tip of the prod swept toward the woman's eyes, but there wasn't so much as a flinch. Just for safety's sake, he touched the prod against her shoulder. The body jerked slightly, but he'd seen that before. The electricity that surged through the corpse was enough to do that. The hair on the dead woman's head shivered and even floated a bit with the static.

"She's dead," Maddox said, forlorn. "What the hell do I do now?"

He was about to prod her eyes when a thought

occurred to him. Maddox turned and looked at Brossi.

"Or is she?" he said, grinning. "I mean, *he* never comes here, right? We'll just lock it up again, leave them here."

Brossi's expression was grave. "When the new Slayer shows up, he'll know."

"We could be gone by then," Maddox replied sharply. "It's a big world."

Brossi hung his head, all the tension going out of him. In the corridor, the other guards were wide-eyed with the realization of their fate. One of them, Haskell, cut and ran right then, his footsteps echoing back down the corridor. For a moment, Brossi turned in that direction, then regarded Maddox again.

"There isn't anywhere far enough," he said. "It's over, Maddox."

"I never even wanted this job!" Maddox shouted, his voice echoing in the cell.

Mind spinning, he turned back toward Summers again. Rage and fear building inside him, Maddox swung back his leg to kick the corpse. His boot thunked into her flesh . . . *moving* flesh. As if it were part of his own motion, she closed herself around his leg, crawling halfway up it, and snapped it at the knee.

Maddox screamed.

As he went down, he felt the prod tugged from his grasp, and then Buffy Summers, the Slayer, stood over him, her resurrection as sudden as a vampire's, but far more shocking to him.

Despite the pain of his shattered leg, he grinned. She wasn't dead.

"Maddox!" Brossi shouted.

"Don't kill her!" Maddox roared.

The other guards, against his previous orders, began to enter the cell. They all seemed to be moving in slow motion in comparison to the Slayer, and each had a kind of vacant, frightened look in his eyes. He did not blame them. Summers had only ever been a captive to them, but in all that time, they had never underestimated how dangerous she was.

Once upon a time, Camazotz had kept the existence of the Slayer hidden from his Kakchiquels, but that had changed after her capture. They had all heard tales of the Slayers now, and knew that Summers was among the most dangerous who had ever lived. For their entire community, the girl locked in this custom dungeon had become almost mythical.

Now they had seen her dead. She had taken a hit from the prod and barely reacted. She had lost a great deal of blood. It was almost as though what they fought was a horrible specter of the Slayer, rather than mere flesh and blood. Not a woman, but a bogeyman so terrible even the creatures of darkness feared her.

They had barely kept her caged all this time.

And now she had a weapon.

In the dim light of the stone room, Maddox

reached out for the metal table and struggled to rise. The Slayer moved so fast he could barely keep his eyes on her. All in all, it would have been much better if she had had a stake. Brossi was electrocuted and then decapitated. The other two were disarmed before she broke them. Maddox could only watch.

Then she came for him.

CHAPTER 2

Exhilaration shot through Buffy as she rushed down the corridor toward a red, glowing EXIT sign. The sign itself—an indication that this place had originally been used by humans—made the whole scene almost surreal, and she felt giddy with her freedom.

Freedom.

But she wasn't free yet. Her captors had kept a hood over her head when they brought her here years before, so she had no idea what surrounded the building she was in. Things were bad. That was all she had learned from August, but it was enough to set her nerves on edge.

Thoughts of August made her flinch and swallow hard. Nausea roiled in her gut and bile rose up in the back of her throat. The girl had forced her hand, and

161

even then Buffy had done everything she could to avoid killing her, but August was dead. When she thought of that, and the things she'd had to do to herself to feign her own death, her feet began to slow beneath her.

Buffy could not afford to slow down.

She took a deep breath, picked up her pace again, and silently cursed the vampires for not having any wood around. A chair leg, anything at all, would have made it possible for her to dust them without feeling so much like it had been a massacre.

In her mind, she saw a quick flash of herself slamming the huge steel door closed on Maddox's neck, severing his head. The spray of dust that had resulted was welcome, but despite her years of hatred for her jailer, there was no triumph in it.

Not that she had any sympathy, either. What unnerved her was that the deaths she had dealt out to the guards had been so intimate. She did not want to get that close to the undead. Not ever. They were abominations, unclean things; a truth she had come to realize more and more during her captivity. Her calling was to eliminate them, but it was a filthy job.

The sick feeling in her stomach abated somewhat, but a faint, sour taste remained in her mouth. She shook her head once to clear her mind, then shoved through the door at the end of the hall. It swung too wide, and would have clanged off the wall if she had not caught it quickly enough.

A momentary pause to be certain no one was near,

and then she started up a set of stairs in front of her. A long oak railing was bolted to the wall. Buffy stopped halfway up and lashed out with a snap kick that cracked the railing in two. The halves dangled down, tearing at their moorings. Another kick, aimed at one of the sagging halves, and a fifteen-inch length of splintered oak clattered to the stairs. The Slayer snatched it and continued upward.

It was too thick by far. Her grip did not come close to reaching all the way around it. But it would do. It would most certainly do.

There was a door at the top of the stairs. As she raced toward it, the door began to open. A vampire poked his head into the stairwell with a predator's curiosity, his nostrils flaring as he scented the air. The black tattoo splayed across his features, bat wings extending down his cheeks into a thin beard, made the blazing orange fire of his eyes stand out in ghostly fashion, there in the darkened stairwell.

Those ghostfire eyes widened as he spotted her. "Oh, sh—"

Buffy pivoted and popped a kick at the door. It clanged into his head and the vampire stumbled back into the corridor. She hauled the door open and pursued him.

Though she sensed some alarm in him, the vampire faced her without hesitation. "She's out!" he yelled into the empty corridor. "The Slayer's out!"

"Tattletale," Buffy rasped.

Expressionless, she backhanded him. He tried to

block the blow, but she was too fast for him. Faster than ever before. It had been a long time since she had fought anything but shadows, and it was going to take some getting used to, but she was at almost her most powerful now.

The makeshift oak stake flashed down and punched an enormous hole in his chest. The vampire dusted.

From around a corner off to her left came the sound of running feet. Her eyes flickered closed for a moment: three, no four of them. Though the stake felt good in her hand, and though she wanted to eliminate all of her captors, her priorities began to assert themselves.

Primary among them was simply to get out, to escape, to see the sky again. To breathe fresh air.

Buffy took off down the corridor, away from her pursuers. The structure she was in appeared to have once housed offices, for there were doors and glass windows looking inward all along the hall. Each office was dark and lifeless inside. The hallway itself had no external windows, however. At least not here.

Up ahead, the hall turned right. Buffy rounded the corner just as she heard shouts behind her. The vampires had seen her. That was all right, though. She could practically smell the outdoors now. Nothing was going to stand in her way.

Even as that thought skittered across her brain, she looked up. At the end of the hall in front of her, the structure opened up into a wide lobby area. The door was all glass. The walls on either side of the door were glass. All of it was painted black.

A pair of vampires stood blocking the door, arms crossed. They did not flinch as she approached, did not even attempt the arrogant, menacing grin that their kind had mastered long ago. But Buffy remembered all too well how this breed of vampires worked, these servants of Camazotz. The demon-god who was their master had trained them to be silent and fearless. Yet she had seen fear in the tattooed eyes of the ones she had killed in her cell, and knew that it was there in them.

"You can get away from the door, or you can *be* the door," she told them grimly.

In unison, they unfolded their arms and prepared to fight her. Behind her, Buffy heard more shouts as her pursuers caught sight of her again. Ahead, the door sentries stood firm, eyes crackling with energy.

Buffy rushed headlong at them without breaking stride. She was three feet away when they lunged for her. The Slayer froze in place, both of the sentries' reach fell short. Buffy leaped up, spun into a round-house kick that caught one of the sentries in the jaw and sent him reeling back toward the blacked out glass door.

In the instant before the glass shattered, she punched the splintered oak railing through the heart of the other. As he dusted, his partner crashed through the glass door. The darkness fell away, and the daylight poured in.

The sun.

A grin slipped across Buffy's features as she watched the other sentry scramble to his feet among shards of black glass and try to get inside. He began to smoke, and then to burn, and just before he would have reached the shade, he exploded into a cloud of cinder and ash.

The Slayer stepped calmly out into the sunshine, sneakers crunching shattered glass. Then she turned, bathed in the light, and eyed the bat-faced vampires who had been rushing at her from within. They all stopped short ten feet from the door, avoiding the perilous splash of sun that spread across the floor.

Once upon a time, Buffy would have teased them, said something funny. She didn't feel funny anymore. With a flourish, she made an obscene gesture, turned, and walked away.

But she felt their burning eyes upon her back.

The building she had been in was a three-story office with no name or insignia on the front, and no sign. Only a street number, One Five Seven.

It was a beautiful Southern California day, the kind of glorious day she had always taken for granted growing up. This was, after all, what California was all about. Today, however, she reveled in it. Birds sang. A sparrow glided across the street in front of her. The breeze carried sweet smells to her, like springtime, though she was not sure of the season.

Free.

Though Buffy knew she had to act immediately, to figure out the lay of the land, to find her friends and discover what horror had driven August so wild, she was overwhelmed for several moments simply with being outside again. She had to shield her eyes or look down at the ground for the first few minutes, so unaccustomed was she to the brilliance of the daylight.

A relief surged through her unlike anything she had ever felt. Along with it came a feeling of power, as though some long dead battery within her was being recharged.

The block she was on was lined with faceless buildings similar to the one she had escaped from. Boring corporate shells. As she strode toward an intersection ahead, though, she frowned. Something was not right. Even out here, something was intensely not right.

Disconnected as she had been for so long, it took her a moment to put it together. An ominous feeling descended upon her. Then she knew. It was not the presence of something dreadful, but an absence. The absence of life, of bustle, even of traffic. The birds were the only activity in sight.

Greatly troubled, she began to run again. At the intersection, she glanced both ways along a street dotted with trendy storefront boutiques and sandwich shops. Though she had not been there since shortly after moving to Sunnydale, Buffy recognized the town. She was in El Suerte, maybe fifteen minutes from home.

Hope rose again within her, punctuated by the appearance, far down the street, of several cars crossing at another intersection. Then, off to her left, an engine caught her attention. She turned to see an SUV cruising along among the shops. It halted abruptly in front of a sandwich shop and the driver, a middle-aged man in a well-tailored suit, popped out and took a look around. He spotted her, frowned, then hurried into the shop.

Moments later he emerged again, carrying several plastic bags she presumed were filled with sandwiches and drinks. Buffy's only thought was of home, of getting back to Sunnydale. Quickly, she trotted across the street to catch the man before he could drive away.

"Hey!" she called.

Eyes wide, he stared at her in alarm. Buffy slowed, wondering if he was some sort of paranoid.

"Why aren't you working?" he demanded, gaze darting up and down the street as though afraid he might be seen speaking to someone slacking off.

"Umm, day off?" Buffy shrugged. "Do you know where I can catch a bus to Sunnydale?"

He laughed, but it was a tiny sound, almost as though he were coughing instead. "What are you, some kind of nut? Who in their right mind would ever *want* to go there?"

Again he glanced around. "You better get off the street, sweetheart."

Then he ducked into the SUV and locked the doors even before starting the engine, as though afraid she might try to carjack him. A moment later, he pulled away. Buffy called after him, but he didn't even look into the rearview mirror.

Angry now, she turned toward the sandwich shop, determined to get answers. When she glanced at the door, however, she saw a dark-haired man with a thick mustache turning a key in the lock. He pulled back from the door when their eyes met, as if he did not want to be seen. Then he closed the blinds that hung by the door, and she could not see him or the inside of the shop anymore.

"What the hell's wrong with you people?" Buffy shouted.

But a deep dread had filled her, a horrible feeling that she knew exactly what was wrong with them. It was impossible, of course. A whole town could not be terrorized like this. But they were.

A sudden squeal from a siren startled her. Buffy turned to see a police car cruising slowly toward her. It rolled up beside her. Two cops jumped out with the engine still running and began to walk toward her. They began to reach for their weapons.

"Excuse me, Miss Summers, but we're going to have to ask you to come with us."

Miss Summers. They knew who she was. They were looking for her. Her suspicion of moments earlier had become a reality. The people terrified to be on the streets, the police looking for her. She had not been the only captive in El Suerte. The vampires held the entire town prisoner.

The two police officers drew their weapons and aimed at her.

"Miss Summers."

"I don't think so," Buffy replied. "It isn't as though they're going to let you kill me."

One of the cops, a tall, dark-complexioned guy with sad eyes, looked extremely uncomfortable. His partner was a heavyset man with pasty skin and thick glasses.

Pastyface smiled. "I can shoot both kneecaps, maybe your shoulders. You'll recover, but it'll hurt like hell. One way or another, you're coming with us."

Buffy sighed. "I don't think so. Thanks for the ride, though."

Pastyface looked confused. With a single, fluid motion, Buffy spiraled in the air toward him and kicked the gun from his hand, shattering his fingers in the process. He let out a scream even as the tall man fired. Buffy was still in motion, however, and the bullet whistled past her cheek, close enough that she could feel the air pressure change by her skin.

Then the tall man stared down at his hand, stunned that his gun had somehow disappeared. Buffy showed it to him, then tossed it over her shoulder. As he watched it sail through the air, she punched him hard enough to spin him around. He tumbled like a felled redwood on top of his partner.

Alarm bells continued to go off in her head, but they had nothing to do with the cops. They were practically forgotten already. All she could think of was the reaction of the sandwich man in the SUV when she had mentioned Sunnydale.

Who in their right mind would ever want to go there?

He lived in El Suerte, a prisoner of the vampires who ran the town, and he thought the idea of anyone going to Sunnydale was crazy.

Tendrils of ice spread throughout her body, wrapping around her spine and curling up in her gut. Grim-faced, she went to the police car and slid into the driver's seat. As she put it in gear she caught sight of her reflection in the rearview mirror.

A shock ran through her.

For just a moment, she saw herself at nineteen. Then the illusion faded and she saw the way she truly looked, the hard line of her jaw, the ragged cut of her long, blond hair, the crinkles at the corners of her eyes and mouth, the furious glare of her eyes. It was startling, after so long, to see her own reflection. She saw that it was not only the world they had changed, but her as well.

Buffy hated them all the more for it.

In her mind, she saw again the image of herself at nineteen. That was how it was supposed to be. None of this was meant to happen. For a short while, she had almost forgotten that. Yet again the voice of her younger self rose up within her, took control.

I've got to get back. I've got to fix this.

The words meant so many things. Whatever was happening in the here and now, she had to do something about it, true. But that was the older Buffy's priority. Within her body was also a girl out of time, a college girl who only ever wanted to be normal. A young woman who had been told by a ghost that she would make a mistake that would have catastrophic results. She could not help but think that she lived amongst those results even now.

I have to go back, she thought again. *Figure out what I did wrong, find a way back, and stop it.* It never occurred to her to wonder if such a thing were possible. After all, the being called The Prophet had somehow cast the spirit of her younger self forward to inhabit her future body. If that was possible, there had to be a way to reverse the process.

For the moment, though, she had to figure out just how far the vampires' influence had spread, and stop them. It was what she did, who she was. The Slayer. Before The Prophet had touched her, had sent her forward in time, Buffy had been determined to dedicate herself wholly to being the Slayer, and also to having a life of her own. One hundred percent Slayer, one hundred percent Buffy. An impossible task, but she had done impossible things before. Yet that struggle had frustrated those close to her, and might have indirectly led to her current situation. If she had not made such a mess of things, she would never have been in a position to rely upon The Prophet, would never have ended up here.

A grim smile cut through her melancholy now. For in this future she did not have to worry about trying to live two lives to their fullest, about filling two roles. The things that had made up the life of Buffy Summers seemed to have been torn away, leaving only this monstrous landscape where vampires ruled. No one needed Buffy anymore. She didn't need to live two lives . . . only one.

She was just the Slayer now. There was a freedom in that, and it felt good.

Knuckles white where she gripped the steering wheel, she accelerated and raced out of El Suerte, headed for Sunnydale. Soon enough, they would know she had taken the car. Her only hope was that they would not realize where she was headed.

Though she tried not to, Buffy wondered what had become of her mother and her friends, her old gang. Not only now, but *then*. Willow, Oz, Xander, and Anya. Not to mention Giles, and even Angel. What had happened to them that day, after The Prophet had cast her out of her body?

In the past . . .

It was difficult to breathe. Willow glanced around the dorm room she shared with Buffy, and shuddered. It was a pretty big room, but she felt claustrophobic in it for the first time. Oz sat beside her, and she reached out to squeeze his hand for reassurance. Xander and Anya were there as well. Quite a crowd for her little summoning, in the darkened room, with the shades pulled down.

But even in the darkness, the thing that shimmered in the middle of the room, beside Buffy, was darker still. It made her think of black holes, the way it swirled, oily and black, there in the air, a rip in the fabric of the world.

Willow had summoned Lucy Hanover, the ghost of a long-dead Slayer, who now aided lost souls in the afterworld. The ghost had heard dire predictions from this thing, called The Prophet, and had agreed to try to bring it forth to communicate those prophecies more precisely.

But now that it was here, Willow only wanted to send the thing back. Just being in its presence made her skin crawl like nothing she had ever felt before. And now it seemed to float nearer to Buffy; or, perhaps more accurately, it seemed to consume the space between them, to slither across reality as it reached for her.

No! Willow thought. *Buffy, don't let it near!* But somehow she had lost the strength to cry out.

The specter of Lucy Hanover lingered, hovering near the window, watching the proceedings as Buffy spoke to The Prophet. The entity's words stunned them all.

"The future cannot be prevented now. Already the clockwork grinds on," it said, voice like whispered profanity. *"But I can show you my vision, share with you the sight, so you may see what is coming and perhaps better prepare for it."*

Buffy flinched away from it and glanced over at Willow. Silently, she urged the Slayer to say no. Anxiously, Willow bit her lip. The ghost of Lucy Hanover reached out phantom hands toward Buffy as though she wanted to help. But she was already dead. This was all the help she could offer.

Buffy sat up straighter and stared at The Prophet, the flowing black presence in the room. "Show me."

Willow shook her head slowly, warning, but Buffy did not see. Still, somehow, she felt unable to speak.

"I must only touch you, and you may see."

"Do it," Buffy instructed The Prophet.

The Prophet's slick, shimmering form slithered toward her. The tear in the fabric of the world extended toward her, fingers like tendrils reached for her.

Finally, Willow felt something give way within her, as though the grip of some hideous force had finally loosened.

"Buffy," she said cautiously. "Maybe this isn't such a good—"

But it was too late. The Prophet touched Buffy. And Buffy screamed.

The Slayer's eyes went wide and she stared as though she were seeing a vision of unspeakable horror. Her mouth remained open but the ragged, high-pitched scream died on her lips. Her chest began to heave, and Buffy started to hyperventilate.

"Buffy!" Willow cried.

She ran to her best friend and grabbed hold just as Buffy began to fall limp. Angry, and fearful for her, Willow glanced around the room. Oz was beside her, Xander and Anya behind him, looking on worriedly.

Otherwise the room was empty.

"Where . . . where'd they go?" Willow asked softly.

The others glanced around as well, apparently equally mystified.

"That's just like a disembodied clairvoyant," Xander muttered. "Offer up the ominous future, then skip town before the questions start rolling in."

"I'm going to open the shade now. I've had enough darkness for today," Anya said in clipped tones.

When the shades were up, and the sunlight streamed in, Willow felt a little better. Buffy was still breathing, though her eyes were closed and she was pale. Her skin felt too cold.

But she was alive. And she was the Slayer.

"What do you think's up?" Oz asked.

Willow swallowed hard. "Well, I'm sorta hoping I'm wrong. And it bothers me to think about how often I feel that way. But I'm guessing whatever future that thing showed Buffy, it was too much for her to handle. Kinda think she's in shock."

"Whoa. Red light," Xander said. "She's the Slayer. How could just seeing something put her into a state of shock?"

"I'm thinkin' it depends what she saw," Oz noted.

Anya threw her hands up in exasperation. "See! Why does this stuff always happen?" She rounded on Xander, a small pout on her lips. "Why do we live *here?* In all the world, *this* is where you want to live? Can't we go far away from the impending apocalypse?"

"You could," Willow said sadly, still gazing at her

best friend's pale features. "But that wouldn't keep it from coming."

For another few moments, Willow cradled Buffy gently in her arms. Then, with a suddenness that gave her a start, the Slayer opened her eyes. Her skin was still cold and white, but her eyes were as fierce and determined as always.

Fierce and determined . . . and yet there was something else there as well.

"Buffy!" Willow cried.

"See!" Xander said. "She's okay."

Buffy sat up and shook Willow's hands off her. She stretched like a cat, as if testing her body to see if she was harmed in some way. Flexing her fingers, she stared at her hands as though they were some newly invented marvel. Then she stood up carefully, a bit off-balance. She nearly collapsed, and Willow thought of a foal just testing its legs for the first time.

"You are okay, right?" Xander asked doubtfully.

The Slayer glanced around the dorm room. A sly grin stole across her features for one moment, and then was gone. She went to the closet, reached inside and grabbed a black leather jacket, though it was too warm outside for the coat.

"Buffy?" Willow asked. "Come on. I know you want to protect us, but we're part of this. It's our future, too. What did you see?"

As she slipped the jacket on, Buffy turned to regard them all. There was no emotion on her face now.

Her eyes flickered with some sort of light, as though from within.

"Everything will be fine," she said, a peculiar slurring to her voice.

"You're not all right," Willow told her. "Come on. Just give yourself an hour's rest. Then we'll figure out what to do about Giles. You've got to talk to us, Buffy. Let us help."

But Buffy shook her head. "There is nothing you can do."

"So you're going to go after Giles alone, after all this?" Xander demanded.

He sounded ticked off, and Willow didn't blame him.

"Do not concern yourself," Buffy said bluntly.

With that, the Slayer turned and left the room, not even bothering to close the door behind her.

"Great," Xander sighed. "Now she's back to that again. Omnipotent Slayer-girl. Taking it all on herself."

"I don't know," Willow said slowly, staring at the half-open door.

Oz sidled up beside her. "What don't you know?" he asked, brow furrowed.

"I don't think this is about that," she said. "This is something else. Something new and family-size creepy. Or, okay, could be just Willow-paranoia. But I'm thinking The Prophet touching Buffy? Possibly more to it than just a Viewmaster of Doom."

"There was a sinister vibe around that thing," Anya agreed. "But what do you think it did, exactly?"

Willow stared at the door. "Remember the part where I said 'I don't know?' "

"Well, we'll keep an eye on her. See what's what," Xander suggested.

Willow nodded, deeply troubled, and afraid for Buffy. She didn't know if the future was going to be as The Prophet had predicted, but she had a sinking feeling it was going to be ugly, one way or another.

As she drove along nearly deserted roads, Buffy was chilled by the changes she saw around her. A few cars passed by, and some stores were open, but many others were boarded up. The skating rink just off I-17 had been partially destroyed by fire, and the parking lot was cracked and overgrown. There were no rollerbladers, no joggers, no bicyclists. Other than those few cars, the only people she saw were a pair of homeless men raiding a Dumpster behind a Chinese restaurant that was apparently still in operation, and they scrambled back through a broken fence behind the place when she drove by.

Buffy decided it was perhaps best to enter the town quietly, perhaps even invisibly. They'd be looking for the car, after all. Buffy ditched the El Suerte police car in the overgrown lot that had once been the Sunnydale Twin Drive-In.

It rolled across the cracked pavement, four-foot weeds whisking against the grille of the car. Buffy killed the engine, took a long breath, and laid her forehead upon the steering wheel for a moment. A slight motion, and she flinched at the sudden pain in her broken nose. Along with her other wounds, it had begun to heal quickly. That was part of being the Slayer. But it was still very sore.

Resolute, she popped open the door and climbed out, then hesitated. Inside the police car was a shotgun locked in a brace between seats. It would be a simple thing to snap the brace and take it with her. Buffy glanced into the car and looked at the gleaming barrel of the gun. Then she shook her head. What she wanted was a crossbow. Maybe even a sword. But after all this time she suspected that the weapons caches at Giles's apartment and her mother's house, not to mention her dorm room back at U.C. Sunnydale, would have been cleaned out. Even if they were still there, the Kakchiquels, Camazotz's vampire followers, would likely be keeping an eye on those places in case she should return.

Without those weapons, without even a knife, she would have to fashion some crude, makeshift stakes, and hope that was enough.

Buffy left the car where it was and began to walk back toward the road. After a moment she paused and glanced back at the concrete structure on the far side of the lot that had once served as both projection booth and concession stand. Once upon a time, like any abandoned structure in Sunnydale, it had been a prime nesting place for vampires and other creatures of darkness.

Best to make sure, she thought.

In a light jog, she crossed the lot without any attempt to hide herself. If anyone were inside the bunker-like edifice, they would already have seen her. The metal door was rusted and hung off its hinges. The sky above was blue as a robin's egg, the wind whispered through the overgrown brush in the lot, the sunlight painted the world around her in bright hues. But the beauty of the day ended at that rusty door. The gaping maw of the place almost seemed to swallow the sunlight. Within was impenetrable darkness.

Nothing moved inside.

Buffy kicked the door loose and it crashed down onto concrete inside. She paused for a moment, then slipped into the dark. It took a moment for her eyes to adjust. Blinking, she ventured farther into the now gray, dusty interior of the building.

Nothing. Something scuffled in the walls, but that was all. It was little more than a tomb for several generations of mice. There were counters of shattered glass where concession snacks had once been offered. Empty now.

Head cocked to one side, Buffy listened, searching for some sound that did not represent rodents. Convinced she was alone, she turned to leave and then thought better of it. Upstairs in the projection booth she was likely to find furniture of some kind. And it was easier to turn smashed furniture into stakes than to forge them out of downed tree limbs, particularly when she had nothing to whittle with.

Sure enough, at the top of the stairs, in the box of a

room where the projectionist had once done his work, she found a small table and several wooden chairs, the legs of which would be satisfactory for her purposes. Buffy crossed to the table, pulled out the nearest chair, and froze with astonishment as she gazed at what lay upon it.

A crossbow.

More accurately, *her* crossbow, the one Giles had given her when they first began to train together. Beside it, a folded bone-white card with two words printed neatly on the front: FOR BUFFY.

Doubt flooded her and she glanced around anxiously, suddenly sure she must have been mistaken. Someone had to be here—otherwise how could she explain the weapon's presence?

Yet her senses confirmed it. She was alone.

Tentatively, she reached out to pick up the crossbow, studying it intently to be sure there was no tripwire or other trap involved. There was not. Only the crossbow, and on the chair opposite that one, a small quiver containing bolts for it.

Profoundly unnerved, a thousand questions in her head, Buffy shattered one of the chairs, snapped the legs and back into half a dozen usable stakes, and carried them under one arm with the quiver. In the other hand she held the crossbow. On alert, skin prickling as she searched around her for any sign of another presence, she hurried down the stairs and out into the sun.

With the blue sky above, she felt a little better, but

not much. This was a mystery that disturbed her deeply. Someone had known or at least suspected that she would find her way to this spot, or had been here upon her arrival and left these things for her to find.

And all across the lot, the shadows cast by nearby trees and the remnants of the drive-in screens had grown longer. The afternoon was waning, and night was only a few hours away.

Buffy hurried to the police car again. She opened the trunk, and was relieved to find a canvas bag that had belonged to one of the police officers inside. There were cotton sweatpants and a sweatshirt in there, as well as a large pair of sneakers. She dumped the clothes out, dropped the weapons into the bag, then noticed a small box of roadside flares and took those as well. She slung the bag over her shoulder and headed, not for the road, but for the chain link fence at the far side of the lot.

It felt to her as though there were eyes upon her, now. The crossbow was almost warm in her grip. Buffy vaulted the fence and set off through a stretch of woods that would lead up to a power plant, from which she could work her way eventually into Hammersmith Park, and then into the backyards of residential Sunnydale.

Stay off the street, she told herself.

CHAPTER 3

If the silence in El Suerte had been surreal, the ravaged streets of Sunnydale were all *too* real. As Buffy made her way through back alleys and across fire escapes, hugging the shadows to keep out of plain sight, a constant current of alarm and abhorrence ran through her body. Her town had become an abomination.

The parks were ravaged, statues destroyed. Every few blocks she passed a row of buildings or houses that had been burned out completely, leaving a charred shell behind. It was unnerving, seeing some shops and markets apparently thriving, while so many other businesses had been ransacked, shattered windows in the front a sure sign of what she would find inside.

Three times she had entered such a store, and each time the result was the same. Christabel's Consignments, The Flower Cart, and Quarryhouse Pizza. Each store had been torn apart, ripped and shattered, but it had obviously happened long ago and a thick layer of dust, umblemished by the footprint of a single intruder, lay upon everything. In the back of each of those businesses, Buffy discovered the remains of the owners, so decayed that there was no way to tell how they died. She could only assume the vampires had killed them.

And yet the others, the stores that were still running, were equally disturbing to see, for Buffy knew that their proprietors must be cooperating with the vampires, serving both the humans who still lived in Sunnydale and the monsters who ruled it.

With each block she drove, Buffy's mood became even more grim. Questions about her mother's fate, and that of her friends, kept forcing their way into her mind, but Buffy pushed them away. Before she could help anyone, she had to know exactly what the situation was, what she was dealing with. Someone had been there, at the Twin Drive-In. They knew she was on her way here. No way could she risk going by her house just yet.

In a way, despite her horror at the devastation that had occurred in some places in town, it disturbed her even more deeply when she saw that other businesses and homes seemed remarkably well-preserved. Downtown was deserted, and yet many of the businesses actually still had lights on. Curious, Buffy broke in through the back door of the Espresso Pump. The machines hummed quietly, the coolers still working, red lights winking on coffee machines, ready for business.

Buffy made her way through the darkened store to the front door and looked at the posted hours of business. There were three words printed there: OPEN ALL NIGHT. Simple enough, but they created more questions. The Espresso Pump was still in operation, as were most of the bars she had seen, as well as video stores, a couple of small markets, and the Sun Cinema. But were they run by vampires or humans? *Were* there many humans left?

As she had made her way around town, she had seen several police cars cruising slowly down deserted streets. *Probably looking for me,* she'd thought. But she had also seen a few other vehicles, including two gray vans with no rear windows and blacked-out windshields.

Just inside the Espresso Pump, Buffy stepped back a bit from the door when she saw another of those gray vans cruise by slowly. It seemed too quiet, almost as though it were rolling along without an engine. Ridiculous, of course. She had not heard anything because of the hum of the many machines inside the café. But eerie nevertheless.

A car pulled up in front of the Sun Cinema across the street. Buffy was only slightly surprised to see a haggard-looking middle-aged couple climb out together. They walked around to the trunk, from which they retrieved a trio of large film canisters. Revulsion rippled through her as she realized what was going on. These people were collaborators. Whatever was in the canisters, they were films that had been brought in to be screened for the vampires that now populated Sunnydale.

Maybe they had no choice, Buffy thought. But she knew that they all had a choice, the people who still lived in this town. Some of them might not be cooperating with the vampires, but rather were paralyzed by their fear, too terrified to fight. The people remaining in Sunnydale could have banded together and killed their masters, or simply run off while the sun was up. Some probably *had* fled. But Buffy knew that she would have to be careful. Whether collaborators or simply ruled by their fear, she could not afford to trust anyone who was still here.

The whole town belonged to the monsters now, one enormous lair for the vampires she had come to know as Kakchiquels, the servants of Camazotz. With this as the epicenter, they were building a kingdom, an empire even. Their control extended at least to El Suerte, probably farther.

Buffy needed answers.

As soon as the human couple had disappeared inside the theater, Buffy went back out into the alley behind the Espresso Pump again. With the canvas bag of weapons slung across her back, she moved lithely through the hidden places of Sunnydale, always alert for watchful eyes. Even the humans here could not be trusted, that much was now certain.

The going was slow due to the need for stealth, but within twenty minutes she found herself on a block of warehouses, factories and office buildings that ran parallel to the street where the Bronze sat. There were other bars there as well, and it stood to reason she might be able to catch a human out during the daylight.

Answers. The need to hear it from the lips of a living, breathing human being was strong in here. Her instinct, and her own memories of the place, had suggested this would be a good neighborhood to start. If that didn't work, she might try at the college, or simply break into a home that looked as though it were still occupied.

It had occurred to her that the initial skirmishes she'd had with the Kakchiquels all those years ago had been in Docktown, but it would take too long for her to get over there. She had a couple of hours, probably less, before dark. If possible, she wanted to be out of Sunnydale by then. Otherwise she would need a safe place to use as her base, and had no idea where to begin.

Buffy slid between an enormous trash bin and the brick wall of a warehouse. Fifteen feet above the ground was an iron ladder that led to the roof. Without hesitation, she splayed her hands against the brick on one side and the metal bin on the other and crawled up between the two. Muscles rippled like cables in her arms.

With a push off the wall, she landed atop the trash bin, balanced on the metal lip of the thing. Buffy sprang from her perch and both hands locked around the bottom rung of the ladder. Feet against the building, she pulled herself up and then was scrambling hand over hand to the roof.

Crouched low, she sprinted across the rooftop to the opposite corner, where she could see the street that ran in front of the Bronze, as well as the alley beside the building she was on. Disappointment deflated her. The street below was empty of movement of any kind. A stray beer bottle, pushed by the wind, rolled across pavement with a tinkle of glass. Otherwise, all was silence.

For ten minutes or more, Buffy sat there at the edge of the roof. From that height, she could see almost as far as Docktown to the east, the blazing sun on top of the cinema downtown off to the north, and to the south, the tops of houses in residential neighborhoods.

It was as though the entire town had been killed, drained by a vampire. Yet it seethed with menace, as if at any moment its eyes would open, burning orange, and it would rise with fangs gnashing, thirsting for blood.

Anxious, Buffy bounced on the balls of her feet and glanced time and again at the deepening hues of blue on the horizon and the long afternoon shadows on the street.

"I've gotta get out of here," she whispered.

Almost as if on cue, the sound of a distant engine came to her. Buffy crouched down even farther and glanced furtively up and down the street. A moment later, she saw the same gray van—or another exactly like it—cruising toward her.

With a small squeak of brakes, it stopped in front of the Bronze. There was a moment's pause and then the horn blared twice and the passenger door opened.

The figure that emerged from the van made Buffy shiver, though the sun shone warmly on her. She could not see if it was male or female, but it was clothed in a silver radiation suit that covered it from head to toe. Only the black goggles across its eyes broke up the endless silver. Not an inch of skin was visible.

Vampire, she thought, and instantly knew it was true. Daylight reflected off the folds in its silver suit, but the monster was safe within that protective garb.

The driver of the van beeped again and the front door of the Bronze slammed open. A tall human man with black hair came out of the club, hands in the air.

"All right, all right! Keep your shirt on!" he snapped.

The vampire walked around to the back of the van and opened the door. From what Buffy could tell from that angle, there was nothing inside the van. Then the man turned back toward the Bronze and shouted inside.

"Move it! Come on, kiddies. Everyone has to take a turn."

Almost immediately, six more people came out of the club, all in their late teens, early twenties. Three male, three female. One of the girls began to sob and hesitate, unwilling to climb into the van with the others. The dark-haired man went to her, held her face in his hands and whispered something that made her stiffen, wide-eyed. After that she went meekly to the back of the van and climbed in.

The vampire returned to the front of the van, climbed in, and then the vehicle rolled away.

For a moment, the dark-haired man stared after it. Then he went to the door of the Bronze and locked it up before walking to a brand-new convertible Mercedes parked along the road amongst several other cars.

He got in and started the engine. Then he took a moment to tilt his head back and regard himself in the mirror, fussing with his hair.

Which was when Buffy recognized him.

"Oh my God," she whispered. *"Parker."*

The last time she had seen him he had been a freshman in college. He had seduced her, used her, and then pretended he had done nothing wrong. Now he was five years older, and Parker Abrams was not only collaborating with the vampires, he seemed to be enjoying himself.

"Son of a bitch," Buffy muttered angrily.

She withdrew from the edge of the building eight or ten feet, paused, then ran full tilt. With a grunt of effort and anger, she sprang out across the narrow alleyway below. The gap was broader than she had judged and she extended her body forward, turned her leap into a dive. Buffy made it across with room to spare, hit the roof of the Bronze and tucked into a roll.

Without a pause, she flowed back to her feet and ran across the building to stare down at Parker's car. The Mercedes slid into reverse, but moved only two feet as he attempted to pull out from between two other vehicles.

He was right below her.

Buffy leaped out into open air, her hair whipping behind her as she fell straight down, canvas bag dragging behind her like an unopened parachute. Though it lasted only a heartbeat or two, the fall seemed extremely slow to her. Parker had turned the steering wheel and put the car in drive again, and even as she fell he began to pull forward slowly, at pains to be sure he cleared the bumper of the car in front of him.

Her boots slammed the hood of the Mercedes with a loud crumpling noise. The impact made her teeth clack together and drove her to her knees.

Parker screamed in surprise and fear and for just a moment, forgot he was driving. The bumper of the Mercedes rapped lightly against the car in front of it.

He didn't even notice. He only stared at her. "What—" he muttered. "Who the—" Parker's eyes went wide, and she knew then that he had recognized her.

"Oh Jesus. *You.*"

Buffy rose from the dented hood and gripped the top of the convertible's windshield. Parker gripped the wheel, cut it as far to the left as he could, and pressed the accelerator. He clipped the other car's bumper again, but Buffy flipped herself over the windshield and into the passenger's seat.

"No!" Parker yelled.

Beside him now, Buffy shot her right hand out and latched on to his throat, squeezing.

"Stop the car."

Parker slammed on the brakes. "Buffy, please," he rasped hoarsely, eyes roving desperately, searching the streets.

It turned her stomach to think that he might be hoping the vampires might still be there, might protect him from her.

"You remember me. You know who I am. Let me ask you, do you know *what* I am?"

Choking, he managed a wheezing "yes." His eyes were on her, and Buffy stared back at him until Parker looked away. She released his throat and he began to massage it, almost whimpering. When she reached around to pull her canvas bag into her lap, he flinched.

"I'm going to ask questions. You're going to drive. If I think you're lying, I'll snap your neck. Any doubt in your mind that I mean what I say?" she demanded.

He hesitated. Then he smiled, as if relieved. His eyes still had the sparkle that had charmed her once upon a time. "Buffy," he said amiably. "You don't have to threaten me."

Nostrils flaring, she turned to glare at him. "You took advantage of me once, Parker. But that was a long time ago. Do I look like that girl to you now?"

Cowed, he gave her the once-over, then shook his head.

"I'll break you," she promised. "Just drive."

"Where to?"

Her thoughts skittered off in several directions at once. There was no way to know how far Camazotz's influence had spread. But she was certain that there was no way a city the size of Los Angeles could have been overrun. If it had, they wouldn't still be based here in Sunnydale.

"South," she said.

Parker drove.

A car passed going the other direction. She watched to be sure Parker made no attempt to signal the driver, likely another collaborator on his way to open up some business that would serve the vampires. The shadows had grown longer. The sky on the western horizon had begun to darken.

Nightfall was imminent.

"Faster," Buffy instructed.

"Your wish is my command."

"Guess you're pretty good at that response," Buffy snarled. "How long have they been in control here?"

"In Sunnydale? Going on four years, I guess. It started small at first, a few people here and there disappeared. Then the cops and the professors up at the college started acting weird. The new mayor, too. Night classes. Evening press conferences. At some point, there were enough of them to just take the town. They did it all in one night, after that. The winter solstice, y'know? Longest night of the year."

The wind seemed almost chilly as it whipped around the convertible.

"How many are there?"

Parker shrugged. "No idea."

"My friends. My mother. What happened to them?"

"I never met your mother. And I haven't seen Willow or that other guy since before that night."

Buffy winced, hurt by his ignorance. She wanted so badly to know what had become of her friends. But Parker could not help her.

"How far does their influence extend?"

"I heard they've turned the governor. But that's just the beginning of the king's plans for the state. Same as he did here, he's gonna turn officials and people in power, then build up enough of an army to take the whole state at once. Right now it's just around here. Sunnydale's like ground zero, with maybe thirty square miles in his control. He's smart about it, though. Keeps other towns functioning, even has people in some of them thinking nothing's changed, not even knowing the vampires have taken over. Morons. The leeches keep reproducing, though. It's only a matter of time."

His words chilled and infuriated her.

"Those people, the ones you gave to the vampires, who were they?"

Parker swallowed loud enough for her to hear it. He twitched a little. "They're . . . like me. We play along, we live pretty good. But we all have to take turns going to the lair. They . . . use us. Drink, whatever else they want. One night only. Then they throw us back until it's our turn again."

Bile rose in the back of Buffy's throat and her stomach convulsed. She nearly threw up right there in the car. Her nose crinkled with her distaste. Then she remembered something else he'd said.

"King."

"What's that?"

"Camazotz has them all calling him 'the king' now? It wasn't enough being the god of bats?"

Parker actually chuckled and shook his head. "You really have been away, haven't you, Buffy?"

Buffy frowned. "What the hell's that supposed to mean?"

But he did not answer. The evening had darkened the eastern sky to a bruised purple, though to the west it was still a baby blue. Minutes left before true night.

Ahead was the intersection with Royal Street, which ran alongside the north end of Hammersmith Park, a quarter of a mile from her mother's house. The light was yellow.

Parker began to slow down.

"Don't stop."

But he only smiled. Alarmed, Buffy turned to see a gray van speeding up behind them.

"Go!" she snapped at him.

Up ahead, a second van barreled down Royal Street. Its brakes squealed as it came to a shuddering halt, blocking the way in front of them. The van behind them slewed sideways, preventing them from retreating.

Furious, Buffy shot an elbow into Parker's side, then punched him in the side of the head. The car was hemmed in front and back. Resigned to a fight, wary of the encroaching dark, she grabbed her bag and leaped up to stand on the seat. Her hands went into the bag and withdrew the crossbow, nocking a bolt into place. She shot a glance at Parker and saw that he was groggy, but conscious. He reached for the steering wheel and the gearshift.

With a grunt, Buffy kicked him in the head and he slumped over the wheel. The car horn began to blare incessantly.

Ahead of her, four vampires in silver suits climbed out of the van. Three others emerged from the vehicle behind her.

Seven. She'd faced worse odds.

The sky seemed to grow darker in the space between one blink and another. It seemed to Buffy that eyes stared ominously down at her from the windows of every building around her. She thought of her mother's house, so close and yet impossibly far, and tried not to think of what she might find if she dared go there.

On the corner was a coffee and doughnut place she and her mother had been to a hundred times. Its familiar presence seemed almost to mock the way she knew the world *should* be. The nineteen-year-old soul that shared a double existence with its older counterpart inside her retreated even farther within.

"Come on!" she cried, outraged, prepared to tear down this ugly new world and rebuild the old, even if she had to do it alone.

The four vampires in front of the Mercedes started toward her. Buffy laughed darkly and shot a crossbow bolt at the one in front. It exploded into a burst of dust inside its silver suit, and the suit crumpled to the ground, empty. Buffy had nocked another bolt into the crossbow in an instant.

Then the vampires began to remove their goggles and hoods. It was dark enough now, and it was as though they wanted her to see them, to realize that they did not fear her. She might kill them, they seemed to be saying, but she was in enemy territory, surrounded now, and with more on the way.

Buffy fired again, but this time the vampire that was her target moved swiftly, dodging the bolt.

She nocked another one, prepared to fire as one by one they removed their hoods. With a harsh intake of breath, she recognized two of the vampires in front of her. One was a female with green-dyed punk hair, face covered in garish, red and white greasepaint. The other was an ugly male who seemed always to accompany her. Though Buffy did not know their real names, during their skirmishes—years ago—she had come to think of them as Clownface and Bulldog.

They knew, she thought. *Knew where I was, all along.* It could not be coincidence that of all the vampires in Sunnydale, these two were the ones who had caught up with her.

Out of the corner of her eye, Buffy caught motion behind her. Alert, ready to defend herself, she spun to see that the other three had also begun to approach her. They had already removed their hoods and goggles.

She knew them all.

Blond, bubbly Harmony had been in her high school class. The dead girl waved almost shyly, a sweet, stupid grin on her face. But Harmony did not worry her. It was the other two that made Buffy curse out loud.

Spike and Drusilla.

Willow sat in her dormitory room amidst a circle of white candles, their flames casting a sickly yellow glow upon the walls, flickering shadows of things that had no form. It was dark outside, but clouds blotted out the stars.

Something prevented her from summoning Lucy Hanover. For more than an hour she had tried. Now she bit her lip and fought the despair that threatened to overwhelm her.

"Lucy, please," Willow whispered into the seething shadows. "I need help. You're the only one who might have answers. Please."

With her heart and soul she reached out into the dark, into the spiritual ether she had mentally touched several times before. Something cold touched Willow's back, and she flinched in fear and shock.

"Lucy?"

As one, the candles blew out, smoke wafting up from each of them, glittering in the dark. The tendrils seemed to reach out to one another, to twine into a web of smoke, to spin and weave together into a hideous shadow face, a snarling, horned thing whose eyes seemed like endless black pits.

"Noooooo . . ." it groaned with pain and anger.

Though the windows were closed, a sudden wind rushed through the room and the smoke dissipated. Willow shivered as the temperature dropped precipitously. She blinked, searching for some sign of that malevolent presence.

Lucy was there, hovering half a foot above the ground. Her spectral form seemed even more faint than ever, a ghost of a ghost. Willow whispered her name and the spirit smiled weakly.

"I am here, friend Willow," Lucy said, her otherworldly voice quavering.

"What was that?"

"The creature was a soul-eater. My will proved too strong for it, but it has been thwarting my attempts to reach you. It attacked me here on the Ghost Roads, in the moment just before The Prophet showed the Slayer the future. I fear that it may not have been coincidence."

Willow slumped over, one hand over her mouth, and squeezed her eyes shut. Only for a moment, though. Then she stood, determined, and faced the ghost.

"You've gotta help me figure out what's going on," she said. "Ever since that night, Buffy's been all wigged. At first I thought maybe she was just pushing us away, that she was gonna go all Lone Ranger, take Camazotz down herself and get Giles back."

Something rolled over in Willow's stomach and she shuddered.

"She hasn't even tried, Lucy. I live here. I see her. She goes to half her classes, and she's looking over her shoulder all the time, paranoid, like any second, hello, ambush! But she's the Slayer. She gets ambushed all the time. Comes with the territory. And not usually during the day. It just isn't like her."

Willow paused, a chill creeping through her. When she looked up, she saw the phantom of the dead Slayer gazing dolefully down upon her, swaying slightly in the dim room.

"Lucy?"

"Where are your friends? Do they agree?"

"Definitely. It's been two days and Buffy hasn't done anything about Giles, so we're going to do it ourselves. Oz is tracking down the ship, and Xander and Anya are getting some weapons from Giles's apartment. We're going in tonight to save him, with or without her."

"Of course I will aid as best I can," Lucy agreed. *"But what of Buffy? Your words have given rise to a terrible suspicion. I think it best we find her and put that suspicion to the test before even attempting the rescue you have planned."*

Willow hesitated. A whispered voice in the back of her mind told her that it was already too late for Giles. But she would not listen. She was determined to find him and bring him back alive. The last thing she wanted to do was to wait another day.

"We're going in after Giles in the morning," she said. "I don't know what to do about—"

A key rattled in the lock. The door opened, and Buffy walked in. Willow's breath caught in her throat as she saw her friend stiffen, a dark look spreading across the Slayer's face.

"Buffy," Willow whispered.

"No," Lucy Hanover said, her voice like a breeze rustling through the trees. *"That is not Buffy Summers."*

Willow shot a glance at the ghost, then back at the doorway. She shook her head, not understanding. Buffy shot the gossamer spirit of the former Slayer a hard look, then smiled grimly.

It was the smile that convinced Willow.

"Oh my God."

Buffy crossed to her bed, bent down and reached beneath it, and retrieved a duffel bag. Willow could only stare at her, frozen with shock and grief.

"It is The Prophet," Lucy said. *"Whatever she is, the creature has taken Buffy's physical form."*

The Slayer began to open drawers and throw clothes into the bag. "It was foolish of me to think I would be able to stay here. Though it would have been more convenient, it is simpler to start over."

Willow could only stare as she zipped the bag, but as soon as The Prophet began to move toward the door, she moved to block the way. Fear and disbelief were supplanted within her by a kind of anger unlike anything she had ever known. She shook her head, jaw clenched tightly.

"You're not leaving," Willow said. "Not until you bring Buffy back."

A brittle, severe expression settled upon Buffy's face, and Willow wondered how she could not have noticed the change in her best friend. This thing in front of her was not Buffy.

"Move, witch."

Willow glanced once at Lucy, hoping that the ghost would have some way to remove The Prophet. But the specter only floated, a soul-haze and nothing more. She could not help. Willow swallowed hard and begin to inscribe arcane symbols upon the air with her fingers. Her lips moved silently as she mouthed a spell that would lock them all in the room.

With a guttural laugh, The Prophet backhanded Willow, who staggered backward and slammed into her desk before crumbling to the floor.

Dazed, she dragged herself to her feet.

But the door hung open, and The Prophet was gone. Buffy was gone.

And if Willow did not catch up with her, she might never know what had truly become of her best friend.

The car horn kept blaring. Parker, unconscious, was slumped over the wheel and Buffy could not spare even a moment to slide him off.

Spike and Drusilla.

"Well, well, Dru, look what we've got here," Spike called happily, preening like a rooster as he took a few steps toward the car. His hair was longer now, almost shaggy, giving him a more feral aspect. "That little Summers girl, isn't it? I thought she was a house pet now. Soft little kitten."

Drusilla's mad eyes widened and she made tiny

scratching motions in the air, then licked her lips. "Ooh, I love kittens. We know just what to do with kitties, don't we, Spike?"

There was bloodlust in Spike's eyes. "Oh, we certainly do, pet. We certainly do."

Harmony stared at Drusilla. "You don't hurt kittens. Tell me you don't hurt kittens."

Dru seemed shocked. "Only when I'm hungry. I'm not a monster."

It took Buffy only a heartbeat to calculate the odds. These three behind her, three more in front. Parker's Mercedes was hemmed in on both sides. Six of them. She'd killed six at once before. More than that, in fact.

But not *these* six.

Harmony and the stranger wouldn't be a problem. But Buffy knew from experience that Clownface and Bulldog were tough enough. Spike and Drusilla, though, that was the final nail.

I'm not ready. Not now. The world had changed and she had to find her place in it. At the same time, she knew that another world awaited her in the past, a place . . . a home . . . where she was desperately needed. She had to return there.

What had she told Faith, so long ago? The first rule of slaying: *Don't die.*

Once the decision was made within her, Buffy acted in an instant. She ratcheted around, fired a crossbow bolt at Spike. He snatched it out of the air, and then glared at her as though his feelings were hurt.

Buffy dove across the unconscious Parker, who slid off the horn. She popped open the door, then used her prodigious strength to shove him out onto the pavement. Her bag dropped onto the seat beside her with the crossbow, and she reached into it for one of the stakes she had made.

The vampires saw that she intended to flee, and rushed at the car.

"Dammit, Buffy! I never took you for a coward," Spike snapped at her. "I'm disappointed."

Buffy slammed the Mercedes into reverse and floored the gas. Spike and Drusilla had learned to be fast. It was part of the reason they had stayed alive as long as they had. They split up, each diving out of the way of the car in opposite directions.

Harmony stood frozen behind the car, her mouth open as though she were somehow offended. The Mercedes slammed into her, drove her back with all the horsepower the engine had. The car crashed broadside into the van with Harmony in the middle. There was a sickening crunch and she screamed, a shriek so wild and agonized that it seemed to be tearing her throat apart.

Buffy spun the wheel to the right in order to avoid running over Parker, dropped it into drive, and floored it again. Spike and Drusilla had gotten up and were rushing at her from either side, but the tires spun under the Mercedes, laying a black rubber patch on the pavement, and the car lurched forward, away from them.

Behind her, Harmony tumbled to the ground, the

top and bottom of her body only connected by torn flesh and a crushed spine. Her upper torso twitched as though she were having a seizure, but her legs lay still.

In the rearview, Buffy caught a glimpse of Spike and Drusilla running to their van.

The Mercedes raced around to one side of the van in front, but the other three vampires were there already, coming for her. Buffy lifted up the crossbow in her right hand, targeted the one she did not recognize, and fired even as he leaped toward the car. The bolt found its mark and the monster dusted, orange-blazing eyes the last to disintegrate.

Buffy tossed the empty crossbow into the backseat as Clownface jumped onto the hood of the Mercedes at the last possible moment. Then Bulldog leaped onto the trunk and tossed himself into the backseat. The Slayer swore loudly.

Her right hand gripped the stake that lay beside her. With all her strength, she stomped on the brake.

Clownface sailed off the hood and rolled onto the pavement, even as Bulldog was thrown into the front seat. The pug-faced vampire slammed his head against the dashboard, but struggled to right himself.

Buffy punched the stake through his heart and he imploded, scattering dust all over the upholstery.

She accelerated again. Just as Clownface was getting up, Buffy ran her down. The car rocked as she drove right over the vampire, and then she was away, leaving them behind. Spike and Drusilla gave chase in the van, but they had no hope of catching up to her. Not in the Mercedes.

Clownface wasn't dead. Buffy knew that. But three out of six wasn't bad for a girl who was only trying to get away. *Maybe I should have stayed,* she thought. But she pushed the idea away. *Priorities.*

A few miles and a left turn out of view, and she had lost Spike and Drusilla. As she drove through the darkness, streetlights flashing across her face, Buffy kept an eye out for other gray vans, or any vehicle that might try to get in her way.

She had gotten away, but she wasn't free. Not until she had traveled beyond the area Camazotz controlled. And Buffy had a feeling that was not going to be easy.

CHAPTER 4

The houses on Redwood Lane reminded Buffy painfully of the neighborhood where she had lived during high school. Perfectly groomed lawns, a smattering of trees—though none of them redwoods—and a minivan or SUV in every driveway. She had abandoned the Mercedes three blocks away, and as she skulked along from house to house, it unnerved her how silent they were. No loud voices, no radios. The few lights inside barely showed through the curtains and shades drawn across every window.

Six miles from the center of town, and still no one dared breathe loud enough to attract the vampires' attention.

Halfway down the block, Buffy paused in front of an imposing Spanish-style house, and put her back against the stucco just beside a side window. From within, she could just barely hear a television set. In the driveway sat a Volvo sedan, maybe three or four years old.

She hesitated only for a moment. Then she slipped around the back of the house and across the patio to the rear door. A heavy wooden door, not a glass slider. That was good. Less noise.

Buffy kicked the door open and the three locks on it splintered the frame with a tearing of wood. It crashed open, the sound echoing out into the night. She only hoped that, locked up tight in their homes, no one would hear it.

"Oh God, no!" someone cried within the house.

Buffy rushed through the kitchen and into the living room where a haggard looking couple in their late forties cowered in a corner by the television set.

"How . . . we didn't invite you in!" the man shouted, panicked.

They thought she was a vampire.

"No," Buffy said, both hands up as she approached them. "Just sit tight, right there, and I won't hurt you. I swear I won't. Cooperate, and maybe I can even get you out of here."

They stared at her as though she were mad.

"Where's the phone?"

"What do you mean out of here? You're not trying to leave, are you?" the woman said, horrified.

"You *want* to stay?" Buffy asked. "Where's the phone?"

"On the wall in the kitchen," the man said. "You passed right by it. But please don't talk to anyone like this on our phone. They'll hear you. They'll think we're involved."

Buffy had already started back toward the kitchen, but paused at his words. She turned to stare at him again.

"What do you mean 'they'll hear'?"

"They listen," the woman replied.

With a sigh, Buffy shook her head. "Of course they do. Can't have anybody spilling the blood-soaked beans, now, can we? Still, they can't listen to every phone twenty-four hours a day. They've got you scared 'cause you never know when they're listening.

"Look, it doesn't matter anyway. We'll be gone by the time anyone can get here." She regarded them closely. "I'm Buffy. What are your names?"

The couple exchanged a tired, frightened glance. The woman stood up first, followed by her husband, but they kept their distance.

"I'm Nadine Ross. This is my husband Andrew."

"Nice to meet you. Sorry about the door. Come into the kitchen." Buffy led the way, and the Rosses followed. "Have a seat," she said, gesturing toward the breakfast table. They slid chairs out and stood gazing at her anxiously as she picked up the phone.

There was a strange clicking sound before the dial tone.

Buffy stared at it for a second. Of all the phone numbers she knew by heart, most of them would be useless now. Her mother's. The numbers of all her friends in Sunnydale. But there were two others, one that she had used only a few times, and another she had never even dialed, yet she knew both of them by heart.

The first was a Los Angeles number. Angel's number. Holding her breath, Buffy dialed, but the number was out of service. She closed her eyes and held the phone against her forehead.

Where are you, Angel?

"Please," the woman whispered behind her.

Ignoring her, Buffy dialed information for Los Angeles. She asked for the number for Angel Investigations, but the operator said there was no listing under that name. Wesley Wyndam-Pryce? Again, no listing. Cordelia Chase?

Unlisted.

As disappointed as she was, this last bit of information fanned a tiny spark of hope in Buffy's chest. It might be unlisted, but Cordelia had a phone number. Somewhere in this insane world, someone she knew still lived.

Buffy thumbed a button on the phone to disconnect, then waited for a new dial tone. There was only one other number she might call for help. It was a long sequence. Time might have caused part of it to change. Given that she had only memorized it, but never used it, she feared that she might have gotten it wrong.

Her chest rose and fell more quickly as she punched in the numbers. She felt the eyes of the people whose home she had invaded, and she shifted uncomfortably under their fearful, accusing gaze.

Somewhere on the other side of the Atlantic, a phone began to ring. Buffy let out a shuddering breath of relief as the tinny sound reached her ears. There was a click as the call was answered.

"Yes?"

The voice was British. Buffy had never heard such a welcome sound.

"This is Buffy Summers."

A pause, a harsh intake of breath. "That isn't funny. Who is this?"

"Who the hell is this?" she snapped, angry and frustrated. "Put Quentin Travers on the phone!"

Another pause. "Dear God, it really is you, isn't it? My name is Alan Fontaine, Miss Summers. Quentin Travers is dead. Where are you?"

"Behind enemy lines and headed south," she said. "Can you help?"

"Hold on."

She heard a muffled sound and assumed he had put a hand over the phone. Dull voices could be heard, and a moment later, Fontaine came back on the line.

"Do you know Donatello's? An Italian restaurant just off your one-oh-nine freeway?"

Buffy thought about it, found a vague recollection of the place. "I think so."

"That's the border. We can have an extraction team waiting for you there. One hour."

One hour, Buffy thought. A smile spread across

her face. One hour, and then she could begin to make sense of this insane world, this horrid future.

"If I'm not there it means I'm dead," she replied. "Oh, and this line is bugged. There could be a Welcome Wagon there waiting for me and for your team."

"One hour," Fontaine repeated. "And Buffy?"

"Yes?"

"I'm glad you're alive."

He hung up, and before she could do the same, Buffy heard a series of rapid clicks on the other end. Though she knew there was no way the vampires could monitor all calls at all times, a dreadful certainty filled her that they had listened to at least part of *this* call.

One hour.

She hung up the phone and turned to the Rosses. They flinched, and would not meet her gaze.

"Keys to the Volvo. Now."

Andrew Ross shook a bit as he stood to face her, face growing red. "Just a goddamn second. Maybe you scare me. Hell, you kicked in a door with three deadbolts in it. But I'm not just going to hand you my keys."

"Are you kidding?" Buffy asked, amazed. "I'm not going to leave you two here. You're coming with me."

"They'll kill us," Nadine hissed, scandalized.

Andrew crossed his arms defiantly. "We're not going anywhere."

Buffy gaped at them. After a moment, she shook her head in astonishment. "All right, look, I'm not going to make you come. The last thing I need is to wrestle with people I'm trying to help. And maybe you're right, maybe you're safer here until the nest is destroyed. But I need your car, and I'm taking it.

"Now, keys."

"They'll . . . they'll think we helped you," Andrew stammered.

With a sigh, Buffy strode across the room and decked him. She pulled the punch, but it would leave a hell of a bruise. Andrew moaned as he sat up on the linoleum. Nadine just stared at them both.

"*Now* they won't think you helped by choice. I don't have time to be nice. Give me the keys."

Nadine hurried across the kitchen and picked up her purse, rifled through it and dug out a key ring. She tossed them, jangling, to Buffy.

"I'll be back," Buffy told them.

The couple only stared at her, Nadine with her purse clutched defensively in front of her and Andrew on his butt on the floor, one hand over the rapidly rising welt on his face.

"What's wrong with you people? I want to help."

"No one can help," Nadine whispered.

"This is helping?" Andrew snapped. "You can go to hell."

"This *is* hell," Buffy told them grimly. "And I've already stayed too long. I'm outta here."

She went out the front door and loped across the lawn to the Volvo. As she drove, Buffy tried not to think about the Rosses and the fear that kept them from even trying to run away. Her destination, Donatello's, was about nine miles away. If the vampires were listening, they knew where she was headed. The only advantages she had at the moment were that they did not know what she was driving, and that she knew the roads. There were half a dozen ways to get where she was going.

The hard part was going to be guessing correctly which one of them would get her there alive.

After high school graduation, Xander Harris had retreated to the basement of his parents' house and a series of dead-end jobs, not because he could do nothing else, but because he was burdened with a depressing ambivalence. He just had no idea what he wanted to do next. All he did know was that he did not want to sit in another classroom as long as he lived. And, while hanging out in the cramped, damp space he called an apartment while his parents battled it out upstairs was not his ideal living arrangement, it had a certain charm in the area of personal finance.

Still, he knew there was more for him to do in life. It was only that he could not figure out what that might be. Thinking about it made his head ache, but once he started, it was impossible to turn the flow of thoughts off. *Ironic,* he thought, given that his girlfriend was curled up naked under the sheets, half asleep with her head on his chest and one leg thrown over his torso.

"Mmm," Anya purred.

Xander sighed. Between his general dissatisfaction with the way his life was headed and the fact that despite her vow to rescue Giles, Buffy hadn't done a damn thing to get him away from the demon Camazotz, he could barely concentrate on Anya. Buffy was acting so weird, that they were all going to go after Giles tonight, to rescue him themselves. He and Anya had even done a little old-fashioned trespassing at the ex-Watcher's house to gather up the weapons they'd need.

It's not fair, he thought sullenly.

His eyes fluttered closed. Anya snuggled up closer and Xander felt himself at last begin to relax. Though he knew Willow and Oz were due in the next hour or so, sleep seemed to be his only escape from the confusion and worry that plagued him.

Bamm! Bamm! Bamm!

His eyes snapped open and he stared at the ceiling for a minute, wondering if he had dreamed the knocking. Anya had not stirred at all. Then it came again, a hard rapping at the door that led out into the backyard, the door people used if they wanted to visit him. Willow was early.

Anya shifted, moaned a bit, and one eye slitted open. "Make them go away or I'll put a pox on them."

Xander smiled down at her uncertainly. "You're not a demon anymore, sweetie, remember?"

She sighed. "There are times . . ."

But Anya did not finish the thought. Xander climbed out of bed and pulled on sweatpants and a tee shirt as he went to open the door. As soon as it was open a crack, Willow pushed her way in. She had an enormous red welt on the side of her face, and a crazed look in her eyes.

"Xander, we have to find Buffy. She's not Buffy. I think she's going to try to leave town and we have to stop her."

Oz followed her at a more leisurely pace. Xander stared at Willow for a second, then glanced at Oz.

"Hey," Xander said.

"Hey."

"What's all this about not-Buffy?"

Oz nodded. "Possessed, apparently. Body thief, I'm guessing."

Anya sat up in bed, covers clutched at her throat, and glared daggers at all of them. "You are early."

Willow shot her a hard look, then rolled her eyes and looked at Xander again. "Come on. Saddle up. We're not gonna let this happen. If Buffy—or whoever hijacked her—gives us the slip, we may never get our friend back."

"Okay, okay, we just need to get dressed. But what about Giles? I mean, not that I was looking forward to sashaying into the lair of the ancient bat-god with a passel of vampires running around the place, but someone's gotta get him out."

Oz raised an eyebrow. "Sashaying?"

Willow rounded on Xander then, but there was no anger in her eyes, just fear and a lingering sadness. "Confession? Always kinda hoped I'd leak our plan to Buffy and she'd feel all guilty and go do the rescuing herself. Apparently no longer in the cards. I don't even want to think about Giles right now, Xander. I can't, because then I'll remember how I'm thinking, hey, he's probably dead, and I can't handle that grief. It would paralyze me, you understand?"

It was as though, with Buffy and Giles out of action, Willow had just stepped right up to the plate. She was in charge, all of a sudden, and Xander was surprised with how all right with that he was.

"Poor Giles," Anya said. "It's Buffy's fault, you know. If she hadn't been all high and mighty—"

"*If* Giles is still alive, we have to pray he lasts until morning," Willow went on. "Whatever this thing is that's taken Buffy over, Lucy Hanover is following it. Following . . . her. Right now, that's our priority. We're going to find a way to expel this thing out of Buffy. You and Oz may have to hold her long enough for me to do the spell, but—"

Xander held up a hand. *"Un momento,"* he interrupted. "Some evil spirit is holding the reins on Buffy's Slayer-powered figure, and we're supposed to hold on to her."

Willow shot him a withering glare.

"Just checking," Xander added quietly. "Wouldn't miss it, personally."

On her way south, Buffy passed through Citrus Beach, a tiny, trendy little hamlet with a single block of bistros and shops frequented only by the wealthy and their parasites.

In that respect, it had not changed.

As she drove along the strip in Citrus Beach, Buffy slowed the Volvo and peered out the window. The sidewalks were swarming with nightlife, packs of drunken Kakchiquels, their trademark black tattoos gleaming as headlights splashed across them. They sat in outdoor patio dining areas at the bistros, served by human waiters, many of whom had wide, terrified eyes, though others only looked numb, shell-shocked. The vampires roamed the streets in packs like Mardi Gras revelers, crying catcalls at passing cars.

It wasn't just vampires, either. For each clutch of undead, there were humans as well. Men and women who fawned over the Kakchiquels or gazed at them like obedient lap dogs. Buffy spotted a man on a leash, his head shaved bald, clothed only in ragged blue jeans and garish, obscene tattoos that had been etched into his skin, presumably by his masters.

Amongst the throng she spotted several demons as well.

I should stop, she thought. *These people . . .*

The thought dissipated. *First rule of Slaying.* Buffy gripped the wheel tighter, her knuckles whitening, but she kept driving, even accelerated. Several of the Kakchiquels hooted at her as she passed, beastly vampire faces on display for the world to see. Buffy flashed back to the others of their tribe she had known, the grim, silent, deadly killers. These were nothing like the others, and she wondered why.

Questions. Too many questions in her head.

A pair of blond, female vampires clad in tight, red

leather pants and matching tops began to move into the street ahead of her. There was menace in their gaze and their stride, and Buffy had to speed up and swerve around them. She checked the rearview mirror and saw one of the twins make a gesture, but they did not pursue her.

Even so, Buffy did not slow down.

Now, more than ever, she wanted to put Sunnydale and Citrus Beach and the Kakchiquels behind her. The lights of the town flashed across her face, but soon she traveled into darkness again. The road wound south, away from Citrus Beach.

I'll come back, she thought, a silent vow to everyone still alive behind her.

It wasn't long before she came in sight of Freeway 109, but Buffy did not dare go that way. More than likely, the Kakchiquels would be waiting to ambush her there. Instead, she said a tiny prayer she would not get lost, and took a left onto a secondary road she thought would eventually take her, in a roundabout way, within a quarter mile of her destination.

For several minutes, she drove in silence, not even the radio for company. The smattering of neighborhoods and gas stations gave way to trees on both sides of the road. A gentle rise curved around and through the thick woods, and Buffy became alarmed. She did not recall a forest on this road and she could not afford to become lost.

Keep going, she told herself. *South. Just get out of here. A few more miles.*

The Volvo crested the hill. The road curved again as it began its descent on the other side. There were a few homes in amongst the trees, but these had lights on inside. She was not out of their territory yet, but those lights gave her hope.

The headlights washed over the trees, then the road straightened out. In the darkness far ahead, three cars were parked at odd angles, blocking the way completely.

"Dammit," Buffy whispered, there in the glow of the dash.

Instinctively, she reached out to shut off the headlights, but stopped herself. It was too late. They would have been watching for her, would have seen her coming long before she had noticed them. Her mind whirled. The Kakchiquels must have set roadblocks up along every route south. They were a couple of miles from the restaurant where she was supposed to meet the extraction team.

Her foot came off the brake. Almost before she knew what she was doing, Buffy floored the accelerator. Her seat belt was cinched tight, her hands gripped the wheel, and she aimed the nose of the Volvo right at the point where two of the cars ahead met grille to grille.

Don't die! an alarmed voice cried in her mind.

Working on it, she silently replied.

Vampires popped up from behind the cars. Doors opened and others stepped out. From the forest around the roadblock, others appeared, moving slowly down toward the road. Buffy's fingers flexed on the wheel. The headlights seemed to grow brighter, silhouetting each one of them, and the engine roared as she built up speed.

Buffy grinned.

She was doing better than sixty when the Volvo crashed into the roadblock. Buffy was thrust forward, the seat belt grabbed hold, bruised her, broke a rib, then the airbag erupted into her face and pushed her back against the seat. There was a screeching of metal like nothing she had ever heard, a shattering of glass as the Volvo rammed through the two cars, battering them aside, crushing at least one vampire.

The Volvo's bumper was caved in, scarred, twisted metal thrust down, punctured the tire. It blew, and the car slewed to one side, then flipped. Buffy struck her head against the driver's side window hard enough to break it as the Volvo rolled toward the tree line, and for a moment, she was unconscious.

When her eyes fluttered open she heard shouts of pain and fury. Her ribs hurt, and it felt as though someone had hammered a nail into each of her temples. She squeezed her eyes shut, then reached up to wipe the blood from her face. It was a surprise to find that the car had come to rest right side up. The airbag pressed her against the seat, but she reached out, clutched a large shard of glass, and punctured it.

As she looked out through the shattered glass, the vampires began to cluster around the ruined vehicles they had used for their roadblock. It was steel and fiberglass carnage. The headlights of the one car that was mostly intact shone in oily sparkles off the gasoline that seeped from the other two ravaged cars. The Kakchiquels seemed stunned for a moment, as though they had no idea how to proceed.

Then, among them, Buffy saw a pale, raven-haired creature rise up, gossamer gown fluttering around her. *Drusilla.*

Perhaps thirty yards separated them. The others were dazed, but in a moment, they would come for her, surround the car, drag her out. She counted at least a dozen. If she didn't move quickly, by numbers alone they might have her.

Her chest hurt with every breath, but Buffy built a wall between herself and that pain. There was no time for it. With the shouts of the vampires in her ears and the ghostly image of Drusilla rising from the wreckage burned into her mind, Buffy released her seat belt and lunged for the canvas bag that lay on the floor. Her fingers closed around the strap and she tried to pop open the door.

It was jammed shut from the crash.

She swung the bag out the broken window, then climbed out, tiny shards of glass pinpricking the backs of her legs. The wound she had gotten in her side while fighting August earlier that day—it seemed like forever to her now—tore open again.

"Smell her, puppies!" Drusilla cried in her singsong voice, hoarse with desire. "Like cinnamon and nutmeg. A fox hunt, now! A taste of her boldness to the first to make her scream, but save the eyes for me!"

Buffy shuddered, but would not look away from Drusilla's crazed, wide-eyed gaze. They thought she was going to run away.

No more running.

Instead, Buffy strode purposefully across the pavement toward them. The vampires had begun to lope toward her, but they paused in confusion when she did not flee. Even Drusilla cocked her head sideways, where it lolled as though broken.

"What's this?" the lunatic inquired in a childlike voice.

"This?" Buffy rammed a hand into the canvas bag and pulled out a road flare. "This is for Kendra."

She ignited the flare, then threw it skittering across the pavement into the pool of gasoline that spread across the road beneath the cars and around the feet of the vampires. There was a heartbeat when nothing happened, and all eyes turned to the blazing flare.

Buffy sprinted toward the tree line.

With a sound like an enormous flag flapping in the wind, the gas ignited into a sheet of flame. Vampires screamed as the fire engulfed them. Then the first of the gas tanks exploded, and the force of it thumped through Buffy's chest like the thunder of fireworks on the Fourth of July multiplied a thousandfold. She was thrown off her feet into the undergrowth at the edge of the woods, where she kept her head down.

The other two cars exploded in quick succession

and blazing chunks of their frames struck the pavement all around. Buffy felt the heat even through her clothes, and her arms felt as though she had been sunburned. She bled from dozens of tiny wounds, and ached as though she'd been worked over good.

But she was alive.

Buffy stood up, glanced down in surprise to find the canvas bag still clutched in her hand, then surveyed the conflagration in front of her. Most of the vampires had been incinerated already. On the other side of the inferno she could see four or five of them running up the road in the other direction.

Sudden motion, much closer, caught her eye. In the midst of the blaze, burning wreckage all around, Drusilla twirled in a mad ballet of fire, her arms flung out like a little girl, her head back. The vampire's hair had been scorched from her head and her entire body was in flames, yet she danced and giggled in a high, wild, disturbingly beautiful voice.

Then she burst into a swirling tornado of burning embers, ash and charred bone fragments . . . and then she was only dust, spinning still, blown about and then drifting across the night sky like confetti.

"For Kendra," the Slayer whispered.

Buffy turned and ran up into the trees, still headed south.

CHAPTER 5

The inside of Oz's van smelled like pine trees. When his band, Dingoes Ate My Baby, had a gig, he usually ended up carrying either the rest of the band or a lot of their equipment back and forth. Not one but three cardboard air fresheners hung from the dashboard to combat the smell of sweaty musicians and beer.

Willow liked the pine scent. It comforted her, the way anything about Oz did. He was not a big guy, not a particularly strong guy, but he was resolute as stone. She had no doubt at all that he would always be there to watch her back.

As Oz drove toward the Sunnydale bus station, Willow glanced at him from time to time. In the soft glow from the dash, his face was expressionless as always, but his eyes were alive, intense and filled with a fierce tenacity. Simply having him there with her made Willow think it was all possible. They could save Buffy.

They had to.

Anya and Xander had been silent in the backseat, but now Xander shifted forward.

"Where do you think she's headed?" he asked.

Willow shook her head. "I don't know. If we knew who she is . . . what she is . . . but we don't. And we've run out of time for research."

"Does it matter where she's going?" Anya asked. "It's almost ten o'clock. There can't be many more buses leaving tonight. The L.A. express, the airport shuttle, and probably one to Las Vegas. There's always one to Las Vegas. For the gambling and carousing."

Slowly, Willow turned to regard her quizzically.

Anya shrugged. "I've left town in a hurry once or twice."

"But you came back," Xander said softly, and slipped an arm around her.

As the lampposts above the bus station parking lot came into view ahead, Oz leaned forward and killed the headlights. He braked, and pulled to the curb before turning the engine off.

"How are we doing this?" he asked.

Willow took a calming breath, a bit unnerved by her sudden, unwanted promotion to leader-girl. Buffy was supposed to be the boss, Giles the strategist. *But they're not here,* she told herself. *It's on you, now.*

Self-conscious, she reached up to gingerly touch

the bruise on the side of her face where this not-Buffy had struck her. It hurt far more than had the older, fading bruise where her best friend had accidentally hit her days before. Willow wondered why that was, but thought she knew. This new one ached deeply, all the way down to her heart.

Another breath, as she forced the coming moments into a semblance of logic in her mind. Lucy Hanover had appeared to them while they were doing research and told them that the thing that had hijacked Buffy's body had come to rest at the bus station, where she now sat waiting for her bus to arrive.

"We have to assume that Buffy . . . that she didn't take off in the few minutes Lucy's ghost was with us. If she's still there, inside the station, I'm going to try the spell from the parking lot, out of sight of the windows. Anya's going to help. It may be that she'll sense me trying to drive her out. That's where you guys come in," Willow said, glancing from Oz to Xander and back. "If she runs, you have to stop her. Keep her down long enough for me to finish the spell."

Xander cleared his throat. "But you said 'cause you don't know what this thing is, you're not even sure it's going to work. What happens if it doesn't?"

Anya smiled at him. "Well, you two will be brutally thrashed, of course. This thing has all of Buffy's gifts as the Slayer. On the bright side, though, Willow and I will think you both incredibly brave."

Xander did not smile in return. "I'll try to remember that during the thrashing."

For a moment, the four friends seemed to take a collective breath. Then, as one, they slipped out of the van as quietly as they were able and started off toward the bus station. The parking lot was far too well lit for them to simply walk across it without drawing attention to themselves. A chain link fence ran the entire perimeter.

Xander was in the lead, and he paused and gestured toward the fence. "We'll have to go around," he whispered. "Anybody notice, no buses? That's a good thing, I think."

The bus station was bordered on this side by a corporate office complex. The drive that led up to the darkened buildings had lights as well, but they were far enough away that the four of them were able to slip along the outside of the chain link fence in relative darkness. They went all the way around to the back of the station, then climbed the fence and dropped down in the parking lot. The rear of the station was plain brick, unbroken by windows, with only a rear exit door Willow thought was likely for maintenance use.

Out in the open like that, the lights of the lot spotlighting them, she felt exposed and vulnerable. With a bag of items she had collected from her own stash and Giles's apartment, she sprinted across the lot toward that rear wall. The others followed quickly. As they reached the station, the ghost of Lucy Hanover appeared suddenly among them. In the glaring overhead lights, the phantom of the dead Slayer shimmered, barely there, as though her form had been woven with spiderwebs.

"She's still here?" Willow asked.

"Indeed," Lucy confirmed. *"She awaits within, anxious and angry. I believe that she can feel me watching."*

Willow stood before the ghost, aware that the others would not come closer. Though they rarely mentioned it, not even Xander, they were always deeply disturbed by Lucy's presence.

"Whatever happens now, we wouldn't even have gotten a chance to save her without your help," Willow said. "Thanks."

"I wish I could do more," the specter whispered in her eerie voice.

"Stand by. You might get your chance. If we can drive her out, it's going to be up to you to make sure she doesn't try to invade anyone else."

Lucy nodded wordlessly and simply hovered there, the solidity of her form wavering as though the breeze disrupted it. Willow turned to her friends, smiled encouragingly, then set her bag down gently. As she reached in and withdrew the contents of the bag, she glanced up at Oz and Xander.

"Go around to either side. Just be ready. But don't pass by the windows. Don't give her a chance to see you."

They complied without another word. Willow was tempted to kiss Oz once before he went, for luck, but he was gone too quickly for her to act on the impulse, and she dared not call him back. Instead, with Anya and the ghost watching over her, she laid out the contents of the bag carefully. A small ampule of white rose oil had made it intact, despite the jostling the bag had taken. Willow daubed a bit of it on her forehead, throat and wrists, then gestured for Anya to do the same.

Quickly as she could manage, she took a small cone of black construction paper and set a piece of incense within it, then repeated the process four times. Willow drew a power circle around herself, and a star at its center, then placed the incense at each of the points of the star. With a deep breath, she sat cross-legged at the center of the circle and glanced up at Anya.

"Go ahead and light them," she said.

Anya complied quickly, using long wooden matches to set fire to the paper the incense was in. The tiny blazes flared up quickly, the paper burning, and the incense in each began to smoke.

"*Wormwood,*" Lucy Hanover observed.

"Artemisia," Willow corrected, using a more modern name for the herb in the incense.

"*What you attempt is dangerous, friend Willow,*" Lucy cautioned. "*If you do not know the name of the spirit you are trying to draw forth, you may succeed only in drawing it into yourself rather than simply expelling it from your friend.*"

Willow paused.

"You didn't tell us that," Anya said, suddenly alarmed. "We should have used a different spell."

"Yeah, with all that extra time we had for research," Willow replied dryly.

"But . . . what if that happens? If this thing comes out of Buffy and into you, nobody else is witchy enough to get it out of you."

Willow was touched by the girl's concern, particularly in light of Anya's tenure as a demon. But she had no satisfactory answer.

"If it possesses me, Buffy will go rescue Giles and he'll figure it out."

"Not if he's dead," Anya muttered.

Willow shushed her, closed her eyes to calm herself, inhaled the fumes rising from the artemisia burning all around her. "Infernal power, you who carry disturbance into the universe, you who have intruded upon the flesh of the living, I call you forth."

As instructed, Anya scattered powdered lodestone around the circle.

"Be you *exurgent mortui,* shade, or demon, leave your somber habitation within living flesh and render yourself back unto the spirit world," Willow continued.

Anya lay a branch of hazelwood upon the pavement, pointing from the magick circle toward the brick wall of the station. The smoke rising from the burning incense seemed to pause in the air, and then to flow as one in a line along the path pointed by the hazel branch.

"Render yourself back unto the spirit world," Willow repeated.

As though it were her will alone and not the power of the spell, she could feel the magick prodding Buffy's body. In her mind's eye, she could picture the inside of the bus station as though she were truly seeing it herself.

The incense smoke is invisible now, but inhabited by the spell Willow had cast, and it works against Buffy's flesh, into her mouth and nostrils and eardrums, circling like tentacles around the thing that has possessed the Slayer's body.

Buffy tenses. Her eyes snap open.

Outside, under the glare of the lampposts, Willow stiffened at the center of the magick circle. "Uh-oh," she mumbled.

"Uh-oh?" Anya demanded, alarmed. "What's uh-oh?"

Both of them glanced over to where Lucy Hanover had been observing them, but the ghost was suddenly gone. Willow had known she would be, for in that last moment she had felt Lucy trying to help her push the invasive entity out of Buffy's body.

But they had failed. The thing had sensed her, and pushed back.

"Come on!" Willow snapped.

Anya was right behind her as they ran around the side of the bus station just in time to see Buffy—or whatever wore her body—slam the door open hard enough that the glass in it shattered. Xander was there, only a few feet away, and he leaped at her. Guilt surged up within Willow, for Xander had been badly injured only days before.

Still, they had no choice.

"We have to help him," Willow said.

But it was too late. Buffy hit him once, twice, then spun and kicked him hard enough that Xander sailed off the concrete walk and into the parking lot. Oz came running around the front of the station then, but there was nothing he could do. Nothing anyone could have done. Willow had known from the beginning that if her spell failed, they were lost.

"We're not going to just let you take her body and leave!" Willow shouted angrily, tears beginning to well up in her eyes.

The thing that was Buffy froze, turned and looked at her, almost kindly. "I have no choice," it said. "And neither do you. Try to restrain me, and I shall kill you all."

The half-dozen other people who had been inside the bus station stood just inside the panoramic plate glass window now, watching the action unfold. Willow looked from Buffy's face to the people inside. She could cast a glamour on them later to make them forget. For now, she couldn't think about what they might see.

"If I can't stop you, I can hurt you," Willow said, wiping at her eyes. She prayed now that pain might drive the thing out.

With a single gesture, her moderate magickal ability amped up by the adrenaline rushing through her, Willow caused all of the broken glass to levitate off the ground. A flick of her wrist sent the hundreds of pieces scything through the air at Buffy, who dodged what she could, and screamed as the others sliced into her.

The beast that lived in her now glared at Willow

with red-rimmed, furious eyes. "If you had walked away, you would have lived."

"That wouldn't have been living," Willow said, fighting back the fear that rose up in her then. She felt the presence of her friends around her. "Take her down now, or we've lost her forever."

Together, the four of them rushed at Buffy.

With a loud pop, all the power in the bus station and the parking lot went out. The lot was cast into darkness, the building's interior dark as pitch. Shouts of alarm came from the travelers inside. Willow and the others all faltered, keeping their distance in a rough circle around Buffy in a bizarre standoff.

"Will," Xander began, "did you—"

"Not me," she said quickly.

"Somebody cut the power off," Anya added.

Oz moved toward Willow, still keeping his eyes on Buffy, just as they all were. "Or blew the transformer out on the street," he suggested.

Inside the bus station, people began to scream. They all glanced over to see blood spattering the plate glass. Motion drew Willow's attention off to the left, and then all around.

A band of vampires swarmed across the parking lot toward them. Others slipped slowly out of the bus station, hands covered with the blood of the dead travelers.

"No!" Buffy snapped, exasperated. "What have you done?" she sneered at Willow. "He has found me."

"Indeed," came a slithering voice from within the darkened station. "I have."

With the dry whisper of ravaged wings that beat uselessly at the air, a creature Willow knew must be the bat-god Camazotz stepped out into the lot. He pointed at Buffy with a long, tapered claw.

"She's mine. Kill the others."

Buffy crouched in the darkened interior of an abandoned gas station and peered across the street at Donatello's Italian Restaurant. The place was all white stucco, glass, and brass, the sort of place where local high school kids might have their prom if their class was small enough. It disturbed her to find that the restaurant was open for business.

She had broken into the gas station almost twenty minutes earlier and found cobwebs gathering in the darkest corners. The cooler at the front was still packed with soda, and the racks under the cashier's counter still loaded with candy bars.

There were no looters in Kakchiquel territory.

Yet the place was dark, not even the hum of electricity to indicate that it might come alive again. Buffy suspected it might be used to refuel now and again, when the vampires needed it. But like so many other businesses in the region they had laid claim to, its owners had either been murdered or had fled. This close to the edge of things, Buffy suspected the latter.

And it was close, indeed. Donatello's was perhaps two hundred yards up the road, and the taint of the undead had not yet fallen upon it. *Creepy and strange,* she thought. Parker had said the vampires' expansion had been methodical, but this brought it home to her more than anything else.

As Buffy watched, late dinner customers emerged from within the restaurant. Even across the distance, a seemingly unbridgeable gulf between them, she could hear the echo of their laughter like a cold blade knifing into her gut.

Though she had somehow managed to combine the two personas within her, the two spirits, the two Buffys . . . there was no denying that there were indeed two. To the older Slayer, who had spent so long as a prisoner, that glimpse of normalcy was the first hint of happiness she had seen in more than five years. To the younger Buffy, it was a painful reminder of all she had lost by being thrust into this dark, malevolent future.

It drew her with a magnetic allure. Her heart ached to be across the invisible barrier that marked the border of Kakchiquel territory. The temptation to simply run for it was enormous. But she had told the Watcher on the phone that she would wait for the extraction team he promised to send, and she knew it was sensible to do just that. Particularly given the half-dozen cars parked on either side of the road between the abandoned gas station and Donatello's.

Though she could not really see into the interior of those ominously silent vehicles, cigarette embers burned inside three of them, and there were at least a dozen vampires that stood sentry around the cars, watching for her. Even a conservative bit of mathematics gave them more than twenty against her one, and she suspected that if she tried to cut around the intersection by diverting behind buildings and into a neighborhood, they would have scouts on the lookout for her there.

It didn't matter. They had heard the phone conversation. They knew she was coming here. Knew that the opposition was coming to bring her out.

At some point.

Another hour passed and Buffy's patience crumbled. Carefully, she slipped out of the darkness of the gas station and ran in a crouch to the silent gas pumps. It had brought her only a dozen yards closer to her goal, but that was something. In a minute or two, she was going to take the crossbow and makeshift stakes out of the canvas bag in her hand and walk right down the middle of the street toward the restaurant.

When the momentum that was tugging at her, the yearning to be free, could not be put off for one more second, she stepped out from behind the pumps and began to sprint.

They were slow. She had counted to nine in her head before the shouting began, before the car doors opened and more vampires leaped out. She had been too conservative. There were enough that she could not count them with a simple glance, and she was going to have to fight them hand to hand. All of them.

Should have waited for the extraction team, Buffy thought.

But it was too late, and she cursed herself for her impatience. She had been through too much to have it end now over a stupid mistake, her own impatience and arrogance.

Not the first time they've gotten me into trouble, she thought, as her younger self recalled her conflict with Willow and Giles only days before, and yet also many years before. Days, years, were one and the same. *No, not the first time. But maybe the last.*

On the other side of the street, the driver's door of the last of the cars opened and Spike stepped out. A lit cigarette dangled from his mouth. His face was misshapen, the countenance of the vampire within him, and in contrast to the furious rage of the others who scurried around preparing to fight her, he walked calmly away from the car, his jacket flapping behind him.

The others had swords, axes, some even had guns in spite of the vampires' usual distaste for such things. Spike was empty-handed. Dead, face as pale as his bleached-white hair, he seemed to drift along the street toward her like the scythe of the Reaper himself, gliding toward her.

Spike raised a hand and the rest of them froze, waiting for his command. He took a long drag from the cigarette and then flicked the ash away.

"You killed her." Spike did not even look at her as he spoke.

A bitter taste in her mouth, Buffy felt a hate rise up in her as powerful as any she had ever known. She remained silent, glaring at him until at last Spike turned to meet her gaze.

"She was dancing when she died," Buffy told him. A smile flickered at the corners of her mouth. "I thought you'd like to know."

Spike took another long drag, then glanced at a clutch of vampires to his right. "Kill her."

"But we're not supposed to . . ." one of the creatures replied hesitantly. "I mean—"

"Oh, bloody hell. Right, then, catch her, and bring her to me."

They moved as one, running and loping and scuttling toward her, a pack of wolves and vermin. Buffy stood her ground, lifted the crossbow, and dusted the foremost from twenty-five yards away. She nocked and aimed and released twice more, killing both her targets, before they were too close for the crossbow.

It clattered to the pavement as they swarmed her, and she pulled the stake she had brought from the rear waistband of her jeans. This was it. Five years of shadow-boxing and private *kata*, of exercise and anger.

Buffy began to move. They came at her and she flowed in a dance of death, kicking and thrusting and spinning, using their numbers against them, drawing them close to keep the others away, slaughtering them in a cloud of their own ashen remains. Gunfire erupted and a bullet grazed her shoulder. Warm blood spilled down her back, but it did not slow her. A sword point punctured her side, just below the rib cage, but she was fluid, in motion, and its owner was dead before he could harm her any further.

Then Buffy had the sword. The stake was forgotten. The sword flashed and vampires died and she choked on their floating, snowflake flesh, the nuclear fallout of slain undead. It stung her eyes and forced her to hold her breath.

Another gunshot.

A bullet through her back.

A club across the back of her head.

Buffy staggered. Fell to her knees, the sword wavering in her hands.

Spike stood over her, an ax in his hands. "So much for the not killing you thing, eh?" he asked sweetly. Cigarette firmly clenched in his lips, its tip flaring bright, he snarled at her. "Your turn now, Buffy. Let's see if you dance."

The others all stood back, but none of them dared to challenge his action. Dazed from loss of blood, Buffy was still able to make a rough guess that she had killed over a dozen of them. That was good. That was something.

But it was not going to keep her from breaking the first rule of Slaying. Spike raised the battleax, and Buffy knew she was about to die. The blade gleamed in the moonlight and somewhere nearby, probably from the parking lot at the restaurant, she heard the echo of several people, normal humans, shouting in alarm at the grotesque, macabre tableau being played out in the street.

But they were on the other side of the border. There was nothing they could do.

The blade fell toward her. The other vampires seemed to pull back even one step farther. There seemed to be more of them now, as though others had arrived, reinforcements.

Buffy tried to lift the sword.

Spike grinned.

Then his eyes went wide and his lips dropped open and the cigarette fell end over burning end from his mouth. His body jittered a little bit and he dropped the ax and stumbled toward her. Buffy aimed the blade of the sword at him and it sliced right through his abdomen, impaling him.

"Kill them!" the vampires screamed.

That woke Buffy up. *Kill who?*

She shoved the moaning Spike away from her and struggled to stand. The Kakchiquels closest to her attacked. Though she was wounded, slowed, still she spun and decapitated the nearest one, who exploded into dust. With an elbow, she drove a second back. The third grabbed her from behind, began to choke her, then he too began to jitter madly.

This time she felt the surge of electricity pass from the vampire and into her. The shock made every muscle in her body contract and ache, made her eyes go wide and her teeth feel like she had just bitten through aluminum foil. The vampire went down at her feet, and Buffy looked up to see a grim-faced man standing before her with a taser gun. A long crescent-shaped scar striped the left side of his face, cutting into the bristly stubble on his chin. His black hair was too long, hanging as a curtain that nearly hid his eyes.

It had been this man who had saved her.

"Thank you," Buffy rasped as she shook off the electrocution.

He shocked the fallen vampire again, blue electricity arcing from the weapon into the Kakchiquel on the ground. As he did, this grave, scarred warrior shook the hair back from his face and regarded her with an urgency in his sad eyes.

"We need to go," he said.

Buffy froze, staring at him, not breathing. Joy and grief clashed within her as she recognized the man.

"Xander," she whispered. "Oh my God. Xander."

"We need to go," he replied sternly, not even a flicker of a smile.

Though she bled now from so many wounds, she stood tall, held the sword up and ready, and nodded at him. "Let's go, then."

The vampires were all around them, but they were being driven back by other men and women with taser guns and crossbows. Their numbers were deteriorating even as Buffy followed Xander . . . this sad, brooding man she had once known . . . in a run for the invisible border. In the parking lot of the restaurant, she now saw a pair of black sedans and a military troop carrier that had not been there before.

Engines roared, headlights flashed, and more cars came racing down from the north, from vampire territory. They slewed sideways and bat-tattooed Kakchiquels with orange, jack-o'-lantern eyes burning, piled out with weapons in hand.

"Go, go, get the Slayer to safety!" snapped a commanding female voice behind her.

Buffy turned, saw the extraction team still fighting, but now withdrawing. The command had come from a woman with long red hair tied in a ponytail. The lithe woman raised her hands, gestured madly in the air, and cried out something in Latin that Buffy did not understand. Three vampires within several feet of her turned to glass and another member of the team shattered them all.

Her voice still echoed in Buffy's mind.

"Willow," she whispered to herself.

"Come on!" Xander snapped, grasping at her arm.

She shook him free, staring at the back of the extraction team commander. The woman turned, then, and Buffy saw her face. Willow Rosenberg at twenty-four, determined, very much in charge. When she saw Buffy looking at her, she grinned.

Buffy grinned back.

But then the newly arrived cadre of Kakchiquels rushed into the fray, and Willow's attention was back on the fight. One of them was Clownface, white greasepaint ghostly in the dark. Buffy went to go back, to help out, but Xander grabbed her with more strength than she would ever have imagined.

"No. We're not here to win. We're here to get you out."

For a long, last moment, Buffy watched. Willow set a pair of vampires on fire simply by touching them. Then she screamed out a name Buffy knew.

"Oz!"

From the midst of the melee came a sudden howl that made the hairs on the back of Buffy's neck stand up. Amidst the vampires, one of the members of the team changed in an instant. In the confusion, Buffy had not noticed him. Now there was no mistaking that it was him.

The werewolf raged, its black snout glistening, its ears twitching, teeth gnashing at the air as it charged at the approaching group. Clownface was in the lead and the werewolf rose up on its hind legs, grabbed the vampire, and tore her head off.

Oz? Buffy thought, horrified by how savage he was. The beast within him had been set loose at Willow's order, though the moon was not full.

He began to attack others, using powerful jaws and claws to tear into them, but then Willow shouted for them all to fall back. The extraction team complied instantly. Xander hauled on Buffy's arm, and then she was running toward the restaurant parking lot, mind spinning, almost blacking out. It was all too much for her.

Then they were at one of the sedans. Xander shoved her into the backseat, then jumped in front and started it up. Through the tinted windows Buffy watched the vampires give chase, but only for a few seconds. The team loaded into the military transport and the other sedan, and the vampires stopped as though they had also been ordered to fall back.

The passenger door opened and Willow dropped into the seat beside Xander.

"Spike," Buffy said. "Did you get him?"

"He disappeared," Willow replied. "He'll always save his own ass first." Then she glanced at Xander. "Move out."

He complied instantly, tearing out of the restaurant parking lot with the other sedan and the troop transport close behind. As they went, Buffy craned her neck to look out the rear window. The vampires who had survived were also retreating. They had climbed into their cars, both those that had been on sentry and the late arrivals, and begun to return the way they had come, as though the carnage had never happened, as though the people in the parking lot had not witnessed something horrible.

One car had not moved. It seemed aimed at them, headlights on high beam. They were several hundred yards away now, but Buffy could make out the form of a man standing in front of the car, his body silhouetted by the harsh lights, backlit so that he seemed more like a dark hole in the air than a man, like a thing of darkness painted over the face of the world.

Whoever he was, he stood calmly and watched them drive away.

Buffy shivered, there in the car, with these people who had once been her friends but whom she now barely knew. As they rounded a corner and the dark figure slipped out of sight behind them, she thought of the feeling she had had in the projection house at the drive-in. She thought of the crossbow that had been left there, just for her.

The two spirits that coexisted within her exulted simultaneously. Buffy was free. Yet somehow she felt her fear even more keenly than before, and a terrible dread was born within her.

CHAPTER 6

Willow felt frozen in place, there in the darkened parking lot of the Sunnydale bus station. She did not know if Camazotz's vampire followers had cut the power, or if the outage was simple coincidence, but she knew that in the end it would not really matter. The vampires scrambled across the lot from both sides, fifteen, maybe twenty. They were silent as wraiths. The night air crackled with menace.

The half that were nearest to Buffy formed a sort of semicircle around her, even as their master, the bat-god Camazotz, sprang toward her on cloven feet. Whatever had possessed Buffy, it was clear that the thing was running from Camazotz. Now that he had found her, the demon thing planned to destroy her himself. Buffy would die so that Camazotz could destroy the entity inhabiting her body.

Camazotz moved in to attack her. Buffy blocked his lunge, then shot a hard kick at his midsection that drove the bat-god backward.

"I came a long way to take the Slayer's body," the thing inside Buffy snapped. "Now you'll see why."

The vampires around her moved in, but Camazotz snarled at them and they moved back. The other cluster of vampires rushed at Willow, Oz, Xander, and Anya, who stood their ground, though they had no weapons at all. Xander and Oz had already been battered around by the Slayer. Even if they were fresh for the fight, and these were normal vampires—which, given their tattooed features and blazing orange eyes, and the way their bodies seemed to spark with energy, they most certainly weren't—even then the odds would have been against them.

With a single, muttered word and a wave of her hands, Willow drew upon the heat in the air around her, and a wall of fire suddenly blazed up from the pavement, a barrier of raging flame that gave the predators pause. They seemed, just then, like some species of ancient animal, these creatures who stared across the wall of flames, their flickering fire-eyes purely evil within the pitch black of the bat tattoos on their faces.

"Way to go, Willow!" Xander cried happily. "Torch 'em all!"

But she knew she did not have the mastery of magick to be able to do that. She had risked setting herself and her friends on fire with the spell she had just cast. Willow shot a quick glance at Buffy. She was in motion, kicking, punching, parrying blows, but Camazotz had already slashed her and she bled from several wounds.

No choice. They had no choice at all. Willow turned to her friends. "Run!" she barked.

"What about Buffy?" Oz asked, where he stood just beside her.

"We'll come back for her."

With that, Willow turned and ran toward the street side of the parking lot, toward the fence on the other side of which the van was still parked. Oz was right behind her, but Xander and Anya hung back a little, slowed down as Xander was by the beating Buffy had given him.

Willow glanced at Oz. "Get to the van. Start it up. Break out the weapons."

He sprinted even faster, and she dropped back to help Anya with Xander. Behind them the fire barrier had diminished and the vampires surged across, still unnervingly silent. Willow wished they would scream or make threats. Quiet as they were, the Kakchiquels made her mouth go dry and her skin prickle with cold fear.

"Willow, they're catching up!" Anya snapped, both petulant and afraid. "Some more fire would be nice!"

But Willow said nothing. It was hard for her to concentrate right now, and she needed focus to do magick. Without the van, without weapons, they would die. Simple as that. Her magick could protect them briefly, but that would not be enough. And even if she could keep them safe until sunrise, what about Buffy?

"Willow!" Anya shouted.

"Just run!" Willow replied curtly.

They were rushing along, Xander's arms over their shoulders, helping him to stay up and keep moving.

"Just go!" Xander said. "I'll catch up!"

Willow glanced at him, saw everything in his eyes in that one moment, his fear and courage, and his determination. But she knew Anya would not leave him behind, and neither would she.

Which was when Xander stopped. He simply planted his feet and pulled himself away from them. Before Willow or Anya could say anything, he had turned to face the Kakchiquels, who were closing in now. One of them, perhaps the hungriest, was far ahead of the others.

Xander crouched in a fighting stance. "Come on, then, you son of a—"

The vampire leaped on him, drove Xander down hard on the pavement. His head struck the ground with a loud *thunk* that seemed to echo in the silence. Anya screamed his name.

But Willow could not speak, could not scream. She saw them coming, smiling grimly now. Saw the one on top of Xander as it gripped his hair and dropped its fangs toward his throat. No words came up from within her, but something did, a dark anger she could barely control.

Her hands twitched, then lashed at the air as though it were the object of her rage. The vampire on top of Xander burst into flame, shrieking in agony at its immolation. Xander's clothes began to burn and he too cried out in pain as the heat seared his hands and face.

Anya kicked the vampire down onto the ground and began to beat at Xander's burning clothes. In an instant the flames were out.

"Not so quiet now," Willow said to the blazing Kakchiquel.

It glared at her, black tattoo blistering, and then it disintegrated in a puff of embers. The others who ran toward them faltered when they saw this, and Willow turned to face them, hands raised, ready for a fight. She wasn't exactly sure how she had managed to pinpoint that spell, knew she had nearly killed Xander, and was far from sure she could manage it again.

But they didn't know that.

"Come on, then!" she snapped.

Which was when the roar of an engine surged through the dark behind them. Headlights washed across them and Oz's van barreled into the parking lot.

Anya hustled Xander to the rear doors, opened them, and then helped him in. The Kakchiquels stood there, staring nervously at Willow, but then they began to inch closer.

"Willow," Oz's voice called from behind her. "Down!"

She dropped to a crouch on the pavement. Two of the vampires were struck in the chest with crossbow bolts. One dusted, but the other was not hit through the heart and grunted in pain instead, clutching at the wooden bolt in his chest.

Willow turned and ran for the van. Oz leaned out the driver's side window with a crossbow and fired again. Anya was in the other window, fitting a bolt into another.

"Go!" Willow said. "Can we just go, please?"

Oz pulled back into the van, put it in drive, and swung around just as Willow ran up toward the back. The rear door was open and she dove inside, then pulled it shut behind her.

Xander sat, face contorted with pain, leaning against the wall of the van.

"Hold on," she told him.

"Buffy," he muttered through gritted teeth. "We can't just leave her."

"We're not," Willow promised. Then she called to Oz up front. "Run them down. Get to Buffy."

"On it," Oz replied as he floored the accelerator.

The van rocked as he slammed into several of the Kakchiquels. Willow moved up between the front seats in time to see them smashed down under the van's wheels. They attacked the sides, and at least one of them managed to get on top and hold on.

The van raced toward the bus station and plowed through several of the Kakchiquels who had gathered as spectators around Camazotz's fight with Buffy.

They were not dead, but some at least were broken and out of the fight.

Oz said her name and Willow's heart broke. Her boyfriend felt things very deeply, but his expression and tone almost never revealed those feelings. Now, though, with just the two syllables of her name, he communicated all too much. Horror, grief, the desire to protect her from the scene that was playing out before them.

Willow sagged against the seats, her heart breaking.

As though they were actors on a stage, pinpointed by the headlights of the van, Camazotz held Buffy two feet off the ground, her feet kicking uselessly beneath her. One of her shoes had come off.

While Willow watched, tears beginning to slide down her face, Camazotz pulled Buffy toward him. A long, forked tongue snaked out of the bat-god's mouth and slipped down inside her throat. It was obscene, an intimate intrusion, a violent attack as vicious as if it had been a blade. The demon's tongue thrust between Buffy's lips and she choked and gagged. Her eyes rolled up in her head.

Willow and the others saw it all, a grotesque tableau before them. The van shook as more vampires attacked it. The passenger window cracked. The rear doors were dented.

Her heart was broken, but an even greater horror threatened to break Willow's spirit. For she understood with perfect clarity that they were too late. There was nothing left for them to do.

The passenger window shattered. Anya screamed as vampires reached in. Oz shot a crossbow bolt at one of them.

Willow did not even look. Her eyes were still locked on Buffy and Camazotz.

Suddenly, the bat-god's tongue began to slither back, inch after inch pulling out of Buffy's throat. The dead, scorched wings on Camazotz's back fluttered obscenely, like the wagging of a dog's tail. The orange fire that sparked in its eyes and those of its servants now seemed to blaze up all over the thing's body, as though electricity were passing all through him.

Buffy went rigid in Camazotz's grasp, as suddenly a dark, writhing, oily thing began to slip from her open lips, dragged out of her by the bat-god's probing tongue. It was an ephemeral thing, a dark ghost of boiling tar, a twitching, roiling cloud of blackness.

Willow had seen it before. *The Prophet.*

Somehow, Camazotz was tearing the entity right out of Buffy.

A pair of arms surged through the passenger window, grabbed Anya by the shoulder and by the hair, and began to pull her out. Her shoulder was slashed with broken glass and she cried out.

Suddenly Xander thrust a hand up from the back of the van and slapped a crucifix down on the vampire's arm. It smoked and burned and the van was filled with the smell of rotten meat cooking. The vampire withdrew, but there were others waiting.

Buffy hung limply in Camazotz's grasp as his tongue dragged the black thing from within her.

"We can't win this," Anya snapped. "We've got to go!"

"Not without *her*," Willow insisted. "Oz, run them both down. Camazotz *and* Buffy!"

"But Willow—" Xander began.

"She'll survive it. She has to. But it's the only way to buy us a few seconds to drag her in here."

"What if she *doesn't* survive it?" Oz asked calmly.

Willow didn't answer.

In the backseat of the sedan, Buffy shifted painfully on the seat, her blood sticky on the leather upholstery. Willow, beautiful and confident, watched her with great curiosity from the front seat.

Xander drove and said nothing, never even turned his head.

"You ran me over?" Buffy asked, stunned. A great deal of the story Willow was telling—of the night five years ago when they had tried to save her from Camazotz—stunned her. "I don't remember any of that."

Willow offered a brief smile. "You weren't yourself, Buffy. First you were possessed by Zotziloha, and then you were unconscious."

"Zotzil-who?" Buffy asked.

The sedan knifed through the darkness. But it was a darkness lit with streetlights and businesses and homes, a place where real people lived out from under the control of the vampires. Through the windshield, Buffy saw a large, ornate church ahead, its stained-glass windows gleaming in the night. It heartened her to know that there were still people who had faith in something.

"Zotziloha was Camazotz's wife. You knew her as The Prophet. She was a noncorporeal goddess entity, a demon yes, but not as evil as her mate. She fled him, but knew he would eventually catch up to her. Which was why she possessed you."

"Then he drove her out?" Buffy asked.

"That's one way to put it."

And then they captured me, and kept me locked up all this time, Buffy thought. But the other Buffy inside her had more questions, and other priorities. Throughout the trek she had made to get away from the vampires, the two personas' priorities had been the same, and it had been simple for them to coexist. Now, though, they were split again.

"I remember coming around while they were bringing me to my cell," Buffy said, her voice a low rasp. "But nothing before that."

Even as she said it, the younger Buffy within her knew that it was no longer as simple as returning to her own time. Given what Willow had told her, she knew that her spirit—the spirit of Buffy at nineteen—would eventually be drawn back to the time and the body it was supposed to inhabit. But she did not know *when.* Any day, any hour, any minute, she could not know when. This Zotziloha entity had been driven out of her that night five years earlier, and her spirit returned. But now, in this dark future, she could not simply wait for that to happen. Unless she could find a way for her displaced spirit to return to her correct time earlier, *before* The Prophet, Zotziloha, possessed her body, then this future could not be avoided.

"God, my head hurts," Buffy whispered. Then she looked at Willow. There was a hesitation between them, an awkwardness that five years apart had created. But Willow was still her friend, and Buffy knew that she had all the help she needed, the greatest ally she could ask for. "You and I have a lot of things to talk about, Will."

"Yeah," Willow agreed. "And soon. You have a lot of catching up to do, a lot for me to tell you. A lot of it bad. But at the moment . . ." she turned around to look out the windshield again. "Here we are."

The sky had been lightening as they drove, and now the eastern horizon was bright and blue. The sedan pulled into an unmarked street. A line of trees had been planted along the road. They drove along until they came to a building that looked like a hospital or office complex, the other vehicles close behind. The troop transport went past them, into a large lot beside the building, but the two sedans parked right up in front among some other cars.

"This is home base," Willow said.

Buffy stared at the front of the building. "Big operation."

The three of them climbed out of the car. Without a

word or a glance, Xander started for the building, but Buffy and Willow hung back, walking slowly side by side. After a moment, both women paused. Buffy and Willow turned to gaze at each other. The Slayer was overcome with emotion, a release of despair that she had fought against for so long. Willow bit her lip, a tiny smile twitching at her lips, and then the women embraced. Best friends, too long apart, they had built up walls around their hope that they would be together again. Buffy still felt some distance between them, knew that it would take time for them to be comfortable with each other again.

But this was a start.

After a moment, they stepped back from each other. Buffy began to walk toward the building, but paused again and glanced curiously at this woman Willow had become.

"I know we have a million things to talk about— you have no idea—but you know what's nagging at me? If all Camazotz wanted was his wife back, then why did he capture me afterward? Why bother with me at all? He could have just killed me and gone home. All this conqueror stuff, I mean, what does that have to do with chasing his wife?"

Willow's eyes went wide as Buffy spoke. When only silence hung between them, Willow lifted a hand to her mouth as though afraid of the words that might come out. After a moment, she shook her head.

"God, Buffy, I'm sorry. I . . . it never occurred to me that you didn't know."

Icy tendrils of dread clutched at Buffy's heart. "Didn't know what?"

"Nobody's seen Camazotz for years. If he's still alive, he's probably as much a prisoner as you were."

Buffy frowned. "I don't understand."

The van rocked back and forth as the Kakchiquels tried to tip it over. Anya held up a crucifix in front of her broken window. Willow stared through the windshield and saw Camazotz retract his tongue. The black, viscous thing that had been pulled from inside Buffy's throat undulated at the end of the bat-god's tongue. Buffy was limp in his clutches but the thing was out of her body, at least.

Camazotz sucked the twitching black thing into his mouth and swallowed it whole. The bat-god's withered wings fluttered mightily and he threw his disgusting head back and laughed, needle teeth flashing in the starlight.

"Run him down," Willow said, stomach roiling in disgust. "Go!"

Oz put the van in drive and was about to floor it when there came a soft tap at the driver's-side window.

They all glanced that way at once, surprised by the subtle noise amidst the violent cacophony around them.

Giles stood beside the van, just outside Oz's window. He no longer wore his glasses, and his eyes blazed brightly with orange flame. He bore no tattoo on his face, but when he smiled at them, Willow saw the pale outline of fangs.

Something crumbled inside her then. "No," she whispered, shaking her head in despair. "No, no, no!"

"Giles," Anya said. "He's a . . ."

"You can't win," Giles called amiably, loud enough to be heard through the window. "You can only die. Don't worry, though. Buffy will live. I wouldn't dream of killing *her*."

With that he turned away from the van and strode toward Camazotz. Through Anya's shattered window they heard Giles shout at the bat-god.

"Careful with her! Don't forget, if you kill her, another will rise in her place. The only way to defeat the Slayer is to cage her. If we can't send her to Hell, bringing Hell to her here on Earth is the next best thing."

Camazotz hesitated, but after a moment he dropped Buffy on the ground. Giles motioned to several of the others, who picked her up, and then they all retreated into the night, beyond the reach of the van's headlights, carrying Buffy with them.

In a moment, the van idled in the parking lot, and they were alone save for the dead travelers inside the bus station.

They had been left alive, but Willow knew it was not because the monster who had once been their friend had spared them. It was because they were an afterthought. With the Slayer a prisoner, they didn't matter to him. Not at all.

"Oh, man. Giles," Oz said, voice hushed.

"What do we do now?" Xander asked. "We are *so* screwed."

Willow began to cry, there in the back of the van, great heaving sobs that seemed to be torn right out of her. She didn't think she would ever be able to stop.

Buffy stared at Willow, eyes wide. She had never felt so cold. Of all she had seen and heard in this horrid future, this was the hardest blow of all. She bit her lip, tears slipping down her cheeks, and shook her head slowly.

"No, Willow. Oh, no," she whispered. "Not Giles."

For Willow, that night was five years in the past. And yet the pain of it still haunted her eyes. She pulled Buffy to her again, held her for a long moment. Suddenly Buffy pulled away.

"Giles," the Slayer said, wiping at her eyes. "Giles is a vampire."

Willow paused, then glanced away. "Not just a vampire," she said. "The most brilliant, most evil, most dangerously organized vampire who has ever lived. He's their leader.

"Their king."

To Be Continued . . .

Part Three:

KING OF THE DEAD

CHAPTER 1

Drusilla's dead.

Spike roared through downtown Sunnydale in a silver Camaro with blacked-out windows. Dawn had come hours ago, and the sun glared down upon the windshield, streamed in through the small splotches that had not been painted black. He had to see to drive, after all.

Behind the black aviator sunglasses he wore to keep the sun off his eyes, tears streaked his face. His jaw was clenched tight, his knuckles white on the steering wheel. Though he would usually have something on the radio, all was silent in the car. No music. Not even the sound of breathing. Not from him, for after all, wasn't he a dead man?

Yes, of course he was. Yet somehow he had never felt quite so dead as he did this awful morning.

The Slayer. That little bitch.

But it had not been only the Slayer's fault, had it? No,

not at all. When Giles had split them up, sending Dru with one team and him with another, he ought to have balked, but he did not. Giles was the king, wasn't he? He hadn't steered them wrong yet.

Till now. Now he'd steered them all kinds of wrong. *Bastard.*

There were big plans. Spike wanted to be a part of it. But now Drusilla was dead and everything they had worked for with Giles was in jeopardy. For millennia, vampires had dreamed big but acted small, never able to agree on anything long enough to get it together, to pull off a scheme bigger than a simple slaughter. Rupert Giles was different. Using the addictive blood of the bat-god, Camazotz, to ensure loyalty among the Kakchiquels, he wanted nothing less than the world. Unlike so many vampires and demons, he had achieved the level of patience that immortality afforded him. What he had in mind would take time to do right. He would wait.

But now this thing with the Slayer. What the hell is this all about?

Images of Drusilla sifted like kaleidoscope images through his mind. He could hear her mad little laugh, remember what she looked like naked and spattered with blood, recall the scent of her, like freshly pressed antique lace with just a hint of lilac.

Fresh tears sprang to his eyes and he let them stripe his cheeks like war paint. They dripped onto his black leather jacket and he let them dry there, a sort of offering to the ghost of his dead love.

If only vampires had ghosts.

Spike drove out of downtown, haunted as an empty circus tent, awaiting the mad revelry that night always brought. The Kakchiquels kept the residents of Sunnydale about for their own amusement. Blood slaves. Sex slaves. Torture victims. Yet for every human they killed, two more would drift into town on the current of whispered gossip and the desire to discover the truth, to subject themselves to the rule of the vampires. These humans would do anything to be tasted, to be bled, to have a Kakchiquel lover, and if having their guts strewn across the sidewalk downtown or their heads rammed onto a fence post at the edge of Hammersmith Park was a moment by moment possibility, that was a small price to pay.

Then there were the original Sunnydale residents, the people who hadn't had the courage to run away. Most of them cowered in their homes, even now, or operated their businesses with the permission of the dead who slept while the sun was high. Those were the ones Spike understood the least and disliked the most.

Cowards.

In silence, he drove to City Hall. It was warm inside the car and though it didn't really bother him, there was something wrong with that today. His chest felt hollow, as if a slender surgical blade had somehow been slipped into him and his heart carved out, cold and dead but still saturated with other people's blood. With Drusilla's death, he had become a shell of himself, a mask with no face beneath it.

How can it be warm?

Spike was certain that he ought to feel cold, and so he turned the air conditioner up as high as it would go and relished the stiffness in his fingers as his body temperature began to dip even lower.

Spike pulled into the underground garage beneath City Hall and parked in the spot reserved for him. He was ice now, a brittle, hollow sculpture of frozen pain shaped like a man. At some point his tears had stopped and now as he stepped out of the car, jacket cascading behind him, there was only his grief to mark Drusilla's passing.

From a pocket inside his jacket he pulled out a white plastic key card. At the door that led into the complex he slid the card into a slot and a light burned green. The door clicked and he pushed it open and entered the warren of corridors beneath City Hall. There were tunnels from there that would lead to the basement of the courthouse, the police station, even the town library.

Spike clutched the key card and strode along one of those tunnels, the scrunch of leather the only sound to accompany him. At a junction in the corridor, he turned left and walked to a bank of elevators, where his key card was needed to call an elevator down.

He stepped in and pressed the button for the third floor, then waited as the elevator glided upward. In the corner there was a security camera. Spike was a shadow of himself, a kind of ghost in his own right, and as he glared at the security camera from behind his dark sunglasses, he wondered if the guards in the monitor booth could see the change in him. He wondered if they saw him coming, and shuddered.

He hoped that they did.

The elevator *shushed* to a halt and the doors slid open. A pair of burly Kakchiquels stood blocking his exit, their eyes crackling with energy, their tattooed faces impassive. Spike was not at all surprised to see them.

"You are not expected until dusk," one of the Kakchiquels said, voice emotionless.

"The master does not need you until then," added the other.

Spike cocked his head to one side, regarding them through the tinted glasses. He slipped his key card into his pocket. The elevator doors began to close and he punched the button to open them again.

"Yeah. He mentioned that. Wanted me to take a little time, cool off a bit, right?" Spike nodded, but then stopped abruptly. "Bugger that."

With one swift motion he reached out, grabbed the one on the left by a clump of hair, and hauled him forward, driving his knee up into the Kakchiquel's crotch. The vampire doubled over and Spike yanked him into the elevator, then stepped off. The other Kakchiquel was ready for him, or at least thought he was. Spike took one blow to the temple that knocked his sunglasses spinning through the air, then grabbed the vampire by the face and squeezed, breaking his jaw and fracturing his cheekbones. He knew his own eyes flickered with the blazing power of Camazotz, just as his enemy's did.

With a low snarl, Spike rammed the vampire back

against the wall, then grabbed his hair in a tight fist and shoved the guard's head through the emergency glass covering a fire extinguisher. Broken glass sliced his hand but Spike barely felt it as he snapped the heavy fire extinguisher from its moorings and began slamming it into the Kakchiquel's skull until it was mashed to pulp and splintered bone.

The guard dusted.

A ding sounded behind him and Spike turned to see the elevator doors opening again, the guard he'd kneed standing inside. With a twist of his arm, he swung the extinguisher again and shattered the guard's nose. Spike struck him again and again, beating him down, then pressed all the numbers on the elevator before stepping off. The elevator moved down, taking the bloody, crippled Kakchiquel with it.

Spike did not smile. He no longer had anything to smile about. No one with whom to share the exhilaration of a good fight, a good kill. Instead he picked up the black glasses from the floor and slipped them back on. He reached into his coat, took out a box of cigarettes and a metal lighter, and fired one up.

He strode down the hall and around a corner that led him to the huge double doors of the courtroom. There another pair of Kakchiquels were standing guard, and they snapped instantly to attention, ready to stop him.

Spike took a drag on the cigarette, blew out the air, and gazed at them coolly from behind his shades, where he hid the telltale spark of power that bound him to these other creatures.

"I know, I know," he said. "You're supposed to stop me, yeah? Bloody hell, mates, have at it then. But think about it this way. Mood I'm in right now, you'll have to kill me to stop me. If you can. And if you do, well, he's gonna miss me, isn't he? Then he'll kill you blokes sure as I'm standing here. His lordship is fickle like that. On the other hand, you stand aside and he'll punish you, sure, but you'll live."

Spike took a long drag on the cigarette, blew rings of smoke into the air and barely even glanced at the two Kakchiquels as they exchanged a nervous glance. After a moment, they actually opened the large double doors for him.

He winked at the larger one and went into the courtroom.

The rows of seats were filled with vampires, eyes crackling with orange fire, black bats seared into the tender flesh of their faces. Spike found that there were fewer and fewer familiar faces as the months went by. Giles sent those he trusted out on errands of vital importance. They were part of the plan. But he had always kept Spike and Drusilla close at hand, either because he felt he needed them or because he didn't trust them, or both.

The lights were dim in the huge room and the only noise was the shifting of the Kakchiquels in their seats as Spike entered. They were a motley collection of vampires, from those who had been servants of Camazotz when the bat-god had come to Sunnydale, to existing vampires like Spike himself who had been recruited by Giles, to new creatures made only recently.

Giles sat on the dais—where the judge would have presided, if there were any judges left in Sunnydale. His eyes glowed only very dimly. His graying hair was combed neatly back and a soft, benevolent smile turned up the corners of his mouth. He wore a thin green V-neck sweater with a white tee shirt underneath. To those who had known him as a human being, only the fact that his glasses were missing would have shattered the illusion that he had not changed at all.

Brilliant, kindhearted, self-effacing. That had been Giles the man, the Watcher. It was a face he wore still, though no one knew what sort of pleasure he derived from the façade.

Of all the vampires in the chamber, only one other besides Spike was standing. He was a dark-skinned leech whose ritual tattoo had been seared into his face with white ink instead of black. The bat-scar was the color of milk and it set him apart from all the others. Giles called him Jax. Spike did not know if he had any other name. He had simply appeared one day, a creature sired by Giles and then suckled by Camazotz as was their tradition. But Jax had quickly become far more than simply another recruit. He was Giles's right hand.

Spike hated him.

Jax glanced once at Spike, a small smile flickering across his features, then he gestured at a female vampire in the front row.

"Valerie? I believe your report is next."

"I don't think so," Spike snapped as he strode up the aisle toward the judge's bench.

Hushed mutterings filled the room.

"Spike. You're half a day early. You have a private audience scheduled at dusk today."

"Bollocks," Spike replied happily.

He walked right up to Jax. No one tried to stop him. Jax moved to block his way, hate simmering in the other vampire's gaze. Spike took another drag on his cigarette, plucked the butt from his mouth between two fingers, and pressed its burning, ashen end into the middle of Jax's forehead. The leech snarled in pain and anger, his features contorting into the bestial face of the vampire.

Spike decked him.

He stood before the bench and glared up at Giles, whose eyebrows shot up with curiosity Spike found insulting.

"She's dead," Spike said, voice a rasp. "You might as well have struck a match to her yourself, you bastard. What are you playing at with this Slayer? You could've had her a dozen times since she got out."

For a moment, just the tiniest flicker, the mask slipped. A shadow of menace seemed to fall across Giles's features. The smile gave way to a lip-curling snarl. His nostrils flared and the orange fire in his eyes became tiny embers. Then it passed and the kindly, almost paternal smile returned to his features.

Giles leaned toward him and gazed down from the judge's bench. "Go. Sit. Valerie is next. When she's done, we'll talk about what went wrong last night, and what we've all lost."

As though Spike had suddenly disappeared from the

room, Giles gestured for Valerie to come forward. Jax rubbed at the burned spot on the white brand on his face, but he, too, gave his attention to the Kakchiquel girl. It infuriated Spike to be ignored like that, but he supposed it beat having Giles order a room filled with vampires to kill him. Still, Spike did not sit as Giles had instructed. He might take orders from the big boss, the king, but he was still his own man. He had a legend of his own to maintain. Giles knew that . . . he constantly used Spike's status as an object of fear to his advantage.

Jax might be the master's right-hand man, but Spike was his enforcer, his assassin. *At least when Drusilla was alive. Now, though . . . Giles has a lot to answer for.*

Valerie, one of those whom Giles had trusted and promoted, glanced uneasily at Spike as she stood. He flashed the girl a grin born from his savage heart and she flinched and looked quickly away. Valerie moved forward and stood beside Jax, staring up at Giles in total subservience. She even bowed.

"Lord and master," Valerie said, her voice sweet and yet confident. "The Los Angeles operation proceeds as per your charted strategy. LAPD sirings are at twenty-two percent. Complete departmental takeover is scheduled for next Wednesday, with the mayor and the commissioner twenty-four hours previous."

Giles stroked his chin thoughtfully, his gaze distant. Half a minute ticked by and no one dared interrupt his thoughts.

"Oh, all right, you pompous git. Get on with it," Spike snapped. He rolled his eyes and crossed his arms, feeling self-conscious there at the front of the courtroom.

He expected a flare of anger, but Giles did not so much as blink. Valerie glanced at Jax, then shifted uncomfortably from one foot to the other. Jax seemed unwilling to even acknowledge there was something odd about the master's behavior. After another half minute ticked by, though, he moved into Giles's field of vision.

"My lord?" Jax ventured.

"Hmm?" Giles muttered. Then he glanced down at Spike and Valerie and blinked several times. "Oh, right. Sorry. Late night, wasn't it?"

Valerie giggled like a schoolgirl and Spike wanted to rip her heart out for it. The king was getting a bit dotty. They all had to see it. Ever since Buffy had broken out of her cell, Giles had been scattered. Never mind that he'd turned up missing from his chambers half a dozen times, not telling anyone where he'd gone.

"Valerie, I don't believe you mentioned the studio heads," Giles reminded her.

"Last night, my lord," she replied. "Just as you instructed. We missed at Paramount, though. He took some unscheduled personal time, went to a spa in Nevada. A team has been dispatched."

"Excellent initiative." Giles stood up. The instant he did so the entire room also rose. "We'll pick this up tomorrow morning. Any urgent reports or requests can go to Jax." His smile grew wider as he looked at Spike. "In my chambers, now, William. And we'll discuss your bereavement."

Jax shot Spike a withering glance as he moved into the aisle, only to be surrounded by those Kakchiquels who felt that their business with the king could not wait. Spike caught Valerie studying him with fascination. Another time he might have flirted with her, strutted for her. But the tears were dry upon his cheeks and Drusilla's death was too fresh for him, too close.

Giles stepped down from the high chair and went to the heavy wooden door that led into the judge's chambers. He opened it and stood aside, waiting for Spike. The smile was still there, but a chill ran through Spike when he caught the glint in the other vampire's eyes. Though he remembered well when Rupert Giles was the Watcher, a stuffy Englishman who relied more on knowledge than on violence, this creature was not that man. Not a man at all. It retained Giles's memories, his intelligence and cunning, and it had turned them to its advantage.

But this king of vampires had not become lord and master to thousands by chance.

That knowledge calmed Spike somewhat as he stepped past Giles and into the darkened chambers beyond. The windows had been blacked out and the three lamps that burned in the room were unable to dispel the shadows there. In the corner, the skeleton of Judge Warren Hester had been arranged in an embrace around a coat rack. Tufts of hair and dried skin still clung to the bones. At night the windows were opened to air the rooms out, but over the years the smell had mostly dissipated.

"Hello, your honor," Giles said to the bones.

Then he turned and leaned against the desk, crossed his arms and gazed at Spike with sympathy in his glittering orange eyes. Sympathy as false, as feigned, as the benevolent mask he always wore.

"Have you got another cigarette?" Giles asked.

Spike raised one eyebrow in surprise, then shrugged and tugged the pack from his pocket. He held it out and Giles took a cigarette. Spike lit it for him, clicked the lighter closed, and slid it back into his pocket with the cigarettes.

Giles inhaled deeply, cig clutched between two fingers. Then he let it dangle in his hand as he leaned against the desk once more.

"You know how important Drusilla was to me, Spike," he said, as the ash lengthened on the cigarette. He did not take another drag from it, however, only let the ash grow longer. "Honestly, I find it more than a bit disturbing that you'd accuse me of having some sort of responsibility for her destruction. Why would I do something like that?"

Feeling more than a bit petulant, even childish, Spike glanced at the ground. "Not saying you did it on purpose, Ripper. But, look, you're playing with the girl. Me, I always thought it was brilliant, keeping Buffy locked up like that. You don't kill her, they don't get to train another one. But she got out, didn't she? Not sure it was too bright an idea puttin' that new one, the little cutie came along after I took care of Faith, in with Buffy. Gotta figure that was a mistake, but it's too late to do anything about it now. Right. Fine. But they could have caught up with Buffy five minutes after she was out the door, or any time while she was on her way to Sunnydale. You told 'em to wait. More'n that, you left her that damn crossbow."

A ghost of a grin whispered across Giles's features. "You knew about that?"

Spike shrugged. "Saw you leavin' with it, put two and two together. At the time I figured you were just toying with her, having a bit of fun all your own. I can understand that. Once upon a time, she was your girl, yeah. In a way, you were her sire the same way Angel was mine. He didn't make me, but he trained me to be what I am. You did the same for her. So maybe you play with her a bit, give the mouse a little string, but you don't let her go."

Spike took off his sunglasses, stared hard at Giles. "You don't let her run around killing your best people. Harmony was an idiot, but she was vicious. Matthias and Astrid, they were the best of the ones who came here with Camazotz. And Dru—" his voice broke off.

"I should've been there!" Spike snapped, shouting at Giles, who watched him impassively. "You had us all spread out, but I think you knew just what Buffy'd do. You trained her, after all, right? Who'd know better than you. You probably predicted every move she made. You played with her, but you gave her too much rope and now Drusilla's dead."

Giles nodded slowly, reasonably. "True," he said. "All of it. You know, you've always been underestimated, Spike. You're really far more perceptive than you get credit for."

Spike shook his head, not knowing what to say next. The last thing he had expected was that Giles would simply agree with him, taking responsibility for Drusilla's death.

The vampire lord rolled his eyes. "Oh, please, Spike!" he cried with frustration. "What would you like me to do about it? I'm sorry Dru's dead. Truly. She was always a source of great amusement. Couldn't find any better. And the occasional vision, when it wasn't too truncated by her lunacy, was helpful as well. But she's dead. So now what? You stomp around like a five-year-old and then go huffing off to Greece or Brazil to lick your wounds? Feel free, if you need to."

Spike flinched. He felt the anger boiling up inside him, dwarfing anything he had felt before. This wasn't just the pain of his loss, the void in his gut where his love for Dru had been ripped from him. It was more visceral, more personal even than that. He had spent over a hundred years proving his worth after Angelus and Darla had disparaged him. He had killed more Slayers than any other vampire he knew of. But Giles had just brushed him off as though he was worthless.

"I'll tell you what you do," Spike snarled. His face changed with his anger, his fangs lengthening, his brow contorting into the face of the beast. "You get a posse up like an old Western, as many of your loyal subjects as you can pull together on short notice, then you track her down and you kill her before she can do any more damage. Or maybe you don't remember the habit Buffy has of interfering with the fun?"

Giles's upper lip twitched once. He glanced away and idly reached up toward his face as though he were about to remove a pair of eyeglasses. His fingers paused inches from his face and he made a fist, then dropped his hand. Spike frowned as he took note of this strange behavior. It was, in that moment, as though Giles had forgotten that he no longer needed glasses. An echo of an instinctive nervous behavior that he had engaged in when he was still human. Still alive. Still really Giles.

"You don't want to kill her, do you?" Spike asked, astonished. "What's got into you, Ripper? You gone soft?"

A shudder seemed to pass through Giles. He bent over slightly, staring up at Spike from beneath heavily lidded eyes. His face changed, became monstrous, lips curled back to show his elongated fangs. Slowly, he took a step toward Spike.

"You have a certain value to me, Spike. I gave you a great deal of rope because of it. No more."

Spike tried to protest, but Giles was too fast for him. The vampire lord darted in and grabbed him by the throat. Lifted off his feet, Spike beat at Giles's head and arms, trying to break his master's grip. Giles gave him a swift head-butt, connected with a loud, solid crack, and then slammed Spike into the dead judge's desk.

"It is not your place to question!" Giles roared as he kicked Spike in the ribs once, twice, a third time.

Bones snapped.

"Somebody's gotta do it," Spike snarled, not sure if

he felt brave or just stupid. He clutched at his side and tried to rise, and Giles grabbed him by the front of his jacket and threw him hard enough that he crashed into the coat rack and the wall and sent the dead judge's skeleton clattering in pieces all over the floor.

When he looked up, Giles stood over him. The vampire lord kicked him in the face and Spike felt his cheek give way.

"Son of a bitch!" Spike grunted in pain.

Giles crouched beside him. His face was human again, his features soft, the mask back in place. Somehow that was more terrifying to Spike than anything else.

"Everything she is, she owes to me, just as though she were my own daughter. She is a more perfect creature, a more effective predator, than any of the beasts who follow me. I wanted to see that beauty, the flow and rhythm of it, again. To know that it is still there."

Spike wiped the back of his hand across his mouth and it came away bloody.

"Yeah, that's brilliant," he muttered. "Things are going too well for you, too smoothly, so you've got to muddy the water a bit. Seen it a million times. Done it myself, even. Winning's no fun if you don't have someone to beat. Doesn't mean it isn't stupid."

Giles kicked him in the gut, then bent to pick up a length of broken coat rack. He turned and strode away, as if Spike were little more than a nuisance, now almost forgotten.

"I toy with her. For my own pleasure. It isn't your

business. But if you must know, I don't intend to kill her, not really. I didn't want her to escape, but now that she's out, she'll never let herself be captured alive again. I want to see if she's still as deadly. It seems all her time in that cell has made her even more so. Buffy Summers is the perfect killer. Imagine what she could be if I turned her."

Spike's eyes widened. Painfully, clutching at his broken ribs, he climbed to his feet. "You're gonna make her a soddin' vampire?"

Giles glanced over at him and smiled sweetly. "Of course I am. Anything else would be a terrible waste, don't you think? Besides, I'm going to have to have someone to replace you."

"What—" Spike began.

He was not allowed to finish. Giles darted across the room at him, broken coat rack in his hands. It whistled as it cut the air, then collided with Spike's skull. He staggered backward, lifted his arms to try to defend himself, and Giles broke his right hand with another swing of the coat rack.

"No!" Spike roared.

"I have to set an example," Giles said simply, coldly. "If only you hadn't been so fresh."

The vampire lord jammed the coat rack into Spike's gut and propelled him with a mighty thrust back through the blacked-out windows. The painted glass shattered and Spike tumbled out into the daylight. He fell three stories, twisting himself in midair, trying to control the descent. When he struck the pavement below, he dislocated a shoulder and his broken ribs tore up his lungs. Pain erupted in him like fireworks and he blacked out for a second or two.

His clothes began to smoke and then tiny flames erupted all over his body. Spike started to burn.

His eyes popped open and he screamed in anger and agony. With some difficulty, he got to his feet and ran for the entrance to the underground parking garage.

Self-righteous bastard, he thought as he slipped into the cool relief of the garage, out of the sun, slapping at his clothes and hair to douse the flames. His keys rattled in his pocket.

Can't kill ol' Spike that easily.

Giles had slipped into the shadows quickly enough that he was barely scorched by the sunlight that streamed in the broken window. His face and hands felt warm, but that would pass in moments. The window would have to be replaced, of course. He could have had it boarded up instead, but he thought, perhaps, that his affection for the symbolism of painting the windows over might have finally waned. No, this time he wanted a real window, with a fine wooden frame and heavy drapes to block the sun during the day. That way, should he ever have occasion to enter that chamber after dark, he could look at the stars.

Spike would probably survive, he knew. But despite his swagger, Spike had never been the most courageous of creatures. Self-preservation was always his greatest motivation. Without Drusilla to trail along behind in puppy-dog fashion, he was likely to grumble under his breath and wander off, go on an intercontinental rampage or the like, then come back in ten or fifteen years with his plumage showing, all cock of the walk.

When he did, Giles suspected he would take Spike back into the fold. By then he would appear to have been properly chastised. And he was useful, after all. His legend was more substantial than he was, but Spike was an excellent hunter, a bright boy, and a decent strategist when he set his mind to it. A bit too emotional, but then, Giles was not entirely without guilt in that area himself.

He thought of Buffy again, and smiled to himself. Never had he seen another creature so resilient, so durable. In his secret heart he had been disappointed that it had taken her so many years to escape, though she was quite a nuisance. Now that she was out, though, he rejoiced in the carnage she had caused.

Always, she had been like a daughter to him. Soon enough, she would be his daughter in truth. His blood would make it so.

Careful to avoid the sunlight, Giles went to the corner where Judge Hester's bones had been scattered, and he began to tidy up. He whistled happily while he put things back in order, thinking about the evening to come, and the brief journey he would make that night.

A journey south.

CHAPTER 2

In her dream, there are two of her.

Buffy-at-nineteen seems to float in a current of darkness that rustles her hair and clothes, pushes against her. She can feel it dragging against her from behind as well, particularly at the base of her skull, as though some unseen thing has violated her flesh, painlessly plunging a hook through the peak of her spine. It tugs on her, but the flesh and bone are uncomfortably numb.

Amid the darkness that sweeps by her there is a bright core, a deep purple vein that surges with electricity and menace. Now that she has noticed it, she can see that it disappears into the distance ahead of her and behind, weaving in serpentine fashion and yet following the same path as this river of darkness that pulls at her.

A chilly certainty shudders through her and Buffy traces the purple vein with her gaze, follows it until she realizes that it runs right up to her chest. Suddenly it is warm there, where the energy cable enters her, and she feels stronger, more aware. How she did not notice before that this power touches her, she has no idea. But she also suspects that the feeling at the base of her skull, the fishhook that is tugging her along the river of darkness . . . that feeling is there because the bruise-colored, thrumming energy stream that enters through her chest exits her body right at the top of her spine.

This thing. This is what's pulling on me, *she thinks.*

Yet something holds her in place, floating there. Something has anchored her here.

Buffy-at-nineteen glances downward. A kind of spotlight is shone in this dark place, and she sees Spartan living quarters, a hard bed, a rough blanket. Upon the bed, Buffy-at-twenty-four rests uneasily, dreaming, twisting beneath the blanket. Her features are beautiful, but hard-edged like diamonds. Her arms where they snake out from beneath the covers are corded with sinewy muscles, her fingers leathery with callus.

Me, *she thinks.* That's me. Or it will be.

No. No, it *is* me. It shouldn't be, but it is.

Buffy-at-nineteen blinks, and she truly sees. The purple vein snakes from her, back through the darkness, where it attaches to Buffy-at-twenty-four like some monstrous umbilical cord.

And she knows what it is.

This is the power, *she thinks.* From the first Slayer to the last, this is the power of the Chosen One. *And on the heels of that thought, another.* Why is it so dark?

"Buffy?"

A voice swirling in the river of darkness.

She turns to look back along the rushing river, the serpentine vein twisting in the flow, and she sees a face back there. For a moment it is vague and out of focus, but then the features shimmer and become clear. Waves of blond hair, a kind but tired smile. So familiar, so intimate.

"Mom?" Buffy asks. "Where are you?"

The tired smile disappears. "Here, now, honey. Just here."

"I need to see you," Buffy whispers. "I have to find you."

Joyce Summers shakes her head, even as the current begins to take her, dragging her back and away, along the river and into the void.

"Faith tried to save me. I thought you should know," Joyce says.

Buffy's eyes widen. Her heart clenches painfully in her chest. She tries to swim the current, to go after her mother as the woman begins to diminish in the distance. But she is anchored now to Buffy at twenty-four, and cannot follow.

Still, there is something she must know.

"Who?" Buffy-at-nineteen screams after the dwindling figure of her mother. There are the ghosts of tears on her cheeks. "Who killed you?"

The tears were still wet on Buffy's cheeks when she woke. She had kicked off the covers and the sun shone through the window, casting a distorted square of warmth and light across her legs. It was too warm and she pulled her legs up in front of her, curled into an almost fetal position there on the bed. The sun felt wrong to her. Too good; too healthy; too rich with heat and life. It was as though the sun itself were unnatural, merely a hesitation between stretches of night, a gasp of brightness and false security before the dark came again.

That was what Giles had done.

Giles, Buffy thought. It was a joke cast down by the cruelest of gods, that her former mentor and friend should become this thing, should be transformed into the most vile example of the monsters he had fought his entire life.

In her mind's eye, Buffy could see a clear image of Giles, a kind, decent man who had been more of a father to her in her teenage years than her own father had been.

Oh, Giles, she thought again.

Through some dark and powerful magick, a being called The Prophet had thrust Buffy's soul five years into the future, so that she now existed inside her own twenty-four-year-old body. Twin spirits, one younger, one older, thrived within her and though their memories and thoughts were sometimes in conflict, for the most part they had merged. Buffy had reason to believe it was a temporary situation, but she resigned herself to growing accustomed to it, just in case.

In this dark future, Buffy had spent the previous five years imprisoned by the vampires, and had escaped to find that her best friend, Willow Rosenberg, had grown wiser and more powerful and was now a major player in the war against the darkness. Willow had told Buffy how it had all come to this, or at least as much as they could guess. The god of bats, Camazotz, had come to Sunnydale followed by his Kakchiquels, a breed of vampires somehow enhanced by his own demonic power. Striking out at the Slayer, Camazotz had ordered Giles made a vampire.

It was the greatest mistake the god of bats had ever made. Giles was brilliant and cunning, with an encyclopedic knowledge of demonology and a violent, dark streak he was at pains to keep hidden. Once the vampiric spirit had taken up residence in the dead man's psyche, adopting as vampires usually did the knowledge and personality traits of the victim, Camazotz had created his worst enemy. Giles established himself as king of the vampires.

What happened to Camazotz, no one really knew. But the Kakchiquels, old and new alike, still seemed to shimmer with the power of the god of bats, and so Willow and the others presumed the Mayan deity was still alive.

Yes, Willow had told Buffy all of that, and more, and it had broken the Slayer's heart. But there were a great many things Willow had not told her. She had not, for instance, said anything about the murder of Buffy's mother. Had talked around it, in fact, changing the subject at least twice to avoid it.

Only through her dream had Buffy learned the truth.

The dream, she thought now. *The line of the Slayer's power stretching into the future and back into the past.*

A thousand questions filled her head, but she pushed them all away. They could wait until later. Wait until she had spoken to Willow.

The night before she had been rescued by an extraction team led by the girl who had once been her best friend—the young witch nineteen-year-old Buffy *still* thought of as her best friend. Xander and Oz had been with the group as well. All of them had been different, changed by time. Hardened. Yet after an awkward first few moments, Willow had softened. Buffy thought that she had seen within this powerful witch the girl she knew so well. It felt as though they had reconnected.

But now Buffy was not certain. Her mother was dead and she felt sure that Willow had known it.

All of these thoughts weighed heavily upon her as she rose from bed. The small room she had been given had a full bathroom and though she had showered before falling asleep the night before, she did so again now. The water was hot and the steam swirled in the room. She breathed the warm air in, and it felt as though she were scouring not only her body but her lungs as well.

In the closet Buffy found some clothes that had been left for her the previous night. Nothing was her size, but that was not a surprise. It was not as though they had had much time to prepare for her arrival. She managed to find jeans, a tee shirt and a hooded navy blue sweatshirt that fit her. In the stale-smelling room, she bounced on her toes and spent a few minutes doing stretching exercises.

Somehow, she had to find a way to explain to Willow what had happened that night five years ago, to make her understand how two versions of the same mind, two moments of the same soul, could exist in one body. With Willow's help, Buffy had to find a way to separate her twenty-four-year-old body from the nineteen-year-old soul inside her, find a way to return her younger self to its rightful place.

It would happen eventually, Buffy knew that. It was already history. But she did not know how to make it happen, or even how long her younger persona was meant to stay in this hideous future.

With a leap, she balanced on the metal frame of the bed, crouched with her arms out. Then she executed a perfect backward somersault, and swept through a series of shadow-boxing jabs and kicks that shook her loose, got her blood flowing.

Somehow she would figure out how to get her split soul back to where it belonged. But for the moment, there were things that had to be attended to right here.

Five years earlier she had taken on too much, tried to force herself to live two lives at one hundred percent each. Ironic, given her current predicament. But she was only one person. Buffy Summers was the Slayer, and her life had to be broken up accordingly. That meant that she had to have help sometimes. That night, years ago, she had tried to do it all herself. Her insistence upon that had probably led to Giles's initial capture, and her efforts to free him had led to everything else.

If she had been more practical, more honest with herself, from the beginning, this future would never have come to pass.

Now that it had, however, she was not going to rest until she set things right. She had to find the lord of vampires, Rupert Giles.

And dust him.

Buffy took a last glance around the small room they had given to her, and smiled softly. Whatever her resentments, whatever her fears, this tiny room was a vast improvement over the much larger cell she had spent the past five years in. The window alone, with the sun shining through, made all the difference. More than that, however, was the simple fact that she could open the door and walk out.

Curious and almost trembling with momentum, with the desire to take action, Buffy went out into the corridor. Whatever this installation was where the Council had set up its task force—if that was what they were—it was cold and featureless, almost military. The floors were covered in gray industrial carpet, the walls painted a sort of jaundiced white that made Buffy think of old bones.

On impulse, she started off to the left. She passed an open door and saw a thirtyish guy doing pull-ups on a bar inside the room. When he spotted her walking past, he lost his focus and let go of the bar. He watched her, but Buffy glanced away. Several others passed her as she wandered, all of them in drab gray paramilitary uniforms or neatly pressed business suits.

At a junction in the corridor, she caught the scent of food off to her right. The cafeteria, she assumed, and so headed in that direction. Her stomach rumbled loudly as the thought of food drew her on.

As she approached the open double doors of the cafeteria, however, a small door opened on her left and a familiar figure emerged. Oz wore droopy denim pants and a green cotton V-neck shirt that hung loose on him. It occurred to Buffy that they both looked like they were wearing someone else's clothes.

In the moment before he saw her, Buffy studied Oz's face. His hair was longer than it had once been, swept back from his forehead in shaggy waves, and there was a reddish stubble on his chin. Though as always his expression revealed nothing of his inner emotions, there was a melancholy in his eyes that gave her pause.

Oz sniffed the air, then glanced up at her sharply.

"Buffy," he said, as if it were hello.

"Oz," she replied.

They shifted uncomfortably for a moment there in the hall, half a dozen feet from each other. Buffy broke the silence.

"I was just wandering around. Trying to orient myself."

Oz nodded once. "You want the ten-cent tour?"

"I'd like that."

For twenty minutes they walked the halls of the installation together. Though his narration on the tour consisted mostly of things like "library" and "training area," Buffy enjoyed his company. She sensed no guile in Oz at all. But there was more to it than that. As they walked down a long flight of stairs she thought would eventually lead them back to the corridor where they had met up, she paused and turned to him.

Oz arched an eyebrow.

"You trust me," she said, and it wasn't a question.

"Yeah?"

"Why?"

Though his features were fully human there was something of the wolf in the way he cocked his head just then. "Some reason I shouldn't?"

Buffy sighed. "No. It's just, last night I felt this kind of static from Xander and even from Willow. It's been a long time, I know. But this seems like more than that. Not that I'm expecting everything to be the way it was—"

"Nothing is," Oz interrupted.

"I know. I understand that," Buffy insisted. "Just feeling a little like the wicked stepsister here. I don't know if it's resentment or what, but it's like they don't want me here."

"Willow led the extraction team," Oz reminded her.

Buffy nodded, smiled awkwardly. "Yeah. Yeah, she did. Maybe I'm just wigged because it's been so long since I've seen you all. Since I've seen anyone who still had a pulse."

"Maybe," Oz replied. "Maybe not. Life went on, Buffy. Willow always believed you'd come back, but in the meantime, we've got this war. Whole big machine pretty much running on its own. My guess? It's gonna take some time to figure out where you fit into it."

Buffy understood immediately what he meant, for she had been feeling almost exactly the same things. She had to figure out what her role was supposed to be now, and so did Willow and the others on the Council. Awkwardness was inevitable. She just had to have the patience to ride it out.

Oz turned and started down the stairs again. Buffy followed him quickly and grabbed his shoulder, still intent upon speaking to him. When Oz snapped around to glare at her, there was a snarl on his face, his lips pulled back to expose his teeth. Buffy flinched and drew her hand back, and Oz's expression softened immediately.

"Sorry," she said.

"It's all right. I don't like to be touched. You didn't know."

And there it was, exactly the sort of thing that she had been thinking about seconds before. The way things were right now, she didn't fit in. She only hoped that would change.

"I guess there's a lot I don't know," Buffy replied. "How . . . how did you get control of your wolf side?"

Oz's nostrils flared. He scratched the back of his neck idly, as if she had not asked the question at all. At length he glanced at her again.

"Had a situation where it was either let the wolf out or die. So I let it out. Been working on it since."

"And it wasn't the full moon," Buffy pressed.

"No moon at all. Breakfast time, actually. Never did get to finish that cinnamon roll." The corners of Oz's mouth twitched briefly, as close to a smile as anyone was likely to get from him. "You want to know why I trust you?"

Slowly, Buffy nodded.

"We've all changed. Maybe on the face of it, so have you. But there's something in you that's just the same, like a flashback to when things weren't quite so nasty. I've got to get going. We all have responsibilities here."

Oz started down the steps away from her again. Buffy could only watch him go, turning his words over in her head.

"Welcome back to your war," he said as he reached the bottom of the steps and began to walk off.

"Wait, Oz," she called after him.

A pair of older men in suits hurried by as Buffy went down the stairs after him. They barely spared her a glance.

"Why is it my war? Why not yours, too?"

"I only stay for Willow. Not sure she notices, though."

Then Buffy understood the sadness in his eyes. Whatever was between him and Willow now, it was not what it once had been.

"Well, what about Willow?" she asked. "Why does she stay?"

Expressionless, Oz studied her for a moment. Then he inclined his head, just slightly. "She stays for you."

The cafeteria reminded her an awful lot of high school. She passed over some of the less identifiable foods and opted for a chicken Parmesan sandwich. It was not quite cold and the cheese had all but congealed on the top, but as hungry as she was, Buffy barely noticed. There were French fries as well, and those, at least, were hot.

When she turned to glance about for a place to sit, Buffy became extremely self-conscious. She caught several people staring at her, but most of them looked away the instant she noticed them. A pair of young, lean guys watched her for a few moments too long, then turned to each other and began to whisper.

Suddenly she was back at Sunnydale High again. The new girl, with a reputation that had preceded her. *Rumor has it she was booted out of her old high school in L.A. for burning down the gymnasium. What a freak.*

Buffy shook those feelings off. High school had been a long time ago, and after the years she had been without any human contact at all, even curious stares and rude whispers were better than isolation. Though she was tempted to take a seat with one of the scattered groups in the caf, she had too many questions in her head, too much on her mind to simply socialize.

In the middle of the room, she found a small round table that was empty, and sat down alone. A short time later, while she was peeling an orange she hoped would get the greasy taste of the chicken out of her mouth, Xander came into the cafeteria. Relief washed through her. She was pleased to see someone she knew, someone who was a friend, despite the grim demeanor that now seemed almost constant for him.

Though she had seen him clearly enough last night, she was not at all used to his appearance. At twenty-four, Xander barely resembled the boy she had first met back in sophomore year of high school. All the lightness, the sense of jest, had gone from his eyes. He had often worn his hair too long and unruly. Now it was shorn only a few inches off the scalp, which only served to exacerbate the severe cast to his features that was punctuated by the crescent-shaped scar on his face.

He spotted her and strode over, his gait hurried and stiff.

Xander did not sit. It pained her, that little detail. The visible changes in him seemed confirmed by this. Yet with Xander she did not take it personally. Whatever experiences had caused his personality to be altered so dramatically, this behavior was not aimed at her. This was simply who Xander was now. Once upon a time, he would have sauntered into the room and dropped himself like a particularly agreeable rag doll into the chair.

No longer.

"Willow asked me to tell you there's a debriefing in five minutes if you want to attend."

So many things she wanted to say to him, to ask him, but Xander seemed like a wall to her, and all Buffy could do was nod. "Where?"

"I'll take you," Xander replied.

When Buffy did not rise to follow him, at last he reluctantly sat down across from her. The last of the peel came off the orange and Buffy tore the fruit in two. She handed half across to him. For a moment Xander only stared at the sticky, dripping orange as if it were some foreign object. Then he took it from her.

"Thanks," he said, as he popped a piece into his mouth.

"It speaks," Buffy said, almost afraid to tease him but more afraid of not trying to break the ice between them.

To her great relief, he smiled. For just a moment, she saw the old Xander in there.

"I missed you, Xand," Buffy told him, though after all the time she had spent alone the words were hard for her. "I missed all of you."

He swallowed hard and put the rest of his orange down on the table, uneaten. Xander rose and faced her.

"We should go."

"God, what happened to you?" Buffy asked him, frustrated.

He hesitated, then shook his head. "Another time, Buffy."

When Xander led her into the conference room, Buffy was at first startled by how many people were crammed inside. Though the room had clearly been intended for smaller numbers, there were at least twenty people standing around a long wooden table. Nine others were seated around the table, at the far end of which there was one vacant seat. Buffy glanced back at Xander curiously, but he only nodded for her to proceed. He would not be sitting, apparently.

Which made her wonder exactly how one earned the privilege of a chair. Willow was seated at the table, dressed in a brown suit that was quite flattering on her. It made her look even older than she was and reminded Buffy that this was not the teenager who had been her best friend. A buzz of conversation filled the room as Buffy looked around at the others at the table. At the end, opposite the empty chair that had been left for her, sat a sixtyish woman with her hair in a tight bun and her hands folded primly on the table in front of her. Her eyes had a ferocity in them that was anything but prim. To her left was a large man in paramilitary garb whose nose had clearly been broken several times. It was flattened and skewed to one side. He had the look of an old-time boxer, but beyond that his most prominent feature was that his hands were enormous. Buffy did not think she had ever seen a human with such large hands.

They made him look dangerous, even monstrous.

The biggest surprise for her was on the other side of the older woman, however. There sat an Asian girl with pink hair pulled back with barrettes. She could not have been more than fifteen. The girl met her gaze and some indefinable connection was established between the two of them, a sort of primal recognition. Even if she had not felt that, she would have known why the girl was present. Why else would they have a girl that age at a gathering like this?

The Slayer, Buffy thought. *The one replacing August.*

It gave her a shock to see the girl, to remember the other recent Slayer, whom she had accidentally killed.

And beside the new girl, the only other familiar face in the room. He had grown a neatly groomed beard and there was some gray at his temples now, but Buffy would have recognized him anywhere.

"Wesley?" she said, surprised to find herself pleased by his presence.

"Hello, Buffy," he replied, not without warmth. "Why don't you have a seat so we might begin?"

The older woman at the head of the table cleared her throat. "Or, rather, conclude, as the case may be," she said as she gazed at Buffy. "Miss Summers, my name is Ellen Haversham, and I am the director of the Council's operations here in California. To my left," she said, motioning toward the man with the pugilistic features, "is Christopher Lonergan, my chief of staff and tactician. To my right, Anna Kuei, the current Slayer."

Buffy furrowed her brow deeply.

"Oh, my apologies," Ms. Haversham said, almost amused with her slip. "I meant other than yourself, of course."

Buffy wanted to punch her.

"Of course you already know the present Watcher, Mr. Wyndam-Pryce, and our sorcerer, Miss Rosenberg."

Willow looked up and smiled and Buffy felt a moment of relief. Maybe things weren't as strained as she had thought after last night.

"We have a great many questions for you, of course—"

"You do, huh?" Buffy asked, a bit incredulous.

"Buffy—" Willow warned.

"'Cause, gotta say, I have a big batch of questions for you guys, too." Buffy shouldered through those gathered around the table until she reached the long windows on the other side of the room. She opened them all, and fresh air began to circulate.

"A little stuffy in here, I thought," she explained, and glanced pointedly at Ms. Haversham.

Then she walked over to the empty chair, ignored it, and perched on the edge of the table. Though there was a great deal she needed to talk about, she wasn't about to do it in front of all these people.

"I've been in a cell for five years," Buffy said, her eyes on Ms. Haversham and no one else. "Not that I don't appreciate the assist last night, but I think maybe before you get to debrief me, I should at least be able to get answers to a few simple questions."

Ms. Haversham's face took on a decidedly sour expression. Then, to Buffy's surprise, the older woman fidgeted slightly, and then glanced down the table to Willow, as though seeking permission. It took Buffy a second to realize that everyone in the room was watching Willow, and then she knew that the real power in the place did not sit at the head of the table.

"What about it, Will?" Buffy prodded.

Willow nodded, but she was not smiling. "Whatever makes you the most comfortable."

"Fine," Buffy said. "Why didn't you tell me my mother was dead?"

Out of the corner of her eye, Buffy saw Xander reach up to touch the scar on his face. She turned toward him but he only stared back at her, so Buffy returned her attention to Willow.

"How did you know?" the witch asked, her expression softening.

"I had a dream."

Willow nodded.

"Why didn't you say anything?" Buffy asked, and in

her own voice she could hear a plaintive tone that she did not like. It was an appeal not to the room but to the woman who had once been her best friend.

For just a moment, Willow glanced away. Then she met Buffy's gaze and sat a bit straighter in her chair. "I didn't tell you," she said, voice steady, "because we were there and we didn't save her."

Despite the strength in her voice, there was pain and sadness in Willow's eyes, in the set of her mouth. In that moment Buffy felt as though they were communicating not across the room but across the years they had been apart. Emotion charged the air between them; sorrow at what they had all been through. Yet there was something else there as well. Whether it was simply her own sense of guilt, her own mind at work, Buffy could not say, but she felt certain that in Willow's eyes she saw disappointment and a troubling question. *Why weren't you here?*

"It was a long time ago, only four or five weeks after you were captured," Willow went on, "but it cost us a lot."

Willow's gaze ticked toward Xander and then back to Buffy.

"What's a lot?" Buffy asked, intuiting that the conversation was painful for her friends, but not able in that moment to let concern for their pain supplant her own. Somehow she had to fill the hollow place within her created by this confirmation of her mother's death, and yet she knew that was something she could never do.

"Your mother," Willow replied. "The scar on Xander's face. And Anya. If it hadn't been for Oz, we'd *all* have died that day."

Had a situation where it was either let the wolf out or die, Buffy thought, remembering Oz's words.

"Anya . . ." Buffy said, almost to herself.

She looked over at Xander. He met her gaze without wavering, no expression at all on his face. Whatever he had seen that day his girlfriend died, Buffy thought it had killed something in him, like deadening the nerves in his soul.

"Who?" Buffy asked Willow, her voice cracking. "Who killed them?"

"It was Spike," Xander answered from amid the crowded room. "Giles gave the order, but it was Spike who did it."

Twice in the previous two days, Buffy had been close enough to Spike to kill him and had not been able to do so. A shudder went through her now and she clenched her right hand into a fist at her side. For a moment, all she could do was breathe. Then she stared at Willow again.

It was as though everyone else in the room had disappeared, and it was just the two of them, trying to make sense of what the world had become, what they had become.

"Angel?" Buffy asked, dread filling her. "If he was alive he would have come after me, right? When did he die?"

"We don't know that he did," Willow told her, her tone regretful but unwavering. "I called him the day you were captured. He came the same night, went out looking for you, and never came back. As far as we know, Giles never said anything about it to anyone, at least not in earshot of Faith, or any of our spies in Sunnydale."

Buffy felt sick. *Faith.* Just another on a long list of people she cared about who had died because she wasn't there to save them. She had a thousand other questions but did not think she had the energy for them. Grieving, she at last slipped into the leather chair and leaned forward to gaze at Willow.

"What is all this?" she asked. "The Council was never this militant."

"We never had to be," the big man, Lonergan, intoned.

His voice destroyed the illusion that this was a conversation between old friends. Buffy wished it really were just the two of them, but she understood that was not how things were done with the Council. It never had been, really, and now Willow was one of them, if not actually a member of the Council, at least working with them.

Reluctantly, she turned her attention to Lonergan.

"We never had to deal with an infestation like this before," the man continued. "Leeches generally keep to themselves, but this group's different, yeah? More powerful, more organized, and Giles at the top of it all."

"We've got the full cooperation of the U.S. government," Willow added. "The military influence is theirs. After Giles and the Kakchiquels started taking over Sunnydale, we found out that, hey, surprise, the government had been running a kind of monster research facility right there in Sunnydale. All roads lead to the Hellmouth."

"You're kidding," Buffy said.

Willow's dubious expression told her all she needed to know.

"They had to pull the plug on their project when the Kakchiquels killed the entire staff on site. The people running that show couldn't get more funding. They were supposed to be primarily a research group, not a combat unit, which was what was needed. That's where the Council came in. I had contacted Quentin Travers when Angel didn't come back, but by then Wesley was here. The rest is sort of history. The federal government doesn't want the rest of America to know what's going on, so they've helped fund the Council operations. They've provided special forces training, weapons, and a jurisdictional freedom not even the DEA has, as long as we help them pretend there isn't a thirty-mile-square block of southern California enslaved to vampires.

"Of course, they could just go in some morning with a battalion of marines, but there's the matter of those pesky civilian casualties. They're hoping we can clean this up without it becoming any messier than it already is. They've given us two more months."

Buffy blinked. She had not been expecting that last bit of information.

"Then what?" she asked.

Willow shrugged and glanced away sheepishly, a bit of her old self coming out. "I'm guessing napalm."

"What about the people?" Buffy demanded.

"Yeah," Willow agreed. "Time is running short now. We're going to have to go in sooner rather than later. If you learned anything while you were in enemy territory that could help us, well, that's why we hoped you'd be willing to answer some questions."

"Anything," Buffy told her.

The questions began. From Willow. From Ms. Haversham. From Wesley. From Lonergan. Buffy told them everything she could remember about her captivity and escape, and ignored the stares she received when she revealed the circumstances of August's death. She told them about her journey to Sunnydale, her conversation with Parker, the deaths of Harmony and Drusilla, and everything leading up to the moment when they arrived to help her at the border.

Somewhere in the midst of all of that, Wesley asked her where she had gotten the crossbow.

The crossbow. Buffy hesitated, glancing uncomfortably around the room.

"On the way into Sunnydale I stopped at the old drive-in there, thinking there might be something I could use for a weapon. I broke up a chair for some stakes. In the projection room, upstairs in the concrete building there, someone had left me a crossbow."

"You mean someone had left a crossbow behind," Wesley corrected, running his fingers through his beard.

"No," Buffy said firmly. "Someone had left it for me. There was a note. 'For Buffy.' "

Everyone in the room stared at her.

Willow broke the silence. "Was it signed?"

Buffy shook her head and then the debate began as to who might have been the one to leave the weapon there, who could have known Buffy would even stop there. It soon became clear that no one could have known such a thing.

"Whoever it was must have been there with you, or right before you. Close enough to've seen you in the parking lot," Lonergan reasoned.

"It was the middle of the day and I didn't see much cover," Buffy noted.

"You never know," Willow told her. "You've seen their sunsuits for yourself. Not high fashion, but they can move around during the day if they're motivated enough."

"But why would anyone do that?" Buffy asked. "Someone was watching me, no question about that. But if it was a vampire, why would they try to help me?"

Willow stared at the table, brows knitted in contemplation. No one else would meet Buffy's gaze. All of them seemed stumped. A low rumble of muttered conversation filled the room. Then Buffy glanced at Wesley, and he was the only one not looking away.

"What if it's Angel?" he asked.

Several people began to talk at once, some to argue the question as ridiculous, others to support the possibility. Buffy's mind was awhirl as she considered it. *Could Angel be alive?*

Before she could respond, however, Lonergan swore

loudly and shot to his feet, one hand clamped to his forehead. He bumped into Ms. Haversham's chair and nearly knocked her over.

His nose had begun to bleed.

"What?" Willow demanded. "Christopher, what is it?"

Lonergan wiped the blood from his upper lip, his expression grave.

"We've got a vampire on the premises."

CHAPTER 3

Bloody hell!

The bedspread was on fire. It was a delicate pastel floral pattern with black scorch marks, flames licking up from those charred spots. *Of all the soddin' indignities I've had dumped on my head today,* Spike thought. *Hell, of all the drawbacks to being a vampire in general, running about draped in flowery linens is the worst.*

The burning didn't send him into giggling fits, either.

Spike whipped the spread off him and tossed it to the floor, then stamped furiously, almost petulantly on it to put the flames out. Gingerly, he felt his face and found that his eyelashes and eyebrows were little more than tightly curled ashes now. His skin was stiff and cracked and it felt as though if he moved too quickly it might split right open. He did not even want to touch his hair.

He seethed with thoughts of vengeance. Nobody

treated him like this, tossed him out some window to torch in the sun like so much garbage. The loss of Drusilla had left a void inside him, a cold, rotting place where despair and bitterness festered. But that void was not really empty anymore. Hate and rage had seeped into that place and now it was boiling over.

Giles had vision. He had a dream. Spike usually ignored the big-talking vampires; silly gits usually had lots of swagger but little sense. Any tosser could wax poetic about a world crushed beneath the heel of vampire rule, human cattle, an endless feast of babies and virgins. Just a whiff of that sort of bluster usually sent Spike packing, chuckling all the way.

But Giles, now. Rupert Giles had had a plan. Spike had plenty of plans of his own, mind, and the Big Bad was not about to sign on to play lapdog—or even foxhound—to a vampire fresh out of the dirt. Thing was, this was Giles, and Spike and Drusilla had both believed he could pull off this grand scheme.

And what a world that would have been.

Now, though . . . now Spike was pissed. And his day was just getting worse and worse. Flowery linens just one example of the way the world had suddenly turned against him. How he was supposed to look fierce hiding his precious mug from the sun under embroidered carnations and lilies . . . *well, you just can't, is all.*

When Giles had thrown him out the window he had been burned badly. But even with the spread covering him, the time he had spent outside before breaking into the Council installation had been worse, trying to be all sneaky in a decorative spread that also happened to be *on fire.*

Now, to top it all off, he had a sudden craving for a cigarette that he found cruelly ironic, but he had dropped his cigs somewhere along the way.

Giles, he thought. *Bloody bastard.*

In his left hand he held the key card he had taken from a guard on the grounds outside. He was tempted to toss it away but then reconsidered. It had gotten him into the building, and there was no way to tell if it would come in handy later. Spike slipped the plastic rectangle into his pocket as he surveyed his surroundings.

A wide corridor, rear of the facility. The building seemed sterile and utilitarian, almost like a hospital. Once upon a time that might have been exactly what it was. *Could do with a visit to the burn center right about now,* he thought, with a smile that cracked his scorched skin and made him curse through gritted teeth.

There were several doors with square glass windows in them along this corridor. He glanced into each room as he moved farther into the building and found mostly abandoned offices and several that seemed like they were still in use. He passed one room in which dozens of white boxes had been stacked floor to ceiling, but did not stop to see what was being stored. To his left, a stairwell led up. Spike figured he was less likely to run into sentries upstairs, and that was probably where he would find personnel quarters.

The Slayer's quarters.

With every step, he winced at the pain in his slowly

healing skin. By the time he reached the top, he was practically snarling. His desire for a cigarette had grown almost obsessive. He knew it was probably just his mind trying to think about anything except pain, but the pain was good in its way. It gave him something to focus on so he wouldn't think about the humiliation.

Spike could take the pain just as well as he could hand it out. There had been plenty of times when pain had been a recreational sport for him and Dru. Pain was a friend, old and dear. Every time he winced and ground his teeth in agony, he could think about other times when he had been the *giver.* Those were sweet memories.

So Spike could take the pain.

The humiliation, on the other hand . . . well, nobody made Spike look like a weakling and lived to boast of it.

There were windows along the second floor corridor and so he hugged the walls to stay out of the sunlight. What he needed now was to find someone to torture information out of. *Shouldn't be too difficult,* he thought. The place stank of humans.

As though he had summoned them by the strength of his will alone, he heard voices beyond a pair of doors ahead that led into another part of the facility. For just a moment, Spike grinned, but it hurt too much.

He threw open the doors.

On the other side was a broad, diamond-shaped atrium where four corridors came together. Several stories up was an enormous, many-paned skylight that spilled sunlight all the way down to the first floor. A balustrade ran all around the atrium, except straight in front of him, where stairs led up from the ground floor.

The atrium was full. Perhaps two dozen Council operatives waited there in the sunshine. Guns cocked. Crossbows were aimed. Several flamethrowers puffed to life. But the worst were the small clutch of people standing just at the top of the stairs, directly across from Spike.

The witch, Willow Rosenberg. A grim-faced Xander Harris, who had proven to be almost supernaturally lucky, practically unkillable. That Watcher, Wesley, who had once run with Angel. A petite little Asian girl he guessed was the latest Slayer. And, of course, the real Slayer. Buffy Summers.

"Hail, hail," Spike said dryly. "The gang's all here. Warms the cockles, it really does."

Then there was Christopher Lonergan, who had a bit of blood just under his nose.

Spike ran a hand over his burned, ragged hair. "Hello, Chris. Didn't know you were in the country."

"Guess you didn't," Lonergan replied. "Else you wouldn'a tried sneaking about in here."

Spike grinned. "Got an extra ciggie?"

The witch took a step toward him. The sunlight gleamed off her red hair and Spike shifted uncomfortably just looking at it. He stood in the shadow of the corridor now, but if they dragged him into the atrium . . . well, he'd had enough sun for one day.

"What are you doing here, Spike? A long way to come just to commit suicide," Willow said curtly.

"Is that what I've done?" Spike asked.

Xander nodded. "Oh, yeah."

"Maybe so," he allowed. Then he tilted his head and shrugged, as though none of it mattered to him in the least. "Gotta say, though, I think you've got bigger fish to slay. You're about twenty steps behind Giles by now, kids. The old sod's got his people in place all over the state. Only a matter of days now before he's got Los Angeles. Blink and you'll miss it."

"Why tell us?" Willow asked.

Spike narrowed his eyes, blistered skin cracking, and studied Buffy. Thus far she had not said a word, but she glared at him with such ferocity that he began to wonder if it had not been a mistake after all, his coming here.

He shrugged. "Bugger pissed me off. He's got big plans, he has, but they don't involve me. I'm off now to redder pastures, but before I left I thought I'd see to it that you did my dirty work for me. In all our best interests, of course."

No one spoke. No one moved. The operatives barely seemed to be breathing. The young Slayer looked a bit nervous, and Spike gave her a friendly smile. The hate-filled sneer he received in return chilled him. But not nearly as much as the expression on Buffy's face.

"Right then," he said with a shrug. "My mistake. You all might want to take a last trip to Disney before the Mouse sprouts fangs." He raised a hand in a small wave. "Ta."

As Spike began to turn, Xander broke ranks and sprinted across the atrium to the double doors. Willow shouted something after him, but nobody else moved. Spike only smiled as he lashed out at Xander.

But he was still healing. His flesh was tight, burned, and those injuries sapped his speed and strength. Xander gripped his throat, drove his head back against the post between the double doors. Spike struck him once, hard, but Xander only grunted and cracked the vampire's head against the post again. Groggy, Spike tried to pull the enraged man's hand away.

Xander struck him in the face, shattering his nose and splitting the burned skin on his cheek. Another blow fell, and another, and all the strength ran out of Spike. When his eyes fluttered open, trying to focus, he saw the stake in Xander's hand.

"This is for Anya, you son of a—"

The stake fell.

Buffy was there. She grabbed Xander's wrist, stopped the point from puncturing Spike's chest, his heart.

Xander spun toward her, practically spitting with rage. "What the hell are you doing?"

Buffy's eyes were dark with painful knowledge. Spike was fascinated by the girl now. He had not gotten a good look at her in the dark the night before, nor on the street during their previous skirmish. In fact, this was the first decent look he'd had at her in years. Her face had thinned slightly, and it made her look meaner. Or maybe that was just her eyes.

"You want to win this?" Buffy told Xander. "We need the information he has."

"Thattagirl," Spike cooed, there on the floor. He sat

up, grimacing with pain. "Knew I could count on you to see the sense of it. Not the first time we've done business, after all. Better the devil you know, yeah?"

In a move so swift Spike barely saw it, Buffy spun and shot out a hard side kick that cracked his cheekbone and slammed him back on the floor. Groaning, Spike tried to rise, tried to scuttle away from her, but the Slayer swept in and kicked him in the side, splintering several ribs.

Enraged and confused, the vampire reached out to her and Buffy snapped his wrist. Then she grabbed him under his chin and, with the prodigious strength of the Chosen One, lifted him off the ground. She carried him back into the atrium and dangled him there, in the sunlight.

Again, Spike began to burn. He screamed in agony this time, for he could feel his skin bubbling, could feel himself start to cook from within, the sun searing the evil in him. It occurred to him, mind reeling from the pain, that there were worse things than flowery linens. That perhaps he was not quite so intimate with pain as he had imagined.

"Bloody hell," he croaked. "Stop!"

Buffy tossed him into the shadow of the double doors where he crumbled into a blackened, whimpering heap.

The Slayer stood over him. "My mother," she said, voice thick with disgust and hate.

Spike grimaced. "Heard about that, did you? Just doing what I was told. Giles gave that order. He was real specific about it."

Ignoring him, she turned to Xander. "We'll find out what he knows. After that, I don't care what you do to him."

Willow stared out her office window at a trio of gulls that circled lazily in the sky. The ocean was thirty miles away and it always made her curious to see the sea birds inland. She wondered if something had drawn them here, or if they had simply become so distracted by their interplay that they had drifted far from their usual haunts. They had a freedom Willow envied.

There was a rap at the door. Willow turned her attention back to her office, which—with its potted plants and the art that hung on the wall—was just about the only room in the entire facility with any warmth. It was her retreat, a place for contemplation, and she rarely liked to have difficult conversations there. But for once she thought that she ought to extend the warmth of this room to another.

"Come in," she called.

The door clicked open and Wesley poked his head in. "We're a bit early, Willow. Sorry about that."

"It's fine," she replied.

He smiled and opened the door all the way to reveal Anna Kuei in the hall behind him. Then Wesley stood aside and ushered the nascent Slayer into the office. There were a pair of black leather chairs in front of Willow's desk, and the two visitors sat and faced her.

"Anna. I'm sorry if this morning's debriefing disturbed you," Willow said kindly.

The girl twirled the fingers of her left hand in the

short tufts of her shocking pink hair. She had the appearance of the rebel, but Willow knew her as a sweet girl, almost an innocent.

"It's all right, Miss Rosenberg," Anna said. Always soft-spoken, her voice today sounded more girlish and wispy than ever.

"Willow, Anna. You're the Slayer now. Call me Willow."

The girl smiled and sat up a bit straighter. "Willow. I just . . ."

When her words trailed off, Wesley jumped in for her. "Anna had a few questions about the, shall we say, dynamics of the Council's efforts here, now that Buffy has returned to the fold."

Willow's brow furrowed. "Shoot."

Anna shrugged, glanced away. "I mean, I know she's the Lost Slayer and everything, and it's like this big deal. But she isn't anything like Faith, is she?"

A tiny smile played upon Willow's lips. During the months of training Anna had spent in this facility with several other Slayers-in-Waiting—girls the Council had pinpointed as having the potential to become the Chosen One—Faith had taken a day to instruct them each time she returned to the facility.

"No," Willow agreed. "She's nothing like Faith."

Anna nodded emphatically. "No kidding. I mean, Faith was all about discipline and focus, and the Lost Slayer—"

"Buffy," Wesley quietly corrected her.

"Buffy," Anna continued. "She's, like, totally unhinged. Okay, nobody's crying over Spike getting his ass handed to him. As long as he ends up dusted, he deserves whatever he gets beforehand. But there's more to it than that. In the debriefing, I just . . . when she talked about August . . ."

The girl's eyes became moist and she wiped a hand across them. Willow's heart went out to her. Anna and August had been close friends during their training, before Faith's death had led to August's being Chosen.

"She killed August," Anna said, hurt and angry. "And now it's supposed to be August's fault, but August isn't here to defend herself."

Wesley reached out and touched Anna's hand to comfort her, but his eyes never left Willow. "She doesn't realize how close you and Buffy are," Wesley said.

"It's all right," Willow said, gaze still on Anna. "I understand what you're feeling. I really do. In high school, Buffy was my best friend. I guess she still is. But it's going to take time for all of us to adjust. There's no way to know what her years in that cell might have done to her. But, for what it's worth, the Buffy Summers I knew would never have killed a human, never mind a Slayer. I believe it was an accident. You know as well as I do, Anna, that August was having problems with the pressure of being Chosen even before she was captured."

"Okay, maybe so," Anna said, her Cupid's-bow lips pinched into a round little pout. "But I hope nobody expects me to be friends with her or something."

"No," Willow said carefully, "but Buffy is a part of the team now. Probably going to be an important part. You could learn a lot from her."

The girl opened her mouth and then clamped it shut tight, and Willow knew she probably had a dozen sarcastic retorts that were bursting to get out.

"The team was fine," Anna said at last. "I mean, if you've got Buffy, what do you need me for? And why does it seem like she's suddenly in charge? Like everyone's looking to her for the next move? You're the one in charge. I don't understand why—"

"Actually, Ms. Haversham is the director of this operation," Willow corrected, feeling a bit awkward.

"Oh, that's crap," Anna snapped. "You're in charge and you know it. Haversham hardly even pretends to be the boss anymore, except in meetings. Even Lonergan looks to you. But Buffy's got this air about her, like everyone should follow her lead."

Wesley scratched at his beard and shifted a bit in his seat. "Her presence does seem to have upset the balance of power somewhat. There's the potential for great confusion there, and in an operation of this magnitude, confusion could be deadly. The mission parameters clearly state that Anna and I are to lead the main unit when the assault on Sunnydale is finally launched. Why do I have the sense that Buffy's arrival is sure to throw a wrench in the works?

"I must confess, Willow, I'm concerned. My experiences with Buffy were limited, of course, and there was always the question of how much of each mission's planning was Buffy's doing and how much was Giles's strategy. Certainly Buffy never allowed *me* to truly lead. My point is that she is rash. The deployment of forces and the creation of layers of strategy for contingencies are hardly her forte. She leads by charisma and passion, by inspiration. Those are enviable traits, to be sure, but leadership also requires forethought, the ability to envision and consider the big picture. Logic, reason, intuition and, frankly, the capacity to outthink your enemy.

"You are far younger than I am, Willow, but I have never questioned your leadership skills. There is a reason why those who were put here to run this operation have tacitly acknowledged you as the de facto commander of this little outpost. You may not give the orders, but you make the decisions.

"It would not only be a travesty to have your leadership jeopardized by Buffy's arrival, formidable warrior though she is, but in my humble opinion it could also have a catastrophic impact on our chances of success."

Wesley paused for a moment, then nodded his head once, brusquely, as if physically punctuating his thoughts on the matter. Then he took a deep breath and let it out slowly as he sat back in his chair.

Willow placed her elbows on her desk and leaned forward, fingers steepled under her chin. She studied the two of them closely. Anna's emotional response to Buffy's revelations—even her mere presence—was understandable and genuine. Wesley, on the other hand . . .

"Are you concerned about Buffy stealing *my* thunder, or your own, as the current Watcher?" Willow asked him.

Wesley sputtered a bit, muttered something about the question being preposterous, but he would not meet her gaze. He had always been easy for her to read.

"You were *her* Watcher briefly, Wes, or don't you remember?" Willow prodded, her gaze roving from him to Anna and back again. "I don't know how the years she's been gone have affected Buffy. Goddess knows I hope my friend is still there. I'm going to try to find out."

Willow hesitated for a moment, unsure whether or not to confide in them. Of late, there seemed no one she felt comfortable confiding in. When she had first seen Buffy again she had been so thrilled that she had let all the intervening years drop away as if they had never been, but it had not taken long for her to put walls up around her heart again. She wanted her best friend back so very much, but she would not allow that desire to override her common sense. She had responsibilities that were greater than her own needs.

At last, she decided that revealing her own fears to these two would be harmless enough. Willow glanced at Wesley, but then regarded Anna more closely.

"I knew Giles very well before," she said. "Wesley did, too, but he likes to pretend Giles wasn't as cunning as we both know he is. I have a confession to make. I've believed for a very long while that it was only a matter of time before all this blew up on us, and the U.S. government would have to essentially declare war on southern California. If Spike's telling the truth about L.A.—hello! A little more right than I ever wanted to be."

The young Slayer's eyes sparkled with fear. She shook her head in denial. Wesley cleared his throat, but did not argue.

"The thing is, if Buffy's really back, I mean, y'know, if she hasn't slipped a gear after all that time to herself, she may be our best chance at stopping this before we reach the point of no return. I don't know about Buffy now, but Buffy *then*, my friend? If anyone can stop Giles, she could."

They stared at her.

Willow smiled. "If that means the balance of power is going to shift? Not exactly going to argue."

As soon as Xander hauled open the steel door, Buffy caught the scent of burned flesh from within the room. Her stomach convulsed and her nostrils flared with disgust. From that point on, she breathed through her mouth.

At dusk, Willow and Xander had come to fetch her from her quarters and then escorted her down to dinner. Things were awkward. Though she wished for the closeness and humor they had once shared, it was almost all business. After they had eaten, Xander had led the way down into the basement and to a wing to the rear of the building that had been transformed into holding cells.

There was one door that had several dents in it and Buffy could hear something huge grunting and shambling within. She glanced at Willow, but her friend had not even seemed to hear it. Buffy decided not to bother asking.

Now, though, they had arrived at the cell where Spike had been imprisoned since early that day.

When Xander pulled the door open the rest of the way and flicked on the lights, Spike was crouched in a defensive posture in a far corner of the room. The extensive burns that had covered his body earlier were not gone, but they had improved significantly. His hair had even begun to grow back somewhat. There were places on his skin where the flesh was raw and wet, pink and vulnerable. Healing.

Spike's face changed instantly, his brow thickening, fangs lengthening. He snarled, low and dangerous, as Xander approached.

"You had me at a bit of a disadvantage before, boy," Spike said, voice a rasp. "I'm feelin' better now. You shouldn't have left me alone all this time."

Xander grinned, and the expression was so haunting that Buffy shivered. Then he pulled a simple plastic water pistol from the small of his back as though it were a real gun. He leveled it at Spike and fired several hissing squirts of holy water into the vampire's face.

Spike's flesh bubbled and steamed as though the water were acid, eating into his skin. With an agonizing scream, the vampire covered his eyes. Xander clasped his hands together and brought them around in a single, massive blow to the side of Spike's head. Spike went down, clutching his ribs where Buffy had kicked him earlier. Xander crouched in front of him and aimed the water pistol at his face again.

"I never liked it when you called me 'boy,' even when I was one," he said pleasantly. "You want to know why we let you heal? It's 'cause you were so far gone that we didn't think torture would be effective. You're living in the past, Spike. Not so much your glory days anymore, as your final hour."

Spike managed to lift his chin but his defiant expression did not reach his eyes, which were filled with fear. The room suddenly seemed too small, too close. The atmosphere had turned ominous, even cruel. This wild thing they had trapped was a vicious, savage beast, but there was nothing honorable about these proceedings now.

They were in a killing box.

"You used to be funny, you know that?" Spike sneered at Xander. "Not very, and stupid humor, yeah, but at least you had a soddin' *sense* of humor. That water gun gag? That wasn't funny."

"I haven't felt funny in a long time." Xander squirted holy water into Spike's hair and the vampire swore and started slapping at his head to stop the burning. Xander chuckled softly. "Now that, though? That's funny."

The twin souls that existed within Buffy were in conflict as she watched. The older Buffy, who had truly experienced the years of imprisonment and torment, the electrical prods and beatings, the knowledge of her own defeat, had not a moment's hesitation about Xander's treatment of Spike. But Buffy-at-nineteen felt differently. To her, only weeks had passed since a simpler time. It seemed almost perverse now to look back upon that chaos and realize that it was, indeed, simpler. Better. Brighter.

"If this is bothering you, you can step out," Willow suggested quietly.

Buffy flinched and turned to stare at her. It occurred to her that as Willow developed her magick more, she might well have found herself able to read thoughts, or at least sense emotions.

"I'm fine," Buffy replied, somewhat defensive.

"You seem pretty conflicted." Willow gazed at her with obvious concern.

"It's . . . it's not this. We'll talk later," Buffy promised.

"All right."

"You done?" Xander snapped. "Can we get on with it?"

Buffy narrowed her gaze. "Why don't we? In fact, why don't we just get right to it."

"Do your worst," Spike grunted. "I woulda just told you everything you'd like to know and got the hell out of town. But now? You get nothing."

Willow shook her head and *tsk*ed like the teacher she briefly was, once upon a time. "You don't really think we could let you go?"

"Did once," Spike replied with a sniff of hauteur. He looked at Buffy. "Me and the Slayer had a deal back then, didn't we, Buffy? Weren't too good for old Spike in those days."

"I had to choose between killing you and averting the

Apocalypse, Spike," Buffy said. "It was a harder decision than you'll ever know, but I figured I'd always get another shot at you."

"And here we are," Willow said, but without humor.

Buffy was relieved to see that, unlike Xander, she did not seem to get any pleasure out of this situation.

Slowly, defiantly, Spike struggled to stand. "To hell with the lot of you," the vampire said. "Do it."

Xander raised the water pistol again, but Buffy had had enough. She reached into the deep pocket of her oversize sweatshirt and pulled out a stake Willow had given her, then shoved past Xander and grabbed Spike by the throat for the second time that day.

He did not even bother to defend himself. "What are you gonna do, Slayer?"

Buffy slammed him against the wall, held him there, and drove the long stake right through the center of his chest, splitting ribs. Spike roared with the pain of it, but his eyes were wide with surprise as well, for Buffy had purposely avoided his heart.

The stake jutted out four inches. With an open palm, Buffy slammed it home, drove it deeper into his body until it was buried all the way. Spike growled and tried to move, and only then did he realize that the stake really had gone *all* the way through.

Buffy had pinned him to the wall.

She put her face up, only an inch from his. "Remember me mentioning how you killed my mother?"

Spike sagged a bit, hung there on the stake.

"Xander isn't pretending, Spike. Neither is Willow.

Things have changed. You better wake up to that right now," Buffy told him. Then she glanced over at the others. "Hurt him. Do whatever you have to do to get the information we need and do *not* let him die until we have it."

Buffy turned away from him, crossed the room and leaned there, opposite Spike, her arms crossed.

Xander and Willow started toward him, and Spike's bravado collapsed. "All right," he said. "All right!"

For hours they asked questions about Giles's operations in Sunnydale and beyond, and Spike answered. The Council had spies there, of course, mostly humans posing as vampire worshipers. They had been able to provide a great deal of information about the various nests and lairs that Giles's minions had established in Sunnydale, and Spike confirmed all of that information. A great deal of what he told them, the Council already knew. But he also revealed that Giles had already turned a sizable percentage of the LAPD, a number of Hollywood executives, and the mayor of Los Angeles. With that kind of infiltration already in place, L.A. might well be under tacit vampire rule within months, or even weeks. And that was only the beginning.

A shiver went through Buffy. Giles had the wisdom and the patience to fulfill his ambitions. Unless someone stopped him, he would slowly, inexorably, take over the state of California and then spread his influence from there.

Buffy knew that the federal government had secretly

told the Council they would resort to full-scale military assault if necessary. The civilian casualties would be enormous and there was no guarantee that Giles himself would be destroyed. Even worse than that, however, was Buffy's fear that the government would not act quickly enough, that they would be so afraid of public backlash at massive destruction on American soil that they might hesitate to act.

If Spike's information was right, if he were telling the truth, the Council had to act quickly. Any other resolution to the situation would be disastrous.

It was after ten o'clock at night when they were through with Spike. He was still pinned to the wall. Buffy stretched, stiff from standing in one place for so long. When she glanced over at her old friends, she found them both watching her expectantly, particularly Xander.

Buffy nodded grimly.

Xander did not smile. Instead he reached for a stake he kept in a sheath clipped to his belt at the small of his back. He brought it out and Spike grimaced when he saw it, as though even now he did not really believe it was over.

Buffy expected to feel something, some emotional conflict or simply melancholy. But for all his charisma, all the times it had seemed he might be an ally, Spike was a vampire. He had slaughtered Buffy's mother, and Anya, and hundreds, probably thousands of others.

There was only one way the night could end.

"This is for Anya," Xander said.

He staked Spike through the heart. The vampire's eyes went wide and he snarled at Xander.

"Oh, you rotten bast—" he said.

Then he exploded in a puff of cinder and ash.

They agreed to return to their rooms to wash up, and then reconvene in the conference room in half an hour, just the three of them.

But when Buffy got back to her quarters, Giles was waiting.

CHAPTER 4

A ripple of disquiet went through Buffy as she pushed open the door to her room. It was dark within, and the feeling that some peril lurked there was instant and certain. Buffy stepped inside and reached for the light switch, but she hesitated. Something moved in the dark, then, a figure unfolding from the shadows, silhouetted only by the starlight from outside the window.

The window where there was no longer any screen.

"Shut the door," whispered the figure in a voice so familiar that Buffy forgot to breathe.

Her hand fell away from the light switch and her eyes began to adjust to the dark. "Why would I want to do that?"

"So we can talk. I think it's time, don't you? Time we talk?"

Despite the glare of the lights from the hall, she could see enough now to know that it really was him. Rupert

Giles made no attempt to remain in the shadows. He slipped away from the wall and leaned, instead, on the sill of the open window. There was still a smattering of gray in his brown hair. He wore tan pants and a rust-colored V-neck sweater pushed up at the sleeves. In short, he looked for all the world like the man she had abandoned to Camazotz years before, save for one detail.

He no longer wore glasses.

Guilt cut Buffy deeply, for she had blamed herself from the moment Willow had told her Giles was a vampire. Though she had been following every lesson he had ever taught her by doing so, she had left Giles behind five years ago. This was the result.

Not just the monster he had become, but the nightmare he had made of what had once been her world.

"Oh, come now, Buffy," Giles said, his tone as impatient as she remembered. "Far be it for me to tell you not to feel badly, but at least try to focus, please? Now, why don't you close the door so we can have a civil conversation without being interrupted."

Buffy's throat was dry. She swallowed, stood up a bit straighter. *It isn't Giles anymore,* she reminded herself. *This is not him, not any more than Angelus was Angel. It's just a parasite, a thing living inside his remains, making it walk and talk, like a marionette.*

She had to remember that. In some ways, she knew, the vampire even *thought* it was Giles. It had his memories, his personality traits, but it was not him.

"All right," she said, blinking as though waking from a dream. "Let's talk."

Buffy stepped aside and closed the door, casting the room into deeper darkness for a moment. The eyes of the vampire flickered orange in that darkness, cruel pinpoints like poisoned stars in the night sky.

Then she turned on the light.

Giles smiled sheepishly. "Well, that's better, isn't it? Does take away some of the mystery though, doesn't it?"

Buffy snaked a hand into the deep front pocket of her oversize sweatshirt and withdrew the stake. Her fingers flexed around it, testing its weight.

"Tell me why I shouldn't just kill you right now? All our problems would be over."

Giles had been studying her, a smirk on his features. Now his gaze seemed to linger on her for a moment too long before he blinked and a quizzical expression came over his face.

"Hmm?" he asked.

A chill deep as the marrow swept through her then. *It's not him,* she insisted to herself. But that hesitation, that moment lost in thought, was such a part of who Giles was that it unnerved her even more. She considered the possibility that it might have been a bit of show for her benefit, but it had seemed so real, so unconscious. Ever since the world of vampires had been revealed to her she had believed that the creatures were just spiritual squatters, taking up residence in empty husks. She had needed to believe that in order to fulfill her duties, to dust vampires without hesitation.

But this thing . . . that single moment made her realize that in all the ways that mattered, all the ways that would hurt her, it *was* Giles. Not the man she had known, not her Watcher, but somehow Giles nevertheless.

Buffy felt as though she were being torn apart.

As though he knew precisely what she was feeling, Giles's expression softened. Again, it was a look she was so familiar with, as though he wanted to reach out to her but was troubled by the emotions at hand, not at all adept at offering comfort.

The look was a lie. A mockery of all that Giles had once meant to her. It shook her free of her pain. Her fingers gripped the stake and she launched herself across the room at him.

His evasion was so swift that he seemed to slip between moments. Buffy struck out with her left fist, then her right, she whirled into a kick that had so much force it ought to have decapitated him.

Not a single blow struck him.

Giles did not smile now, did not mock or taunt her.

But he hit her, a backhand that sent her pirouetting down to the floor. Sweeping around like a scythe blade, she tried to knock his legs out from under him, but he danced lightly away.

Again, she pressed the attack. Once, twice, her blows missed. But now she had extracted herself from the moment, examining the conflict as though it were a chess match. Her attack now was merely a feint to draw another punch from Giles.

When he struck out at her a second time, she was ready. Buffy sidestepped, grabbed his left wrist and then twirled into his arms as though they were engaged in a macabre waltz. The stake held tightly to her, she wrapped herself in his left arm and then thrust the stake at his chest.

Giles stopped the wooden point with his right hand; it pierced the palm and then the tip appeared at the back of his hand, protruding from the skin. Buffy withdrew the stake and stabbed it down again, but the wraithlike vampire slipped away from her.

"Well done, Buffy," he said. "Bravo, truly. I couldn't be more proud. It makes me realize that coming here was precisely the right thing to do."

Wary, Buffy stood ready for another skirmish. Giles gestured toward the bed.

"I brought you a gift."

Even as she glanced over toward the bed, the vampire crossed the room and lifted a sword from the mattress. Its hilt was steel and wood and leather, not at all ornate and yet somehow elegant. The scabbard was black and plain, but when Giles drew the sword out, Buffy saw that the blade was inscribed with runes all along its length.

Giles turned the sword in his hand and starlight glimmered off the blade.

"For you," he whispered.

"I don't want anything from you," she snapped.

"But I insist."

"Fine, give it to me. Just the thing I need to cut your head off."

He smirked. "What else would you say?"

Suddenly there was no trace of the old Giles in his

features, in his stance. It was as though the evil that burrowed inside him had emerged for a moment to gaze upon her with its own eyes.

The air seemed charged with the power that crackled within him, his eyes flickering with jack-o'-lantern flame.

"You might be able to kill me, Buffy," he confessed, though without losing his haughty air. "But it won't be easy. You think it's only speed that saved me tonight? You're nearly as fast as I am, maybe faster. But I trained you, remember? I'm inside your mind, crawling inside your skin. I'm the only real father you ever had, the only one who cared about you. I know every move you'll make before it's even been born in that ferocious brain of yours.

"Still, you might be able to kill me. If you really want to."

Suddenly it was too warm in the room. What little air rustled the curtains was stagnant and damp. Buffy felt her breath hitching in her chest; a vein pulsed in her temple; her heart beat too loud inside her head.

Hate and despair filled her in equal portions, but were inextricably tangled.

"What makes you think I won't?" she whispered.

Giles smiled, cocked his head to one side like a wolf listening for the steps of its prey.

"Hope," he said. "I forged you just as that sword was forged, Buffy. You belong at my side just as it should hang at yours. I was curious how you would change after so long without human contact. When you finally escaped, I observed you closely. I aided you as best I could. I had to see with my own eyes that the weapon I had forged had retained its fine edge. And you have, my dear. Truly, you have."

Horrible understanding bloomed in Buffy's mind. "The crossbow. You're the one who left it for me."

"Of course," Giles said, seemingly offended. "Wouldn't have been sporting if I hadn't given you a fighting chance. And now you have a choice to make. I am a creature out of time, Buffy. The years have no bearing on me. I can afford to be patient as I spread my influence slowly, quietly, until the world is roughly awakened one night to discover that their lives are no longer their own.

"You should be with me, Buffy. You may not be my daughter, but you *can* be, if only you surrender yourself to fate. Can't you hear the voice of destiny in this?"

Her fingers gripped the stake in her hand. "Oh yeah," she said. "I hear it. It's saying maybe you should start watching the clock again, 'cause your time is up."

Cautiously, her eyes on the sword in his hands, she slipped toward him.

"Ah, well," he said, a mischievous twinkle in his eyes. "Perhaps you require a bit more time to contemplate the future."

With a single fluid motion he cocked his right arm back and hurled the sword at her as though it were a spear. Buffy sidestepped the ancient blade, her left hand whipped out, and she plucked it from the air, then turned to face him with the sword in one hand and the stake in the other.

But Giles was gone.

The curtains billowed as the breeze picked up, but only the stars and the broad lawn behind the installation were visible through the screenless window. Buffy went and leaned on the sill. For a moment she was baffled as to how Giles had made his entry. Her room was much too far above the ground for him to have climbed. Then she glanced up, and understood. Somehow he had reached the roof, come across the top of the place and then hung down to her window from there.

There was no sign of him on the grass below save for the screen he had torn from her window. At least, that was what Buffy thought at first. Then she noticed a dark form a ways from the building, the starlight not enough to make out much detail.

Her gaze fell upon a second. Then, far off to the right, only a few feet from the building's foundation, a third.

Council operatives. Sentries.

Dead men.

The moon was little more than a sliver as the werewolf trailed the scent Giles had left behind. The incongruity of it still astonished Buffy. It was not supposed to happen this way. Yet Oz had strolled casually out onto the lawn with twenty people in tow, found a spot roughly beneath Buffy's window, and sniffed the air.

He had glanced at Willow with eyes heavy with warning. "Keep them back," he had said.

Then he had changed. Buffy had seen him transform under the power of the moon before, but this was different. It looked more painful, and that was saying quite a bit. His body contorted, his facial structure stretched and popped, and as the fur sprouted all over his flesh, Oz arched his back and snarled with the effort of it.

When the transformation was complete, Oz had growled low and dangerous at the people gathered around him. The Council operatives backed off and the werewolf set out on the trail.

Now they followed him as he tracked an invisible trail across the ground. Buffy wrinkled her nose at the werewolf's musky odor and wondered how Oz could smell anything other than himself. When the wolf came to one of the dead sentries, he nudged the corpse a bit, snuffled in its clothes, and then glanced toward a stand of trees on the far side of the property. Oz began to lope toward the small wooded area and then it was just a matter of the rest of them keeping up.

The operatives spread out to run. Buffy found herself in the lead with Willow and Xander to her left and Christopher Lonergan to her right. Wesley and the new Slayer were there as well, but they were back among a group of Council agents who trailed slightly.

Out of the corner of her eye, Buffy saw Willow watching her.

"So, I'm guessing we don't have to invite them in," she said as she ran.

"It was a hospital once. Anyone is welcome in a public place like that. When we first moved in, I tried half a dozen times to cast a spell to revoke that general invitation, but it never took. When a hospital is built, the intention of everyone involved is that it be open to anyone. I think that intent of purpose is too strong to override."

Ahead, Oz had reached the line of trees. The werewolf paused and stared back at them, poised impatiently as they hurried to catch up.

"Meaning any vampire can stroll right in at any time," Buffy said. "Nobody thinks that's a security risk?"

"Of course it is," Lonergan grunted, obviously a bit annoyed. "That's one of the reasons they've got me around here. Bloodsuckers nearby, I sense it."

"So I noticed," Buffy replied. "But you didn't sense Giles, did you?"

Lonergan shot her a withering glance. "Didn't know you'd dusted Spike, did I? Gift I've got can't distinguish one from the other. Just tells me when there's evil about. Look, we've got enough manpower to repel a demon or vampire assault. But, hell, nobody ever thought the leeches'd come in one at a time. Suicide, isn't it?"

"Or it should be," Xander muttered darkly.

Buffy shot him a sidelong glance. "What the hell's that supposed to mean?"

"Nothing."

At the edge of the trees, the Slayer stopped. The other operatives went on around them, but Willow and Xander hung back. The three of them studied one another warily. Buffy could not even bear to argue with Xander. Instead, she looked at Willow.

"So you think, what, that because it's Giles, I let him go?" she demanded.

Willow met her gaze evenly, though she replied with some hesitation. "It crossed my mind."

Xander was more direct. "You can't tell us it wasn't difficult for you, seeing him like that."

"Of course it was!" Buffy snapped, shaking her head. "But that only makes me want to destroy that thing even more. He was too fast for me. That took me by surprise. He trained me, and he used that against me. But if you guys think I just let him go, after all he's done . . . I don't know what you've gone through the last five years that's changed you so much, but you don't know me at all anymore."

Xander stared at her. "Maybe we don't," he said. Then he turned and jogged into the trees after the others.

Buffy watched him go, then stared at Willow. A bitter sort of anger rose up in her and she turned to follow Xander. After a few steps, though, she changed her mind, turned and confronted Willow.

"When they put me in that cell, they didn't just take away my freedom. They stole so much more from me. My mother. Giles. Faith. Angel. And five years of my life. I guess I didn't realize they'd stolen you from me, too."

Willow blanched, all the wary hesitation going out of her expression in an instant. She took a quick, unsteady breath and shook her head almost imperceptibly. Buffy waited for a few seconds for her to speak, but when Willow said nothing, she turned to follow Xander through the trees. The woods weren't very deep, perhaps thirty feet. On the other side was an office park. The werewolf was crouched on a spot in the parking lot, sniffing the pavement. He glanced up expectantly. In that form Oz could not speak, but his meaning was clear.

This was where the trail stopped.

Buffy hung back, watching Xander and Lonergan and the other operatives begin to scan the lot for any sign of Giles, but it was clear they all knew it was a futile pursuit.

There was a rustle from the woods behind her, and then Willow laid a hand on Buffy's shoulder. The Slayer turned to face her old friend, and was surprised to see that Willow seemed almost angry.

"There's something you should understand," Willow said. For a moment, she glanced away, then fixed her gaze upon Buffy again. "After they took you, it was a while before we realized what was really going on. Giles took his time, covered his tracks. During that time before it all really went to hell, there wasn't a day that went by that I didn't think the next phone call, the next knock on the door, was going to be you. That you'd find a way to get free, to come back. That you'd have a plan.

"When Angel went looking for you and he didn't come back either . . . I still tried to tell myself it would be all right. We searched for you constantly, interrogated every vamp and demon in Sunnydale. I tried to use magick to find you, but I knew that was probably useless. Giles would have expected that."

Willow pressed her lips together and turned away, wiping at her eyes.

"A little more than a year after they took you, the vampires rose up and took Sunnydale. It happened in a single night, and we had no idea there were so many of them. A lot of the cops. The mayor. People's parents. *My* parents, Buffy."

With a small shudder, Buffy put a hand over her mouth. "Oh God, Willow."

"I hadn't been by the house for a couple of weeks," Willow went on, eyes narrowing with grief at the memory. "That night, they came to see me."

"What . . . what did you do?"

Willow shook her head and glanced off at some point in the distance, as though she could still see the horrors she had witnessed that day.

"Not me," she said softly, the burden of her memories clear in the set of her shoulders, the cast of her eyes. "Oz. He dusted them both. It's never been the same with us since then. I never stopped hoping you would be all right. But after that night, I couldn't wait for you anymore, you know?"

Regret weighed heavily upon Buffy and she cursed herself for being so selfish. She was not the only one whose world had changed.

"I'm sorry I wasn't there for you," Buffy said. "But, Willow, I'm here *now*."

A tiny, hopeful smile twitched upon Willow's lips. Her hand shook a bit as she held it out. Buffy took it, their fingers twining together. Then the two women embraced briefly.

"I'm so glad you're alive," Willow whispered.

"Join the club," Buffy replied as they separated again. "So what's our next move?"

"You're asking me?"

"Seems like you're the girl to ask around here."

Willow furrowed her brow in contemplation. "If even half of what Spike said about Giles's advancements in Los Angeles were true, and after this thing with Giles, I think we have to accelerate our plans. But I want to talk to Christopher and Ms. Haversham first."

Buffy nodded slowly, then paused. "Before you do that, though? There are some other things we should talk about."

Willow stared at Buffy, astonished and baffled. "Is that even possible?"

Buffy threw up her hands, a kind of lost expression on her face. "Apparently."

They sat on the sofa in Willow's quarters, shoes off, feet drawn up beneath them as they faced each other. After they had come back inside, Willow had brought Buffy here. The Slayer had been distracted as she complimented Willow on how nice the suite was, the way Willow had acquired some of the things that decorated the walls and shelves. Though Willow had known Buffy was stalling, putting off getting around to discussing whatever was on her mind, she could never have prepared herself for the sheer incredulity of it.

"Are you sure it isn't . . . well, no offense, but some

kind of psychosis from being a prisoner so long?" she ventured.

Buffy shook her head. "It would be easier if I was crazy, huh? Tell me about it. But, not, sorry to say."

Willow rested her chin atop her knees, arms wrapped tightly around her shins, and stared at Buffy as she turned the extraordinary story over and over in her mind.

"Tell me that look is from you puzzling out how to fix it," Buffy said hopefully.

"Sort of that," Willow replied hesitantly. "And sort of . . . there are really two of you in there?"

"Yep. *Dos* Buffys."

"There's no conflict, though? No struggle for dominance or whatever?"

Buffy gave her a sheepish look. "Haven't thought about it much, to be honest. Been a little busy. But it isn't like having two different minds in one body. Two sets of memories, yeah, but not really. I mean, the stuff that happened five years ago . . . all that's a lot fresher in my mind than it should be, because in a crazy way it just happened a few *weeks* ago. I know there's this doubled up thing happening, but both of the souls in me *are* me. Y'know?"

"If I say I do, will you not try to explain it anymore? It's making my head hurt."

"I know how you feel," Buffy said. "I mean, some of the things that I do, I'm not even sure if my instincts and emotions come from version nineteen-point-oh or twenty-four-point-oh, or some combination of both. But it's not like I'm all Jekyll and Hyde or anything."

Willow nodded, but her mind was already skipping tracks, examining other aspects of this bizarre phenomenon. "Let me think out loud for a second." She stood up and paced around the room a bit, reaching out to touch familiar, comforting objects, thoughts swirling. At the same time, even though she was contemplating Buffy's situation, in the back of her mind a warm, joyful feeling had begun to grow now that the awkwardness she had felt toward Buffy had been dispersed.

"This is thinking out loud?" Buffy asked.

"Oh, sorry," Willow replied quickly, waving at something in the air around her. "It's just . . . a little overwhelming. It's hard to put any of it into words."

Buffy leaned forward on the sofa. "Those telepathic powers I had once? Long gone."

"I know, I know. All right, since your *now* self remembers being thrown into the cell in the first place, and since I'm pretty sure you were *you* for a second there after Camazotz ripped Zotzilaha out of you, we know this, um, overcrowding thing is temporary. Which means we're destined to figure out how to send you back."

With a sigh, Willow reached up and took the clip from her hair, then shook it out. Her head hurt, and though she doubted the clip was responsible, it felt better to have her hair down.

"That's not right, is it?" she asked.

Buffy shook her head. "I wish it was that simple. But

no, that's not right. Even if you can figure out how to separate me, or us, or whatever, and send me back to where I belong, if you just put me in at that moment, nothing will have changed. Everything will happen the same way."

Willow nodded. "Which means that Camazotz exorcising The Prophet from your *then-body* is the catalyst, the thing that draws you back from this time." Alarm bells went off inside her. "And we have no way of knowing when that will happen. It could be years or seconds from now."

"Exactly," Buffy said. "The clock is ticking but we don't know how much time we have. Before I get pulled back, you've got to figure out how to override it all and send me back farther, back *before* The Prophet Zotzilla or whatever took over my body. Zotzilaha said I made a mistake that led to this. I hate to say it, but I believe that. Which means I have to go back and stop myself from making that mistake; I have to pick the right moment."

Willow pressed a hand to her forehead. "Which is?"

Buffy sighed. "I don't know. I guess I made a lot of mistakes. The thing that sticks out in my mind was that night at the harbor master's office, when Giles was captured. I . . . left him behind."

"You had to," Willow told her. "You'd probably both have been killed right then and there. What could you have done differently?"

The Slayer lowered her gaze and a shadow fell across her face. "I don't know. Maybe it wasn't that moment.

Maybe the specific moment was before that. Or even after it. But what could I have done differently? I want you to use your magick to give me a chance to find out. I'll tell you this much, though. If I get a second chance, I'll never leave Giles behind again."

"I wish I had as much faith in me as you do," Willow said with a soft laugh. "But Zotzilaha did this to you. Once we understand exactly what she did and we can figure out how she did it, hopefully we'll be able to reverse it. If we can get you back far enough, none of this will ever have happened. Everything in my life will be different."

Buffy frowned. "Will, I'm sorry, I didn't even think about that. But—"

Willow interrupted firmly. "Anything's better than this." All the heartaches of the past five years came to her then with crystal clarity. The death and loss and disappointment, and the loneliness.

"I'm so glad you're here," she said.

Buffy gave her an emphatic nod and a sweet smile. "Never thought I'd say this, but me too."

"I'm going to get on the research right away," Willow promised.

"Good. While we're waiting around for that, we can work on the plan."

"Plan?"

"How to take Sunnydale back and kill Giles."

"Ah," Willow nodded. "That plan."

Over the years since Sunnydale had fallen to the vampires, its downtown area had become like Bourbon

Street in New Orleans. While some shops and restaurants still had windows boarded up, there was more life here than anywhere else in town.

After dark, at least.

The old Sun Cinema was technically closed, its façade falling apart, but they still showed movies all night, every night, thanks to one enterprising demon who saw a need and filled it. Establishments that had been trashed or abandoned had been replaced over time with others, mostly bars and strip clubs and such.

Giles rode north through town on a refurbished thirty-year-old Norton motorcycle that was his pride and joy. He had first spotted the machine in Aaron Trask's garage eighteen months earlier. Trask was the human mechanic who cared for all the vehicles used by Giles and his most trusted aides. For more than a year, in his spare time, Giles had admired the mechanic's handiwork as he restored the Norton. When it was finished, buffed to a high shine, ready to go, Giles let Trask take it out for one ride before he demanded the motorcycle as tribute to the king.

Frankly he thought the whole king thing was a load of crap, but he found that vampires and humans were, as a general rule, stupid, and royalty was something they could understand. That, and fear. Giles had a feeling it was more the latter than the former that convinced Aaron Trask to hand over the Norton without a word of argument.

Trask hated him, that much was clear to Giles. For that alone, he would have killed the man, but he was a very good mechanic.

A short time later Giles parked the motorcycle in its

spot in the garage under City Hall. The guards all inclined their heads as he passed. Aaron Trask was there working on a limousine as Giles walked to the elevator bank, past a pair of sentries on duty there. He smiled and waved to Trask. Trask returned the wave but not the smile.

When the elevator doors slid open on the third floor, Jax was waiting for him.

"Did you enjoy your trip, my lord?" he asked, eyes blazing amid the white tattoo across his face.

"Very much, thank you, Jax."

"You have supplicants waiting for the brand, master."

Giles paused to glance at Jax, then scratched his head thoughtfully for a moment. "Let's move them to tomorrow night. I'm feeling a bit hungry, and thought I might go down for a bit of rejuvenation."

"I'll take care of it," Jax promised.

"Excellent," Giles replied.

He reached into his pocket for a ring that held keys to the Norton, a Jaguar he particularly liked, and a few others. As he walked down the hall to a different elevator, he spun the ring on his finger, the keys jangling loudly.

The elevator doors opened immediately when he pressed the button. Giles stepped in, selected the appropriate key, and inserted it. After he turned the key, he pressed the button marked "BB" and the elevator began to descend to the subbasement.

A very interesting night, he mused. Buffy's response had not been what he had hoped, but it had been precisely what he'd expected. He only dreamed that in time she would surrender to the conclusion that he was right, that she was meant to be a part of his regime. Still, it had been wonderful seeing her again. He had nearly been able to taste her blood even from across the room.

A good night.

Giles was humming as the doors slid open again.

Time for a visit with the god of bats.

Time to drink of power.

CHAPTER 5

Home.

As Buffy opens her eyes her senses are suffused by the atmosphere of home that surrounds her. Soft jazz on the radio floats up to her along with the scent of something cooking. Pancakes, she thinks. Or not thinks exactly, so much as registers, 'cause thinking would require too much effort. Sunday morning, then, with pancakes and that jazz radio show that runs until noon.

The sheets smell fresh and clean and she burrows a little deeper under them, enjoying the feeling of the cotton against the side of her face. A strand of her hair is across her face and it tickles her nose so that she must blow it away with a puff of breath.

It's bliss, really, but somehow she cannot slip back into unconsciousness. Sleep has fled now and though she is warm and content, her mind has begun the day already without her cooperation. A bemused, drowsy *grin steals across her face and, lazily, she opens her eyes.*

It is bright outside her windows but there is no breeze. Her stuffed pig, Mr. Gordo, is a pink lump half hidden between her pillow and the headboard. Her alarm clock has numbers on it, but Buffy finds she cannot read them. She blinks several times, convinced it must be after nine o'clock because of the jazz. Then her vision seems to clear—though there wasn't anything wrong with it before—and the numbers on the alarm clock read "12:00." The numbers blink off and on like the clock on a new VCR.

Power's out, Buffy thinks. But she knows it can't be, because then where is the music coming from?

Her bliss ripples like the wind across the surface of a pond. With a sigh, she sits up in bed, and it is then that she notices the splash of purple on the wall. She recognizes it immediately, a carnival mask hand-painted in vivid colors. Her father brought it back from Venice for her when she was twelve years old.

During the move from L.A. to Sunnydale, it was shattered in the box. A box scrawled with the word FRAGILE on the top, bottom and on every side. Broken, this gift from her father, that he brought back specially for her from his business trip.

But here it is. Whole and unbroken.

Buffy is staring at it when her mother pops into the room, a bright smile on her face.

"You're up!" Joyce Summers says, her astonishment only half mockery. "The smell of pancakes luring you from bed?"

"Yeah," Buffy says slowly, but she is still troubled as her gaze returns to the purple and pink mask. There's some red in it, too, she notices for the first time.

Slowly, Buffy turns to focus on her mother. Joyce is almost bubbly. She loves Sunday mornings, the jazz and pancakes tradition, the time to share with her little girl who isn't so little anymore.

But now Joyce stares back at Buffy and the smile melts from her face as though it were a mask of ice, revealing an expression of despair beneath. She tries to hide the look, but cannot.

"Did I spill something on my blouse?" Joyce asks, picking at her shirt anxiously.

"Mom," Buffy begins.

"I should get back to the pancakes. They'll burn."

"Mom—"

"No!" Joyce snaps, panic flooding from her eyes. "Don't!"

"Mom—" Buffy's heart is breaking.

"Don't say it, Buffy!"

"You're dead, Mom."

Her mother's face goes slack and her arms drop to her sides as though all the energy, all the life, has been sucked from her. Drained from her. She shakes her head slowly, softly, and her words come out as a moan.

"Why did you have to say it?" Joyce Summers asks her daughter, weeping now. "It's Sunday morning."

Behind her, in the darkened hallway, Buffy sees another figure moving. Someone else in the house.

Daddy? *she thinks. But that has to be just because of the mask, because her father isn't here. Doesn't live here. Never has. Never even calls anymore.*

Then he steps into the room.

Giles.

Glasses on. Patient, knowing smile.

"Maybe you should go back to sleep now?" he suggests kindly. Paternally.

He takes Joyce in his arms and she collapses there, weeping, asking him why.

Buffy glances at the windows. The sun shines through, warm and bright. The wind had been dead before, but now a strong gust blows in and the carnival mask falls from its nail on the wall and shatters on the floor. Tsking in sympathy, Giles moves to pick up the pieces. When he reaches to touch the shards of her father—her father's gift—he slices his index finger.

He does not bleed.

"You're not dead," Buffy says to him, eyes welling with tears.

Giles glances up at her as though he has not quite heard.

Buffy narrows her gaze as she studies him, and she sees it then. The glasses and the benevolent gaze are a mask of ice, like the one her mother had worn.

"No," Giles agrees. "Not dead."

"But you should be," Buffy tells him.

And his face begins to melt, but now it is not ice melting. It is his flesh, peeling and blackening in the sun, running like wax. Still, there is no blood.

Another voice, off to her right, by the windows. "Buffy."

She turns toward the voice and sees Angel standing in front of an enormous pane of glass. Not her room. Not her windows. The shine burns through the window and silhouettes him and he stands with his arms out as though crucified, his eyes closed.

Buffy says his name. Angel opens his eyes and gazes down upon her, but he does not smile.

"He thinks like a vampire now. He doesn't understand love."

She realizes then that Angel's clothes hang heavily upon him because they are sodden with blood. It drips steadily from the edges of his jacket and the cuffs of his pants.

A noise by the door, and Buffy turns to see that her mother and Giles are gone. The room is dark now, no sun, no light, yet somehow she can just make out the shape of her door and the end of the bed.

Downstairs the music has died. The acrid odor of burning pancakes fills her nostrils and bile rises in the back of Buffy's throat. She closes her eyes against the darkness.

Buffy woke with her head under the pillow, the stiff, starchy sheets wrapped around her legs. The smell of burned pancakes was still in her nose. She sat up quickly and swung her legs over the side of the bed, then rubbed her face vigorously with both hands as though she could erase the dream.

Her hands were dry.

Surprised, she glanced at her palms, then gently traced the skin under her eyes. No tears. And yet she was sure she was crying, had felt the tears welling in her, even subconsciously. When she woke she had known that if she opened her mouth it would be to sob.

But no tears.

Somehow she knew, then, that it was the younger Buffy in her, Buffy-at-nineteen, who was crying. But those tears never appeared on the cheeks of the woman whose body she inhabited. After all she had been through, Buffy-at-twenty-four was harder, more callous.

An image of Xander swam into her mind, and she understood that if it were not for the bizarre twinning of her soul, Buffy would have been like him. Without her younger self to temper the bitterness within her, she might have been just as numb and cold as he had become. As long as he had no hope, he had nothing to survive for. His despair might well get him killed.

All or nothing, Xander thought. The day had finally come when they would stop all this sitting around crap, saddle up, and head across the border. They would take Sunnydale back, kill Giles and every other leech that got in the way, or they wouldn't be coming back at all.

Which was just fine with him. Xander had been waiting for this day an awfully long time.

He had woken up hours before dawn, checked and double-checked his gear with only the light slipping under his door from the hallway to guide him, then suited up. When he knew there was nothing more that he could do, he popped *The Wild Bunch* into the DVD player and lay back on the bed. He didn't want to bother anyone else, so he left the sound off. Not that it mattered. He had seen the film dozens of times and knew most of the dialogue inside out.

The Wild Bunch. The Outlaw Josey Wales. Once Upon a Time in the West. Red River. Stagecoach. Nearly every DVD on the shelf was an old Western. He watched them over and over. Regular television was no distraction, for it was a joke to him to watch the news or even a sitcom, and think that the world on television was one that most people believed in.

They had no idea.

He might have read a novel, but he found that he had no patience for books anymore. His mind tended to wander into places he never wanted it to go.

On screen, the climactic battle erupted. Even without the volume, Xander could hear the gunshots. A bunch of men with no ties, nothing to lose, dying because they finally found something to stand up for.

A knock at the door. He glanced at the clock. 4:57 A.M. Xander slipped off the bed, grabbed his gear and opened the door. Oz stood in the corridor with Abel and Yancy. The werewolf was jittery, like he'd had too much caffeine, but over the years Xander had come to recognize that trait in him. He always got that way before a fight.

It was the animal in him.

"Time to roll," Oz said.

"Rolling," Xander replied.

Down the corridor, they met Buffy and Willow on the way down the stairs. All the other operatives were already outside, Xander knew. Or on the way out there. The grunts had been ordered to have everything prepared to move out at five A.M. precisely. But the group led by the Slayer was supposed to be different. Special. Ms. Haversham had handpicked this little squadron for the main event, the attack on Giles himself. So the rules that applied to everyone else didn't apply here.

'Cause we've been doing it longer, Xander thought. Killing monsters. We're better at it 'cause we know how they think.

Buffy hung back. "Xander. Got a minute?"

He glanced at her, then at Willow. She seemed surprised. Xander nodded toward Oz to let him know he and the others should go on, and when he went down the stairs, Willow went with him.

"Yeah?" he said, studying Buffy.

There was a kind of anger in her eyes that was not really anger. Something she wanted to say, maybe a lot. Xander had the feeling whatever it was, it wasn't anything he wanted to hear. For a moment he thought she was going to spill it, all the things that were on her mind.

Then whatever tension had built up in her seemed to subside. Buffy smiled, but there was no amusement in it.

"I wish I could bring that wall down," she said.

"What wall?"

"The one around you."

Then she reached up to grab him behind the head, stood on her tiptoes, and kissed him once, gently, on the lips. There was no romance in it, no passion, but he swallowed hard and forced himself not to look away.

"I love you, Xander," she said. "I did then and I do now. You still have people who care about you."

Her smile went away. Now her expression was grim, eyes dark. With the strength of the Chosen One, she gripped the back of his neck and shook him once.

"Don't die."

In the room that had once been the mayor's office, Giles sat across a small table from a Borgasi demon named Ace Tippette and sipped tea. Ace was not a tea drinker, but Giles had provided him with a glass of Kentucky bourbon. They had been in that room, across that table, long enough for the tea to get cold and the bourbon to get warm. The Borgasi seemed to wish he were elsewhere, but Giles would not relent. He gazed at the demon expectantly.

Ace ran a hand over the porcupine-like quills on his head and the back of his neck, and sighed for perhaps the thirteenth time. The black, wet nostrils that were about all he had for a nose twitched, and both sets of slitted eyes gazed about the room, avoiding Giles's face until at last he had no option but to respond.

"Ya gotta understand, the Borgasi ain't exactly a war-like race. I mean, all right, we understand the need to break kneecaps now and again, and we've buried our share of problems in the desert, but our clan has been living pretty peaceably alongside the humans in Vegas for, what, fifty, sixty years. Hell, they're most of our business these days. Since organized crime let us have a piece of things, Vegas runs smooth. Thanks to us, the place calmed down enough to become a freakin' tourist mecca, you know? We don't wanna mess up a good thing."

Giles nodded once, then took a sip of his tea. He grimaced at its temperature and set the cup down on the saucer. Contemplatively, he tapped a finger against the tip of his nose.

"You do seem to have quite a comfortable life out there in the desert, Ace. But let me suggest that perhaps you really aren't considering the larger picture here. You've seen a great deal of my operation on your visit tonight. I have revealed even more of it in some detail as I laid out the part I wish the Borgasi to play. Too much, I fear."

"Whoa, hold on there, chief. Nobody saw anything you didn't want them to see. We're here to parley, not to stick our noses in," Ace protested.

The vampire king smiled thinly. "Yes, well, putting that aside for the moment, let me see if I can cast this in a slightly different light for you. I'm expanding. Slowly, but quite inexorably, I assure you. I have one hurdle in my way. Much like walking a dog in Los Angeles, it is a mess I cannot avoid but am prepared to clean up after. I expect to have overcome that hurdle and have the detritus of its destruction cleared away within three or four days. After that time, I will continue to expand my sphere of influence. You could count on two hands the number of days before Los Angeles is in my hands. When I am done there, I will visit Las Vegas and I will take it."

Ace held up a hand, narrowing his gaze. "What the hell do you mean you're gonna 'take it'? You think we're just gonna clear out?"

A soft chuckle escaped Giles's lips. He did so enjoy Ace's company. "Perish the thought," he said as he steepled his fingers beneath his chin. "You *could* run, of course. Or I could destroy you all. But there is a third option I think we would both find preferable. As I complete my infiltration of Los Angeles, it would be simpler if, with your assistance, Las Vegas were already under my control. Simpler, and healthier, I think. For the Borgasi. After all, wouldn't you rather live as lords above the humans than as shadows among them?"

The vampire king had recently had the black paint scraped off one of the windows, and he could see that the sky was lightening outside, dawn sneaking in as if to catch the odd, errant night creature unaware. Now Giles offered a half-smile to the demon as he rose and went to close and latch the steel shutters that had been installed to block that single, clear window.

Giles turned and glanced at Ace again. "Put another way, my friend, wouldn't you rather live?"

For a second, he thought the Borgasi might snap. They weren't a warlike race, true, but they were dangerous when the spirit moved them. And proud, too. That was the real peril in baiting Ace, that Giles would tread too roughly on his pride. On the other hand, perhaps peril was not the right word, for Giles had laid out the future for the Borgasi in no uncertain terms. Despite his mannerisms and the absurdity of his nickname, Ace Tippette was not a stupid creature.

So Giles was not at all surprised when the demon shook his head and threw his hands up. "Not much use arguin' with that kinda logic, is there?"

"None," the vampire lord replied.

Ace stood and held out his hand. "All right, Giles. You give the orders, but you'll leave us alone to run things, yeah?"

Giles shook his hand firmly. "Agreed."

The Borgasi smiled, his hundreds of tiny, jagged teeth glistening damply. "Gotta say, it's gonna be interesting. Some of the boys got a problem with change. This'll throw 'em for a loop."

Ace paused and all four of his slitted eyes widened. "Say, when you get all the way to Atlantic City, you think we could have first dibs?"

"Dibs," Giles repeated. "By all means, Ace. By all means."

"Excellent." Ace shot him a thumbs-up.

The Borgasi turned to head for the door.

"One more thing," Giles said.

Wet nostrils sniffing the air as if sensing a change in the atmosphere of the room, Ace turned back to him.

"From now on, you will refer to me as 'my lord' or 'master.' Even 'majesty' is acceptable, though it always makes me feel a bit, oh, I don't know . . ." Giles tossed a hand in the air and grinned mischievously, ". . . self-conscious, I suppose."

Ace grinned back, misreading him. "You gotta be kiddin' me."

Giles glared balefully at him. "Decidedly not."

The quills on the Borgasi's head stood up slightly and he reached up to brush at them, forcing them to lay down again.

"Yeah, no, I mean . . . not a problem at all. You're the boss, right?"

"Not the boss," Giles replied. "The king."

There came a sudden rap at the door and then it was opened before Giles could even ask who it was. Jax glided into the room, practically crackling with anxiety.

Giles stared at him. "Jax," he said, the single word enough of an admonition to stop the servant in his tracks.

"Forgive me, my lord Giles," Jax said quickly, ducking his head in a rapid bow. "There's a, uh, a matter that's come up. An urgent matter."

Ace cleared his throat. "Know what? That's no problem. I'll just find my own way out, all right?" The Borgasi glanced anxiously at Giles. "We're at your service . . . my lord. Y'know, just buzz me when you want us to do it. We'll be ready."

Giles narrowed his eyes. "Excellent, Ace. I accept your mangled oath of fealty. Please wait in the corridor and Jax will escort you out momentarily."

The demon waved his hand in the air. "Nah, that's all—" He paused, glanced sheepishly back at Giles. "Right. I'll wait outside."

When Ace had left the room, Giles crossed his arms and glared expectantly at Jax. "What is it that couldn't wait?"

Jax glanced at the door and lowered his voice in almost theatrical fashion, apparently concerned that the demon would overhear.

"They're here, majesty. Five border sentries have called in to report a massive incursion along the southern border. As many as fifty to sixty vehicles thus far, separated into seven different groups at this count. Estimates have their individual numbers as high as three hundred."

"Excellent," Giles replied as he moved to the high-backed chair behind his desk. "A single-front battle. I had thought they would muster up enough operatives to attack from the north as well."

Jax stared at him. His expression was almost comical. "But, my lord, there are so many. We can only put a handful of your soldiers against them. There aren't more than twenty or thirty sunsuits."

"Oh, stop being such a mollycoddle, Jax. Granted, despite their vows of loyalty, most of the humans are unlikely to risk their lives to defend me, but some will. Enough to slow them down. And it isn't as though the demons I've been so careful to pamper are going to let their livelihoods be taken away. Under my rule, this is paradise for them. They can't afford not to help."

To his credit, Jax made an effort to quell his anxiety and stood a bit straighter. "Your orders, my lord."

Giles sighed. "We've planned for this eventuality,

Jax. Give the order. We'll see who obeys it. Losses are acceptable, even significant losses. But *loss* is not. I will be in the court in ten minutes. The battle will be conducted from there."

"Yes, my lord."

"Oh, and Jax? Make certain everyone is aware that the Slayer is mine. I want her captured if possible, but under no circumstances is she to be killed. Even if it means giving her safe passage to this building."

Now Jax dropped all pretense of calm and stared at him in horror. "But majesty, she'll ki—"

"No," Giles replied firmly. "She will not. I've seen it in her eyes now, felt it in her hesitation. She will do everything she can to stop me, but she will *not* kill me. That is the chink in her armor, Jax. She will be one of us before we see another dawn."

There were five vehicles in the phalanx that entered Sunnydale on the shore road, three Humvees and two troop carriers. There was a sense of urgency about the proceedings, but no one was in a hurry. They could not afford to be. Undercover operatives in Sunnydale had pinpointed at least a dozen major nests in town, and each team had been assigned two. They were to clean out the nests, taking out any opposition they met along the way, and then rendezvous downtown to exterminate the opposition they were sure to encounter there.

Ms. Haversham had ordered that the nest in the Sunnydale Museum was to be left untouched for the moment, because the Council of Watchers could not abide the destruction of such valuable antiquities. When human control had been restored to the area, then the vampires in the museum would likely flee anyway. The older woman and her aides had established a command center at the Council building. From there they were in constant contact with the field units via headset communications systems.

One unit differed from the others, however, a small force whose mission was to proceed directly to City Hall. There they were to locate and destroy Rupert Giles, no matter the cost, eliminating any vampiric resistance they found along the way.

Buffy rode in the back of a troop carrier, engine rumbling loudly, rattling ominously. A castoff from the U.S. army, she suspected. But that was all right. They didn't need to go much farther. She glanced around her. Willow, Oz, Xander, and a dozen operatives handpicked by Ellen Haversham. Christopher Lonergan was in front, behind the wheel.

Just before their departure, Wesley had created a stir, protesting loudly to Haversham and Willow that he and Anna, the younger Slayer, were not part of this primary unit. There had been a lot of talk about the practical and effective dissemination of their forces, but Buffy didn't buy it for a second and she doubted Wesley did either.

The difference was that she suspected Wesley thought it was about him, that he was taking it personally. Buffy figured it had more to do with Haversham wanting to keep the Slayers separated to lessen the risk that they would *both* be killed today.

Up front, Lonergan cursed loudly and jammed on the brakes. The truck shuddered to a halt and Buffy held her breath.

"Abraxis demons. Four of them and a handful of humans," Lonergan explained.

Buffy glanced forward through the windshield and saw that they were in Docktown. A run-down tenement building ahead had been identified as a nest by Council spies. This was the moment when their smaller team was meant to break away from the phalanx, but there were yellow-skinned demons and some human collaborators in the way.

"Go," Buffy said.

Lonergan glanced at her in the rearview mirror. As a Council operative, he certainly had seniority in terms of years. But she was the Slayer, and the field leader of this mission.

"Beta team can handle this resistance," she pointed out. "That's what they're trained for, right? They'll firebomb that nest inside of ten minutes and be moving on. Let's go."

After only a moment's hesitation, Lonergan nodded. Gunfire erupted outside the truck and Buffy could hear the *whoosh* of flamethrowers as Lonergan accelerated, steering the groaning truck around the other vehicles and on toward the center of Sunnydale.

On toward City Hall.

The truck engine revved as they hit a straightaway. Out of the open back, she saw humans coming out of their homes and standing in the street to stare after the truck, and she wondered if they were relieved or terrified that help had finally come. If they even wanted help.

As Buffy glanced around at the operatives in the truck, one of the guys caught her eye. Yancy, she thought his name was. He was staring at Buffy as though she were a riddle he just could not unravel. The others were lost in their own thoughts, in preparation for the fight to come, and did not seem to notice Yancy's preoccupation with her. Even when Buffy stared back at him, the operative did not turn away.

"Can I help you with something?" she asked.

Yancy flinched, as though he had been unaware that he was staring. "Sorry," he said uncomfortably. "I was just thinking. I understand that you're the Slayer, and all, but this seems a bit kamikaze to me. The place will be well-guarded. They won't simply let us drive right in."

Buffy stared him down. "I think he will," she said. "Oh, he'll put up a fight, but I don't think he cares if we get in. That's the easy part. The way he talked to me the other night, I think he wants me to come."

"He *wants* you to kill him?" Yancy asked, incredulous.

"You're out of line, Yancy," Xander said curtly. "You don't have the first clue what the deal is here. It isn't your place to know. And it isn't your place to question. Buffy's got field command of this unit, and she knew what she was asking of us when she picked this team. You knew the risks when you agreed to be part of it. You want out, we'll stop the truck and you can walk back to base."

They all stared at Xander. Everyone except for Yancy, who had dropped his eyes and shifted his gaze away. Buffy smiled softly, silently thanking him. For the first time since she had come into this harsh world, she felt like they were all together again. It wasn't like it was, and it never would be. But they were together.

"I didn't mean anything by it," Yancy said.

"It's all right," Buffy told him. "It's a lot to ask anybody, to go on this mission."

"Trouble," Lonergan said abruptly. He gripped the wheel hard and hit the brakes.

Buffy swayed as the truck shuddered to a stop. She looked out through the front again and saw that there was a roadblock ahead. There were humans with assault weapons, and at least five vampires in protective gear.

"Fine," she said. "Trouble's just fine."

CHAPTER 6

The sun gleamed off the vehicles parked across the road, and off each fold in the silver protective suits the vampires wore. Buffy crouched between the seats of the truck and stared through the windshield at them. The vampires weren't her concern, not when they were only lightly armed and the sun was up. The humans, though, the traitors who worked for them, they were going to be a problem.

"Buffy Summers!" a tall, bearded human shouted. "Come with us, right now, and everyone else in the truck gets to live. All we want is you."

"I'm all flattered," Buffy muttered.

There were nine humans that Buffy could count and at least six of them carried semiautomatic rifles. Assault weapons weren't something she was used to having to deal with. The forces of darkness tended to rely on more archaic weaponry, either out of a sense of style, an ap-

372

preciation of antiques, or simply because they were too damn cocky to realize an Uzi was a more effective tool of destruction than a sword.

Sword, Buffy thought with a tiny smile flickering upon her lips. She reached under the bench in the back of the truck, just under where she had been sitting. Wrapped in a green blanket was the ancient, rune-engraved sword Giles had left for her. She had brought it along, wondering about it a great deal. Wondering if he had left it to give her an edge, or really, truly, as a gift. Or if, perhaps, there was something about the sword that was meant to hurt her. Some enchantment or curse. Some sort of trap.

Quickly, Buffy slipped a leather strap through the steel ring on the scabbard and then looped it over her shoulder, the sword lying across her back. Suddenly she was aware of eyes upon her. She glanced up to find everyone in the back of the truck staring at her. All of them, Willow, Xander, Oz, and the Council operatives, seemed coiled and ready to strike. The air crackled with the violence about to erupt, like the static electricity that hung in the sky just before a thunderstorm.

Through Lonergan's partially open window Buffy could hear music, a heavy-thumping blues-rock tune that filled the vacuum created by the tension between these two opposing forces.

The music was incongruous, and yet it wasn't.

In some ways, it was just what Buffy wanted, a sort of affirmation of the beating of her heart, the blood rushing through her. She glanced at Willow. "What can you give me for a diversion?"

As though their minds were cogs in the same machine, Willow scrambled into the midst of the troops, there in the back of the truck. On one knee, she glanced around at them.

"Buffy's going to walk right up to them," she told the others. "They will not attack her unless she draws the sword. They might try to make her disarm herself, but she won't."

Willow paused, glanced at Buffy. "Don't."

Buffy smiled. "Check."

"All right, then. Here's what we'll do . . ."

The music on the radio blaring from one of the cars in the roadblock had given way to screeching guitar from some seventies' rock band Buffy could not remember the name of. It ought to have seemed incongruous this early in the morning, less than an hour after sunup, but in light of the circumstances, there wasn't a lot that would have stood out as odd. As Buffy climbed out of the back of the truck, she could smell fire from somewhere not too far off. A vampire nest, she knew. Burning. The leeches dying, maybe wondering where Giles was when they needed him.

No way, she thought. *No way to make the world what it was. No way to ever make it right.* What Giles and his lackeys had done to southern California was akin to tearing a wound in the flesh of America. No way was this going to heal clean. But if they could cleanse the wound, purify it, then it *would* heal.

All that would be left behind were the scars.

Buffy picked up her pace, walked a little faster as she

went around the truck. A couple of the vampires swore when she appeared in their line of vision. One of them even took a few steps back. Before Giles took over, when this clan still answered to Camazotz, the demon-god kept the Slayer's existence a secret from them so that they would not be afraid. The Kakchiquels knew of her now, though. Giles had not taken that same precaution.

That was good. Their fear gave her an edge.

"Take the sword off and leave it on the pavement!" shouted the burly human who had called out before.

The mouthpiece, Buffy thought. The others might be there just because they thought that it was the safest way, the way to survive. Working for the vampires. But this guy, he clearly was into it. He was a part of the dark, rotten thing that had spread its filthy tentacles all through this town.

She kept walking.

All of the assault rifles swung around, their barrels aimed directly at her. Two of the human collaborators who had not yet shown weapons now pulled pistols. She thought she recognized one of them as a cop she had met once in Sunnydale. The other, though. She recognized him right off the bat.

Parker.

"Drop it, now, or we bring you to him dead," Mouthpiece shouted, a bit of panic tinging his voice.

If anything, her gait accelerated. Buffy strode toward them without the slightest hesitation. "I don't think so," she replied, close enough now that she barely needed to raise her voice. "He gave me this sword himself. It was a gift. I'm sure he wanted me to bring it when I came for a visit. And here I am."

Buffy ignored Mouthpiece as he struggled to figure out what to say next. The humans seemed more and more jittery as she closed in. The vampires moved slowly toward her as she approached. They were faceless behind the hoods they wore, and Buffy could imagine that there were no bodies in those silver suits, just the darkness, just the evil demon parasites that lurked in every vampire.

That's all they were, in the end, really. Corpse squatters. The image was gruesome, but it helped to think of Giles that way. *No, not Giles.* She wanted to stop herself from even thinking of the thing as Giles, but somehow she could not.

Maybe a dozen feet from the roadblock, Buffy stopped. The human collaborators—in front of the cars, behind them, standing on the hoods—seemed to hold their breath. Buffy saw Parker's eyes darting over toward Mouthpiece and then back to the sword that hung at her side. The vampires—*walking silver body bags*—encircled her like a pack of coyotes, exuding quiet malice, studying her, waiting for an opening.

"The sword," Mouthpiece said again, but this time his tone was uncertain. "On the ground."

Buffy smiled. With a small shrug of acceptance, she reached over her shoulder for the hilt of the weapon. The vampires twitched, drew back a step.

The tips of Buffy's fingers touched the sword.

The signal.

Buffy closed her eyes.

There was a burst of blinding light and searing heat that made her skin prickle. Screams of pain and alarm erupted all around her. Even with her eyes closed, she squinted harder against the brilliance of that light.

And she moved.

Etched upon her mind's eye, she could still see the vampires around her, the position each of them had stood in before Willow had cast this spell of illumination. Even in the daylight it was blinding, bright enough to sear the eyes of the humans, and even momentarily to stun the vampires despite the shaded face masks of their sunsuits.

With a sound like a bow across the strings of a violin, Buffy slid the sword from its scabbard. As it sliced the air she stepped forward and swung the blade. It connected, but was sharp enough that she felt only a small tug as one of the vampires was decapitated.

The sound was not unlike hearing someone close by biting into a crisp apple.

All around her, gunfire erupted. Buffy flinched, but only just barely. She had been prepared for it. Bullets tore the ground and she heard at least a few windows breaking around them. The human collaborators were firing, though they were all but blind in the glare of Willow's spell.

With their backs to the glare and their eyes squinted, the Council operatives could see well enough, and they began to fire back with far greater accuracy than their enemies. Someone cried out in pain and surprise. Buffy opened her eyes even as she spun and brought the sword across the neck of a second vampire. She squinted, and could barely see through her slitted eyes, but her instincts guided her well enough to make use of the advantage Willow had given them.

In all her time as the Slayer, she doubted she had ever moved so fast. One of them lunged at her; she brought the sword down as though she were chopping wood. Another had turned to run away from her; she sliced at it from behind, the silver protective hood staying on the head as it bounced off the ground, just before the entire creature turned to a small whirlwind of dust.

Only one remained. The vampire raised his weapon and fired two wild shots. She thought she could practically feel one of the bullets go by her head like a hornet. The cut from her sword was so fast, so clean, that for a second the head of the vampire remained on top of his shoulders. Then both head and body tumbled to the ground and disintegrated into embers.

Buffy slid the sword back into its scabbard. As she turned to face the collaborators, the Council operatives came up all around her. Willow and Oz and three others were on her left. Xander came up on her right with Yancy and a couple more. They seemed like little more than silhouettes in the bright glare of magickal light.

One of the operatives, a good-looking blond guy named Devine, took a bullet to the shoulder and went down hard. But the bullet had to be a stray, Buffy knew. The collaborators were firing blind, blinking rapidly as they tried to get their vision back. One of them stumbled off the roof of a car.

Backs still to the glare, the Council operatives rushed the roadblock and fired pistols, mostly to keep their enemies off guard. The idea was to disarm them without killing them.

Or it was, until Buffy saw a round red bullet hole appear in the center of Mouthpiece's forehead. He staggered back two steps, then fell against the passenger door of the car behind him with a *crump* of metal. He didn't move again.

"Hey!" Buffy snapped.

Beside her, Willow's hands worked quickly in the air. Even as Buffy watched, the Uzi in the hands of one of the humans turned to ice and shattered. The guy turned to run.

The power of the spell began to diminish and the brilliant, glaring illumination to fade back to normal daylight, but by then Buffy and her comrades had reached the roadblock. Even as she lashed out and cracked the jaw of a man in front of her, she saw Xander attacking and disarming a couple of others.

Willow had given them a vital advantage, allowing the confrontation to be dealt with quickly and without losing any of the members of their unit, but there was more to her than her skill as a sorceress. She was swift and graceful, a much better hand-to-hand fighter than she had been when they were younger, and she took the gun away from the man in front of her without him even really noticing he had lost it. To her left, Oz dove across the hood of a car and tackled a woman. But he was just Oz, not the wolf. Buffy had been clear about that. She wasn't sure the wolf could be trusted not to kill.

Someone *had* killed, though. Buffy glanced around, trying to figure out who it had been, and then she saw Yancy, a satisfied expression on his face. Before she could say anything, the human collaborators tried to grab her again. With a quick elbow, she cracked a nose, knocked someone unconscious. She spun around, and found Parker aiming a pistol at her from six feet away.

"You shouldn't have come back," Parker told her.

Hate and disgust filled Buffy then. He had always been a lowlife, but what he had become was worse.

"You don't think I can take that from you?" she asked him.

Parker smiled.

Then, from amid the chaos of the roadblock, Yancy appeared almost right beside Parker, and shot him in the side of the head.

"Yancy!" Buffy shouted as she watched Parker's corpse fall to the ground. "What the hell was that?"

The collaborators who weren't unconscious or dead took off running. A pair of Council operatives helped Devine to stand and began to examine the bullet wound in his shoulder.

Yancy holstered his weapon and the others began to crowd around, yet of all of them only Willow seemed even vaguely uncomfortable with what had happened.

Yancy gazed at Buffy expectantly. "He could have killed you. If you're the key to this thing working, we can't afford that. Not that I expected slobbery kisses, but a simple thank-you wouldn't have hurt."

Buffy glared at him. "You shot that other guy, too. The one who was doing their talking for them. Maybe you're just slow, but I meant what I said before. These are the people we're supposed to be trying to save. The only thing that matters here is that we get into City Hall, dust Giles, and, if we can manage it, get out alive."

Yancy's eyes grew stormy and his nostrils flared with anger. "Yeah? I'm sorry, I was under the impression that the people we were trying to save were the ones who weren't trying to kill us."

With that, he turned and marched back to the truck.

"Let's go," Buffy snapped at the others, and they all ran back to the truck.

"It did look like Parker had the drop on you," Willow whispered beside her.

"Not for a second," Buffy replied, though in truth she was not as certain as her tone implied.

She had not realized Xander was behind her, but now he jogged up next to her. "This isn't like it used to be, Buffy. Nobody *wants* anyone to get killed, but they've thrown in with the Big Evil; they know that's a risk. Maybe it's been conducted in secret until now, but this is a war. There have already been plenty of human casualties. The faster we end it, the fewer there will be in the future. Keep your head on straight, keep your eyes on the goal."

Difficult as it was for her, Buffy realized that Xander was right. Harsh, even callous perhaps, but right.

As they climbed into the back of the truck, Lonergan leaned around from the driver's seat and waited for instructions.

"You're supposed to be able to sense vampires, Christopher," Buffy said. "Try not to run us into any more. You see another roadblock, drive right through it. Just get us to City Hall."

As the truck rumbled on toward City Hall, Xander sat on the bench and glared at Tim Devine even as Hotchkiss cleaned and dressed the other man's bullet wound.

"You will stay with the vehicle, Devine. I'm not taking a liability into that building, and with that hole in you, that's exactly what you are," Xander told him, clipping off every word with his teeth.

He could feel the tension in the back of the truck and it pissed him off. Wasn't it bad enough, the pressure of what they were about to do? First Yancy squares off against the Slayer, and now Devine had to give him this crap. Out of the corner of his eye, he saw Buffy and Willow, side by side. Both of them seemed poised to speak up, take some action, and he shot them a quick, sidelong glance to let them know he would handle it. Buffy might be field commander, with Willow running a close second, but Xander and Lonergan were the ones who were really responsible for these grunts. Xander was not about to let the operatives in his unit forget that.

Devine grimaced as Hotchkiss wrapped the bandages tighter across his shoulder. Then he narrowed his gaze and stared at Xander. "Don't get up in my face, Harris," Devine said. "The coagulant stopped me from bleeding too much. I'm right-handed, which means I can still fire my weapon. And you are *not* running this mission."

With a soft chuckle, Xander shook his head. The Council had worked with the U.S. government to develop a chemical treatment that acted as a coagulant upon their blood when it was exposed to air. The army had recently begun to use the same treatment. If they were wounded, it caused the bleeding to stop quickly. It also made it decidedly unpleasant for a vampire to drink from them. Devine was right about that, but it didn't change his mind.

"First of all, it's *Mis*-ter Harris to you, Devine. I may not be your direct commander, but I am your superior on this mission. Do you hear anyone in this truck contradicting me? What it comes down to is this: you are wounded, and therefore at least partially impaired. You are not one hundred percent. Could cost your life, but that's your risk. The thing is, you're in there covering somebody's flank, they are trained to be able to rely on you. If they can't, you're a liability.

"You stay in the truck."

Devine practically snarled in response, but Xander held firm. A second later the truck's brakes squeaked and it rattled to a stop.

"We're here," Lonergan said from the front. He touched the headset he wore and listened for a moment. "From the sound of things, all the other units have reached their initial targets and have started to exterminate the nests. At this point, even best case scenario, Giles either knows we're coming or knows we're here."

Xander glanced over at Buffy and Willow. "Drive by?" he asked.

The two women looked at each other, and in that moment, memories flooded through him of his childhood with Willow, and of the way things had changed after Buffy had come into their lives. Things had been so simple once upon a time, even after they had discovered what really lurked in the shadows of the world. They had been teenagers, then, tangled in emotions and hormones and a belief that they could keep the monsters at bay.

They had failed.

But now, looking at the women his friends had become, at cool, confident Willow with her red hair tied back in an oh-so-serious ponytail, and at edgy, wiry Buffy, her features somehow more beautiful despite the ghosts that seemed to haunt her eyes . . . now Xander believed that it was possible for them to win.

And he was not going to compromise that hope for anyone.

Willow nodded to Buffy.

"We're doing the drive-by, Christopher," Buffy told Lonergan.

"Done," the man replied.

Lonergan put the truck in gear again and floored it. Xander turned to Alex Hotchkiss, an operative he'd trained with when the Council had first set up shop for real in California, and held out his hand.

"Let's knock," he said.

Hotchkiss grinned, then reached under the bench and produced a long plastic cylinder. He uncapped one end and slid out a 66mm M72-A7 disposable antitank weapon. What always amazed Xander about these things was that they looked harmless enough, more like a fat telescope than anything else. Hotchkiss handed it to him and Xander slipped the strap over his shoulder. He sat on the floor of the truck with his back braced against one bench and his feet steady on the floor.

"Five seconds," Lonergan warned. He spoke quickly into the headset to the drivers of the other trucks that were rolling in even now to back them up.

"Gimme a window," Xander snapped.

Yancy and another operative, Darren Abel, scrambled to unhook a set of latches on the wall of the truck. They bracketed—and held in place—a four foot square section of the sidewall. Behind Xander, Buffy and Willow undid a matching set on the other wall. When the latches were open, Hotchkiss shot Xander a look.

"Ready!" Xander shouted.

"Go," Lonergan replied, barely a second later.

The two operatives shoved the unlatched section of wall and it swung out and down, even as Buffy and Willow did the same on the other side. They leaped out of the way. Xander saw guards running toward their transport and the two other trucks that were rolling in. A pair of Draxhall demons lumbered menacingly in front of the doors to City Hall. Xander peered through the M72's sight, saw the elegant granite steps in front of the building, aimed at the Draxhall demons and the huge double doors right in the center of the building's face, and fired.

The four-pound missile roared out of the M72's fat barrel with a hiss like God opening a God-size can of soda after the Devil shook it up. The backfire roared flames out the rear of the barrel through the opening behind him. Xander slammed against the bench and he knew his back would be badly bruised from the force of it.

The front doors of City Hall exploded, shattering the stone frame around them and ripping the Draxhall demons to shreds.

Lonergan kept driving, but he cut the wheel, turning the truck in a hard circle to bring it back around toward the front. Operatives fired their weapons through the now open ports in the truck's walls, and out the back. Several human sentries went down, but the others turned to run.

Xander glanced at Buffy. "Couldn't be helped," he told her. "But at least the others are running."

She nodded grimly.

Then the truck slammed to a stop again.

"Go! Go!" Willow shouted. "Stay together."

They leaped out through the openings in the wall, and through the back, hustling as fast as they could. The other vehicles were also disgorging their troops. At the rear of the truck, Xander turned and shot a last look at Tim Devine.

"Get behind the wheel. Don't let them take the truck. If any of us lives through this, we'll need a ride home."

Devine, resigned to being left behind, nodded grimly.

The sword banged against Buffy's back as she ran up the granite steps. It had worked so well that she was tempted to use it now, but in close quarters with the rest of her team, she did not want to risk it, so instead she clutched a stake in her hand as they ran through the debris of the ruined doors. Then they were inside, leaping over large chunks of stone and shattered wood.

Buffy blinked, her eyes adjusting, and then she saw them. At least twenty vampires were gathered in the huge foyer, and more were scrambling down the stairs and running along distant corridors to join them, to save their master, their king.

Around her, she glimpsed Xander, Willow and Oz, Christopher Lonergan, Yancy and Abel, Hotchkiss and the other members of the squad. More were pouring in behind them. There was a sort of pause, just a tiny moment where time seemed to be suspended, where no one moved.

Buffy glanced at Willow.

"Oz," Willow said.

In an instant of howled pain, Oz transformed. Then the moment broke and the vampires rushed forward and the fight began. The operatives were in close quarters battle. No rifles or assault weapons here. There were crossbows and shotguns and some pistols, and there were stakes.

Oz leaped into the fray first, slashing at two of the vampires before driving one down to the ground and ripping its throat out with a single thrust of his enormous jaws. Buffy cringed when she saw it, for she had a sense that Oz hated what he was. He would use it to help make things right, use it maybe just because Willow asked him and she still had a hold on his heart, but he hated it. Buffy could see why.

Then she was in the thick of things and had no more time for thought. A high side kick drove one of them back, a quick elbow cleared the way, then she staked two in quick succession. Long, filthy claws raked at her back and she dusted a third without even glancing back at it, instinct alone helping her locate its heart.

Around her, the fight raged, dark and savage and throwing dust all about. It clogged Buffy's throat and nostrils and she nearly vomited on the floor as she realized she was breathing vampires.

Yancy died, screaming as a pair of vampires tore into him . . . the scream cut off abruptly when one of them broke his neck. Then Xander was there, dusting Yancy's killers, grim and silent. He wore a crossbow slung over his shoulder on a strap, but for the moment he was using a stake. He liked to get close to them, he had said, to make sure the job got done.

But still the vampires came. There were just too many of them, a building filled with them.

Of course, that was exactly what they had expected.

"Now?" Willow asked.

"Do it," Buffy replied.

With a wave of her hands and a shout in some ancient tongue Buffy could not even identify, Willow cast a spell that set half a dozen vampires near her ablaze. The fire roared up from them and reached the ceiling, and then the ceiling itself started to burn. Fire licked across the wood, raced as if alive to the edges of the ceiling and began to incinerate the walls as well. It was unnaturally fast, a ravenous flame. It was exactly what they wanted.

The vampires continued to fight, but tried to shy away from the fire. They began to cluster near the middle of the room.

As if on cue, the emergency sprinkler system in City Hall turned on, spraying hundreds of jets of water down upon them, just in the massive foyer alone.

Some of the vampires had begun to look frightened of the flames, but now those same leeches laughed and smiled, and the menace came back into their faces. Orange electric fire burned in their eyes, like distant stars in the black abyss of the tattoos they all had across their faces. Once it had been the symbol of Camazotz, but no one knew what had become of the god of bats. Now, though, that symbol was the brand of Giles.

Bloodlust filled the vampires. Power crackled all through them as the water doused the flames. They knew their numbers were greater, knew that they would triumph eventually.

Which was when Christopher Lonergan stepped forward, a crucifix raised in his hand, and began to recite a prayer in Latin. He blessed the water that fell from the sprinklers above.

Blessed it, and made it holy.

Christopher Lonergan was a priest.

The holy water burned the vampires, their skin steaming. They started to scream. All the bravado and power that had been in them a moment ago evaporated and they looked almost foolish with the tattoos across their faces, like children at Halloween.

Some of them tried to run, but the operatives moved in. The vampires shrieked with agony from the water that fell even as Buffy and the rest of the team began to eliminate them, to scythe through them like a field of wheat.

It was a massacre after that.

In that moment, the reason for this attack hit Buffy hard. *Giles,* she thought. In her mind's eye she saw him, a thousand shards of memory, images of him with Jenny Calendar, or in battle, or standing up to the bullying of Quentin Travers. She thought of Giles with his nose stuck in a book, face scrunched up in contemplation, of the glances of half-feigned shock or disapproval he so often shot at Xander or even Buffy herself, and of the way that he had always been able to comfort her, sometimes even without saying a word.

Somewhere in this building, the evil that had usurped her mentor's body lurked, waiting. She had no doubt that the thing that Giles had become would find a way to shield himself from the holy water. But she also knew that it would not run. It wanted her to find it, to find him. It wanted to face her. The very feelings and memories that filled her now, those were the things that Giles relied upon to throw her off-balance.

Buffy spotted Willow and Oz, still a wolf, not far away. She ran to her friend. Oz turned with a snarl, then sniffed at Buffy and was calm.

"Let's go," the Slayer said. "Let's find him now. I want this done with. We'll start in the basement. No windows, so he'd think that was the safest place for him. If I'm wrong, we'll work our way up from there."

Willow nodded, turned to beckon for Xander to come with them.

Then Buffy shouted to Lonergan. "You've got command! Scour the place. Don't leave any of them. We're starting in the basement and we'll catch up when we can."

Lonergan gave her a wave and Buffy nodded in satisfaction as Xander ran over to join them.

"All right. Let's go," she said, then led the way down the corridor toward the stairwell that would take them to the basement.

It was just the four of them—Buffy, Willow, Xander, and Oz—but that was okay. Once upon a time, she could remember having thought that in order for her to be an effective Slayer, she had to learn to operate on her own. But now she realized how foolish that was. *This is the way it's supposed to be. This is right.* The same way that Xander had insisted Devine stay behind, so that no one had to count on someone who might not live up to expectations, that was how she felt now.

She knew she could count on her friends to back her up, no matter what, and no matter how long it had been since they had been in the midst of such anarchy together.

They passed right by the elevator banks. With the fire alarms blaring and the sprinkler system on, chances were the elevators would have opened on the nearest floor and then frozen in keeping with safety regulations.

A red EXIT sign ahead marked the door that led to the basement. Buffy didn't even bother trying the knob. She popped a side kick at the metal door, right beside the knob. Metal shrieked and tore and it banged open.

Buffy led them onto the landing, out of the shower of water from the sprinklers. The stairs were unattractive, concrete and metal. A three-foot number one was painted on the wall. With a quick glance upward, Buffy started down toward the basement. Oz followed right after her, sniffing the air and the stairs as they went. Willow was behind him, and Xander covered their flank. He had the crossbow dangling from a leather strap around his shoulder like a rock star with his favorite guitar, but he let it hang there as he pulled a nine millimeter Glock from its holster at his side.

Not a word was spoken as they descended.

At the bottom of the stairs was another door. A huge letter *B* was painted on the wall, but other than that there were no markings. No guards. Nothing out of the ordinary at all. Buffy paused on the last step, feeling the damp heat of the werewolf's panting breath on her back. Oz sniffed the air several times in quick succession and began to growl low.

Buffy nodded. "I smell it, too," she said.

"What?" Willow asked.

"Don't even know what to call it," Buffy told her. "Static. Like the bug zapper in Xander's backyard."

"Electricity," Willow said, her voice a sort of hush.

"Exactly."

Willow stepped past Oz. Buffy noticed the sorceress's

hand stroking the werewolf's neck gently as she went by him. Willow studied the door for a moment, then glanced over her shoulder at Xander.

"I'm a little tired already," she told him. "Catch me if I fall."

"Always," Xander replied without emotion. It was a simple statement of fact.

"Hey," Buffy said. "I can do it if it's too much—"

"No," Willow said quickly. "We need you in front. Just be ready."

A small smile flickered on Buffy's features. "No such thing. But let's do it anyway."

Willow took a deep breath, sketched in the air with her hands, muttered perhaps four words in what sounded like Greek. Buffy felt a wave of absolute, bone-chilling cold push past her, and she shivered.

The door turned to ice and there was a crackle and pop as the electricity running into and around it shorted out. Willow swayed slightly, but her arm shot out and she leaned against the wall. Buffy grabbed her arm and Xander moved in from behind, but she shook it off after a moment. They were on the landing at the bottom of the stairs now, and Oz moved around them, closer to the door. The werewolf's growling grew louder and more menacing.

"Oz," Buffy said.

The wolf turned, black lips curled back from gleaming teeth. She saw no human intelligence in his eyes, but she knew that he at least partially understood what went on around him.

"Giles is mine," she said.

Then Buffy glanced back at Xander and Willow. Without another word, they both nodded. She took a deep breath, faced the frozen door again, then leaped at it in a high drop kick. The ice shattered into a million tiny shards. The door was gone. They were in.

The basement was dark save for the amber glow of emergency lights on the walls. It was practically a dungeon; not fit for a king. Clearly this was not Giles's lair. There were other corridors that led to this place, other doors on the other side of the vast chamber in the basement, but this was the main room. Once it had undoubtedly been a massive storage area of some kind.

In some ways, it still was.

Half a dozen Kakchiquel sentries, their eyes blazing orange in the darkened room, moved to attack them. But the sentries could not keep them from seeing what lay in the basement.

Bats hung from the pipes that ran all across the ceiling. On the floor beneath them, shackled and chained to iron rungs sunk deep into the concrete, was the god of bats, the demon Camazotz. His green, pocked flesh was obscenely bloated, like a leech that had feasted until it was ready to explode. The demon-god's withered wings were barely visible underneath its grotesque bulk. There were sores on its flesh. Its wide eyes were milky white. Blind. Its tongue slithered over its needle teeth and dry, cracked lips.

Yet Camazotz himself was not the thing that horrified

Buffy the most. For around the swollen, distended demon, seven vampires were latched onto his putrid flesh, sucking at him like newborn kittens, crackling with the energy they siphoned from the captive demon's blood.

Buffy shuddered, stomach convulsing at the sight.

"Now *that* is really gross."

At the sound of her voice, the suckling vampires glanced up, mouths smeared with demon blood. The sentries surrounded them. Camazotz began to cry out in a high, keening, lonely wail that sent a chill through her. *The god of bats,* she thought, *has gone insane.*

And Giles was nowhere to be found.

. . . TO BE CONTINUED

Part Four:

ORIGINAL SINS

CHAPTER 1

"All right. Let's go."

Buffy led the way down the corridor toward the stairwell that would take them to the basement of City Hall. She quivered with an electric awareness of her surroundings. Of all the horrors she had faced in her time as Slayer, it was possible that as a vampire Rupert Giles was the deadliest, not due merely to his cunning, but because Buffy loved him.

It was broad daylight outside, the midmorning sun glaring down upon the town as squads of Council operatives attacked nests of Kakchiquels, the vampires who were loyal to Giles. Communications had been silent with other units for several minutes as the operation unfolded in earnest. Buffy had helped to formulate the plan, so she knew that the nests would be burned where possible and the vampires attacked one-on-one only where necessary. The numbers were against the Council, but the sun gave them the edge they needed.

Or at least that was the hope. Buffy had a feeling that it was going to be a closer fight than any of them had admitted. If she could dust Giles, however, that would be the end of things. Without the vampire they looked to as a king, the Kakchiquels would lose their cohesion and it would be every leech for himself, the way it always was before Giles came along.

When they had stormed City Hall, Willow had used magick to burn some of the Kakchiquels. The flames set off the sprinkler systems on the first floor of the building and Father Christopher Lonergan—who was both a Council operative and a Roman Catholic priest—had spoken the words to the penitential rite, turning the spray into holy water. Vampires had screamed and run but the water was everywhere and it made their flesh bubble and steam and finally disintegrate.

Lonergan was a psi-operative who had a specialized ability to psychically sense the presence of vampires. Now, upstairs, he led the rest of the unit through City Hall in a room by room search, exterminating vampires as they went. They would work their way up, and inform Buffy immediately if Giles was located.

It was just the four of them—Buffy, Willow, Xander, and Oz—but that was okay. Once upon a time, she could remember having thought that in order for her to be an effective Slayer, she had to learn to operate on her own. Now she realized how foolish that was. This was the way it was supposed to be. This was right.

With the fire alarms blaring and the sprinkler system on, they passed right by the elevator banks. A red EXIT sign ahead marked the door that led to the basement. Buffy didn't even bother trying the knob. She popped a side kick at the metal door, right beside the knob. Metal shrieked and tore and it banged open.

With a quick glance upward, Buffy started down toward the basement. Oz followed right after her; the werewolf sniffed the air and the stairs as they went. Willow was behind him, and Xander covered their flank. He had the crossbow dangling from a leather strap around his shoulder, but he let it hang there as he pulled a nine-millimeter Glock from its holster at his side.

At the bottom of the stairs was another door. A huge letter B was painted on the wall, but other than that there were no markings. No guards. Nothing out of the ordinary at all. Buffy paused on the last step, feeling the damp heat of the werewolf's panting breath on her back. Oz sniffed several times in quick succession and began to growl low.

Buffy nodded. "I smell it too," she said.

"What?" Willow asked.

"Don't even know what to call it," Buffy told her. "Static. Like the bug zapper in Xander's backyard."

"Electricity," Willow said, her voice a sort of hush.

"Exactly."

Willow stepped past Oz, studied the door for a moment, then glanced over her shoulder at Xander.

"I'm a little tired already," she told him. "Catch me if I fall."

"Always," Xander replied without emotion. It was a simple statement of fact.

"Hey," Buffy said. "I can do it if it's too much—"

"No," Willow said quickly. "We need you in front. Just be ready."

A small smile flickered on Buffy's features. "No such thing. But let's do it anyway."

Willow took a deep breath, sketched in the air with her hands, and muttered perhaps four words in what sounded like Greek. Buffy felt a wave of absolute, bone-chilling cold push past her, and she shivered.

The door turned to ice and there was a crackle and pop as the electricity running into and around it shorted out. Willow swayed slightly, but her arm shot out and she leaned against the wall. Buffy and Xander both moved to steady her, but she shook it off. Oz moved around them, closer to the door. The werewolf's growling grew louder and more menacing.

"Oz," Buffy said.

The wolf turned, black lips curled back from gleaming teeth. She saw no human intelligence in his eyes, but she knew that he at least partially understood what went on around him.

"Giles is mine," she said.

Then Buffy took a deep breath, faced the frozen door again, and leaped at it in a high drop kick. The ice shattered into a million shards. The door was gone. They were in.

The basement was dark save for the amber glow of emergency lights on the walls. Clearly this was not Giles's lair. There were other corridors that led to this place, doors on the other side of the vast chamber in the basement, but this was the main room. Once it had undoubtedly been a massive storage area of some kind.

In some ways, it still was.

Half a dozen Kakchiquel sentries, their eyes blazing orange in the darkened room, looked up and snarled in alarm as they entered. But the sentries could not keep them from seeing what lay in the basement.

Bats hung from the pipes that ran all across the ceiling. On the floor beneath them, shackled and chained to iron rungs sunk deep in the concrete, was the god of bats, the demon Camazotz. His green, pocked flesh was obscenely bloated, like a leech that had feasted until it was ready to explode. The demon-god's withered wings were barely visible underneath its grotesque bulk. Around the swollen, distended demon, seven vampires were latched onto his putrid flesh, sucking at him like newborn kittens, crackling with the energy they siphoned from the captive demon's blood.

Buffy shuddered, stomach convulsing at the sight. "Now *that* is really gross."

At the sound of her voice, the suckling vampires glanced up, mouths smeared with demon blood. The sentries surrounded them. Camazotz began to cry out in a high, keening, lonely wail that sent a chill through her. The god of bats, she realized, had gone insane.

Xander stepped up beside her. "Giles isn't down here. Let's make this quick."

The vampire sentries rushed at them, eyes blazing, fangs bared.

"You read my mind," Buffy told Xander. A part of her wanted to warn him, to warn all of them, that the demon energy coursing through the Kakchiquels made them stronger and quicker than average vampires, but she thought better of it. They knew, after all. They had been fighting Giles's minions for years.

"You dare?" one of the sentries snarled, fangs bared as he lunged for her.

"Yeah," Buffy replied curtly. "We dare."

She had her sword in a scabbard slung across her back, but did not bother to reach for it. Once she had used that same sword to draw Angel's blood. Only recently, Giles had slipped into the Council headquarters and brought her the sword as a gift, as though daring her to kill him with it. Buffy would use the sword when she had to.

But she did not have to just yet.

She ducked under the vampire's outstretched arms and shot a kick up at his chin. Her heel connected and the impact shook her bones. He staggered, but only barely, and his eyes blazed and sparked even brighter. In an elegant, murderous ballet, Buffy took one step out from in front of him, then whipped her leg around again in another kick that cracked the back of his skull, knocking him forward. She slammed her stake through his back with enough force to separate the bones and push through to the heart. He exploded in a cloud of dust.

"We dare," she whispered to herself.

All around Buffy, her friends moved into action with a fluidity that exhilarated her and shamed her all at once. The four of them moved so well together, and yet she could not help but recall the days when she had attempted to push them out of her life as the Slayer, as if she had suffered from multiple personalities of a sort; as though she could truly separate Buffy from the Slayer. Ironically, it was that very attitude that had led to her present predicament, with the soul of her nineteen-year-old self thrust into the future and now sharing the body of a Buffy who was five years older.

They made her proud now, her friends, so that she could barely imagine going into a major conflict without them at her side.

Willow sketched sigils in the air and snapped off shorthand incantations in ancient tongues with an air of confidence Buffy herself envied. Her red hair was tied back in a long ponytail that swung with every graceful movement. A wave of cold slivered across the room as one of the sentries turned to ice. Another burst into flame, the blaze hungrily licking at his clothes with a low roar of fiery consumption.

The seven vampires who had been suckling at Camazotz's flailing, pustulent body had begun to come out of the daze of contentment they were in. They seemed almost bloated themselves now by the power they had leeched from their former master, now simply their battery. Buffy had always wondered where the demonic energy came from that had enhanced the Kakchiquels, gave them their additional speed and strength and the electric fire in their eyes. Now she had seen firsthand.

The feeders, surfeited upon the power of the god of

bats, thrumming with that dark might, moved to join the sentries in battle against these intruders.

Gunshots punched the air in the basement, and Buffy could feel the subtle changes in air pressure against her skin and her eardrums. The bats hanging from the pipes all along the ceiling shrieked at the loud noise and some of them took flight, but settled again seconds later.

Buffy spun to see Xander firing again and again into a pair of sentries with his Glock. The bullets wouldn't kill them; he was using the gunfire to hurt them, to set them off guard. Then he slid the gun into the oiled leather holster and snatched up the crossbow that hung from the strap across his shoulder.

There was a roar off to Buffy's left and she whipped her head around quickly, expecting an attack. But it was not one of the remaining vampires who thundered with such savagery. It was Oz. He tore the head off a sentry as Buffy watched, bone and flesh ripping with a sickening noise, and then the vampire crumbled into gray soot. The werewolf moved on to the vampires who had been feasting on Camazotz, claws flashing and tearing.

Two of the feeders leaped across the air at her and Buffy dodged. In her life, she had never been in better physical condition. Her muscles rippled as she moved with the deadly precision of a scalpel. With a flurry of blows, she kept them both off-balance for several vital seconds. One of them, a pale blond female, became so enraged that she simply reached out for Buffy's throat.

The Slayer let her come, felt the vampire's grip on her throat, cutting off her air. Buffy smiled as she slid the stake between the Kakchiquel's ribs, its glowing eyes going wide as it felt the penetration. Then it was dust.

The other, a copper-skinned bald man, got a handful of her hair and yanked. Buffy did not fight his strength, but used the momentum. As he hauled her backward and down, she bent farther and flipped into an aerial somersault. In his surprise, he let go, but not before his hold on her hair tugged painfully at her scalp and it began to bleed. He held strands of her hair in his hand as Buffy landed on the concrete floor behind him.

The bald vampire turned toward her, a bewildered expression on his face, and Buffy struck him twice in the face in quick succession, batted his arms out of the way, and then rammed the stake through his rib cage and into his heart. When he burst into a tiny whirlwind of cinder and ash, there was an audible pop, as though all the energy he had sucked from Camazotz had suddenly been released.

When she turned again, crouched in a battle stance, she saw Xander fire a bolt from the crossbow. It struck home and the leech was dusted. The other was nowhere in sight, and Buffy had to assume Xander had gotten them both.

The sounds of their combat seemed to resonate there in the basement, but they were like an echo now. Buffy sensed that it was almost over. Prepared to slay the remaining few vampires opposing them, she turned to see that Oz and Willow had cornered two Kakchiquels who cowered behind the corpulent, writhing form of Camazotz. The demon-god was chained to the floor and he alternated between a catlike mewling and a sinister snicker that made Buffy wonder if he was not quite so unhinged as she had imagined.

Oz leaped over the captive demon and upon one of the Kakchiquels, a huge claw slashing right through the bat-shaped brand on its face as the werewolf drove it to the ground.

Willow faced the other, lifting her hands, her clothes rustled by an invisible wind that often accompanied her sorcery these days.

Buffy began to relax and to think ahead to their next step, linking up with Lonergan and the others again in the continued search for Giles. She began to turn toward Xander to tell him to contact Lonergan on the headset he wore.

An alarm went off in her head, spurring her to glance quickly back at Willow. The final Kakchiquel feeder ran along beside Camazotz, probably hoping to use him as cover from the sorceress's magick. Willow seemed to carve the air with her fingers, beginning an incantation.

Buffy saw what was about to happen and cried out, but too late.

The vampire leaped over Camazotz's massive arm.

Willow cast her spell.

It missed the Kakchiquel and instead struck the huge, iron chain that bound Camazotz's right arm to the concrete floor. The heavy chain turned to ice and the demon-god uttered a wet, soul-searing laugh as the ice shattered. With one hand unleashed, the demon began to sit up, tearing at the chains, struggling to free himself.

"Damn it," Buffy muttered. "We *so* do not have time for this."

The Bronze was in ruins. Explosives had blown in the entire outer wall, scattering debris and concrete dust all over the floor and crushing one end of the stage. With the wall shattered, the sunlight had streamed in and incinerated seven or eight vampires quickly enough that Anna Kuei, the Slayer, had not been able to get an accurate head count. It was a comparatively small nest, but there were other Kakchiquels scattered throughout the building, in the kitchen and in storage and office areas.

Or there had been.

Now she crawled out from beneath the shabbily constructed stage and wiped blood from her eyes. When she glanced up, she saw Wesley moving across the floor with his old repeating crossbow in his hands. Other Council operatives moved about the wreckage, searching behind the bar and under toppled tables. Wesley spotted her and an expression of intense relief washed across his bearded features.

"Oh, Anna," Wesley said, hurrying toward her. "When I didn't see you out here . . ." His words trailed off as he focused on the cut across her forehead.

"You thought I was dead?"

He cast a sheepish glance at his feet. "I confess I feared the worst."

A shudder went through the young Slayer. *Does that mean you have no faith in me?* she thought, but she did not dare to ask aloud. Anna dreaded the answer. For all his sometimes amusing mannerisms, Wesley was a skilled combatant and a brilliant strategist with a knowledge of the supernatural that was nothing short of extraordinary. He was not merely *the* Watcher, but had briefly been Watcher to both the Lost Slayer, Buffy Summers, and to Faith, the Prodigal.

Faith. Just the thought of her caused a tumult of emotions to swirl in Anna's heart; warm memories, grim dignity, and despair. The older Slayer had never hidden her past. But when Sunnydale had fallen the Prodigal had returned to the fold and selflessly thrown herself into the effort against the Kakchiquels. Faith had been the bravest person Anna had ever met, and though she had teased him, it had always been obvious that Faith had respected Wesley Wyndam-Pryce.

"Anna?" Wesley prodded now, brow furrowed with concern. He touched at the cut on her forehead and she hissed. "Are you sure you're all right? Do you feel at all disoriented?"

"No," she said quickly. "Sorry. I'm all right. I just . . ." she gestured toward the stage. "I heard something moving in the dark beneath the stage. Once I was down under there, it was easy . . . well, their eyes gave them away. But there wasn't a lot of room and for a second I thought they had me."

Wesley did not smile or try to comfort her with platitudes. That was not his way. Instead, he gave an approving nod and clapped her on the shoulder. "But you're standing right here. Well done, Anna."

The young Slayer slid her stake into the leather sheath on her hip. The other operatives in their unit were still exploring every dark corner and shadow of the remains of the club and she picked her way toward the back to offer what help she could. It helped to turn her mind to things other than death and combat and evil.

For all her training, Anna had almost no experience in the field. The four vampires she had dusted in the past five minutes were more than she had ever previously seen in one place at one time, and here she found herself smack in the center of what some of the Council operatives had referred to as the biggest anti-vampire operation in centuries. Though she would never let Wesley see it in her, Anna was frightened.

But Faith had believed in her. Wesley believed in her.

And Anna Kuei was not going to let them down.

In the balcony that overlooked the main floor of the club, something rustled in the dark. A pair of operatives had already been up there, but Anna knew what she had heard. The hush of clothes moving, someone shifting in a hiding place, the belly of a snake across hard-packed desert.

Her body tensed, muscles coiling. Her gaze ticked toward the stairs and she slipped her stake out of its sheath again. Quiet descended upon the Bronze as the Watcher and the Council operatives noticed her stealthy movements.

"Anna?" Wesley said.

The Slayer went to the bottom of the stairs. She heard the sound again, some dark creature huddling beneath a table perhaps, clinging to the remaining shadows, the threat of the sun far too close.

"Come down," Anna said, her voice hard and cold, though her every nerve seemed to prickle with a combination of fear and exhilaration.

With a bang, a table up on the balcony seating area toppled over. A dark figure rose, whipped a dusty tablecloth around its shoulders, stepped onto a chair and then the balcony railing, and leaped out over the concrete debris-strewn floor of the Bronze.

The vampire, tablecloth over his head, landed in a crouch in the sunlight. Wesley fired a bolt from his repeater crossbow but it went wide. The target was in motion. A Council operative took a few shots at it with a pistol and the vampire grunted in pain as one of the bullets tore through its shoulder. But all the gunshot really did was add to the vampire's momentum as it careened across the rubble for the outside, trying desperately to get away from them.

Anna sprinted across the floor, leaped onto a table and then jumped up into a flying drop kick that cracked into the back of the runner's skull. The Kakchiquel was driven forward, lost his balance and sprawled through the huge opening that had been blown in the wall to land on the sidewalk in front of the Bronze.

In the sun.

The vampire tried to curl up under the tablecloth but one of his legs was already on fire. Groaning, the creature struggled to rise.

Anna tore the tablecloth from its head. The vampire

snarled, fangs bared in blind fear and rage, the sun gleaming off the perfect black of the bat-shaped brand around his eyes. He burst into flame, fire rushing all over his clothes, his hair roaring like an oil-soaked torch. The fire consumed him, and the vampire burst into a small explosion of cinder and ash, like confetti raining down on New Year's Eve.

For a moment she stared at the ash that fell, there in the sun, with the wind swirling it along the sidewalk, carrying the remains of the creature away. Anna shivered. This was her sole purpose, the slaying of vampires and other creatures of the night. But it was a hideous thing to see.

Footsteps crunched the rubble and she turned to see Wesley approaching. He had donned a communications headset.

"Yes, Ms. Haversham. We'll be right along," he was saying. Then he glanced up at her. "I think we're through here, Anna, don't you?"

The other operatives had begun to spread out to the buildings on either side of the Bronze. The mission parameters called for them to check adjunct buildings for any annexes to the main nest. But she had a feeling they'd taken care of the real trouble, so she nodded at Wesley.

"Ms. Haversham has informed me that the unit at the Hotel Pacifica has run into some difficulty. The rest of our squad is to continue on to their next objective, but the group at the Pacifica would appreciate our aid."

Anna's heart was still racing from the thrill and chaos and utter terror of what she had just been through. But she had to confess to herself that, in a way, she liked that feeling.

"Let's go," she said.

Together they climbed into one of the Humvees the unit had at its disposal. Its engine rumbled and the vehicle shook her so that she could feel its power in her bones. On the way to the industrial park north of town, Wesley updated her on communications that were coming over his headset. It seemed that of the five units deployed, two had already moved on to their second targets. Their own unit was soon to do the same. But there were two—one at the new high school, and the one at the Hotel Pacifica—that had encountered great resistance at their initial target locations.

Just words, until they pulled into the parking lot at the Pacifica. The property around the hotel was all lawn, with a broad parking lot in front. The structure itself had a Spanish influence like so many older buildings in the area, but this was a five-story stucco monstrosity painted a pastel tangerine. By all rights, it ought to have been abandoned ages ago, but according to Wesley, it had been in operation right up until the vampires had occupied Sunnydale. From Anna's perspective, it was the sort of place frequented by tourists who could not afford a place right on the ocean, two-bit sci-fi conventions, and real estate salesmen who snuck off for a few hours twice a week with their secretaries.

Not anymore.

Now the only guests at the hotel were vampires.

An enormous hole had been blown around its main entrance, a gray Humvee jammed half in and half out of that hole, its body a burned out husk, still smoking. Several of the white sunsuits the vampires wore during the day lay on the pavement, fluttering empty in the breeze, their owners dusted.

The unit of Council operatives was nowhere to be seen, save for a man and woman who stood behind a green troop carrier, shouting into their headsets.

Wesley drove toward them, and they looked up gratefully as the Humvee came to a lumbering stop nearby. Anna jumped out, Wesley only steps behind her, and ran to the pair. The woman was Terri Blum, but Anna did not recognize the man.

"What happened?" Anna asked quickly.

The man glanced at her and Terri turned to him. "The Slayer," she said.

"Thank God." He heaved a sigh of relief as he studied Anna and Wesley. "Here's our situation. The population of the nest was much higher than estimated and it looks like they were expecting us. They're spread out all through the hotel, but their numbers are much greater than ours. My unit is in there but we've already suffered at least three fatalities, possibly more."

All three of them stared at her. After a moment, Anna met Wesley's gaze. The last thing she wanted to do was go into that building; she did not even want to look at it. But in the back of her mind she envisioned the men and women who were searching the darkness within for vampires, imagined the glowing eyes of the two

Kakchiquels under the stage at the Bronze, and she knew she had to go.

"All right," she said. Then she spun and started for the front of the garishly painted hotel. After a moment, she glanced back at Wesley. "You coming?"

He smiled. "Wouldn't miss it."

CHAPTER 2

Chains snapped, and Camazotz was free.

For a single moment, silence descended upon that dank basement, a quiet interrupted only by the rattling wheeze from the demon-god's throat and the drip of moisture from the pipes that ran along the ceiling of the basement. The tiny sound drew Buffy's attention and she glanced up at the pipes. Dozens, perhaps hundreds of small bats still hung from the metal shafts or clung there, wet charcoal bodies almost blending.

Buffy had almost forgotten the bats. While she and her friends had slain the vampires around Camazotz, the flying rodents had barely stirred. Now, though, they began to emit tiny squeaks, disturbed by the demon's motion and anger. Camazotz was, after all, the god of bats.

"You!" the demon thundered, his voice thick and grating.

417

Though it seemed impossible, Camazotz was not merely more obese than the last time she had seen him, the demon was simply bigger. The basement ceiling was perhaps fourteen feet and Camazotz fell short of striking his head on the pipes by no more than two. His head sagged forward on his shoulders, lips open in a kind of eternal slur, yellow drool sliding over the needle-like fangs in his mouth.

According to what Buffy had learned from Willow and the other Council operatives, the god of bats had made a terrible mistake when he had one of his Kakchiquels make Giles into a vampire. Camazotz had fed his vampire servants on his own blood and it had charged them with a horrible, demonic energy, enhanced them and made them deadlier than their brethren. But given what they had discovered in the basement, it now appeared that once Giles took control, Camazotz had been made into little more than a battery, a thing to be worshiped for the sake of the power he provided, a horrible dark communion of which all Kakchiquels shared.

There was no way to know how long ago Giles had locked Camazotz in this basement, but the shambling, rotting creature seemed a pitiful, lunatic caricature of his former self. The demon moved only a few steps from the spot where he had been chained. The last survivor of the vampires who had been feeding from him when they came into the basement slunk back into the shadows behind him, but Camazotz paid no attention to him. Nor did the demon appear to notice

Willow and Oz, who were only a few feet in front of him.

"Willow, Oz, get back." Buffy motioned for them to come to her and Willow complied immediately, backing away from the demon. The werewolf snarled low and sniffed as if taking Camazotz's measure by scent alone. Then Oz turned his snout away, the awful stench of the moldering flesh of the demon-god driving him back. The wolf trotted over behind Buffy and Willow, and a moment later, Xander joined them.

Camazotz moved slowly, almost staggering. His rheumy eyes glared down at them, but Buffy suspected he barely saw the others.

"You . . ." the demon-god said again, slobber spilling from his lips. "Slayer. Look what you have done to me. I came to these shores to retrieve my wife and your interference led to this. If not for you . . . Zotzilaha would not have had a host powerful enough to resist me. I might have torn her away and kept her with me . . . and punished her appropriately. But with your body as host . . . my only choice was to destroy her!"

Buffy stiffened, reached behind her and drew the sword from the scabbard across her back. "Blah, blah, blah . . . Willow already told me the whole sad story. How you killed your wife . . . twice! And that's somehow *my* fault?"

With her sword brandished before her, in a standoff with the hideous beast, Buffy laughed softly in disbelief.

"I don't think so."

Camazotz began to shriek in a high pitch that drove like nails into Buffy's eardrums, and the demon-god rose up to his full height and started to shake. As an answer to his shriek, the bats on the ceiling began to cry out in return. They fluttered down into the basement in a black cloud of rustling wings and sharp talons, swarming around Buffy and her friends, ripping at their faces and arms as they tried to defend themselves.

With her sword, Buffy rushed at Camazotz, whose eyes crackled with sorcerous energy. Buffy brought the blade around in a low arc that slashed a gaping wound across the demon-god's gut. Blood and noxious bile spilled out onto the floor.

Willow and Xander struggled with the bats, but Oz batted them away, ignored them, and joined the fray. Oz growled as he leaped up onto the god of bats and began to tear at his face. One of the pointed ears on the demon's head was ripped off as the werewolf dug deep furrows into the rotting monster's scalp.

Camazotz cried out in pain and hauled Oz off him, then tossed the werewolf across the room. Buffy swung the sword around her head again and was about to slash the blade down when Camazotz pointed at her and orange, fiery energy lanced across the few feet that separated them. It cut into Buffy and she shouted in pain, riveted in place. She began to shudder with the pain of it coursing through her.

With a roar of agony, she pushed toward him, feeling as though hurricane winds were buffeting her to keep her away. Still she went on. Arms heavy with the effort and exhausted from the bone-deep pain, she brought the blade up and cut off his clawed hand.

"There you go," she said through gritted teeth. "Another stump to go with those stubby little wings."

Camazotz only grunted.

Buffy drove the sword into him and began to cut upward. But even as she did so, she noticed that the first gash she had opened in his torso had begun to close.

"What does it take to kill you?" she yelled.

"Buffy!" Willow called. "Get back!"

The Slayer did not turn, but neither did she hesitate. Once upon a time, despite her love for her friend, she would have wanted to know Willow's plan. But she knew now that that was a mistake. She trusted Willow completely, and it had nothing to do with the authority and confidence in her voice.

Camazotz reached for the Slayer with his remaining hand, fingers crackling with power. Buffy dodged, then backed quickly away, sword held high in front of her.

Gunfire erupted nearby and a quartet of holes were punched into Camazotz's chest. *Xander,* Buffy thought. Across the basement, Oz growled low and dangerous and started toward the demon again.

"Oz, wait!" Willow commanded.

The werewolf froze at her order, yellow eyes on Camazotz.

When Buffy had moved back beside Willow, she

glanced at the sorceress and saw that she held Xander's crossbow in her hands. All around them on the floor were the charred or battered remains of bats. Some of them still squealed and dove at Xander, who was bleeding from multiple tiny wounds, but he easily knocked them away as he took aim at Camazotz again.

"I've got it, Xand," Willow said. "Camazotz is hard to kill, but he has a weakness. It took me a few years, but don't let anyone ever say I don't do my homework."

"What is it?" Buffy asked.

Willow smiled grimly. "Ever wonder why all those ancient civilizations made so many things out of gold?"

With that, she grimaced as though in pain, laid a finger on the bolt nocked in the crossbow, and whispered a spell in what sounded like French to Buffy. The crossbow bolt turned to gold.

"Alchemy," Willow explained as she raised the crossbow and took aim. "The secret is, it only works if you're not using it for personal gain."

Xander shot a bat and it spun away in bloody pieces. "Well, that sucks," he said. "Who made that rule?"

Camazotz screamed furiously and shambled toward them, entire body now crackling with demonic energy. Buffy raised the sword again, but she need not have worried. Willow fired the crossbow and the golden bolt pierced the demon-god's blistered hide in the middle of his chest.

Anna had dust in her eyes.

She did not allow herself to consider that it was the

remains of vampires, of walking corpses, as she brushed at her face and shook the ash out of her hair. The Hotel Pacifica had seemed deserted at first but the instant they entered the stairwell she and Wesley had been attacked by a pair of vampires. For a moment, as she drove one of them down on the stairs with stake in hand, and the other leaped upon her back and yanked at her spiked, pink hair, she had thought it was over for her. In her mind, she had already begun to apologize to the people she felt she would be letting down.

Then Wesley had fired a bolt from his repeating crossbow, and dusted the vamp on her back. A second later she rammed her stake through the heart of the one beneath her on the stairs, and it was done. Anna cursed herself for having allowed her mind to accept defeat so readily.

"Are you all right?" Wesley whispered, his gaze darting about, alert for any further sign of attack.

Anna nodded. She steeled herself and continued upward, with Wesley following close behind. The design of the building's interior was modern and at the second floor the landing opened to a wide, carpeted hall with contemporary art decorating the walls. The corridor was littered with the bodies of the dead.

"Dear God," Wesley whispered behind her.

As they passed the elevator, Anna paused. Voices, shouting from upstairs. The sounds of battle.

"Listen," she told Wesley.

He paused, put his ear to the elevator doors, then his eyes narrowed. "Top floor. Mission schematics indicated a ballroom up there."

Anna punched the Up button. Moments later there was a small ding and the doors slid open. They were both prepared for an attack from within but the elevator was empty. As they stepped in and Wesley pressed the button for the fifth floor, the noises from above grew louder.

"If they notice the elevator coming up?" she asked him.

Third floor.

Wesley slid his headset firmly into place, ready to relay their situation back to the unit commander outside, or to Ms. Haversham at their ops center. He did not answer her, but rather pressed his back against the wall of the elevator as it whirred upward, and lifted the repeating crossbow. Anna saw that there were only four bolts left in it.

Fourth floor.

Soft music poured from speakers above their heads.

Fifth floor.

With another pinging noise, the doors slid open on chaos. In a single glance, she took it all in: three more operatives dead or downed on the fancy carpet, probably twenty or more vampires under the faceted light from the chandelier, seven Council operatives cornered on the far side of the room, axes and crossbows and guns in their hands.

Flamethrowers, she thought. *Where are the . . .*

Then it hit her. One of the dead men downstairs had had an extinguished flamethrower on his back. In the epicenter of the ballroom lay the second of the men in this unit equipped with one, also dead.

"Wesley, the flamethrower," Anna whispered.

As she and Wesley stepped surreptitiously off the elevator, surviving operatives leaped at the vampires, axes falling, hacking. A crossbow bolt whistled into the cluster of vampires and one of them dusted. Someone threw a glass vial of holy water and it burned those it touched, but none severely enough to destroy them.

Anna studied the room quickly, and saw that the wall to her right had once been almost entirely glass. There were boards covering most of the wall now, but in the center was a glass door that had been painted black.

Anna rushed the nearest vampire from behind. Though she was far shorter than he was, she leaped up onto his back and wrapped her legs around him. With a fistful of his hair, she yanked his head back and he fell with her still riding him. He landed on top of her even as Anna reached around in front of him and thrust the stake through his chest.

He dusted, but she was on the floor.

They came at her then, five or six, she could not count. In the false glimmer of the chandelier above, their eyes flickered with unearthly energy. As one, they leered at her, fangs bared, the brands seared across their faces stealing away their individual identity and making them all the more hellishly terrifying for it.

Bracing herself on the ground, Anna swung her foot up into a kick that shattered teeth and sent one of them spitting blood. She tried to spin away from the others but they were on her, hands in her hair and all over her body. One of them slammed her face into the ground and she was dazed despite the carpet.

When she glanced up, she saw Wesley. He had the flamethrower and let loose with a stream of liquid fire as they ran at him. Two of them were set ablaze and ran screaming toward the stairs over near the elevator before bursting into twin puffs of smoke and embers.

As she attempted to shake herself free, she saw a Kakchiquel grab Wesley from behind and sink his teeth into her Watcher's throat. Blood spilled down Wesley's neck, staining his collar. His eyes were squeezed closed, but not the vampire's. The monster's blazing eyes were wide open and staring right at her.

"No," she whispered.

The silent killers turned her over. One of them, an Asian female who had been young when she was bitten, was a mirror image of Anna herself. Nothing had ever unnerved her quite so much as that.

"No!" she screamed.

With every ounce of energy in her, she swung her left hand up into a bone-crunching blow that shattered ribs in the vampire girl's chest and knocked her back. They were still all over her, but Anna was fearless now, with nothing left to lose. She twisted her legs, grabbed up another vamp in front of her in a scissors move and then toppled him into a third.

A massive Kakchiquel with a build and features that made her think of a troll grabbed her by the shoulders and tried to drive her back down. Anna shoved her hand into his mouth, the skin of her palm and fingers tearing on his fangs, and she yanked down hard, cracking his jaw.

Then somehow she was up and away from them, whirling and ready for them, and the Kakchiquels hesitated, giving her a wide berth. The operatives shouted for her, even as they hacked at their own attackers. Two crossbow bolts cut across the room but only one found its mark, and the odds were still against them. Only four operatives were left alive now, not including herself and . . .

"Wesley!"

Anna cried his name and turned to see him sagging in the arms of his attacker. His killer.

No. Not his killer. On the floor five feet away was the corpse of an operative, a shotgun clutched in his dead hands. She ran to the dead man, shot an elbow into the face of a vampire who tried to stop her, picked up the weapon and turned it toward the blacked-out glass door on the other side of the room.

Anna fired and the glass exploded and sunlight streamed in. Its reach was only enough to touch three of the vampires who stood near it, but that was enough for her in that moment. They shouted in agony and began to burn, then scuttled into the shaded parts of the room.

The light also fell on Wesley and the leech attached to him. The vampire grunted and then reluctantly let him fall to the ground, its face charring as it retreated.

Anna ran to her Watcher, crouched over him and felt for a pulse. He was still alive, but she did not know for how long.

Anna glanced around the room again. No one moved. For a moment it was a stalemate, though the Kakchiquels still outnumbered them four or five to one. At length, the troll-face whose jaw she had broken began to hum, low and guttural, like some ritual chant of ancient days, and all the others joined in. The demon magick in their eyes glowed brighter and a sinister calm fell over them; they began to close in.

The Slayer looked down at Wesley, so pale, eyes fluttering under his cracked glasses, and a stillness touched her own heart as well. She stood and faced the leeches, her only weapon herself. The anxiety and fear she had been battling all along dissipated and a certainty grew in her. Anna Kuei was the Slayer, and she was not going to let anyone else die here today.

"Come on, then. Try me."

Their chanting continued and Troll Face even laughed, eyes glowing with magick and menace.

Then the spark went out of his eyes. He grunted and blinked in surprise as the orange glow faded completely. Anna flinched, then looked quickly around to see that all of the Kakchiquels were reacting in shock as they felt the energy leave them, their eyes returning to normal.

The chant died.

Anna smiled. It seemed that whatever had given the Kakchiquels their enhanced strength was gone now.

"Well, this is interesting," she said, standing astride

Wesley. She glanced over at the four surviving Council operatives. The panic in their faces had been replaced by anger and a dark satisfaction. They hefted their weapons and began to move in. Crossbow bolts struck two of the vampires and they disintegrated.

The young Slayer moved toward the others, who had clustered together. The vampires stared at her. With the black tattoos across their eyes all she could think of was a pack of raccoons caught raiding trash cans.

"Don't let any of them leave," Anna told the operatives.

"No problem," one of them, Tom Canty, replied grimly.

The vampires broke and ran and the operatives went after them, Canty shouting into his headset commlink the news that the Kakchiquels had lost the additional power that gave them their edge. The tide had turned. Anna lifted Wesley, put him over her shoulder the way a fireman would have, and ran out after them. Amidst the carnage, she started down the stairs. As she reached the second floor, Anna felt him stir.

"What happened?" Wesley croaked weakly.

"I don't know. Whatever enhanced them, it's gone."

"Do you think we could stop for a Pepsi?" he asked.

Anna laughed as she walked down the stairs toward the first floor, shifting his weight on her shoulder. "I'm taking you to a hospital. I thought you were half dead."

"Certainly not," he protested. "And while I appreciate the concern, you can put me down now."

She set him down, but his legs were weak and he had to lean on her.

"Thanks to you, Anna, the ruffian did not have the

time to drain very much blood from me. Certainly not more than the Red Cross would have. But, you see, I always faint when I give blood. When I come around, I get a Pepsi and a cookie, and I feel much better."

With his arm slung around her, Anna navigated them both around the Humvee and the rubble that blocked the main exit and then they were outside in the sun. She cast him a dubious sidelong glance.

"You want a cookie?"

Wesley smiled, his eyes bright with amusement. "If it wouldn't be too much trouble."

Camazotz died.

With a single gasp of fetid breath, the god of bats rolled his eyes upward and fell back with an impact that shook the floor. A moment later, his flesh began to boil and run as though it had been doused in acid. Then his body collapsed into a pool of mucus, dark energy crackling in it, sizzling, and then dying out.

"Take your time, Willow," Xander muttered. "You couldn't have done that when we came in?"

"Well," the sorceress replied defensively. "He seemed pretty helpless until, okay, the bats."

"And the homicidal demon rage," Buffy added.

"And that," Willow agreed.

Something shifted in the shadows of the far corner, and only then did Buffy remember that there was still a Kakchiquel left alive. Its glittering eyes gave it away. It stared at them, the bat tattoo on its face gleaming black in the dimly lit room.

The vampire tried to slip along the far wall, moving toward the exit.

Oz had taken human form again, though there was still something feral about him. He approached the rest of the group, a dubious expression on his face. "Does he think we don't see him?"

"I've got him," Buffy replied. "We've wasted too much time already."

She started for him, putting her sword back into its scabbard and pulling out the stake. The vampire began to hiss. Then the filthy orange light flickering in his eyes simply died. Stunned, the vampire blinked several times, and glanced over at the exit again.

"You'll never make it," Xander told him.

Buffy saw in the undead thing's eyes that he knew he was trapped. To his credit, he did not try to run. Instead, he lunged at her. Even without the power leeched from Camazotz, he was fast; fast enough to get a grip on her throat before she staked him.

The ash showered down onto the floor, but Buffy had turned back to her friends before the last of it touched the concrete. Oz stood by Willow as though he were some innocent bystander, completely distanced from the savagery of moments before. His oversize tunic hung on him even larger than before, stretched out as it was, and he had his hands in his pockets as though he were bored. Xander had his sidearm out and was popping a fresh clip of ammunition into it.

As Buffy walked toward them, Willow watched her expectantly.

"You're quite the witch," Buffy told her.

A coy smile flickered across Willow's features. "That I am."

With Buffy in the lead, they headed out the door and into the stairwell. The stink from the remains of the demon-god was nauseating and did not go away as they started up and away from the basement. On the first floor, they stopped briefly and moved out into the main corridor. The alarms had stopped and the sprinklers had been shut off. A pair of Council operatives had been left behind as sentries in the fire-blasted main foyer. But they were alone. The rest of the floor had been cleared.

"I wonder if there's a way to set off all the sprinklers in the building at once," Buffy wondered aloud.

"We checked the schematics," Willow replied. "The system isn't set up that way."

"Giles has probably killed the water to the whole building by now anyway," Xander said. "Just in case."

Buffy nodded slowly. Of course Giles had shut the water main off. Or, more likely, had someone else do it. Though her stomach tightened uncomfortably every time she thought of him that way, she knew the monster was still as cunning as her Watcher had been in life. The first floor was clear. They had eliminated a lot of opposition already. But it would be foolish to think that they had the upper hand.

"Check in," she told Xander.

He tapped a button on the side of the headset he wore. "Lonergan, this is Harris. We've swept the basement, fourteen hostiles no longer our concern. One of them was Camazotz."

Buffy could not hear Lonergan's response, but Xander frowned deeply as he spoke.

"Will do," Xander said. "We'll rendezvous with you there." He glanced up at Buffy, Willow and Oz. "Let's go."

It was Xander's turn to lead now, as they headed back into the stairwell and started up at a steady jog.

"They're just hitting the fourth floor," Xander said. "A few stragglers dusted, no losses from our camp, but no sign of Giles or any large contingent of Kakchiquels. The mayor's office is empty. Lonergan's sixth sense is still picking up vampire presence up there, but now he's getting something else, a kind of static, to the south. We'll hook up with them on the fourth floor, complete the sweep, then investigate whatever's blocking him.

"Oh, and looks like the little power drain the vamps are experiencing now that Camazotz is dead is spreading. The last few they dusted had no light in their eyes, and word is coming in from some of the other units. The same thing's happening all over town."

Willow grinned. "Chain reaction. If they're all just ordinary vamps now, our job is practically done."

"No," Buffy said grimly. "Not yet."

They had passed the second floor landing and were halfway to the third when a low growl came from behind them. Buffy turned to see that Oz had begun to change again. This time, however, he did not change all the way. He was hunched over, his face still recognizable despite the fur covering it, his hands curled into claws.

"Oz, what is it?" Willow asked, her voice clipped and heavy with authority.

His words were a guttural snarl. "Caught a familiar scent. Wasn't sure what it was at first. Now I am."

"What is it?" Buffy asked.

Oz stared at her a moment. Then he sniffed the air again.

"It's Angel."

CHAPTER 3

The Humvee rumbled through the streets of Sunnydale and Anna thought of all the times she had turned on the news and seen footage from urban war zones. With her hands tight on the wheel, she could not help but glance around as she drove. On the horizon, above the town, she saw three pillars of black smoke trailing up and away from locations where operatives were burning out vampire nests. She spotted a couple of demons packing some bags in an old Thunderbird, obviously clearing out of town before the Council took complete control. *A good sign,* Anna thought.

"You really have done quite well today," Wesley said happily, between cookies.

They had found a convenience store whose owner had remained in business by cooperating with the Kakchiquels. He had locked the door and hidden inside, but after a few minutes of knocking, he had reluctantly opened the door. The man had not asked a single question nor said a word to them and when Wesley had tried to pay for his Pepsi and a bag of Oreos, the man had waved them away.

"Just get them. Wipe the vermin out."

It had surprised Anna to hear those words. This man was what she would call a collaborator, but the more she thought about it the more she realized that he would have lost everything if he had closed his business down. And without people who were willing to cooperate with the vampires, those who were truly prisoners, living in fear, would have starved to death.

"We're working on it," Wesley had told the man.

Now he had the small bag of Oreos on the seat beside him and was munching away contentedly. As she took a turn past Hammersmith Park, Anna glanced at him.

"I was terrified," she confessed, her voice small.

"You'd never have known it," he said firmly. "Truly. You were magnificent. Faith would have been very proud."

A warm feeling rushed through Anna and she beamed. She was about to respond when Wesley held up a finger and bent forward slightly. A low buzz came from his headset, and Wesley nodded as he listened to whatever message was coming through.

"Yes, of course. Excellent. We're on our way," he said.

"On our way where?" she asked.

Wesley slid the headset down to rest around his neck and grinned at her. He still seemed a bit weak, but his color was coming back. Anna figured Oreos just sort of had a magick all their own.

"Our original unit has their second nest under control. Ms. Haversham has asked us to proceed to City Hall to aid with efforts there," her Watcher explained with great satisfaction. "So it appears we're needed after all."

In the pool of light spilling in from the shattered window at the end of a fourth-floor corridor, Father Christopher Lonergan stood as still as he was able and reached his mind out. He could feel that there were more of them, but while their dark intentions usually gave them away, he sensed only two or three individual vampires still in the building. In the courthouse, however, well, that was another story. It had taken him some few minutes to orient himself, but when he did he realized that there was a kind of psychic screen blocking him from sensing anything in the adjacent building. That was the source of the static he felt.

Giles was hiding, which meant that he *knew* Lonergan was with this unit. It seemed the king of the vampires had his own spies. The thought was chilling.

"Right, then," he called gruffly. "Nothing else up here. All of you with me now."

With Harris, Rosenberg, Osborne and the Slayer off on some quest of their own, Lonergan's unit was comprised of some fifteen operatives, ten men and five women. Minutes before, as the unit spread out to sweep the fourth floor, Harris had contacted him on the commlink again and announced that their little squadron would be delayed. Lonergan wanted more details, of course, but neither Harris nor Rosenberg was willing to provide any. They promised to be along just as soon as they were available. The priest did not like it. What was the point of having the Slayer along, not to mention a werewolf and a witch, if you could not take advantage of their abilities?

Now, alert to any possibility of attack, Lonergan led his unit down the stairs. He carried a metal crossbow with a pistol grip. He had modified the contemporary weapon so that it would fire wooden bolts, rather than trust the antique weapons that many other operatives and Watchers favored. He also wore a heavy two-headed battleax across his back in a leather case.

Then there were the guns. All of the men wore them, but Lonergan had not needed to use a side arm as yet. More useful was the flamethrower Hotchkiss wore on his back, its mouth sputtering as though in anticipation.

On the second floor, they spread out across the corridor, all eyes on Lonergan. He raised a hand and they all froze, waiting for another instruction. Though it was only a faint trace, he sensed a vampire not far away, along the corridor that led west. With nothing but static anywhere else, it was tempting to head in that direction, but reason dictated that such a weak presence could not be Giles.

Suddenly, the priest saw movement back the way they had come, two figures emerging from the open stairwell. Adrenaline surged through him as questions raced through his mind; how had the vampires gotten so close without him sensing them?

"Down!" he shouted as he raised his crossbow.

The operatives in the path of his shot dropped and rolled quickly, coming up again ready for a fight. Others who were not in the line of fire took aim with their weapons, some unholstering pistols, more than one leveling a shotgun.

Lonergan sighted along the length of the crossbow and his finger tightened on the trigger. Then he saw the face in his sights: Wesley Wyndam-Pryce. The Watcher held his hands up as though he were being robbed, his antique repeater crossbow aimed at the ceiling. Behind him stood the Slayer, Anna Kuei. A momentary expression of alarm traveled across her face and then was replaced by a relieved smile.

"Wesley," the priest said tiredly. "Next time, y'might want to give us a shout before you pop your head 'round the corner."

"Yes, well, we thought it best to be as quiet as possible. I was just about to try to contact you by commlink when we heard your lot moving around up here. Like a pack of elephants, really. So much for stealth."

The insult rankled Lonergan and he was about to snap off a nasty retort when he spotted the raw puncture wounds on the side of the Watcher's neck. His respect for Wesley ratcheted up a notch or two and he frowned and gazed at the man again.

"Ms. Haversham informed you of our current situation?" Lonergan asked.

Wesley nodded once.

"Right then, it's what we're here for, lads and lasses," Lonergan told them all. "Let's get to it."

Wesley was exhausted and weak but he would collapse and die there on the floor before he would let Lonergan see it. Even with Anna he had taken pains not to reveal just how debilitated he had been by the bite of the vampire. Now as the Council operatives all hurried down the eastern corridor, then turned right at a junction, it was all he could do to keep up.

But hate drove him on. His teeth were set together, jaws clenched, and he drew the back of his left hand across his mouth, beard scratching his skin. Rupert Giles had never seemed to really respect him, but though Wesley would never have admitted it to his face, the man had been a sort of hero to him. Once he had become accustomed to being Buffy's Watcher, Giles had never toed the line for the Council, never cowtowed the way the Directors so often seemed to demand. Wesley remembered wishing he himself had that sort of backbone.

Now there was nothing he desired more than to drive a stake through the heart of the thing that had infested Giles's body. While he suspected others might have difficulty separating the two, he had no trouble making the distinction.

Rupert Giles was dead.

This thing they called by his name was his murderer.

All morning he had hoped that fate would bring him to this very place, and so it had. But getting here had almost cost him his life. He felt faint, his throat dry, and he stumbled slightly as they ran through the breezeway above the street that separated City Hall from the court-house.

"Wesley?" Anna asked, her strong grip on his arm supporting him.

"I'm all right," he said quickly, straightening up.

He checked the crossbow's chamber. He had nearly run out of bolts back at the Pacifica and had only found a handful more in the Humvee. But it would be enough, he was convinced. Now that he knew that whatever had given the Kakchiquels their demonic energy was gone, he had begun to believe in his heart that he could destroy Giles himself.

At the far end of the breezeway, the doors into the courthouse were propped wide open. Wesley dismissed the idea that they had been left that way by accident. It was either an invitation, or an indication that they were not considered a threat at all. A shudder went through him and he wondered when Willow and the others would rendezvous with them.

Lonergan stopped ahead and motioned for them to go upstairs. The breezeway had been their passage from one building to the next, but apparently the vampires were gathered above them.

On the third floor, Lonergan led them out into the cor-ridor where a massive set of double doors marked the entrance to one of the building's courtrooms. There was a sense of menace all around them now, hanging in the air like the foreboding weight of the sky just before a thunderstorm. The way the operatives moved, their every glance, revealed that they all felt it as well.

The corridor was empty. The room beyond the doors was silent.

Lonergan motioned for Hotchkiss and Bianchi to move up in front of the door with their flamethrowers. Then Quinones stepped between them with his shotgun slung down at hip level. Lonergan gave the signal and Quinones blew a huge hole in the doors where knobs and locks had been a second before. Then Lonergan and another operative kicked the heavy doors open.

Hotchkiss and Bianchi were the first through the door, fire streaming in hungry arcs from their flamethrowers and igniting three . . . five . . . six vampires who rushed them as they entered. The leeches all roared their pain, but two of them actually continued to stagger forward, skin and clothes ablaze, before Quinones blew their heads off.

The courtroom was perhaps forty feet square, the high windows blacked out by heavy tapestries that hung over them. The lighting was dull and flat and gave a surreal, almost two-dimensional look to everything within. But the vicious beasts in that room, the dozens of vampires gathered there for a last stand, were all too real, all too three-dimensional. Though their eyes no longer flickered with the tainted blaze of ancient magick, they were a fearsome sight, the bats tattooed black across their contorted features, fangs bared, all hissing as one hideous, ravenous pack.

The melee began.

Wesley pushed into the room with the other operatives around him. He shot an elbow at a vampire, knocking it back at the cost of a sharp pain that spiked up his arm. Another appeared, leering, before him, and he fired a bolt at its chest and was bathed in a cloud of ash for his trouble. Around him, in his peripheral vision, he saw the battle raging on. The Council operatives kept together in a rough circle, backs to one another, letting the enemy come to them. Lonergan's crossbow was batted out of his hands and the barroom-brawler-turned-priest head-butted the vamp in front of him, then whipped the ax from behind his back, threw off its leather case, and swung it in a wide arc. The gleaming blade decapitated one Kakchiquel and sank into the shoulder of another.

A female vampire, almost completely naked save for a vividly colored serpent tattoo all across her body, lashed her hands toward Wesley. The long clawlike nails of one hand gashed his cheek and jaw, cutting the skin beneath his beard. The Watcher expertly fired another bolt and she was dusted.

Wesley glanced to his left and saw Bianchi driven down beneath a horde of bloodsuckers, and it pained him to know that there was nothing he could do for her. Quinones was there a second later, and he fired the shotgun into them. None of them were destroyed by it, but they scattered, wounded, leaving Bianchi's corpse behind. Wesley felt faint again, sweat dripping down his face, blood matting his beard. Ever since he entered the room he had been gazing around, hoping to see Giles.

At the back of the courtroom, the door that would lead into the judge's chambers opened. A lithe, dark-skinned vampire whose bat-brand was stark white emerged from the open door. Wesley recognized Jax from file descriptions. A moment later, Giles followed. Despite the absence of his glasses, he looked for all the world like the wry, benevolent man he had once been.

Giles spotted Wesley noticing him. One eyebrow raised, the vampire king gave him an ironic smile, and waved.

"So glad you could make it, Wesley!" Giles called across the shattered benches and the corpses and the blood, his voice somehow rising above it all, even the blast of a shotgun nearby.

Bitterness welled up inside Wesley. His gaze was torn away from Giles by another attacker, and he dusted it with the last bolt in his crossbow. He was now weaponless, exhausted, and vulnerable. But he would not give up. With a snarl of hatred he started across the courtroom. A vampire grabbed his shoulder and Wesley shook the thing off, turned and pummeled it with three quick blows that knocked the monster unconscious.

The Watcher wavered on his feet, but he refused to fall.

Then Anna was at his side. One of her arms had a long gash in it, but she seemed not to notice as she brandished her stake in front of her.

"Time for him to die," she said.

Wesley nodded, and together, they started for the dais where the judge would preside over the courtroom. The door to the chambers was behind it, and Jax still stood there.

But the vampire king had slipped away through the chaos of the battle.

Giles was gone.

Buffy could barely breathe. Once again the two souls within her swirled together, thoughts and emotions and memories mixing, making it almost impossible to separate one from the other. Buffy-at-nineteen knew that in her own time, Angel was still alive, fighting for his own redemption in Los Angeles. She had accepted that they could not be together, but her love for him was an ache in her heart that never quite went away. Buffy-at-twenty-four remembered that feeling distantly, but she also felt the long years of her imprisonment, during which she had wondered so many times if Angel would come for her; why he had not; what had become of him.

Together, upon Buffy's escape from El Suerte, the two spirits residing in her body had come to one conclusion: Angel was gone. The only thing that would have kept him from her was death. What little Willow had been able to tell her only seemed to confirm that. Angel had gone to face Giles, to free her, and had never returned.

In his love for her, a love that both of them had sacrificed for the greater good, Angel had risked his life and his chance at redemption. Now Buffy would discover what had become of him. With Xander and Willow alongside her, she followed Oz down a side corridor on the second floor of City Hall. Oz was a werewolf again, and he prowled the carpet, sniffing the air, following the scent he had picked up before.

Angel's scent. Which meant that somehow, Angel was alive.

"Hey," Willow said softly, her hand reaching out, her fingers entwining with Buffy's as they moved swiftly after Oz.

Buffy glanced at her, saw the concern in her friend's eyes.

"If it's him, and he's here . . . and he's still alive?" Willow said. "Gotta consider the possibility that he's evil."

"I know," Buffy said, offering Willow a sad, lopsided smile. She reached up and touched the hilt of the sword that was slung in its scabbard across her back. "I used this on him once before. I'll do it again if I have to."

"Or I could," Willow offered. "If you want."

"Let's see what's what first."

Willow nodded and they kept on after Oz. Xander had passed them by and now he and the werewolf stood in front of a door at the end of the corridor. Oz paced back and forth anxiously, sniffing at the door. Xander gazed at Buffy and Willow expectantly.

"Check this out," he said.

On the door was a red and white metal sign inscribed with the words NO ADMITTANCE. Buffy frowned as she studied it. It was the sort of thing you might see in the back of a restaurant; she recalled a similar sign on the door to the boiler room back in Sunnydale High. But it was awkward and out of place on the upper floors of the neatly appointed government building, and they had not seen anything else like it on other doors, save for the entrance into the basement.

Buffy stared at the sign, then glanced down at Oz. "Angel?"

The werewolf growled low and snapped at the air. The Slayer took that as a yes. She tensed, and was about to kick the door down when Willow called out for her to stop. Buffy looked at her curiously. The sorceress waved her hand in front of the door with a flourish.

"Munimentum prodeo!" she commanded.

With those words, a breeze whirled around them from out of nowhere. A static hiss filled the air and the door was suddenly blocked by a shimmering barrier of crackling energy the dark purple of a painful bruise. The smell of sulfur was in the air.

"Boy, whoever hung that sign wasn't kidding," Xander said in a hushed tone.

Willow gazed at Buffy. "Defensive spells. Not just a ward against entry, but a powerful destructive magick. If you'd touched it, I'm guessing we'd be scraping Slayer off the walls. Not to mention the blood on our clothes? You know those stains never come out."

The dark energy of the barrier crackled from floor to ceiling in front of the door. Buffy glanced at it and then back at Willow.

"Well, good thing you caught it. Y'know, 'cause of the dry cleaning bills and everything," Buffy said, a thin smile on her face as she stared at her friend in wonder. "How'd you know?"

Willow shrugged. "Just sort of sensed it, I guess."

"Oz didn't," Xander noted, gesturing to the werewolf,

who had retreated a few paces down the hall. "And he's got wolf-nose. Pretty cool, Will."

"Can you get us through it?" Buffy asked.

The sorceress stared thoughtfully at the sparking current of magick that barred their way. After a few moments, she closed her eyes and whispered.

"Perfringo contego."

Willow opened her eyes and twisted her mouth into a grimace. Several minutes passed and she merely stared at the door. Twice, her fingers moved and she began to draw symbols on the air, but then stopped and shook her head.

"I can't just shatter it," she said. "And I've tried to come up with a spell that would protect us enough that we could just pass through, but as adept as I've become in certain areas of magick, that's just not something I can do."

Disappointed as she was, Buffy did not fault Willow. If not for her, they would never have even known the barrier was there, and Buffy herself might actually be dead. Still, she was not simply going to stand out here in the hall.

"We could come back," Xander suggested. "The rest of the unit may need our help."

"Lonergan would have contacted us," Willow replied, still staring at the door. "That's what the commlink is for. Your headset is still working, isn't it?"

Xander tapped it, then nodded. "As far as I can tell."

Buffy drew her sword again and took a few steps down the hall. "How long do you think it would take me to get through the wall?"

Willow stared at the sword. "Oh. Wait. A thought is here!" She walked to Buffy and gazed down at the engraved blade. "This thing is already enchanted somewhat, and that might help. But maybe I could put a spell on the sword, a protective ward like the one on the door."

"I get it," Xander said. When he narrowed his eyes in thought, the crescent scar on his face crinkled and seemed almost to shine. "The thing blocking the door is like electricity. If you introduce a separate field of similar energy to it, you might short it out."

Willow grinned.

Oz padded up to them, gazed at each of them in turn, and then went back to his spot just down the hall. He sniffed the air and Buffy realized he was keeping watch for them.

"So what are my chances of exploding when I do this?" she asked Willow.

"Minimal."

Buffy held the sword out in both hands. "Do it."

Willow nodded intently and studied the blade. She placed both hands above it, her fingers perhaps half an inch from the metal, and began to sway slightly as she muttered words in a guttural, ancient-sounding language that Buffy thought might be German or something older. She was never more aware of her own linguistic limitations than when she was around Willow.

A light seemed to glow around Willow's face as she spoke, and then that weird illumination traveled down along her arms and to her fingertips, and finally to the sword. A kind of aura surrounded the blade, tinted green. It sparkled with power, as did the barrier in front of the door, but this spell seemed somehow smoother, calmer.

The hilt of the sword vibrated in Buffy's hand and the skin of her arm prickled. She glanced around at her friends.

"Back up."

They did so immediately, moving away to stand with Oz. Buffy held the sword with both hands and hacked at the magickal barrier. As the blade slashed through the field of crackling energy, a sound like a buzzsaw ripped the air. Light flashed green and black as night, and then the barrier dispersed. The metal NO ADMITTANCE sign fell off and hit the floor. Behind it was a small, simple placard with the words TOWN PLANNING BOARD.

In the corridor, all was still. Buffy reached out, touched the knob, and found that it was not locked. She pushed the door open. The windows inside had been bricked over, but light spilled into the room from the hall. The planning board's office was a shambles, with massive file cabinets tumbled over and papers spilled across the floor. A desk had been turned on its side; a computer monitor lay shattered on the ground.

There was another light in the room as well. A dark, unearthly glow, the same bruise-purple as the barrier in front of the door had been. It emanated from a spot off to the left, out of sight of the doorway.

Buffy stepped inside and the others followed her. On the left side of the room, in the midst of more destruction, she saw Angel.

"Oh God," she whispered.

Angel hung suspended in a sphere of dark magickal energy, his arms straight out from his sides, legs dangling beneath him, as though he had been crucified. He was dressed all in black, his jacket torn and hanging loosely, a long gash across his cheek. But it was his position that stunned her the most, for he hung there just as he had in her dream, when he had advised her on dealing with Giles. There were differences, of course.

A stake protruded from his chest, perfectly positioned to have destroyed his heart.

Yet somehow he lived.

CHAPTER 4

"Angel?" Buffy whispered.

Oz appeared beside her and in a heartbeat he transformed from wolf to man, face contorting, fur withdrawing, as if it were the simplest thing in the world.

"Is it really him?" she asked, staring at her former lover where he hung encased in a shimmering sphere of sorcerous power.

"His scent? No doubt," Oz confirmed. He scratched a bit at his unruly hair. "Really him? Couldn't say."

The vampire's eyes were closed and he looked peaceful, as though he were lying in a casket at a funeral home. The thought came to Buffy unbidden and she pushed it away. Though she wanted to deny it, she felt certain it really was him. The line of his jaw, the strength in his sculpted features.

"Willow?" she asked. "This is the same as the spell out there?"

"I think so, Buffy, but . . ." her words trailed off.

Buffy turned to find all three of them looking not at Angel, but at her. Willow's chest rose and fell unevenly, as though she were overwhelmed with emotion. Oz raised one eyebrow. Xander glanced down and shifted on his feet, then looked back up at Buffy.

"What?" she demanded.

"Not to make a big deal out of it, Buff, but . . . did you notice the stake?" Xander asked.

Buffy sighed and looked to Willow. "It missed. I mean, it had to have missed, right? He's still here."

"Now there's some logic," she replied supportively.

Oz cleared his throat. "And blood. There's some blood, too."

Buffy stared at him. "So?"

"He's been gone five years," Xander said. He rested his crossbow on his shoulder, his expression grim. This was the soldier in him, she knew, the man he had become. "If he's been here all that time . . . I don't know. I just think you should be careful, is all."

"Careful as I can be," Buffy said. She held the sword up to Willow again. "Spell me."

But even as Willow lifted her fingers above the blade and began to chant, Buffy heard the soft rasp of a voice behind her, speaking her name. With a start, she let the sword drop down, the fingers of her right hand aching with the grip she had on it. And she turned.

Angel's eyes were open. A wan smile spread slowly across his features.

"Found you," he rasped, the words laden with static as they passed through the sphere that was his prison.

"Actually, we sorta found you," Xander corrected.

"Semantics," Oz added.

Buffy barely heard them. Willow touched her arm, whispered to her that she should stay away from the sphere, but she could not help herself. Carefully, eyes locked on Angel's, Buffy moved closer. She could feel her hair beginning to stand up with the static energy that emanated from the dark sphere.

"Angel."

Her heart felt cold in her chest and for a few moments she forgot to breathe. No matter how deeply she loved him, she had known those years ago that they were not destined to be together. It seemed fate had other things in store for them. But now . . . he had been a prisoner all this time, just as she had. He had come to find her, to save her, and now it seemed it would be up to her to save him.

"I dreamed I heard your voice," he croaked, smile broadening. "Guess it wasn't a dream."

"Hang on, Angel. We're getting you out." Buffy turned and raised the sword up in front of Willow again.

Crucified, hanging there in perfectly preserved agony, Angel uttered a small, soft laugh. "I wish you could," he said. "But, Buffy, you can't."

She faltered. More than anything, she wanted to argue with him, to tell him that they had broken the magickal barrier protecting this place and they could free him from that same magick. But in her heart she knew that wasn't what Angel was talking about.

Slowly, her throat dry, a chill running all through her, she turned to face him again. "The stake?"

Angel's smile was gone. Some of the light was gone from his eyes. "I came to find you. I don't know how long ago it was. Time does weird things in here. I confronted him . . . Giles. We fought. That's why the place is such a mess. Sorry I couldn't pick up."

He laughed softly, but his expression was still grim.

"He beat *you?*" Xander asked.

"Hardly," Angel replied bluntly, frowning. "I cleaned his clock. But he had this spell all set up. Like a magickal bear trap, and I walked right into it. I was trying to escape as it closed in around me, and he caught me with my guard down."

With a tilt of his head, unable to move his arms, Angel motioned toward the stake.

"Even though he isn't really Giles, he has all of Giles's memories and personality, his grudges. He remembers when I tortured him and he wanted to return the favor. Time is sort of frozen around me. If you try to free me, I'm dead."

Buffy shook her head slowly, fighting back the tears that threatened at the corners of her eyes. The two souls within her were completely unified in their sorrow, in grief. It would have been better, she—they—thought at that moment, if she had never found Angel at all. Then she could have imagined he still lived, somewhere. But this was almost more than she could bear.

"There has to be a way," she said, her voice tight.

"Maybe we can find a way to take the stake out before breaking the spell that's holding you."

"Buffy," Angel said, his voice low and hard now. "Look at me."

She did. What she saw in his eyes made her want to turn away, but she would not do that to him. Not now.

"The damage is done," Angel told her.

Willow came to her then and Buffy hugged her friend close, taking comfort in the familiar feel of her arms, the smell of her hair, the simple caring in her eyes. The Slayer still held her sword, but its tip hung toward the ground, dangling from her hand.

"There's got to be something we can do, Will," Buffy said. "When is it enough? Giles. My mom. Your parents. Anya. Faith. When do we get to the point where we've lost enough?"

Buffy looked past Willow to Xander and Oz. Xander's steely exterior had given way completely now, and she could see that he shared her pain. Oz, though, was not looking at her at all. He looked so deceptively normal, so human, but his brows were knitted and he sniffed at the air. Then his eyes widened.

"Guys?" Oz said.

As one, Buffy and Willow spun toward the door.

Giles stood leaning casually against the wall just inside the room. The moment was completely surreal. He wore soft black shoes, gray pants and a blue cotton sweater that seemed amiably rumpled. As she stared at him, taken aback by his sudden arrival, she almost expected him to be holding a book, or a cup of tea. He seemed startled by the sudden attention directed at him.

"Hmm?" he mumbled absentmindedly, as though he'd been caught not paying attention. Then he straightened up, slipped one hand into his pocket, and scratched idly at the back of his head as if in contemplation.

"Right. Sorry. Just lost in the spectacle. As to the point where you've lost enough? I don't think any of you have reached it yet, really. Not when you consider that you're still alive. I'll guarantee you this, though. I'm working to remedy that even as we speak."

The illusion shattered, along with Buffy's heart. This was the second time she had faced him like this, heard his voice and *known* that the evil she had dedicated herself to combatting had tainted him, reached out and claimed him . . . and just as it had the first time, several nights earlier, it crushed her. And yet it hardened her as well.

"It's over for you," Buffy said, sword at the ready. "Your little kingdom is done."

"Tsk," he said. "No 'Giles, old boy, so good to see you? I've missed you so?' Nothing?"

"You're not Giles."

"Oh, but I am, Buffy," the vampire king said, his tone making the words sound as though he found them delicious. "I always underestimated the process, you see. My soul is gone, certainly. But whether you like it or not, I *am* Giles. If I weren't, if I didn't love you like my own daughter, would you still be alive? Would you have gotten this far? I saved your life, Buffy, I helped you get out of Sunnydale, but only because I knew you would come back. They called Faith 'the Prodigal,' you know. The Council did. But you are the real Prodigal, aren't you? You've come back to me."

The Slayer began to shake her head, revulsion flooding through her, fingers flexing on the hilt of the sword. The vampire king's eyes locked on the blade.

"You know that, though, don't you? Otherwise you would not have accepted my gift. You would not have brought it with you. Did Angel recognize it, I wonder? The very sword with which you killed him, and sent him to Hell. The weapon with which one of us, my dear girl, my own daughter, might very well soon kill the other."

"I'm going to tell you one last time," Buffy snarled. "I'm not your daughter. I brought this just to give it back to you. Blade first."

"As you once did with the knife Faith used to try to kill you," Giles replied.

Buffy blinked, hesitated.

"Surprised?" the vampire king asked. "You shouldn't be. Deny all you want, but I *am* Giles. I made you what you are. You could not kill Faith, and you won't be able to kill me when the moment arrives. I want you to join me, Buffy. Be what you were meant to be. Together we will be unstoppable."

With a shake of her head, Buffy stood a bit taller, held the sword higher. "See, that proves it right there. Giles was never that stupid, or that arrogant."

"Actually, I always thought he was pretty conceited," Xander put in.

Giles glared at him. "I'm amazed you're still alive, boy."

In response, Xander fired a bolt from his crossbow. Giles sidestepped easily and it *thunked* into the wall behind him. With a low, menacing growl, Oz transformed again, and Buffy wondered how much strain it caused him, how much control he had to have to shift back and forth like that. The werewolf stalked forward, lips curled back from its snoutful of gleaming fangs.

Behind them, Angel's voice came weakly through the sphere around him. "Be careful," he said. "Remember what he's accomplished. Don't underestimate him."

"We never have," Willow said, her tone guarded. She lifted her hands and a soft green light began to dance among her fingers.

"Nor have I underestimated you, sorceress," the vampire king said, scandalized. "But I know Buffy. This is too personal for her. She's likely already staked a claim on my head, I'll wager."

Buffy hesitated again. He was right, of course. But if that was what he expected, maybe the best thing to do was surprise him.

"You know what, guys?" she said to them. "Nobody likes a know-it-all. Whoever kills him gets ice cream later."

For the first time since they had discovered him lurking in the room, Giles seemed off-balance. She was glad.

"Dammit!" Xander muttered.

His face was alive with conflicting emotions and he held one hand to the headset against his ear, listening. When he raised his eyes and looked at her, Buffy knew that there was trouble.

"Lonergan," Xander told her. "They need backup or they're dead."

Her gaze ticked toward Giles. He wore a broad, Cheshire-cat grin, and Buffy knew then that this was precisely what he had expected. Even orchestrated.

"They're in the courthouse," Xander added. "Wesley and Anna are already there, but they're seriously outnumbered."

Buffy did not take her eyes off Giles. "Go," she said.

"Buffy, no!" Willow protested.

Oz snarled and began to creep closer to the vampire king, who silently beckoned for the werewolf like a back alley bully, urging him forward.

"Don't take him alone," Angel advised, his voice like some dim, buzzing echo in the room, a radio someone forgot to turn off.

"Go," Buffy repeated calmly. "Camazotz is dead. Sunnydale's pest problem is over. Help Lonergan finish the job on this nest. I'll be all right."

She did not look at any of them again, for she feared that she would see doubt in their eyes; doubt that she could or would kill this thing wearing the corpse of her mentor, her Watcher, her friend. Buffy strode forward, on edge, ready to defend herself, and faced Giles down.

"Out of the way."

"But of course," he agreed happily, and he stepped aside, moving to the other side of the room, away from Angel.

Xander and Oz went quickly into the hall, but Willow lingered, staring back in at Buffy. The Slayer nodded at her, expressionless. After a moment, Willow nodded back. Then she, Oz, and Xander took off down the hall, and Buffy prayed they would be in time to save Lonergan and the others.

And then she was alone with Giles, save for Angel, who could only look on, crucified, imprisoned, and eternally an eyeblink away from death.

Sunshine streamed into the courtroom from a single, tall, shattered window. Dust motes danced on the rays of light and the splash of day into the room was a beacon of safety. In the midst of the melee, as humans and vampires clashed, the undead leeches dodged around that splash of sun time and again. Even if they were backed up toward it, they seemed to feel the burn of it as they got close and managed to slip away.

Anna slid beneath a vampire's attack as though she were a reed bending in the breeze, her right hand whipped up and the stake sank into the vampire's chest with a satisfying thump. Even as he turned to dust, scattering all around her feet, she shot a low kick at another and shattered his knee.

Behind her, Wesley shouted, rage in his voice. "Dammit, no!"

Alarmed, she spun and was just in time to see Jax, one of his eyes blown out and gore streaked across the ivory tattoo on his face, pull an ax out of Lonergan's chest. Lonergan was dead, staring blindly up at his murderer.

The fight had hardened Anna. The death and the blood and the constant motion of her own bludgeoning fists and pummeling kicks had become a sort of song that rose up in her and swept her away from the grief she knew she should have felt at the loss of people who had been at least her comrades, and some her friends.

But with Father Lonergan's murder, she could not postpone mourning. Sorrow flooded her heart and hot, salty tears sprang to her eyes. Almost immediately, though, her anger surged forth. Only a few of her tears fell before the cold fury in her heart dried them.

The Kakchiquels knew she was the Slayer, and so Anna and Wesley were culled away from the other four operatives who still fought. Hotchkiss and Fuchs were across the room with two others Anna did not know. They were in a rough circle, still fighting, probably still alive because of the flamethrower Fuchs had appropriated from somebody's corpse. Liquid fire blazed out like dragon's breath and the vampires knew enough to keep back. One of the vampires had a gun, but only got off a single wild shot before Fuchs torched him. Then the four operatives began to work their way toward the pool of sunlight spilling through the high, shattered window.

Wesley swore again and Anna glanced at him. He had a shotgun that had changed hands twice in the past minute, from operative to vampire and now to Wesley. He blew the throat out of a Kakchiquel in front of him, severing its neck. It collapsed in a tumble of ashes even as the Watcher swung the stock of the shotgun back into the face of another vampire behind him.

Anna took a right hook from a pretty boy vamp with blond hair and bright blue eyes. The punch cost her a fraction of a second and in that time the vampire got his hands around her throat. Furious at this lapse on her part, Anna reached up, grabbed his hair and rammed his head down even as she shot her knee up into his face.

The vampire went down and she was on top of him, stake in hand. He dusted and Anna rolled away instantly, then leaped back to her feet. She found herself side by side with Wesley, a new wave of vampires moving toward them. When she shot another look at the surviving operatives, Fuchs was a corpse, trampled underfoot by vampires going after the other three. But Hotchkiss and the others had reached the sunlight, making them more difficult targets.

Jax capered a bit, prancing merrily with the ax over his shoulder, as he came to join the other vampires who were slowly surrounding Wesley and Anna. With his bloodstained, razor grin and the bone white brand tattooed across his ebony features, Jax was a terrifying, nightmare creature, scarecrow-thin and yet with the grace of a dancer. The Slayer tensed, determined not to let the lives of Lonergan and the others have been lost for nothing.

"Wait for them," Wesley whispered next to her. "Dust Jax quick as you can. It'll unsettle the others."

She nodded, though her newfound confidence was fading. There were a lot of them. Probably too many.

Jax stopped, cocked his head to one side and smiled, the gaping black hole where his eye should have been making Anna shudder.

"Finish them," Jax said happily.

As the Kakchiquels started forward a sudden snarl made them waver. In that instant, Oz was upon them. Hope surged within Anna as the werewolf attacked them, tearing the arm off of one of the vampires before driving another down beneath his primal rage and slashing claws.

"Wesley!"

The young Slayer and her Watcher glanced over to see Willow and Xander come running into the courtroom. Jax and the other vampires turned as well, and Wesley took that moment to attack. With a triumphant roar that thundered from his chest he lunged forward and cracked the butt of the shotgun across Jax's face. The ravaged vampire crashed into the first bench in the courtroom and fell over, dropping the ax with a clatter. It slid under the benches. Kakchiquels tried to help him, and Anna knew that was her cue. She staked one from behind, kicked another out of the way and grabbed a third by the arm, keeping them away from Wesley.

The Watcher looked wild with his beard and his

cracked glasses and his face red from exertion. He shoved the barrel of the shotgun down and pressed it against Jax's throat, and he pulled the trigger.

It clicked on an empty chamber.

Jax grinned, grabbed the shotgun by the barrel, and pulled Wesley down on top of him. Anna tried to scream but no sound would come out. Her eyes were wide and she felt suddenly weak as she grabbed at the back of Wesley's shirt and tried to tug him away from the hideous circus nightmare holding on to him.

With one hand on either side of his head, Jax broke Wesley's neck. The crack echoed through the room. Anna opened her mouth, horror exploding in her like fireworks, but still she could not scream. Distracted, she was not fast enough to stop the three vampires that grabbed hold of her and threw her back against the judge's dais. Jax approached her, licking his lips.

"I've heard such rumors about the blood of a Slayer," he said. "Well, more than rumors, really. I only wish I'd been among those who got to feast on Faith's blood."

At last, Anna screamed. She bucked one of the Kakchiquels away and tried to rush Jax with her stake, but he knocked it from her hand.

They had her.

Willow's heart sank as she and Xander entered the courtroom. So many dead, only a handful left alive. Easily two dozen vampires still in the room, and Oz had dragged three of them away into a corner, where they sparred with him as though playing. But it was not playing. Willow feared for him, but she knew how hard it would be to kill him, and so she pushed that fear away. Oz would destroy them.

But there were more. Maybe too many.

She saw Anna and Wesley across the room, but not Lonergan. With effort she put a wall up between herself and her grief, and she acted. There were three operatives to her right in a pool of sunshine streaming through a shattered window, but eight or nine vampires surrounded them, darting in and out, searing their hands as they tried to reach the trio. Apparently their only remaining weapon was a flamethrower one of them had acquired, and between that and the sunlight, they were barely keeping the vampires at bay.

Willow raced at them. Two of the vampires sensed her or saw her in their peripheral vision, for they turned to her with their fangs bared, hissing. Silently, her whole body aching from the magick she had already performed that day, she cast a long-practiced spell and both of them burst into flames. Another tried to grapple with her, and she turned it to ice even as they fought. When she tore her hands away, it shattered.

Beside her, Xander fired a bolt from his crossbow and one of the Kakchiquels menacing the three surviving operatives turned to dust. He and Willow moved in.

Then Anna screamed.

The cry of anguish echoing in her ears, Willow spun to see what had happened. Jax and the other vampires had the young Slayer trapped, and Wesley . . .

"Wesley's dead," Xander whispered, his voice hollow. Then he shot a quick glance at Willow. "Save them."

With that, he sprinted down the aisle.

"Xander, wait!" Willow shouted. "I can—"

But she could not, for before she could finish formulating the thought, a powerful hand closed on her ponytail from behind and yanked hard. Willow staggered backward, yelping in pain. It was a female vampire, a woman with red hair cut into a rough shag, and piercings all over her face. She pulled hard enough that Willow lost her footing and her head slammed against the wooden floor.

For a moment, everything went black.

Her eyes flickered open and felt the woman's ragged cut hair brush her face as the vampire went for her throat. In that eyeblink, Willow panicked. All thoughts of magick went out of her; she could not remember how to do spells that would destroy this vile thing. Pinpricks of pain on her neck, and Willow closed her eyes again.

"Go away!" she screamed, every ounce of despair collected over the past five years spilling out of her in those three syllables.

The weight was gone from her. The feel of the hair against her cheek. The prick of fangs on her throat. All gone.

Willow opened her eyes and looked around. The vampire woman with the piercings was simply *gone,* but the others who had been clustered around the three surviving operatives were now staring at Willow in abject horror, their fanged mouths hanging open. They looked ridiculous, these terrified monsters, and they began to back away from her.

Willow felt blood trickling from her nose and her legs were shaky. She wasn't sure exactly what she had done, but it had cost her.

She glanced up, saw Oz lunging at the back of a vampire who was fleeing from him; saw Xander pick up a battleax from the floor. The young Slayer with her shock of pink hair and her pretty ceramic doll features screamed as Jax raked talons across her cheek.

Xander was quick and silent as he swung the ax sidelong at Jax's neck with all his might. The vampire's head was cut off in one stroke, and it bounced once on the floor before both head and torso dusted.

Enraged, the other four vampires who had attacked Anna now turned on Xander. Willow shouted in alarm but it was too late. They piled on him, punching and kicking and clawing and Willow saw Xander's arms flail as he tried to beat them away.

Willow ran for him.

Anna rushed at them, tore one of the vampires away. Her eyes went wide when she saw what was under him, what had become of Xander. Willow faltered, her heart seizing in her chest, ice running through her whole body as she saw the look on the Slayer's face.

"No," she whispered.

"The windows!" Anna shouted as she grappled with a Kakchiquel. "There are too many of them. We've got to take out the windows!"

All Willow wanted to do was curl up into herself. The

vampires who had attacked Xander were rising now, done with him. *Done with him.* She could not see him, this man who had once been a boy, once been her best friend, once stolen her Barbie dolls. Once kissed her, no matter the cost.

He was too still.

And Anna was right. Oz was cornered, tearing into one after another, but still there were fifteen, perhaps twenty. And only she, Anna, Oz, and the three operatives remained.

Xander. Oh God, Xander. He had saved Anna's life, taken vengeance for Wesley, and now they might all die anyway.

"No." She spoke the word not in simple denial, but with power. The blood began to flow more freely from her nose now and she felt faint, as though she might fall at any moment. Then a breeze blew up around her, the wind borne upon the magick she now called down to her. Willow held out her hands, closed her eyes and tilted back her head.

It frightened her to call upon the power of the old ones, the elder gods as they were sometimes called, the lords of chaos, because they never gave without a price. It might be paid today, or years in the future. But Willow thought she had paid enough already this day, and so with all the mystic strength within her, she reached out.

"The highest walls, the thickest walls, the strongest walls, like a flood they pass," she chanted, teeth gritted, barely aware of the tears that slipped down her cheeks. "No door can shut them out, no bolt can turn them back.

Like a gale wind they blow amid the places between the places. The sons of Eng, be with me now!"

Her voice rose with each word and as she spoke the power within her increased. Willow gathered it up, and then in one instant, she pushed it away, pushed it out of her. In her mind's eye she saw the room around her, saw the windows with their heavy tapestries, and she *pushed* at them.

She *pushed*.

And the windows shattered, and the tapestries burned and fell, and the sun streamed in the high windows, and the vampires burned and died, and the wind swept in, caught their dust up in eddies and swirls.

It was done.

The courtroom was a shambles, corpses scattered all over the room. The sun seemed almost blasphemous, the warm breeze so sweet and clean and so very wrong. That something like this should happen under the light of a perfect day, while the world rolled on . . . Willow Rosenberg believed in magick and she wielded it with power that surprised even her. But in that moment, she did not believe in plain everyday *magic* anymore.

Slowly, she walked across the room to where Xander's body lay. The other operatives started for her, but Willow ignored them. She heard Hotchkiss talking on the commlink, reporting in to Haversham or someone, but the words sounded foreign to her. Willow glanced at Anna, who knelt by Wesley's corpse and tried to adjust his broken glasses on the bridge of his nose.

"Oh no," Willow whispered, as she stared down at the

broken, savaged form of her friend. "What did they do to you, Xand?"

A thousand images flashed through her mind. She did not remember life without Xander, and the ache inside her when she realized she would now have to go on without him was infinite. He had always been her cavalry, her hand to hold. No more.

Oz, human now, laid a hand on Willow's shoulder. She froze, reached up to grasp his fingers, then let him take her in his arms. A sob escaped her, but only one. Only one.

"He was right, you know," she whispered. "The earth never opens up and swallows you when you want it to."

CHAPTER 5

Angel writhed in torment as hellish as any he had ever known. Trapped within the smothering sphere of magick that yet preserved his life, he struggled. He had spent years in that terrible prison and yet he had survived worse in the past. What made this far more horrible was the stake in his chest, the knowledge that there would be no escape from this torture, for the moment the spell was shattered, he was ash. More than once, more than a thousand times in that five-year span, he had wished for the end to simply come and be done with. His death was inevitable now.

But he had never desired his own death as much as he did in that moment.

In the room that had been his prison, Buffy held the long sword out in front of her, the runes engraved on it dark with age. He knew that sword all too well, for once she had been forced to impale him upon it. Now Angel only wished she could do it again. Much as he tried, he could barely move, not even to lower his arms. He hung there like a scarecrow as he had done for so long, the wooden shaft already in his heart.

In all that time, he had never expected to see Buffy again. Now he stared at her, amazed by the woman she had become, and saddened at the same time. Here was a warrior. Her blond hair was tied back carelessly, her body chiseled with muscle, tight as a whip. Her face was different now, the cheekbones and jaw more defined. Somehow, though, this was the girl who had always been inside her, the woman she was destined to become. This warrior had always been in her eyes, waiting to arrive.

But that had not been the totality of her, for there had been passion and love in her as well. Always, it had been there, and it had made him love her, made her the extraordinary Slayer, the amazing girl that she was.

And now Angel wished that he could crush that spark in her, because he feared that in this moment, it was either that, or Buffy was going to die. All because she still felt love for him.

"Buffy, whatever he says, don't listen!" Angel called to her, though he knew his voice would only come across dimly on the other side of his magickal cell, just as he heard their voices as a distant buzz.

Their voices.

Buffy's voice, and the voice of Rupert Giles. Or at least the monster he had become. Even now Giles glanced at him, an expression on his face that mimicked the intellectual curiosity he had so often shown when he was alive. But there was amusement in that expression now, a cruel humor that made a mockery of the man he had been. Just as the way he chose to dress so carefully mimicked who Giles had been as a Watcher. Certainly it was not an accident; the monster knew that the more he increased the illusion of benevolence, the more it would throw his enemies off-balance.

"By all means, Buffy," Giles said, his voice hushed and placating. "Do as Angel says. Don't listen to me."

The vampire king, so human in his soft cotton sweater, so normal looking, so Giles, strolled toward Angel and stared up at him for a long moment. Buffy could have attacked him then, might have reached him with the sword even before he could turn, but she didn't. She hesitated.

"Kill him!" Angel yelled.

"You could," Giles agreed, not even bothering to look at her. "Or you could join me, as I've asked. You can feel the rightness of it, Buffy. I know you can."

Buffy took a step forward, sword rising. "You're pretty cocky for a guy who's about to be kitty litter."

Giles smiled, chuckling softly. "You haven't changed a bit."

It was so familiar, and Angel could see it working on Buffy even as the alarm bells went off in his own head. She had to see what he was doing, preying on her feelings for him, her memories. She had to know it.

But it was working.

"Buffy!" Angel shouted again.

Finally, Giles turned to her, his back to Angel, who could only watch and listen.

"Give yourself to me," Giles said smoothly, intimately. "It's the right thing, Buffy. Become the daughter we both always wanted you to be, and I promise that after, I'll let Angel go."

Buffy's sword wavered. "You'll just let him go? What about the stake, moron?"

"I did this to him. Do you really suppose I cannot undo it? You know me better than that. Of course, after you're with me, you might change your mind about releasing Angel, but a promise is a promise. I'll let him go even if you don't want me to anymore."

As Angel watched in horror, Buffy lowered her gaze, gnawing on her lower lip, considering the offer.

"No!" he screamed. "Buffy, don't! He can't save me now! He's lying. The second I'm free, I'm dead. The only thing you can do for me now is to kill him!"

Giles spun, enraged, his features contorting as he fought to keep the face of the beast, the true countenance of the vampire, from showing. That would shatter the illusion.

"Oh, *do* shut up!" the vampire king snarled.

Behind him, Buffy raised her sword again.

Angel rejoiced.

Buffy mourned.

It tore her up inside to stand there and look at the two men who had meant more to her than almost anyone else in the world, and to know that both of them were dead. Her grief welled up from a place so deep within her that it was like some newly discovered heart.

Both of the souls within her, the spirits of Buffy-at-nineteen and Buffy-at-twenty-four that were twined together inside her, reached back in time for a memory, the moment that had led to this.

In the harbor master's office. Camazotz held Giles in his grasp, his life in the balance. The demon-god had instructed her to surrender herself . . . just as Giles did now. Camazotz had wanted her to sacrifice her own life to save Giles's and Buffy had known that the monster was lying, that if she gave herself up Giles was dead, that his only chance lay in her survival and the hope that Camazotz would keep him alive to use as bait for her later.

So Buffy had run away, crashed through a window and fled the scene, vowing to return to save him, to wrest him from the clutches of the god of bats. But her mind had been clouded by ominous warnings received from the ghost of Lucy Hanover, whispers Lucy had heard from an entity called The Prophet about a mistake Buffy would make that would have horrifying consequences.

The Prophet had promised to give Buffy a vision of those consequences, and instead had stolen her body, thrust her into this horrible future. For in truth The Prophet had been Zotzilaha, bride to Camazotz, herself fleeing from him. Now both Camazotz and his bride were dead, and so were so many others.

So was Angel, if not in this tick of the clock then in the next. And so was Giles. Somehow Buffy had to separate the two souls within her, her younger self returning to the past, traveling back far enough to prevent this future from ever occurring.

But in order to do that, she had to fall back once more on the first rule of slaying: she had to stay alive. No matter the cost, no matter how it broke her heart, she had to remind herself that this creature in front of her was little more than a demon wearing the mask of affection.

Still, Giles's words had their effect, his gentle, laughing eyes so familiar. The blade wavered in her hand. All was silent around her save for her own breathing and the crackle of magick that kept Angel both imprisoned and alive. And then Angel shouted at her again and she knew he was right.

Giles rounded on him, his voice a bludgeon. "Oh, *do* shut up!"

Buffy felt that voice cut into her and whatever illusion the vampire king had been able to maintain, shattered. He stood only a few feet away, his back to her. Angel hung in the air beyond him in a sphere of bruised light, and her former lover's eyes glowed as Buffy raised the sword and lunged at Giles.

Her arms brought the blade back, its edge whistled as it cut the air.

Giles moved so quickly that she could not counter. He dropped down beneath the arc of her attack and the sword passed above his head, even as he kicked out at her. His foot caught her in the gut, cracked one of her lower ribs, and sent her staggering backward. Buffy nearly fell over, stumbling several paces, and just regained her balance in time to avoid the vampire's follow-up attack. She dodged that blow and brought the sword up again.

He wasn't Giles anymore. His brow was swollen and ridged, his eyes feral, his lips bared to reveal fangs. This was the vampire, then, the mask now disappeared, all pretense gone.

"And I had such high hopes for you," Giles said sadly.

"Happy to disappoint you," Buffy replied.

She pushed away her hatred and anger and grief and focused only on him, on combat, on surviving. Angel exhorted her to action from within his sorcerous prison but Buffy no longer heard the words. All she knew was the tension, the moment between her and the fiend who stood in front of her, the heartbeat before they would clash again.

"Come then," Giles snarled. "If you must die, do it quickly. I've had enough of your interruptions."

Buffy smiled, enjoying his pique. "It burns your butt, doesn't it? You really thought I would give up, give myself over to you? See, in the end, that proves there's no Giles left in you. That's evil thinking, vampire thinking. Maybe you have his cunning, but you don't have his brains."

Her words had shaken him, and Buffy darted forward, slashing the blade down and severing his left hand.

The vampire screamed.

"Moron." She launched a high kick that connected with his chin and rocked him back.

He staggered, clutching at the raw, red stump at his left wrist. Buffy rushed in, her hands tight on the sword. She grunted with the effort as she swung the blade again.

Fangs bared, eyes gleaming yellow in the dim light, Giles leaped at her, disrupting her attack. He slammed his forehead against hers, their skulls clacking together, and then he rammed his knee into her gut and tore the sword from her grasp.

"Buffy, no!" Angel called, his voice so far away.

The vampire king raised the sword in his one hand and brandished it with the skill of the expert fencer Giles had been in life. Buffy backed up, glanced quickly around the overturned desks and cabinets of the room for some weapon, something with which to defend herself.

"You know," Giles said calmly. "I actually think I feel sad to have to kill you. Odd, don't you think?"

He attacked, sword slashing down at her. Buffy leaped back, then ran to her left. She dove over a desk and he pursued her swiftly, confidently. Buffy's heart thundered in her chest but now her emotions were truly clear. There was only necessity now.

Don't die. That was the rule. Survival was all that mattered, whether her younger self ever managed to erase this nightmarish era or not, there was nothing she could do for Angel or for Giles, only for herself and for all those who had suffered under the vampire king's predations.

The sword slashed down and carved a huge chunk out of a wooden cabinet as she ran past. Buffy ignored Giles and ran to Angel.

She stood staring up at him, this good, decent being who had waged such a long war within his own heart. Angel seemed alarmed at first but he must have seen something in her eyes, for he smiled.

"I've always loved you," he said, so quietly that she had to read the words from his lips.

Her entire body was tensed, her senses attuned so that she could practically feel the shift of the air in the room, could hear the swish of the fabric of the vampire king's clothes as he swung the sword straight down. Five years this creature had kept Buffy prisoner, during which she had worked her body every single day. She was faster than he remembered. The blade cleaved the air, falling toward her head.

Buffy moved.

The sword crashed through the sparking energy field that surrounded Angel and the sorcerous electricity surged up the blade as though it were a lightning rod. Giles jittered as the spell he had cast lashed out at him with enough dark power to kill a man.

But this beast was not a man.

With a pop, the sphere collapsed and faded as though it had never been. In that same moment, freed for the first time in years, Angel reached for Buffy.

Her eyes met his and she went to grasp his hand.

Their fingers never touched. Angel disintegrated in a blast of cinder and ash and the stake dropped toward the ground.

Buffy caught it as it fell, that carved shaft of wood with which the vampire king had killed Angel. Giles was stunned by the effect of his own magick but as she turned on him, raising the stake, he tried to block with the sword. She kicked his arm aside, though his fingers were still closed on the hilt, and she moved in close.

His features changed, and once again she was looking into the face of her former Watcher.

"Buffy," he said softly. "Please—"

"This is my mess," she whispered. "Time to clean it up."

Then she staked him, looking into his eyes. The dust of his remains sprinkled on her clothes as it fell to the ground, and Buffy fell with it, going down on her knees, there among the ruins of a fight that had begun years earlier and only ended now. In truth, though, she knew when it had all started.

Just as she knew that it was not over yet.

"Buffy?"

The gentle voice belonged to Willow. The Slayer let the stake slip from her hand to clatter to the floor and she turned to gaze up into the face of this valiant woman, this sorceress who seemed to have less and less of the girl she had once been in her features.

Oz was behind her. Xander was not. As she studied Willow's tear-streaked face, Buffy understood why.

And at last she cried.

Willow came to her and knelt by her and they held one another. Oz stood just inside the door, his eyes rimmed with red, his feelings for once plain to see.

After a time, Buffy stroked the back of Willow's head and whispered to her. "I have to fix this. I have to make this go away and you have to help me. I don't know what it will mean for you, but—"

Willow shushed her and nodded and promised that she would help.

Buffy held her close. "I have to make it right."

CHAPTER 6

It rained all morning the day Xander was buried. The sky hung too low, a sagging gray canopy of clouds that seemed almost close enough to touch. It threatened at any moment to collapse and smother the earth in damp despair. But it was a hollow threat; there was no cataclysm, only the rain.

Only the rain.

Buffy and Willow stood together as the priest spoke at the graveside. Neither woman had an umbrella. The rain soaked their hair and clothes and Buffy felt her shoes sinking slightly into the sodden ground. She did not mind, nor did she even try to brush the wet hair from her face. Though it washed all the color from the world, cast everyone and everything in shades of gray, Buffy knew the color would return. More than that, she believed that this rain would begin to wash away the taint that Giles and Camazotz and the Kakchiquels had left on Sunnydale.

It might take a year of rainstorms, but it was a start.

The priest was Father Luis Vargas, a chaplain in the U.S. military. There were no clergy remaining in Sunnydale, though they were certain to return. In the meantime, however, now that the Council had done all the difficult work for them, the federal government had instituted a clandestine operation to restore the town, offering financial assistance to merchants and homeowners who had been driven out and wanted to return, or to people wishing to relocate there.

No mention of vampires was ever made.

Gangs, they said. Sunnydale had been the unfortunate victim of long-term gang warfare that terrified the citizenry, devastated the town's economy, and forced out many of its residents. This gang war had apparently also had a detrimental effect on surrounding communities, including El Suerte. Now, they said, thanks to a "police action," the gangs had been broken up, their leaders arrested, and a military presence was being maintained to prevent looting while locals and feds alike worked to restore the town to a functioning level.

Soldiers in the streets accepted the thanks of those who had lived in terror, as well as those who had cooperated with the vampires. But they were government soldiers, not Council operatives. After all they had lost, all they had sacrificed, the Council would not even be able to accept the gratitude of those they had liberated.

Buffy stared at the wooden casket and a tear slipped down her cheek. It was lost in the rain.

"It isn't fair," she whispered to Willow. "All he gave, and no one will ever know. His parents haven't even come back to Sunnydale. They should know what he did. That in spite of them, he was so brave and good."

Willow nodded, wiping away her own tears. "*We* know. I guess that has to be enough."

The priest droned on and it seemed to take forever, though Buffy was sure he was hurrying. And why not? He was a clergyman, yes, but he was just doing a job. This wasn't his town and they weren't his flock. The only reason Father Vargas presided over the service was so that the government could keep the cleanup as inconspicuous as possible. A brief memorial had been held the night before for all those who had fallen in the climactic battle in Sunnydale, their remains returned to their own homes for burial. Ms. Haversham had read the list of names and her voice had caught with emotion as she came to Father Christopher Lonergan, and then again when she read the name Wesley Wyndam-Pryce.

Giles and Angel were on that list as well. The reading of their names was the only memorial either of them would ever have, for their names and the memories of their deeds were all that remained of them. Wesley and Lonergan would be returned to their families and given a proper burial, but for Angel and Giles, there were no bodies to inter.

The priest raised his hand and made the sign of the cross over Xander's casket. Buffy gazed at the rain beading up and streaming down the wood and tried not to imagine Xander looking back up at her. To the right of the priest, Ms. Haversham stood with a handful of Council representatives, all of them in black umbrellas and mourning clothes. On Buffy's left, just past Willow, Oz held an umbrella over Anna Kuei's head as if he could protect the girl from not merely the rain, but the world.

Buffy studied Anna and her heart ached for the young Slayer. She remembered what it had been like for her at that age, when she had first discovered her destiny. Anna had seen her Watcher die. Buffy had witnessed the murder of her own first Watcher, Merrick, and now Giles was dead as well. That wasn't how it was supposed to be. Slayers had such a short life expectancy; it was the Watchers who were meant to be left behind to grieve. If it were possible to be trained for such a loss, they were.

As Buffy watched her, Anna glanced up and their eyes met. Though the girl did not smile or even nod, Buffy felt a kind of understanding pass between them and a kinship grew there.

"He'd hate that," Willow whispered.

Buffy glanced at her. "What?"

Willow gestured toward the granite headstone that the Council had rushed into the ground. It was engraved with the years of his birth and death, and with his full name: Alexander LaVelle Harris.

"Alexander," she whispered. "He'd hate that."

Then Buffy understood. "Nobody ever called him that."

"Not in his whole life," Willow said, her voice hitching with emotion. "Except for teachers the first day of school. It's just wrong. It's all just . . ." Her hands fluttered up toward her face as though she did not know what to do with them and then she pushed wet strands of hair away from her forehead.

"Wrong," Buffy echoed.

She stared grimly at the priest, who had completed the service and now turned to walk away. Ms. Haversham crossed toward Anna, spoke softly to the girl and then led her away, the young Slayer's shock of pink hair the one splash of real color on this gray day. Oz gazed for a long moment at the casket and then strode over to slip one arm through Willow's, a gallant gentleman escort.

"Hey," he said, greeting them both with that one word and eyes that had always communicated most of what he felt.

"Hey," Willow said softly.

He stared into her eyes then, perfectly still. "I was thinking it's like all along we've been in this huge house built out of our lives and everything we've been through up till now, and all of a sudden we stepped outside and the door shut behind us and we can't get back in."

A shudder passed through Buffy and she hugged herself, only now feeling the chill of the rain that soaked her clothes and skin. She wondered if she had ever heard Oz put so many words together at one time. He was usually so reserved. When he did speak, though, it was usually to make some wry observation, or to offer comfort. In some ways, his words now accomplished both.

Willow's face crinkled up and she wiped at her tears again and shook her head, her free hand touching her chest above her heart. "But I want to go back in."

"We can't," Oz said. His eyebrows rose and he tilted his head slightly, studying them. "Way I've got it figured, that door's locked now. But the thing is? There's the whole rest of the world."

Then this odd, sweet man who Buffy had known for years but never really *known* turned to her and one corner of his mouth twitched in what might have been a smile.

"At the end? He started to be Xander again, like he'd forgotten how to be and then someone reminded him. For what it's worth, I think that was you."

Her grief welled up within her then and Buffy found herself unable to respond to that. She offered a pained, wan smile, and then slipped her arm through Willow's on the other side and the three of them walked together away from Xander's grave.

"We're going to change it all," Buffy said as they left the cemetery.

"I think I've found a way," Willow replied.

Oz uttered a curious grunt. "I wonder if we'll feel anything."

Three days later, Willow sat at a broad oak desk surrounded by stacks of books and reams of notes in her own scrawl. Though the early morning sun streamed in the row of windows behind her, the green banker's lamp on the desk was still on from the night before. She had not slept.

Nearly a week had passed since the reclamation of Sunnydale and the extermination of the vampires who had inhabited City Hall. A search of the premises had turned up three entire rooms on the third floor of City Hall that were lined with books. Giles's library. He had learned what magick he knew from these ancient volumes and Willow knew that if she was going to figure out how to separate the two souls within Buffy, it would be here.

She set up camp that same night in the first of the rooms. Oz and Buffy took turns bringing her meals, most of which she did not eat. In the wee hours of the morning on which Xander was buried, she thought she found the beginnings of the answer.

Three days later, she was certain of it.

Exhausted, terrified by the thought of looking at herself in the mirror after days of little food and less sleep, she nevertheless felt a rush of excitement. She slid two books off the desk, both of which had pages that were yellowed and flimsy with age.

The previous morning she had allowed herself an hour to shower in what had once been the mayor's private bath and to change clothes, and now her hair was pulled up with just a rubber band. As she walked out of the room, she took the rubber band from her hair and shook it out, no longer needing to keep it out of her face. It felt good. *She* felt good.

It was shortly after seven in the morning when Willow rapped on Buffy's door. She paused briefly before knocking again. The third time around she heard Buffy moving inside and a moment later the door opened. There were several books on the floor next to a lamp but otherwise the room was spartan, a simple bedroll and a small duffel jammed with clothes all that Buffy had to her name.

Buffy wore a baby blue tank top and pajama pants and she stretched as she ushered Willow inside.

"Sorry to wake you," Willow said.

"S'okay," Buffy replied. "I was up late, training with Anna. She's actually pretty good." Even as she spoke, however, the Slayer's eyes went to the books in Willow's hands and then their eyes met.

"This is it?"

Willow nodded. "I had it sort of figured out days ago, but it took me a long time to figure out what to do with that knowledge."

Both women hesitated. After a moment, Buffy shrugged.

"What've you got?"

Willow walked over and set her books on the desk and then leaned against it. "A lot of this you know, some of it maybe you've only guessed. Some of it, honestly, I'm kinda guessing, too, based on what you've told me. The rest I put together based on research.

"Camazotz and Zotzilaha were Mayan deities, lords of the underworld, that sort of thing. Sometimes scholars mixed them up, which was sort of easy to do because they were pretty much a couple. Husband and wife, though obviously not *married* in that sense. He was the god of bats and both were more than demons, ancient beings who existed at the beginning of time but who gained strength from human worship.

"The destruction of Mayan civilization weakened both of them badly. For ages they couldn't even manifest on this plane. Zotzilaha was content with that but Camazotz needed worshipers. Somehow, in the late forties or early fifties by our count, he managed to open a portal to our world and came through. Zotzilaha did not want to come but he coerced her.

"She was miserable here. Hated every minute of it. Eventually she hated *him,* so much so that one night she attacked him and savagely mutilated his wings. Camazotz killed her physical form but her spirit escaped him before he could destroy that as well. As a ghost, if a deity can ever really be a ghost, she ran away, looking for a host body strong enough that she could elude or even destroy Camazotz.

"The demons had of course heard of the Slayer. So the ghost of Zotzilaha set out to find you. She masqueraded as The Prophet and used Lucy Hanover to help get to you, to warn you that you were going to make a mistake with horrible consequences. When Camazotz took Giles, you got desperate and she promised to show you the result of your mistake. All of that was pretty much accurate, but Zotzilaha only did it to get you to open up to her, to let her into your mind so she could force your spirit out."

Willow took a breath. The room was stuffy and the lack of sleep was beginning to get to her. She wished for a glass of water. The blacked-out windows were a harsh reminder of the evil presence that had inhabited this building and she did not like it.

As Buffy watched her expectantly, Willow cast a spell that restored the windows, eliminating the paint on them. It took the paint off the frame, too, but she thought that was a small price to pay for sunlight.

"Pretty much the way I figured it. How can you be sure about the recent stuff, though?" Buffy asked. She gestured toward the books. "You didn't get their lovers' quarrels out of books from the nineteenth century."

Willow smiled. "Vampy Giles was evil, but he still had some of Giles's old habits. He got it all from Camazotz, and he wrote it down."

A sad smile passed across Buffy's face. After a moment, she walked to the window and looked out at the street below.

"Here's what I don't get. The Prophet, whatever her name is, Z-woman . . . she was right. Her prophecy was true. Okay, instead of just showing me this future, she fast-forwarded my spirit five years. But to do that, she had to really be able to *see* this. The future, I mean."

"Exactly," Willow agreed.

Buffy turned to her, shaking her head. "No. You're not supposed to say 'exactly.' 'Exactly' is bad. You're supposed to explain it."

"You just did. Zotzilaha had precognitive powers, Buffy. She saw the future, saw what was to come, and she showed you, just as she said she would. But at that same moment, she used a spell of transference to move your spirit to the place your mind saw. When you first told me about it, I didn't understand how it could be done. What I was missing was how simple it really was. If she could show you the world through the eyes of your future self, she could cast the spell that would transfer you here. In some ways, it's like astral projection, only instead of you willingly leaving your body to wander the spirit realms, she used magick to force you out."

"Then she had to know," Buffy replied. "It was confusing at first when I, the two of me . . . whatever . . . when we both occupied this body for the first few days. But we adjusted 'cause even though there are two souls in this body, I'm still just me. When The Prophet pushed me into the future, she had to have sensed that the older me was really me. That she was no longer using my body as a host by this time. Didn't she know that she'd be destroyed?"

Willow could only shrug. "You know how arrogant those deities can be. I'm guessing she touched your future mind and soul, but just figured that the reason you were yourself in the future was because she had moved on to another host or returned to her own dimension by then. By now, I mean. It probably never even occurred to her that the reason the future you was still you was because Camazotz had killed her."

Buffy crossed her arms, muscles taut as she stared at Willow. Somehow she managed to look formidable even in pajama pants.

"Can you get me back?"

"I think I can undo the spell," Willow confirmed. Her pride and pleasure at being able to help made her smile and knock her feet against the desk on which she sat. "Actually, that's not the hard part."

Warily, Buffy raised an eyebrow. "What is?"

"Once I break the spell, the two souls in you will separate. You . . . the you who's supposed to be here, will stay here. The younger *you* will be pulled back automatically and return to its rightful body five years in the past when Zotzilaha, posing at The Prophet, came to you in our dorm room. But we both remember *when* that happened."

Buffy slumped against the wall again. "The night before I was captured," she said solemnly. "Giles was already dead by then, which means you've got to find a way to get me back earlier, to stop him from ever dying."

"Ex-act-ly," Willow said again, growing excited. "And I think I've figured out how. We just need to know *when*. Whatever mistake you made, you need to go back to that time and either stop yourself from making it or prevent the consequences from happening. We talked about that night at the harbor master's office when Giles was taken and you . . ."

Her words trailed off and Willow glanced away. She had been so thrilled by her discoveries, exhilarated by the sudden realization that she might actually be able to *do* this, that she had nattered on without taking Buffy's feelings into consideration. The last thing the Slayer needed was to be reminded that she had left her Watcher to die, and that because of that, thousands of others had been killed as well.

But Buffy surprised Willow by finishing her sentence.

"I ran," the Slayer said.

"Well . . . , 'ran' might not be, y'know, completely—"

"Okay. I threw myself through a window and killed a bunch of vampires and nearly drowned trying to get away."

Willow flushed.

"But I've been thinking about it, Will," Buffy added. "And I don't think that was it. I think I made my mistake earlier than that."

The early morning sun had warmed the room and it felt good, but still, goose bumps rose on Willow's skin. She waited for Buffy to elaborate, but the Slayer only smiled and walked toward her, picked up the books Willow had brought in, and gazed down at them.

"I'm not sure I ever really understood how lucky I was to have people who loved me for who I am, who were part of my regular Buffy-life and completely dedicated to taking part in my Slayer-life too," she said.

After a moment she glanced up and Willow saw that her smile had turned sad. Buffy proffered the books to her and Willow took them.

"Being the Slayer, the power that gives me, everybody calls it a gift. Way I'm seeing it, most every Slayer who ever lived had this burden dumped on them that they weren't prepared for. They fought the forces of darkness for a few lonely years, pretty much on their own except for their Watchers, and then they died.

"But me? I had you guys. And I never realized *that* was my gift."

Willow grinned sheepishly and suddenly all the sadness was gone from Buffy's face, just as magick had swept away the black paint that had kept the sun out of the room. In that moment, standing there in her tank top and pajama pants, and despite the time that had passed, Buffy looked once more like the new girl at Sunnydale High who had been so kind to her all those years ago.

"So what do we do now?" Buffy asked. "Do you want to talk to the Council or something before we do this?"

"Not thinking they'd believe us," Willow said. "And, okay, assuming they did? Not exactly sure they'd be the cheering section for what we have in mind."

Buffy frowned, shaking her head. Willow studied the Slayer's eyes, wondering if she could somehow see *both* Buffys in there.

"Which part of 'let's never have the army of vampires and avoid the mass murder' don't you think they'll like?"

"It isn't that," Willow said. "It's just . . . from their perspective, they won. What if, by going back, you don't prevent all this? What if you make it worse? And, okay, on a selfish, individual level, some of them might be thinking if you change the past, their present might be different in ways that are . . . unpleasant."

Buffy shook her head. "What could be worse than this?"

"Dying. That is, if you change the past, maybe some of us won't still be alive now."

"I never thought of that," Buffy said. "So what do we do?"

"Well," Willow ventured. "We could take a survey of the entire population of the world, find out if they mind if you tinker with the past to stop Sunnydale's little vampire holocaust. Or, y'know, we could just keep it to ourselves."

"I vote for Plan B."

Willow hugged her books to her chest. "I thought you might. Meet me in my office in an hour."

Shortly after eight-thirty, Buffy strode down the third floor corridor in City Hall. Already it was abuzz with the activities of Council operatives and government employees, both military and civilian, as they attempted to both restore order to Sunnydale and to cover up the circumstances that made their actions necessary. Only one or two people acknowledged Buffy as she passed, but that was all right. She recognized almost no one.

After a shower she had pulled on jeans, boots, and a green silk shirt that was almost too demure for her. It did not really seem to matter much. It had occurred to her that she ought to go and say good-bye to Oz and Anna, but then she had realized that there was no need. Within her were two spirits, and the Buffy whose soul belonged here would not be going anywhere at all. If she failed to alter the past, nothing here would change. And if she succeeded, no one would ever know.

She came to the door of the office Willow had

claimed as her own and knocked only once. Inside, much of the clutter in the room had been cleared, books stacked off to the sides now. White candles flickered, and they seemed oddly out of place in the sunlit room. A breeze blew in from the open windows and the candle flames sputtered but did not go out. Buffy had a feeling they would not go out, even in a hurricane.

Willow wore the same, rumpled clothes but did not look as tired now, despite her lack of sleep. She had been busy in that single hour, and the desk that had been piled with research was now barren save for two small metal dishes with incense burning in them, a small bundle of sticks and twigs tied with a red ribbon, and—lying across the wooden desktop—the same engraved sword she had used in her final combat with Giles.

"Am I late?" Buffy asked.

"You can't be late," Willow replied with a lopsided grin. "It's your party."

"You shouldn't have."

For a long moment they just looked at each other. Then Willow stood up from the chair and reached for the sword. She lifted it and beckoned for Buffy to approach.

"I have to cut you."

Buffy raised an eyebrow, taken aback. "Not that I don't believe you, but . . . why?"

Willow rested the blade point down on the wooden floor. "Souls are a sort of energy. All kinds of energy leaves traces behind. Souls make a mark on the universe, if you want to look at it that way. If you could see time, the energy of every soul living would leave a trail.

Zotzilaha put a curse on you that advanced your soul along the Buffy soul groove . . . and that sounds cool, but you know what I mean."

Buffy smiled. "I'm with you."

"The trick is, once I break the curse, you can't follow that same groove back or you won't be able to change anything. Fortunately, you aren't like most people. The power of the Slayer is a primal thing, an ancient force that is given to each Chosen One in turn, but the power itself never goes away. When a Slayer dies, the power still exists."

"It has its own groove," Buffy said, beginning to understand.

Willow raised the sword again and rested it on her shoulder. "You're groovier than most."

The breeze fluttered the candles again and their tiny flames danced but still did not go out. Willow's expression became suddenly very grim, all trace of humor gone. The time for procrastination, even for questions, was over.

"I'm going to bind you to that power, Buffy," she said. "I have to cut you a little and anoint you with your own blood. The blood of the Slayer, see? Even though it's your own, for the purposes of the spell it should still work. The spell isn't technically for that . . . it's really meant to let sorcerers see through the eyes of their ancestors. But it should make the pull of the primal power of the Slayer stronger than the pull of your physical form when you get where you're going.

"That means you'll have to concentrate on the moment in the past you want to return to, meditate on it with total focus. Once you've done whatever it is you need to do to stop all this from happening, you might not even remember any of this. 'Cause, y'know, it won't ever have happened."

An odd chill went through Buffy as she looked at Willow. "I don't want to forget," she said. "I think I need to remember this."

Willow shrugged. "What do I know? I'm just the travel agent."

Buffy took a long breath. "So where are you cutting?"

"Palm is pretty traditional."

The Slayer straightened up to her full height and held her hand out. Willow took it in hers and squeezed, then lifted the sword and lay it across Buffy's palm.

"Focus on that moment, the point in time you want to return to," Willow instructed. Then she slid the sword backward a fraction of an inch and the blade sliced through the rough skin. Buffy hissed air in through her teeth. Willow winced and glanced up at her apologetically.

"Look upon me as I draw seven drops of blood from you, blood which your ancestors have forfeited for you."

Blood welled up in Buffy's palm. Willow dropped the sword to the ground and took the Slayer's hand again. Cupping Buffy's hand in her left, Willow dipped the fingers of her right hand into the blood and then daubed Buffy's forehead and cheeks, then each of her wrists.

"Open your mouth," Willow said, voice weak.

Buffy did as she was told and Willow smeared her

mouth and teeth, even her tongue. The copper tang of her own blood was strong in the Slayer's mouth.

"From your heart, the blood of your ancestors, from the well of your spirit and the strength of all those who came before, I wed you to the ancient seed of the first among you, the first to bear the name Slayer, and each heart and soul and spirit 'tween she and thee. You are bound one to the other now, the power to the spirit."

Willow paused and for a second Buffy thought there was more. Then a shy smile crept over the features of the sorceress and she shrugged.

"I changed it around a little to make it fit, but that should cover it."

Buffy smiled. "It was great."

With her fingers pointed toward the ground, Willow began to swirl her hand in slow circles. The smoke from the candles and incense seemed suddenly drawn toward the center of the room and it gathered around Buffy, spinning lazily.

"That was the hard part," Willow said.

She gazed into Buffy's eyes, then went to the desk and picked up the small bundle of sticks. The smoke kept twisting around Buffy, though the Slayer could still feel the breeze from the windows. Willow held the bundle of sticks out to her and Buffy took them.

"When I nod, untie the ribbon and drop them," the sorceress said. "Good luck."

Buffy felt the prickly sticks and herbs in her hands, the slice in her palm stinging sharply. Her hand was slick with blood.

"In the name of Light and Darkness, in the name of the Earth and Air, in the name of the World and the Veil, remove thy curse and sting from this heart."

Willow gazed at her for a long moment and Buffy felt her eyes burn with the candle and incense smoke. Then Willow nodded, and the Slayer looked down at the bundle in her hands. She tugged at the red ribbon, felt its satiny fabric, and it came loose. Buffy watched the sticks fall . . .

. . . and fall . . .

Falling.

And yet soon it seemed not like falling at all. Rather it was as though she were deep beneath some red and pulsing ocean, hurtling along with the force of a current of unimaginable power. Yet there was no resistance, no pressure upon her as she was propelled through this ocean. She was not some intruder, but part of this abyss, this void, this sea.

She was water in the torrent, wind in the storm.

A chasm of infinite black yawned before her, and yet it was somehow familiar to her. Once she had felt herself lost, forgotten her own identity. No more. She felt the pull of her flesh on her heart, as though that were where her soul resided. And in her gut, she felt another force tugging at her.

In the blackness around her, lights flickered. Souls. Sparks and thoughts and emotions. The bus station, where Willow, Xander, Oz and Anya fought against the Kakchiquels and bled to try to stop her.

Not her. Not Buffy, but Zotzilaha in her body.

Camazotz was there. And so was the beast inside Giles, the monster, the vampire. The Watcher was already dead.

The god of bats tore the spirit of his demon bride out of Buffy's body . . . and that hollow cavern of flesh was a vacuum. Its emptiness pulled her, tempted her heart, her spirit, to return to its rightful place.

No.

Buffy focused her mind on an earlier point. In her dorm room at U.C. Sunnydale, talking on the phone to Oz. Giles had asked her to track Willow down so that they might perform a spell that would locate Camazotz. She had a list of the materials he needed for the incantation. Yet when Oz told her that Willow was not home, Buffy had let it drop. Even knowing that Giles would be incensed, she had purposely not followed through.

For in her heart Buffy did not want Willow's help, or Giles's, or anyone's. She had convinced herself it was possible to separate the two lives she led. Not merely possible, but preferable. She had come to believe that letting her friends into her mission blurred the lines and detracted both from her efficacy as the Slayer and from the freedom and pleasure she ought to have had in her life as a nineteen-year-old college student.

Now she knew it had been selfish to think she should push them out of her life as the Slayer, and foolish to think that she could, that it was even possible to separate herself from her duty. But in that moment, she had allowed her emotions to cloud her reason. She and Wil-

low had had a silly misunderstanding earlier, and things had been tense between them. Willow was avoiding her, and in that one, brief moment, Buffy had allowed herself to be petty enough to want to avoid Willow as well. When she had the chance to ask for Willow's help, to follow through, she let that petty tension stop her.

So that was the moment. She sensed it approaching, that time when she would be in her dorm room, on the phone with Oz, when she would make the mistake . . . the error that would lead to Giles's capture and eventual death and the horrors of the future she had just experienced.

She would reach out for that moment, join once more with her flesh, and she would change it, averting all that was otherwise to come.

Buffy focused.

Then, suddenly, images began to coalesce in the void around her and for a span that seemed eternal but might have been only a spark of time, she smelled the ocean and heard the ding of a distant buoy. She saw the harbor master's office. While Camazotz watched, the vampire clutched Giles in his talons, prepared to take his life.

In a moment she would flee, crash through the window to escape, and Giles would be taken away to die under the fangs of one of the bat-god's minions.

She had to stop it.

By instinct, Buffy reached out with her whole soul. But this was not the moment. She knew it. If she stopped here she would only repeat the same motions. If she surrendered to Camazotz, she and Giles would both die.

Only by fleeing, surviving, did she have a chance to save him, and see what the future would bring then.

Recoiling, she tried to go on, tried to reach out, back to that moment on the phone with Oz, hours earlier that same night.

But she had lost her focus.

Every fiber of her soul cried out in alarm as she skipped past the designated hour, the day, the year . . .

In an instant that seemed very much like an eternity, Buffy reached out into the ether, the black-red void, and tried to grab hold of her own flesh, the body of the Slayer. A barrage of images assailed her and it was as though in that everlasting moment she could see through the eyes of every Slayer who had ever lived. This was what it meant that Willow's magick had bound her to the primal power of the Slayer.

Demon armies marched across frozen tundra. Villages burned. Horrors unimaginable died beneath her sword, her stake, her cudgel, her bare hands. Men draped in cloaks clutched magick in their grasp. Women in Victorian dress lay bloody in the streets. Dawn rose over ancient Rome and dusk fell across the French Revolution. She was all of them in a single instant. She hated their enemies and loved their lovers, she felt their pain and shared their bliss, and through every set of eyes she saw fangs, the face of the vampire, and the scattering of dust.

It was almost enough to pull her apart, to scatter her soul across the eons, among these thousands of years of Slayers.

No, *she thought, and it echoed over millions of days, infinite moments. I am the Slayer.*

Moment by moment, life by life, in an instant or a fraction of forever, she pulled herself back. Heart and soul she grasped the lifeline that was the primal power of the Slayer and she found herself again, reached up through time and looked through her own eyes the moment she met her first Watcher, Merrick. The moment he died. The moment she first met Angel and the night they made love. All the times she laughed with Xander and cried with Willow, and all the times that Giles silently lent her his strength and faith.

Then she was there, in that moment again, in the dorm room as a ghost, staring down at her own self, at Buffy Summers on the phone, talking to Oz, about to make a terrible mistake. She reached out to touch her own face, to at last make things right, to join her own flesh.

Collision.

She could not enter. Willow had broken the spell Zotzilaha had cast, but it was that very enchantment that had twinned her to her own future soul. Now, in the past, she was unable to enter her body when it already had a soul.

All she could do was watch as Buffy . . . flesh and blood Buffy . . . said good-bye and hung up the phone.

The moment had passed. It was over.

She was lost.

And then, from the mist around her that was partially her dorm room and partially still the abyss, a voice called her name. Slowly a section of the mist began to coalesce into a familiar face, filled with affection but also deeply troubled.

"Lucy," Buffy said.

Once upon a time, this spirit too had been a Slayer. After death, she had lingered upon the ghost roads, where souls traveled to whatever final fate awaited them. Lucy was a guide to them, a lantern held high to light the way for those who became lost.

Just as Buffy was lost.

"How can this be?" the ghost of Lucy Hanover asked.

And Buffy told her, grateful that she was not alone.

CHAPTER 7

In the house Oz shared with several other guys just off the U.C. Sunnydale campus, Willow struggled to keep all the cheese from sliding off the slice of pizza in her hands. Tendrils of it stretched from the slice to her teeth, still attached to the bite of pizza in her mouth. At last she severed the connection and the strings of cheese fell, nearly dragging all of it off the slice so that she had to use one hand to pull it up and plop it back down where it belonged. Her fingers were greasy and red with sauce and as she lifted it to take another bite, she caught Oz watching her.

He had paused in the process of eating his own slice and though he did not smile, his brows were knitted together in an expression of both curiosity and amusement.

"You could fold it," he suggested.

Willow saw that was exactly what he had done, his pizza folded in half like a paper airplane, keeping all the cheese and drippy sauce safely inside.

"I'm living dangerously," she told him. "Throwing caution to the wind. And pizza is supposed to be messy. The folding of pizza for one's own safety is an abomination."

Oz took a sip from the grape soda she had brought him, then gestured toward her with the can. "Plus, you got a big stack of napkins."

"Plus," she agreed, reaching for one off the pile. "But . . . even in the absence of napkins I would resist the urge to fold."

Oz nodded, clearly impressed. "Life without a net."

"It's my way," Willow said happily. She picked up her slice of pizza and bit into it. The cheese, completely loose now, began to slide off again and she was forced to keep the pizza in front of her face as she ate. Oz took two more quick bites of his slice, but he kept watching her.

This was exactly what Willow needed, just time with her guy. Buffy was her best friend and her roommate, but she had been more than tense lately and Willow felt as though she was being pushed away. It made her sad and a little angry at the same time, and hanging out with Oz and eating pizza was just what the doctor ordered.

In the corner of the room—surprisingly uncluttered for a guy's bedroom—sat Oz's guitar and amplifier.

"When we're done, will you play me that new song you've been working on?" she asked between bites.

"More a riff than a song, but if you insist."

"I do."

"So Buffy called while you were out."

Surprised, Willow put down her pizza and wiped her hands on a new napkin. "You didn't say."

"Didn't want to interrupt the feast. She and Giles are working on the Camazotz thing and were hoping you could search manifests, ports of call and such for ships stopped over in Sunnydale."

Instantly Willow's mind began to work, turning the request over, considering the time and difficulty involved. There were unknown variables, of course. She was not quite certain how to go about ascertaining which ships were currently moored in Sunnydale, but suspected it would be possible to find out.

"Did she say how fast they needed it? If it could help them find Camazotz, I guess it's important."

"Maybe. She didn't say."

Willow took a drink of her soda and pondered. The way Buffy had been behaving lately, trying to do everything herself, it was surprising that she would ask for help. *It* must *be important,* she thought.

"I should call her back."

But when she did, there was no answer. If Buffy had called while she was out, it could not have been more than twenty or thirty minutes earlier. A ripple of concern passed through her as the answering machine clicked on and she hung up without leaving a message. For a moment she just stared at the phone, then she picked it up again and began to dial the number for Giles's apartment.

A sudden squeal came from the amplifier in the corner of the room. Willow flinched at the assault on her eardrums and glanced over at the offending box to see that the red light that would have indicated it was on was not illuminated. Confused, she glanced at Oz, who seemed equally baffled. He rose and went to look at the amp and Willow had to hang up and start dialing again because she had lost her place.

The lights in the room dimmed as though the power were being siphoned away. In her peripheral vision, Willow saw something move. On the other end of the line, the phone in Giles's apartment began to ring. She turned, and there in the center of the room, just above the pizza box and the detritrus of their little picnic on the carpet, the ghost of Lucy Hanover hung in the air, her transparent form shimmering with an ethereal light.

Willow hung up the phone. The grim cast of the specter's features sent a shudder through her.

"Were we expecting company?" Oz asked quietly.

"Lucy?" Willow ventured. "What is it?"

"Good evening to you, friend Willow," the ghost began. *"I am sorry to interrupt, but we have little time, and it is not I who needs to speak with you."*

She was about to ask what Lucy was talking about when she realized that there was another form coalescing there in the half-light of the room. Willow held her breath, wondering what this new ghost would be. It took form beside Lucy and even before the features of this spirit had become clear, a terrible knowledge formed in Willow's heart and she began to shake her head.

"No . . ." Willow whispered, shaking her head. "It can't be. You . . . you can't be . . ."

Oz came up beside her and slipped an arm around her waist. Willow was grateful, for she feared she might have collapsed otherwise.

"Willow," the new arrival said, its voice like the rustling of the wind in the trees.

It was Buffy.

Willow felt cold and hollow inside. "Please, no. Buffy, tell me you're not—"

"It isn't what you think, Will," the spirit said. A strange, tinny, static echo came from the powerless amplifier on the other side of the room. *"I'm me . . . sort of . . . but I've made a huge mistake and things are about to pretty much go to hell. I need your help to stop it."*

"I don't understand."

"When I called, I was supposed to ask you to come meet me and Giles to do a spell to find Camazotz . . . to go get the ingredients for the spell, but I . . ." the apparition of Buffy became agitated. *"Look, I can explain it all later, but right now I need you to call Xander and Anya. They're at Giles's. Go pick them up and meet me at the harbor master's office in Docktown. And come armed. Heavily armed. Kakchiquels are stronger and faster than your average vamp and there are going to be a lot of them. Some Molotov cocktails wouldn't hurt."*

Willow's heart was racing. She glanced at Oz.

"I can handle the Molotovs," he said simply.

"We'll be there," Willow told the phantom version of her best friend, whose form looked disturbingly similar to Lucy Hanover's. It was hard for her to shake the idea that both of them were ghosts, that Buffy was dead. "Are you really okay?"

"With you guys to back me up, I will be," Buffy said

in that strange voice. *"But you have to hurry or it'll be just like last time."*

Willow frowned. "Last time?"

"Giles will die," the Slayer told her. *"And that's just the beginning."*

The pulsing abyss of red and black had given way now to a new void, a gray, swirling, formless mist. Buffy was familiar with this place, however. She had traveled here before, not merely as a spirit, but physically. These were the ghost roads. Silhouettes flitted through the nothingness all around her and low voices called out, some desperate and some filled with wonder.

Lucy led the way through the mists and Buffy followed as best she could, walking swiftly, though she knew that walking in this spirit realm was subjective.

"Stay with me," the ghostly Slayer said. *"We cannot afford to have you become lost if we are to prevent the events you described to me."*

She reached one ethereal hand back. Buffy took it, and then they were traveling side by side. It chilled her to make this journey, to realize that though all souls experienced the time after corporeal death differently, many of them walked these paths and some got lost. For the fortunate ones, Lucy was there to guide the way.

"From what you have said, it seems I had a role in enabling Zotzilaha to trick you," Lucy continued. *"You have my regrets."*

"For something you won't ever do?" Buffy replied, *trying to ignore the forms skittering about the gray ether*

around her. "Bygones. If you can get me back into my body, we'll call it even."

Lucy turned to her as they walked and smiled, her dark hair framing her porcelain features. "It won't be my doing, Buffy. I can aid you in manifesting for your fleshly self to see, but then it will be up to you to convince her to allow you to intrude. Just as, in your experience, what is yet to come at this time, Zotzilaha required your consent to touch your soul."

Before Buffy could respond, the mist around them parted and color bled back into the world. Everything seemed two-dimensional, false and thin, like the painted backdrop in an old movie. They were on the street in Docktown perhaps a block away from the harbor master's office. Somewhere nearby a dog was barking and the sound of the surf was a low undercurrent running beneath everything. The sky was somewhat overcast and the stars shone through only dimly. A gull cawed overhead.

Giles's weathered Citroën was parked only a few feet away. Though it was dark, Buffy could see herself sitting in the front seat.

"Come," Lucy said, and she drifted closer to the car.

Buffy followed the ghost until they stood just beside the front door, and now she could see the interior of the car more clearly. It was all wrong, the world inside out, being able to see herself from the outside like that. Her soul quaked and she yearned for the safety of her own flesh, the security of looking out from her own eyes. She was close enough now to see the expression on the face *of the Buffy inside the car, bored and frustrated, and only just beginning to wonder what was taking Giles so long.*

Giles. She turned and glanced along the street at the harbor master's office. A single light burned inside the small structure. On the front stoop, Giles stood, arms crossed impatiently. The sight of him there, alive and well, thrilled her, but there was no time to lose. Any moment now, she knew, the harbor master would drag him into the building where Camazotz was already waiting.

Lucy began to pass through the car as though it were not there at all and Buffy hesitated, her mind unable to grasp that such a thing was possible. She was merely a spirit now, her nineteen-year-old soul free of the limitations of flesh, but it was hard to imagine. Then Lucy reached out and grabbed her sleeve and tugged her into the car after her, and she found herself sitting in the backseat of the Citroën, staring at the back of her own head.

"Buffy," Lucy said, her voice clear and filled with authority.

Simultaneously, both soul and flesh turned to the ghost. In the front seat, Buffy's eyes widened in alarm and then she visibly calmed when she saw that it was Lucy Hanover who spoke to her. Then her gaze ticked to the right and she saw herself.

Buffy watched the shock and recognition in her own eyes.

"What are you supposed to be?" the flesh and blood Buffy asked, steel in her voice, though her spiritual self could see how unsettled she was. No one else would have noticed, of course, but how could she not know herself.

"The ghost of Christmas yet to come," she replied. "Lucy told me ... told you ... something nasty was coming and that it would be your fault. It's true, but I can still stop it if you'll let me."

In the front seat, Buffy narrowed her gaze. "How?"

"Trust me."

For a moment, she feared it would not work, that all she had been through was for nothing. If she doubted, if she thought this was some kind of demonic trick, it would be over. But as Buffy reached out a spectral hand to touch her own face, she again saw recognition in her own eyes and she knew that there would be nothing barring her from entering her body this time.

Her fingers passed right through her skin.

Once more, two souls merged as one in the body of the Slayer. Memories of the days to come, and the nightmarish future she had lived in so briefly, clashed with the mind of a Buffy who had yet to experience any of those things. Confusion overwhelmed her and she groaned and slumped down in the front seat of the car, felt the rough upholstery beneath her cheek.

Seconds ticked by, but no more than that. Her eyes focused on the dials of the radio and then she sat up again. Buffy was unsettled by this twinning of her soul, but at least part of her had felt it before, and so it was not quite as difficult.

In the backseat, the ghost of Lucy Hanover, less translucent in the darkness of the car, watched her curiously.

"Are you all right?"

"We'll find out," Buffy told her. "Make sure Willow and the others didn't get lost."

And then the ghost was gone.

Buffy leaned forward and peered out through the windshield at the harbor master's office. Giles was still there, but even now he reached up and knocked on the door again. She popped the door and jumped out. It hung open behind her as she ran toward him. Buffy was about to call out a warning when the door to the harbor master's office opened and a hand thrust out to drag Giles inside.

She cursed under her breath and ran faster, haunted by the familiarity of these events. The distant ring of a buoy reached her and dread crept through her as she began to fear that she could not change this moment. Every step was one she had taken before. The only difference now was her awareness of what lay behind that door, and of the Kakchiquels lurking in the shadows around the building, readying themselves to move in and surround the harbor master's office.

No, there's one more difference, she thought. *Help's on the way, and this time they know what they're dealing with.*

Xander sat on the floor in the back of Oz's van and held on to the box of Molotov cocktails as they took a hard corner. Glass clinked together in the box and he twitched. "Is there a reason I'm the one with the explosives between my legs?" he asked.

Willow was in the passenger seat next to Oz and she turned around to look at him, one hand propped on the dashboard as the speeding van turned another corner.

"They only blow up when you light them and throw them," she said helpfully.

"I knew that," he replied quickly. "But still, not the most comforting feeling in the world."

No one responded. The sense of urgency among them was grave, and no wonder. He was pretty puzzled by the whole Buffy-mirage thing Willow had told him about, but he'd seen weirder since the Slayer had moved to Sunnydale. What really bothered him was how much importance Willow and Oz were putting on Buffy's suggestion that they hurry. Xander did not like that at all.

He glanced around the back of the van, where Oz often carted his band's equipment around. Now the vehicle was loaded with weapons. No big war hammers, and no stakes. Going up against the Kakchiquels apparently required close quarters fighting without getting *too* close. There were two crossbows, an antique and a more modern version, a long sword, a battleax, and a curved blade Willow had said was a scimitar. If these guys were as fast as Buffy said, the crossbows would get used once and then things would get really ugly.

Anya sat across from him, a look of concern on her face. He loved her, but had not really wanted to bring her along.

"We did remember the lighter, right?" Willow asked suddenly.

Xander had a moment of panic before Anya proudly produced the silver metal lighter, popped it open and lit it. The flame was high and strong and only a few feet away from the Molotovs. He was about to protest when she snapped it shut.

"I'm very helpful," she told him. "Isn't it exciting?"

"Oh yes," Xander replied. He glanced down at the box of liquor bottles between his legs. Oz had made the Molotovs from booze his housemates had lying around. There had to have been an awful lot of it, because he'd been able to pick and choose just the alcohol that was one hundred proof or more, without which the little fire bombs would not work. Then he had ripped up an old bowling shirt and stuffed strips of cloth into the necks of the bottles. *A good job,* Xander thought.

Twelve bottles. He wondered how many vampires.

When the ghost appeared inside the van, he actually shouted in alarm. She was right between Xander and Anya, but he could still see his girlfriend through the dead Slayer's diaphanous form.

"It has begun," Lucy Hanover told them. *"You must hurry."*

Much to Xander's dismay, Oz actually accelerated. They rounded one more corner and then were on the straightaway that shot through the center of Docktown right toward the ocean. At the end of the road was the harbor master's office. Though he was disturbed by the nearness of the dead girl's ghost, the crisis of the moment took precedence. Xander set the box of fire bombs aside and leaned forward to peer between Oz and Willow as the van careened down the street.

"No cops, no cops, no cops," he chanted.

There were no cops.

The street dead-ended at the ocean and it was dark down there, but he saw Giles's car on the left as they approached. And beyond it . . .

"Buffy," Willow said. "She just went into the building."

But Xander was not looking at the door to the harbor master's office. His attention was on the shadows on either side of the building. As he watched, the Kakchiquels appeared, their eyes sparkling orange in the dark, their dark tattoos making their faces barely visible. They slunk out from beside the building and began to gather in front of it in a kind of half-circle, facing the door.

"And here come the rest of the party guests," Xander said.

"I will see if I can help," the ghost whispered.

Xander shivered, but when he turned to look at her again, Lucy was gone.

"Crossbows," Willow said, glancing back at him.

He grabbed the two weapons, made sure bolts were nocked into them, and handed them to Willow. She had one in either hand as Oz aimed the van straight at the front of the building.

"Anya." Xander used his foot to shove the box of Molotov cocktails at her. "Get ready to light a couple. We're going to need the vampires to cluster around us."

"Shouldn't be hard," Oz said simply. Then he laid a hand on the horn. "And now Buffy knows we're here."

At the roar of the engine and the sound of the horn, the vampires all turned. Oz steered right at them and two went down with a crunch of flesh and bone. Xander silently hoped they'd broken something significant enough that it would take a while for them to heal; at least long enough to keep them out of the fight.

Willow handed Oz a crossbow and they each fired out through their open windows. Xander heard a squeak of triumph from Willow and knew that they had both found their marks. Two Kakchiquels dusted.

Even as the front windows were being rolled up, vampires began to pound the sides and back doors of the van. The metal of the rear doors bucked and creaked, but were locked. Xander held a Molotov in each hand while Anya lit the alcohol-soaked strips of shirt that hung out of them as wicks. As soon as they flared up like torches he handed one to her and then slid to the back of the van.

"Anya, door," he said. "Oz, get ready to give me some room."

Oz put the van in gear. "Got it."

Xander tensed, raised his feet. "Unlock it."

Molotov blazing in her right hand, Anya popped the back lock with her left. The Kakchiquels were so intent upon battering the vehicle that it took a moment before they tried the handles again. The doors began to open and Xander kicked out with all his strength. They popped open, knocking several of the vampires aside.

Together, he and Anya hurled the flaming bottles into the crowd behind the van and vampires roared in pain as the Molotov cocktails shattered, spilling burning alcohol all over them. Four of them were set alight in an instant, their clothes igniting and their hair beginning to blaze. As those crumbled to the ground, trying to put themselves out, they blocked the others from attacking.

The passenger window shattered in front and hands reached in, clutching at air as they tried to reach for Willow. Xander did not need to tell Oz to drive. The van lurched forward, rolled thirty or forty feet, then slammed to a halt again.

Xander passed the battleax up to Oz and the scimitar to Willow. The sword he took for himself, though he had little proficiency with such a weapon. The back doors of the van swung open but no vampires approached, after what had happened to their comrades. Even as Willow and Oz got out, weapons in hand, Xander jumped out the back. Anya followed, sliding the box of Molotovs up to the edge. She pulled another out and lit it, even as the vampires began to attack again.

Anya threw the bottle, another Kakchiquel burned. Oz and Willow joined Xander in a rough circle, hacking at the monsters. As Xander watched, a greasy-haired vampire raked its claws across Oz's shoulder and he grunted in pain. Before he could go to Oz's help, Willow was there, her scimitar scything down to decapitate the vampire. More Molotovs shattered around them and vampires burned and turned to dust. Xander managed to down a couple of them, but not to kill them, and he cursed his clumsiness with the sword.

But he took them out of the fight. That's what counted.

A hand grasped his shoulder from behind, fingers digging in. Xander tore himself away, spun, and this time his blade did connect. Bone and muscle crunched but the sword's edge did not pass all the way through the vampire's neck. Sickly orange light burned in its eyes and though he had seen this breed of vampire once before, he was still unnerved by the bat tattoo on its face, seen so close up.

Then it dusted. Although he had not cut all the way through, apparently it had been far enough.

"And they say close only counts in horseshoes and hand grenades," he scoffed.

Behind him, Anya screamed. He turned to see two Kakchiquels grabbing at her. One of them was an olive-skinned woman with close-cropped hair and killer legs clad in leather pants. The other was a skinny guy with his hair in a ponytail. The female ripped an already lit Molotov out of Anya's hands.

Even as he moved to help her, Xander knew he would be too late. In his mind's eye, he had visions of Anya's neck being snapped.

Then the female vampire kicked her companion in the gut, causing him to stagger back, and she threw the Molotov. It burst into flames and the vampire tried to beat at his own chest even as his ponytail lit on fire, burning like a torch. He ran away as though he could escape it, and then exploded in a flash of cinders.

"What the—" Xander began, even as the vampire in leather pants turned to smile at him.

"*I said I would try to help*," the Kakchiquel said in an eerie voice he instantly recognized.

Anya tried to attack the vampire and Xander had to stop her.

"No," he said. "It's Lucy Hanover."

"How's that?" Anya asked.

"I don't know, but I'm not complaining."

The three of them turned back to the fight. Fire blazed and blades fell and vampires died, and suddenly Xander realized they were winning.

The harbor master's office was trashed. Paperwork was strewn about the huge oak desk in the far corner. A lamp lay broken on the floor next to a phone that was off the hook. Both had been knocked off the desk. An old framed painting of a schooner about to crash onto the shore by a lighthouse hung nearly sideways on its hook. A shelf of books had been knocked over. Two other lights still burned in the room, dim, but leaving plenty of illumination to allow Buffy to see the horror that was unfolding before her.

The exact same scene she had been witness to before. Exactly the same.

In a narrow doorway that led into another part of the office, Giles lay half in one room and half in the other. His pants leg was torn and blood had begun to seep through the cloth. He tried to sit up, eyes glazed over as he shook his head, blinking rapidly. His face was already bruised and cut, blood dripping down his chin from some unknown wound inside his mouth.

The harbor master was hunched over Giles, holding him by the front of his shirt. With his other hand, the gray-bearded vampire gripped Giles's throat and snarled at Buffy.

The same.

But then, outside, she heard the loud beeping of a car

horn and the screeching of tires and she knew her friends had arrived. She was not in this alone.

"Let him go," Buffy demanded.

The vampire laughed, a deep, throaty, gurgling sound. "Or what? You'll kill me? And if I free him, what then? You'll let me go? We're not all that stupid, you know."

Words she had heard before.

With a grunt, the creature hauled Giles up and spun him around, holding him as hostage, as shield.

"Buffy . . . you must go . . ." Giles croaked.

The vampire rammed its head into the back of Giles's skull. The impact was loud, and sounded perilously fragile, as though something had broken. Buffy cringed and felt as though she might throw up. She had forgotten that part, that sound. Giles's eyes rolled up to white and he went limp in the vampire's powerful hands.

Now, she thought.

Buffy kept her eyes on Giles and the harbor master but she moved to the right, away from the door. Moments later, a hideous silhouette appeared in the doorway.

This Camazotz was a far cry from the bloated, pitiful beast he would become. Naked from the waist up, the tall, hideous thing was hunched over and his ravaged, skeletal wings jutted up from his back. On his chest was an enormous scar, and at the center of the scar an open wound that seemed partially healed, as though it might never close completely. Buffy had not understood that before, but she now knew the wound had come from his *feeding* of his Kakchiquels.

She had nearly forgotten what he looked like during

this, their first meeting, before his sanity had been lost to him. His hair was black and thickly matted, as was his long beard. He had a short, ugly snout with wet slits for nostrils, and his chalky, green-white skin was pockmarked all over. Upon his forehead were ridges that resembled those of a vampire. From his mouth jutted rows of teeth like icicles, and his fingers were inhumanly long and thin, white enough to have been little more than bones.

His eyes blazed orange fire.

"Join the party, Camazotz," she said amiably, her back to the wall now so that she could see both the demon-god and the vampire who held Giles's life in his hands.

The monster frowned at the familiarity in her voice. "You know me?"

"Better than you think."

The vestigial wings on his back fluttered with a dry whisper and Camazotz narrowed his blazing eyes.

"Those children outside. Friends of yours, I presume? They're going to die, you know."

Of course he had seen Willow, Xander and the others fighting his Kakchiquels as he entered the building. She figured he had dismissed them. They were mere humans, after all, and young at that.

"I think they might surprise you," Buffy told him.

Out of the corner of her eye she watched the harbor master, just in case. Camazotz noticed.

"The man means something to you," the demon-god said, indicating Giles. "Your Watcher?"

The same words.

His voice was wet and thick, something trapped in quicksand and desperate to be free. Again her gaze ticked toward Giles, still unconscious, and back to Camazotz.

"Not my Watcher. A friend," she admitted. She hefted the stake in her right hand, turned its point toward him. Though she had no desire to contribute to the way the scene was repeating itself, she could not help taunting him. After all, she already knew his sore spots.

"So you're the god of bats, huh? Considering the job description, those are pretty pitiful wings."

Camazotz actually flinched.

"The wife caught you napping, huh?" She gestured with the stake at his back. "Can you even fly with those?"

Camazotz lost all of the cool reserve he'd shown, and a primitive snarl split his features. His eyes flared and sparked.

"I knew I would have to destroy you to reach the Hellmouth, cow. I am prepared. My Kakchiquels are bred and raised by me. They do not fear you, girl, because they have never *heard* of you. They will face you without hesitation, down to the last of them, because they do not know what a Slayer is."

"Yeah, yeah. I've heard it all before," she replied, returning his snarl as she relaxed and tightened the grip on her stake. She stared at him, letting the moment of silence charge the air between them with crackling energy. Then she smiled. She knew she would not be able to antagonize him into attacking her, but she had to try.

"Let's get it on, stumpy."

The flesh of the ancient creature seemed almost to

ripple with his rage. He shuddered, nostrils flaring, long needle teeth bared, and he rose up to his full height, about to lunge at her.

Then Camazotz smiled.

Buffy sighed softly, resolved to play it out, praying that the small changes she had wrought on this night would be enough to buy her the moment she needed.

"You want to antagonize me into direct combat, believing you can destroy me and still save your ... friend," Camazotz said, slippery voice tinged with wonder. "And maybe you would at that, Slayer. Maybe you would. But I have—"

"Walked upon the earth since before the human virus blah blah blah. I remember. Just get on with it."

Camazotz stared at her, obviously unnerved that she had spoken the very words that had been about to come from his mouth. His chest rose and fell as he studied her. Then he gestured to the harbor master.

"If she does not obey me instantly, kill him. *Drink* him." Tongue flicking out over his teeth, Camazotz glared at her. All trace of humor was gone from his horrid countenance. "Throw the stake down. On your knees and crawl to me."

CHAPTER 8

On your knees and crawl to me.

So there it was. The same moment, the same situation. Even as the seconds had ticked toward those words, this very instant, she had been turning it over in her mind, examining it, trying to see if there was anything she could have done differently. If she had not broken into the office, Giles would already be dead. If she had charged the harbor master, Giles might already be dead. If she had attacked Camazotz as he entered, the harbor master would have killed Giles immediately. And now . . .

If she did as Camazotz commanded, she and Giles were *both* dead. If she attacked, Giles would be savaged, possibly murdered, before she could reach him. Now, though, she knew that even if she fled, she would be saving only herself. Camazotz was keeping Giles alive for the moment to try to manipulate her, but she had lived this night before and she knew that if she ran,

529

Giles would become something even more horrible than the god of bats himself.

Buffy would not surrender herself, but she had to buy time and hope that her friends came through for her. She had to trust in them. In the vampiric old man's grasp, Giles moaned softly, beginning to regain consciousness. Camazotz stared at her, almost daring her to attack. When she dropped to her knees on the wooden floor, his horrid, inhuman face split into a grin that revealed the rows of needle teeth within once more. A thin line of spittle ran into the matted hair on his chin.

"Now crawl," the demon-god sneered.

On her knees, Buffy stared up at him. Her heart played out a rapid, erratic rhythm and she held her breath. Seconds passed and the energy that sparked in Camazotz's eyes seemed to burn brighter as he grew furious.

"Crawl!"

Buffy did not want to crawl. She put the stake carefully on the floor beside her, praying she would have a chance to use it. Reluctantly, she went down on all fours and began to crawl toward Camazotz.

Out of the corner of her eye, Buffy saw his lackey, the harbor master, relax the hold he had on Giles.

"Buffy, no . . ." Giles murmured weakly.

The god of bats began to laugh.

From the open doorway, the blade of a scimitar swept toward his neck. In the last moment, he sensed or heard his attacker and began to turn, and the curved blade sank into the putrid flesh of his chest.

Eyes wide with fear and shock at what she had just

done, Willow tried to pull the blade from Camazotz's body but it was lodged there. The demon-god screamed in rage and shook her loose. Willow staggered back two steps.

The white-haired vampire gaped at the spectacle of his master reeling, trying to pull the scimitar from his chest. Buffy snatched up the stake from the floor and leaped across the room at him. Giles saw her coming and tried to duck but the vampire held him firmly. The harbor master looked up at Buffy at the last moment, but then she had him. With a short kick, she broke one of his arms and Giles staggered free, still unsteady on his feet.

Shock registered on the harbor master's face as Buffy grabbed him by the throat and rammed the stake through his heart. He crumbled to dust even as she spun away to see Camazotz tear the scimitar from where it was wedged in the bones of his chest. The demon-god roared and hunched toward Willow.

"Hey!" Buffy shouted.

As Camazotz turned toward her, he faltered, unsteady from the wound Willow had given him.

"Where were we?" the Slayer asked. "Oh, yeah, you were gonna crawl?"

The god of bats glared at her with such hatred that Buffy shuddered. But the electric flicker of demonic energy in his eyes had dimmed. He was off-balance, weakened, and apparently the last thing he wanted was to face the Slayer now.

"It was not supposed to be like this," Camazotz muttered.

Buffy started toward him. "Sucks to be you."

Then, as she and Willow both watched in surprise, Camazotz turned and with a burst of renewed strength, leaped up onto the desk and crashed through the window and onto the street beyond.

"No!" Buffy yelled as she ran to the window.

But when she stared down at the pavement in the alley on the side of the building, there was only shattered glass and broken bits of window frame. Camazotz was gone.

"I must say," Giles began weakly as he walked up behind her, "for a moment there . . ."

Buffy turned to him and smiled, shaking her head. Giles had long scratches on his face and neck, a small cut on his forehead that had bled quite a bit, and he hissed in pain as he reached up to touch the spot on the back of his skull where the harbor master had struck him.

"You're a mess," she told him.

"Yes. Well, you don't have to be so happy about it," Giles replied tiredly. He glanced around. "Have you seen my glasses?"

They were on the floor several feet away. She grabbed them and handed them to him, just as Willow called to her.

"Buffy! Out front!"

Together they ran to the door, but when they reached it they were surprised to see Xander, Oz and Anya just up the street, standing by the van and watching in astonishment as the six or seven remaining Kakchiquels fled into the shadows. Bruised and bloody, Xander nevertheless began to give chase.

"Come on!" he cried. "'Tis but a scratch!"

He ran out of steam after half a dozen steps and bent over, hands on his knees, trying to catch his breath.

"Come back and fight, ya bunch of yellowbellies," he rasped.

"Yellowbellies?" Oz asked.

Xander shrugged. "It's a John Wayne thing."

Buffy lent Giles her support as they walked down the steps with Willow. On the street, the others gathered around them. Anya threw her arms around Xander and kissed him passionately until he winced and gingerly began to search his rib cage for some hidden damage.

"Camazotz got away," Willow announced.

"Oh, that's perfect," Anya snapped. "So much for urgent. Xander and I didn't even have time to make Giles's bed. We rush all the way down here, put our lives on the line, waste all that alcohol on fire bombs, and you let him get away."

"Well, *let* is a strong word," Willow said defensively.

Anya crossed her arms and glared at them sternly.

"If it helps any, Willow has impeccable timing and probably saved my life and Giles's," Buffy offered.

But Giles was paying her little attention. He was staring at Anya with a baffled expression on his face. "What about my bed?"

"So!" Xander said abruptly. "How're we gonna find this guy now?"

"Actually," Buffy replied, "I think I know just the person to ask. But we're going to need Lucy's help."

"Ooh, she was so great," Willow said excitedly. "She

possessed a vampire, this trashy girl in leather pants, and was helping us out." She glanced around. "Where'd she go, anyway?"

Xander and Anya turned to stare expectantly at Oz. He stood there with his hands in his pockets and raised his eyebrows as if he had no idea why they were looking at him.

"Oz?" Giles inquired.

"He dusted her," Xander explained.

"You killed her?" Willow asked, horrified.

Oz shrugged. "Accidentally. And, not that I'm not sorry but, last I checked, ghosts pretty much already dead."

"Yeah, but ouch." Buffy shivered and then looked around at her friends, these people without whom she would not have been able to survive this night a second time. She had no idea what she would have done without them. Still, the night was not over yet.

"Come on," she said, heading for Giles's car. "We've got work to do."

Giles lay on the couch and stared around at his apartment. It had never seemed so small to him. The clock ticked the seconds off loudly on the wall and he could not keep his gaze from straying to it from time to time. It was a quarter till midnight and he did not think he had ever seen Buffy and her friends so quiet. The calm was almost enough to make it seem as though the conflict with Camazotz was over.

But the final battle was still to be fought.

They had returned an hour and a half before but it had

taken time for them to cleanse their wounds. Oz had a gash on the back of his head that might need stitches. Giles had washed his own scratches and cuts with alcohol and tried not to whimper loud enough for the others to hear. He would probably have a small scar on his forehead from the harbor master's initial attack, but it would be a near thing. They were all suffering from bruises and aches that would linger for days afterward, but were fortunate that none of their injuries were more serious.

Xander and Anya were curled up together on the floor . . . which was preferable to Giles's bed, as far as he was concerned. He thought Xander might even be snoring lightly. Willow and Oz were at the table poring through books to make absolutely certain the spell that had to be cast would be powerful enough for their purposes. But there was really no way to be sure.

Buffy had placed candles all about the room. There had not been enough white ones so she had been forced to improvise with a small box of birthday candles. Now the Slayer moved quietly from place to place with a silver lighter Anya had given her and lit the candles one by one.

With the corner of his shirt, Giles wiped the lenses of his spare glasses—the others had been cracked—and then slipped them on. He approached Buffy as she lit the last of the candles and when she turned to face him her eyes brightened. It warmed his heart to see the affection she felt for him, but it seemed odd, too, for she behaved as though she had not seen him in months.

"There's a great deal you're not telling me," he said, his voice low.

Buffy nodded. "Pretty much."

"You seem different."

"Older?"

Curious, Giles thought. "Actually, I only meant that you seem like your old self again. Your behavior earlier tonight, well, you seemed impatient and quite rash."

The Slayer only raised her eyebrows. "Yep. You ready?"

Frustrated, Giles refused to allow her to brush him off. "How do you know all of this? About Zotzilaha and Camazotz? Do you really expect Willow to be able to learn alchemy in a matter of hours? How can you be certain the references to gold being Camazotz's weakness are true?"

His mouth opened again but Giles fell silent, embarrassed by his outburst.

A sadness washed over Buffy's features, but it lasted only a moment. "You just have to trust me. And believe in Willow."

That flustered him. "I do, on both counts. But alchemy? Surely there's another, simpler way to find something gold to use against Camazotz. Some weapon."

Buffy raised an eyebrow. "You have a golden dagger around?"

"Well, no, but—"

"Want Willow and me to raid our mothers' jewelry, maybe break into some jeweler's downtown?"

"Of course not! But perhaps if we had enough gold to melt down we could simply *coat* a dagger with it, or a stake for that matter, rather than having a weapon made of solid gold."

"I can't be sure something that wasn't solid would work, but let's say it would. What temperature does gold have to be at to melt?"

Giles glanced away. "Nearly two thousand degrees Fahrenheit."

"Do you know of a working foundry nearby where we could get a furnace up to *two thousand* degrees? Y'know, *right now?*"

"No. Certainly not. But look at it from my perspective, Buffy. In all my years researching the supernatural I have never once seen anyone successfully complete an alchemical process."

"I'm not surprised," Buffy said. "But I know Willow can do it."

The Slayer smiled softly, the flicker of candlelight on her face. Giles did not think he had ever seen her look so tired.

Buffy turned away and clapped her hands together, rousing Xander and Anya and drawing the attention of Willow and Oz at the table. "All right, let's evict the Mayan deities from Sunnydale so we can get some sleep. I still have to figure out how I'm going to convince Professor Blaylock not to fail me.

"Willow, are we ready?"

The young witch nodded. "Giles had all the things we needed to perform the spell. No guarantees, but I'm thinking it'll hold the big stinkin' liar of a Prophet."

"She's channeling her ire," Oz added.

"And we're all grateful," Buffy said gravely. "Now if Lucy isn't too cranky after you cut her head off, this just might work."

Once again, Buffy had the feeling that events were repeating themselves, though in this case the circumstances were not exactly the same. They were in Giles's apartment, for one, and it was night. More importantly, this time around, Giles was with them, safe and sound save for a few scratches and knocks on the head. He had a hard skull, though, her former Watcher. He'd survived plenty of cranial trauma before.

They were all tougher than she had been willing to give them credit for. And they were all here, and alive. Giles. Xander. Anya. Somewhere, Faith still lay in a coma. And down in Los Angeles . . . Angel. Their destinies lay ahead of them, whatever the future might hold, but for now Buffy had prevented the dark fates that had been in store for all of them, for the world. She had her friends again.

Still, though, there was much work to be done.

The candles she had placed in a rough circle around the room burned with white-orange flames that seemed to sway in a breeze that came from nowhere. Buffy and Willow sat opposite one another at either end of Giles's table. Xander, Anya, Oz and Giles completed the circle. It was a sloppy séance, or summoning, or whatever the official name for it was, but they did not have time to worry about the niceties of such things. Buffy wanted to bring an end to things tonight.

"Clear your minds," Willow instructed.

Her voice seemed somehow different to Buffy, deeper, more confident. It took her only a moment to realize that it was the same as the voice of her older self, that future sorceress who wielded her authority with as much grace as she did her magick.

Willow's eyes snapped open, fixed directly on Buffy. "I said clear your minds."

"Oh," Buffy said sheepishly. "Sorry."

Same words. But no longer the same situation. She had altered the past and so changed the future, yet Buffy would not rest until Camazotz was destroyed. Only then would she truly believe it was over.

Eyes now closed, Buffy took a long, deep breath, let it linger within her for a moment, and then let it out as though it were her very last. It was a cleansing, meditative technique Giles had taught her way back during sophomore year of high school. It worked.

"With hope and light and compassion, we open our hearts to all those walkers between worlds who might hear my plea and come to aid us in this dark hour," Willow began, intoning the words slowly.

Buffy felt Xander's hand grip hers on one side, and Oz do the same on the other. It was as though the innate power within Willow, the peace and mystic qualities within her heart and soul that made her so naturally attuned to the energies of the supernatural, had created a kind of electrical charge that ran through them all—a circuit of benevolent magick, a beacon to the souls to whom Willow now spoke.

"Spirits of the ether, bear my voice along the paths of

the dead, whisper my message to every lost soul and wanderer," Willow continued, voice lowering in timbre, becoming not unlike a kind of chant. "I seek the counsel of Lucy Hanover, she who was once a Slayer. She who holds high the lantern to light your path on the journey between worlds."

After half a minute's silence, Willow spoke again, this time her voice barely rose above a whisper. "Lucy, do the lost ones bring my voice to you?"

The answer was immediate.

"That hurt."

Buffy opened her eyes. The others were all looking as well. Lucy Hanover was there, hovering over the center of the table they had created, staring down at Oz with an admonishing look on her ghostly face.

Oz glanced away, looking a bit chagrined. "Sorry."

The candles flickered in the room and the shadows danced, the variations in light washing over and through the ghost. Parts of her misty form seemed more transparent than others. Normally reserved, Lucy smiled.

"All is forgiven. The heat of battle, after all, and all those vampires around. To be honest, it did not really hurt overmuch. I was merely controlling that form, not . . . not living in it."

Buffy felt sorrow for Lucy, then. She had been bodiless for a time, a lost soul in some ways, but she had flesh and blood to return to. She could not imagine what it must be like to be truly dead.

"Good evening once more, Willow," Lucy said. *"I am pleased you are unhurt."* Then the ghost turned her dark

eyes upon Buffy. *"We meet again, Slayer. I believe I know why you have called upon me once more. You wish me to try to lure The Prophet here, to mislead and help entrap her?"*

"If that's all right with you," Buffy replied.

"Oh, it's fine," Lucy told her, a smile on her ghostly features. *"Better than fine. The creature perpetrated a horrible cruelty upon you, and facilitated a hideous future. We have the opportunity to prevent that, and to punish her for her evil deception."*

"Spoken like the Slayer you are. Thank you." Buffy glanced at the table. Upon it lay a snow globe from Aspen someone had given to Giles, a seemingly harmless item. Around it, Willow had laid black yarn in an ever shrinking circle, its inner end beneath the base of the globe.

"Anyway, I don't think you'll have trouble with her," Buffy told the phantom Slayer as she watched the candlelight flicker off the globe. All was still inside it at the moment. "Zotzilaha wants to come."

"She wants your body," Xander observed happily.

Buffy shot him a look and then glanced back up at Lucy.

Lucy seemed almost to bow, though it might merely have been a wavering of whatever ethereal substance comprised her body. "I will seek her." Then, as if she had never been there at all, she was simply gone.

Oz was the first to break the circuit. He let go of Buffy's hand and then Buffy released her grip on Xander's. Anxiously, she glanced beneath the table to be sure the circle of salt Willow and Anya had laid out there was still intact and unbroken.

Though she had felt relieved when Giles had been saved, and quite calm as they prepared for this moment, now that it had come Buffy began to grow agitated again. In her mind's eye she could still recall the pain of Zotzilaha's touch, the terror she had felt as the curse the thing had used upon her became apparent. It chilled her and a sickly feeling began to churn in her stomach.

This was the creature who had started it all, who had stolen her body. Camazotz was a horrifying thing and he had to be stopped, but Zotzilaha was in some ways even more insidious. It occurred to Buffy for the first time since she had saved Giles that there was no longer an echo within her, no more twin soul. She was herself again, whole and complete and alone in that corporeal shell. But she still could feel the cold touch of this thing they had now summoned and she felt tainted by it.

She was the Slayer, and she had all of her friends around her, yet some small part of her was still afraid.

Oz broke the silence. "Well," he said. "That was bracing."

"What now?" Xander gazed at Buffy, sort of nodding his head to prod her to answer the question. His eyebrows went up as further punctuation. "Buff?"

"We wait—"

A gust of wind cut through the room fast and hard enough to scour the walls. Impossibly, though the flames sputtered, the candles still burned. Then, in a single moment, every candle in the roof was snuffed.

The wind swirled tighter and tighter until it no longer touched them, instead creating a miniature tornado in the center of the table. Then the wind itself seemed to bleed an oily black, the oil to spread and flow and take form. The wind slowed.

It *became* something.

"She has agreed to speak with you."

Buffy glanced quickly toward the window and saw the ghost of Lucy Hanover, hovering there, watchful. Wary. Knowing.

When she looked back, the wind had died and the flowing black core of it had coalesced into a figure, the silhouette of a woman. Zotzilaha had no face that Buffy could see, nor flesh, not even the diaphanous mist that gave Lucy shape. Instead, The Prophet was like a female-shaped hole in the room, a black pit that lingered in the air like soot from a smokestack.

But it spoke. *She* spoke.

"Slayer. You summoned me. How may The Prophet be of service?"

Her voice was like the whisper of a lifelong smoker whose throat had been ravaged by cancer. Pained and ragged and knowing, in on the perversity of the joke.

Gotcha, Buffy thought.

"You can tell me where Camazotz is, and then you can go away, pretty much forever, *Zotzilaha.*"

The thing twitched, her obsidian form shimmered where it hung in the room, a wound between worlds.

"I do not know how you found me out," the demon-spirit said, *"but you are of no use to me now. Fortunate for you. I will depart."*

Willow stood up from the table. "No. I don't think you will."

Buffy felt a tiny pang of alarm when the blackness began to flow toward Willow, menace in the way it seemed to consume reality around it. But then it collided with the invisible barrier created by the salt beneath the table and the spell Willow and Giles had performed, and the pulsing void began to pool and bleed around the edges of the table.

"What have you done?" the demoness thundered.

"They have trapped you, false seer, cruel spirit," Lucy Hanover said, floating toward the table now.

Buffy stood up as well. "Where is he? I know you are still linked to him or he wouldn't be able to track you. How far can you run away from someone you're bound to forever?"

The blackness quivered and at last seemed to take a more female shape. There might even have been a face there, vaguely outlined, somehow beautiful in its hatred for them.

"Camazotz sailed to your shores in the belly of a vessel called Quintana Roo, *a vessel that is now moored in the harbor not far from here. I care not what becomes of him. Now free me, Slayer."*

Buffy furrowed her brow. "Like that's gonna happen."

Even as the demon-spirit began to protest, Willow and Giles spoke simultaneously, their words overlapping as Zotzilaha screamed at them in fury. Once more that insidious, amorphous darkness began to churn, a tornado made of oil and tar that spun in upon itself, faster and faster around the center of the table. Around the snow globe. Tiny white flakes began to swirl in the glass ball and the flowing sable twisted tighter in upon itself, following the diminishing circles created by the black yarn beneath it.

With a sound like grease burning, Zotzilaha was gone. The inside of the snow globe was completely black, as though it were filled with ink. It was going to make an interesting paperweight for Buffy's dorm room.

Buffy stared at the globe. "Bet you didn't see that coming," she said. "Hell of a Prophet *you* are."

CHAPTER 9

For the second time that night, Willow rode shotgun while Oz drove to Docktown, once again with Xander and Anya in the back of the van. Some of the students she had met at U.C. Sunnydale who came from out of state had been surprised to find how chilly it could get in Southern California at night, but Willow had lived here all her life. Though they had swung by Xander's for some things, there had been no time to go back to the dorm and Willow regretted that now. A cold wind blew through the shattered window on her side and she shivered, lost in her thoughts.

"So, who else thinks Buffy's acting kind of freaky?" Xander asked from the back.

"I have always considered her somewhat freakish, so I'm not sure I could tell the difference," Anya replied.

"Freak-y, not freak-ish," he corrected.

Anya averted her gaze and was silent.

The van rumbled on toward Docktown and no one else replied. Normally that would not have stopped Xander, but tonight it did. He said nothing more about it. Willow was glad. Though she had a great many thoughts of her own about Buffy's behavior that night, they were not really things she wanted to discuss. It was all so odd.

How did she know so much about Camazotz and Zotzilaha? How had Buffy appeared in Oz's house as a spirit? How had she known the very moment when Giles's life would be in jeopardy, and that Camazotz and his Kakchiquels would be there?

Even as these questions whirled in her mind, they arrived at the wharf. As Buffy had requested, Oz parked back from the docks, out of sight of the ships that were moored there. Giles pulled in behind them a moment later with Buffy in the passenger seat. They all piled out quickly, but as quietly as possible. As the others began to remove the weapons from the back of Oz's van and from the trunk of Giles's car, Willow stood near the front of the van and stared at the stretch of ocean she could see between large shipping warehouses.

The sea was dark and almost invisible in that blackness, but even blind she would have known where she was. The sound of the surf and the scent of the ocean, the cool salty dampness that hung in the air, were all unmistakable. As Willow took it all in, she heard the scuff of a sole upon the pavement behind her and turned to find Buffy watching her, a massive compound bow in her hands. A quiver of arrows hung across her back along with a sword, whose heavy scabbard was tied to a leather thong the Slayer had slipped over her shoulder.

"Hey," Buffy said gravely. The infectious exhilaration she had exhibited earlier had dispersed, and now she was as intense as she had ever been.

"Hey," Willow replied, watching her best friend with concern.

"So you're all set for the spell?"

A wave of uncertainty went through Willow and she shrugged lightly. "I read that alchemy text by Saint Germain and I memorized the spell that seemed like the one you described. But I told you, Buffy. I tried it earlier and it doesn't work. Giles doesn't believe it *will* work."

From where they stood, Willow could hear the wood of the wharves creaking with the ebb and flow of the ocean. In the darkness, the constant blink of a buoy light drew her attention but she forced herself to keep her eyes on Buffy. If the Slayer was right, and gold was Camazotz's one true weakness, their success might depend on her ability to do this spell.

"Giles is wrong," Buffy said simply. "You can do it. As long as you know the secret."

Panic shot through Willow then and her heartbeat sped up. "Which I don't," she said. "I vote for chopping Camazotz into tiny pieces. I gave him a pretty good whack earlier myself. And there was blood! Tiny pieces is a good plan."

Willow would never forget the knowing smile Buffy gave her then. Though it only confused her more, it also helped to dispel the rising panic in her.

"Tiny pieces is Plan B," Buffy said. "Camazotz isn't an ordinary monster, Will. God of bats, remember? Ancient Mayan deity. The tiny pieces strategy would take him out of the game for now, but he could easily come back again later."

"And probably would," Willow admitted. "Mainly 'cause being chopped into tiny pieces tends to annoy the deities."

"That it does," Buffy agreed. "You can do this, Will. You can."

"As long as I know this secret that I don't know."

"I do."

Willow stared at her.

"It won't work if you're doing it for personal gain," Buffy said.

"That makes sense," Willow admitted. "But back at Giles's place, I wasn't doing it for me. I was doing it 'cause you told me to."

"But in the back of your mind, you had to be aware that a big hunk o' gold could buy a lot of hats and shoes."

A twinge of guilt went through Willow. "And books. Don't forget books. But that's not fair. I mean, I wasn't really doing it for personal reasons. How can you not at least be aware of the potential value of gold when gold is what you're trying to make?"

Buffy offered a small smile in return. "Now you see why no one believes in alchemy."

"So how am I supposed to do this spell?"

"When the moment comes, you'll do fine."

"I'm glad you have faith in me, but what if you're wrong?"

Buffy glanced past her, toward the vehicles. "If I'm wrong, it looks like we're prepared for Plan B."

Over at the van, the others were almost completely geared up. Everyone wore black except Oz, who was still in the New York Yankees game shirt he had been wearing earlier. Xander had a pillowcase over his shoulder that made him look like the biggest kid in the neighborhood out trick-or-treating. Anya cradled a pair of crossbows as though they were an infant whose diaper she did not want to change. Oz and Giles carried the weapons they had all used earlier.

The sword that hung across Buffy's back was different. In the shadows of the night, Willow had not recognized it at first, but now she had a glimpse of the scabbard and saw that it was the same sword with which Buffy had stabbed Angel more than a year before.

"I thought you were never going to use that sword again."

"It seemed appropriate tonight. And it goes with what I'm wearing."

The Slayer began to turn, but Willow called her name and Buffy paused to regard her again.

"There's a lot I don't understand," Willow told her. "And I know you're being Coy Woman for a reason. But tell me this much: the secret to alchemy. How do you know that?"

Buffy smiled. *"You* told me."

* * *

The *Quintana Roo* was moored at the farthest end of the wharf from the harbor master's office, in front of an old warehouse that had been gutted by fire years before and never repaired. She was a cargo ship registered in Mexico but owned by a Guatemalan export company that had gone under the year before. All of that Willow had been able to discover with a quick search of records online.

Buffy had no idea if the ship had been bought or the owners and crew slaughtered, but at this point the question was moot. Though her hull was scarred and plated from numerous repairs and she barely looked seaworthy, the *Quintana Roo* had made it to Sunnydale with the dark prince of the Mayan underworld and his minions on board. In mythology, the demon-god presided over a house of bats, and Buffy could still remember that dark future time when Camazotz had been chained in a dank basement where bats hung overhead. She had a sense that if Camazotz were on board, licking his wounds, he would be in the cargo hold.

But she was prepared for that.

Waves crashed the pilings beneath the wharf and one long end of a rope the ship was tied off with slapped against the side of the vessel with the rising of the wind. The wharf and the *Quintana Roo* both creaked loudly as they leaned together, as if whispering the pains of their age to one another. The overcast sky had mostly cleared and the stars shone down, but the moon was only a crescent, torn in the ceiling of the night.

Despite its stated purpose for docking in Sunnydale,

there were no crates on the wharf beside the *Quintana Roo,* nor any evidence that even an attempt had been made to unload any cargo. Buffy was not surprised. Camazotz might be an archaic leftover from a bygone age, but he had been crafty enough to have one of his Kakchiquels turn the harbor master into a vampire rather than simply killing him. They didn't have to unload any cargo, or even pretend to, if they had him on their side.

But the harbor master was dust now. And as far as Buffy was concerned, in the morning the *Quintana Roo* would just be another mystery for the local authorities.

In the shadow of another ship, the *Sargasso Drifter,* Buffy gathered her forces—her friends—about her. With a single glance she let them all know that silence was a necessity. Carefully she slipped between stacks of cargo crates from the *Sargasso Drifter* and then glanced up the wharf at the *Quintana Roo.*

As she suspected, there were sentries posted on either side of the metal gangplank that led from the deck down to the dock. They stood with their arms crossed, straight and solid.

One of them turned to look toward her. Buffy did not move, unwilling to give herself away, and the sentry looked away again. He had not seen her. But Buffy had recognized him. He had a pug nose and a shaved head and once upon a time she had thought of him as Bulldog. The other guard was a female and Buffy could see now that save for the black bat tattoo around her eyes, the guard's features were painted white.

Clownface, Buffy thought. *And Bulldog. I'd almost forgotten about you two.*

She stiffened. A part of her wanted very badly to take these two Kakchiquels down hand to hand. But that was not part of the plan. And, after all, she had dusted them once before, hadn't she? In that dark future world?

Buffy glanced back among the stacked cargo crates at her friends and found them all watching her expectantly. Aside from Buffy herself, Giles and Willow had the best aim, so she had armed them both with crossbows. Anya had the scimitar Willow had used earlier, Oz an ax and Xander a sword. If they were lucky, they would not have a chance to use them.

Silently, she withdrew a few steps from the open stretch of wharf and signaled to Willow and Giles. As planned, they slipped off through the cargo, away from the water and toward the burned-out warehouse. Buffy then gestured for the others to come forward. There were no jokes from Xander, no protests from Anya. No one made a sound.

Buffy slid along the crates again and peered around the edge of the stack. Clownface and Bulldog still stood guard at the gangplank. Up on the deck of the *Quintana Roo,* nothing moved. Buffy reached up and slid a single arrow from the quiver on her back. Most arrows bore metal tips but these were all wood. She fitted the notch at the back of the arrow to the bowstring, took aim and waited.

Patience was the order of the evening. Patience, and silence.

A sudden loud bang echoed inside the ruined warehouse.

Bulldog and Clownface both glanced around immediately. They conferred in whispers and then Bulldog began to walk toward a boarded-up door in the dilapidated structure. He moved like a predator, ready to pounce at any moment.

When Bulldog was perhaps a dozen feet from the front of the building, Buffy whistled at Clownface. The vampire's head whipped toward the piles of cargo crates where Buffy and the others hid, then she glanced at Bulldog. Uncertainty clouded Clownface's features. She turned toward Buffy.

That was all the Slayer had been waiting for. She drew back the string on the compound bow and let the arrow fly with such force that it went all the way through Clownface and *thunked* into a wooden piling behind the vampire. Her white-painted eyes went wide and she glanced down at the small hole in her chest even as she disintegrated, her ashes swept away by the ocean breeze.

Buffy glanced over to see Bulldog six feet from the door. At the sound of her arrow striking wood, he lifted his head slightly. Before he could turn, a crossbow bolt shot between two slats in the boarded-up door and Bulldog was dust as well.

"Yes," Xander whispered behind her.

With a grin, Buffy put a finger to her lips to shush him, and then she led the way out from behind their cover and across the wharf toward the *Quintana Roo*. The creaking of both ship and dock would cover any sound their tread might make, but she still moved as quietly as possible. Moments passed before Willow and Giles emerged from the ruined warehouse and then they were hurrying to the bottom of the gangplank to meet up with Buffy and the others.

The Slayer led them up the gangplank. Xander still carried the pillowcase she had insisted he bring, but Buffy took it from him now. Though they tried to be quiet, feet on metal were bound to make noise. Still, she expected that any sounds would be attributed to the sentries rather than intruders. Camazotz had trained his Kakchiquels to be fearless, but that had made them arrogant as well.

The deck of the old cargo vessel was deserted. Buffy raised a hand and gestured for Xander, Anya and Giles to go to the opposite side of the deck, and she stood with Willow and Oz until the others had taken their position. She handed Oz the pillowcase and he removed its contents, a dozen small round balls whose long wicks had been meticulously tied together. Buffy slipped a hand into her pocket and gave him the silver lighter she had brought.

Then she notched another arrow in her bow.

Again, she whistled. A shout would have brought vampires running. Instead, the whistle was meant to produce idle curiosity. After a moment, when there was no response at all, she whistled once more. To the fore and aft there were doors leading belowdecks. From what Willow had determined of this class of merchant ship, one led to the galley and crew's quarters and the other to the cargo hold.

Finally, a Kakchiquel face emerged from the door on

the left. Giles was nearest and he fired the crossbow the moment he had a clear shot. The vampire exploded in a cloud of ash. Another appeared seconds later from the cargo bay door and Willow took him out. Buffy had seen the power of her compound bow and so she held off, not wanting to make too much noise.

Over the course of the next several minutes, five other Kakchiquels were dusted in that fashion. During that time, Buffy could see Xander fidgeting impatiently. Nine dead. There was no way to know how many more of Camazotz's lackeys there were, and even a long, loud whistle brought no further inquiries. Buffy shot a glance at Giles across the deck and he nodded once.

The Slayer pointed toward the galley door to indicate that they should watch it, then she gestured for Oz to light the massive twined wick on the bouquet of colorful smoke bombs Xander had left over from the last Fourth of July. Buffy kept her bow aimed at the cargo bay door and nodded. Oz left his ax on the deck and ran, the twist of wicks sparking and hissing. He threw the smoke bombs down the stairs and into the hold.

Buffy held her breath.

They did not have long to wait. Cries of alarm rose from below as the smoke began to spread. Those shouts were followed by a horrible screeching and a flurry of hundreds of small, leathery wings. A few bats emerged almost immediately, wings beating the air furiously, and then the rest followed in a dark cloud of vermin.

Across the deck, even in the dark, Buffy could see the anxious expression on Giles's face. The others all stood at the ready, fearful of the bats. Behind her, Oz lit a package of firecrackers and threw them, fuse hissing, to the deck. The bats had begun to circle above, angry and curious and at least partially driven by the sinister intentions of their god, Camazotz.

The firecrackers began to explode. At Buffy's side, Willow flinched. The bats screeched again and fluttered off into the darkness over the ocean in search of quieter places to roost.

But they were the least of Buffy's concerns.

Even as the firecrackers popped and tiny explosions echoed off into the night, the battle began in earnest. Kakchiquels raced up from the cargo hold, their tattooed features contorted in the hideous visage of the vampire. They did not have to breathe and so the smoke was more a nuisance than an actual problem, but they were to protect their master and so they burst out onto the deck in a murderous rage.

More spilled from the opposite door, ascending from the crew's quarters. Six, ten, fifteen. Far more than Buffy would have thought were still aboard. The Slayer cursed under her breath and shot an arrow through the heart of the nearest vampire. It punched right through him and he exploded as if shattered into burning embers. The arrow tore through the shoulder of the Kakchiquel behind him, who shrieked in pain and surprise.

The ship rolled ponderously on the undulating ocean; the cold sea breeze blew across the deck. Under the starlight, the melee took on a surreal atmosphere, as though this were a secret war fought on the edge of some twilight borderland between reality and nightmare. In a way, Buffy thought that was correct.

There came a moment of stillness, when all was silent save for the ringing of a buoy out on the water and the distant screech of bats high in the air. Then the Kakchiquels began the low chant in their ancient language that had so unnerved Buffy once before. This time, she ignored it.

Another arrow flew, another vampire dusted. All around her, the conflict raged. Willow fired the crossbow at a scarred female Kakchiquel in a dirty linen shirt. The bolt caught in the flapping linen and the vampire descended upon Willow, but Oz stepped in and beheaded the creature before she could lay a hand on the witch.

The combat spread out across the deck. Giles used his crossbow and another Kakchiquel was dust, but then it was torn from his hands. Xander and Anya were forced to defend themselves and they hacked gracelessly at their attackers.

A half-naked vampire with gleaming bronze skin leaped at Buffy, eyes glittering with orange sparks. The Slayer had drawn another arrow from her quiver but had no time to use it. Instead she cracked the vampire across the head with the compound bow. It staggered back, disoriented from the force of the blow, and Buffy used that opportunity to slip up to it and drive the arrow into its chest with a single thrust.

Another was dust.

Still, there were at least nine left, and her friends were not faring too well now. As she glanced around, she saw that they were barely holding their own. Staying alive.

Buffy dropped the bow and pulled the sword from the scabbard across her back. Oz and Willow were faring all right and so she sprinted across the deck toward a cluster of vampires who were menacing the others. Xander slashed at one of them, tore it open from throat to belly, but his attack left him vulnerable. Even as Buffy raced toward him the others drove him down. Anya screamed, but Buffy could not make out the words through the noise of her own furious shouting.

A desperate terror was in Anya's wide eyes and the ocean wind blew her hair back as she brought the scimitar down again and again, hacking at the neck and shoulders of one of the vampires trying to dismember her boyfriend. But the ex-demon was just a human girl now and did not have the physical strength to cut the head off a Kakchiquel.

Giles kicked one of them in the head and as it began to look up, he grabbed its hair in one hand and a fistful of its clothes in the other and propelled it over the side of the boat to splash in the ocean below.

The vampire Anya had been bludgeoning thundered his pain and fury and rounded on her. But even as he lunged for the other girl, Buffy swung her blade in a clean, horizontal arc that sliced through his neck with a wet crunch. Through its dust, she saw Giles haul one of the vampires off Xander, who struggled with another, his sword already buried in its gut, the tip protruding from the vampire's back.

Buffy was about to go to his aid when she glanced at Anya and saw the way the girl's face had blanched.

"Uh-oh," Anya said, eyes wide.

Buffy turned away from the battle just as Camazotz emerged from the cargo hold in a crouch. A dark, sickly orange energy crackled all about his body, leaking from his eyes and from the slash in his chest where Willow had attacked him. His green, pock-marked flesh looked black in the starlight and as he unfolded his body and stood to his full height—easily eleven or twelve feet—Buffy could only imagine how horrifyingly magnificent he would have been at the peak of his strength. The god of bats, the prince of shadows.

"Slayer," the demon-god rasped as he sneered at her. His long tongue slithered out over the rows of razor teeth in his mouth and his piggish nose glistened wetly. His beard and hair were filthy and matted, and she thought he had never looked so primitive. Power radiated from him as though he had ripped a tear in the fabric of reality, a conduit into the demon dimension of his birth. With the exception of his mangled wings and the wound across his chest, Buffy thought this must be the primal visage of the god of bats that had terrified the Mayans into worshiping him in the first place.

The wind died.

The air erupted with ear-piercing screeches as the bats began to return.

With her left hand, Buffy reached behind her back and slipped a stake out of the small sheath in her waistband. She glanced over at Willow and Oz. A pair of Kakchiquels menaced them, but all of the combatants in the melee on the deck of the *Quintana Roo* seemed to have frozen with Camazotz's arrival.

"Willow!" Buffy snapped.

Then she threw the stake so that it struck the deck and rolled up to Willow's feet. The witch snatched it up and stared at Buffy.

"Now would be good," Buffy told her.

Shaking her head with uncertainty, Willow held the stake in both hands and whispered something too quietly for Buffy to hear. Nothing happened. Then the bats began to descend and Willow screamed as they dove at her. She tried to slap them away as one of them became tangled in her hair. Oz batted several away from his own head.

The Kakchiquels began to move in.

"Plan B!" Willow screamed.

No, Buffy thought. *You can do this.*

But she had no choice now. With sword in hand Buffy raced at Camazotz. The demon-god lashed out with a long arm and struck her in the temple. Buffy went down, rolled across the deck and was up again as Camazotz reached for her. She ducked and shot a straight kick up into the raw place on his abdomen where his Kakchiquels suckled for his power. Camazotz cried out at this blow to such a tender area, and she knew then that he was vulnerable.

"You hide it well, Camazotz, but you belong on the Mayan pantheon's injured reserve list," Buffy said, staring at the demon-god as he snorted hot, fetid breath in her face.

Buffy leaped into a high spin and brought her leg

around in a kick to the bat-god's filthy bearded jaw. Several of his teeth broke and Camazotz howled in pain.

"You were a crappy husband and the wife Bobbitted your wings, then took off," she said, filled with loathing for this creature. "You should've let her run. Left her alone."

Leathery wings fluttered around Buffy, a bat tore at her hair and scalp. Buffy slapped a few away and ignored the rest, even as one of them tore tiny claws into her neck. Camazotz tried to reach for her, but he was staggering and Buffy was too fast for him. She ducked inside his reach and drove the sword deep into the wound Willow had already made, then twisted the blade and tugged it upward, tearing whatever passed for organs inside an ancient demon-lord.

Camazotz roared and stumbled backward.

Buffy tore the sword out of him and sliced two bats into pieces as they flew toward her. She ripped one off her neck and stamped on it. Around her, she heard the shouts of her friends, still alive, still fighting, but she could not take the time to turn and check on them.

For Camazotz had climbed to his feet, one taloned hand clamped over his bleeding wound. Weakly, he lifted his other hand and pointed at her, sparks jumping from one claw to another. Buffy had seen him use his demonic power before. Whether it was magickal or something innate in him, she did not know. But it mattered not. As a stream of dark electrical fire arced from his hand, Buffy leaped from its path and the deck of the ship was seared and charred where it struck.

But Camazotz nearly collapsed from the effort.

Buffy raised her sword and started for him, ready to finish the job.

The demon-god raised his eyes. "That you have brought me to this is shameful, for my Kakchiquels are like my children. But Camazotz must survive, and you, Slayer, must be destroyed."

The malformed, withered wings on his back seemed to flutter as though he were trying to fly. Then Camazotz reached his hand out again. Dark fire rippled all over him and leaked from his eyes, but instead of power erupting from his fingers, the reverse happened. The six Kakchiquels who remained alive froze, all of them screaming in agony simultaneously as thin tendrils of orange lightning shot from their bodies and into that of their master. They jittered as though electrocuted.

Then, as one, they dusted.

The ocean wind blew, carrying the remains of Camazotz's minions away over the waves.

Above, the bats shrieked and flew off again, seemingly now freed from their god's control.

On the deck, Anya and Xander helped an exhausted, bleeding Giles. Oz embraced Willow as their adrenaline subsided, the fear that they were all about to die giving way to sudden relief. It was quiet, almost as though it were over. And they all seemed to think it was.

Then, one by one, they all turned toward Buffy. Looked at her, then past her.

Buffy knew it was not over.

Whatever of his power had been siphoned by those

surviving Kakchiquels had been drawn back into Camazotz. The god of bats stood tall again now and his entire body seemed bathed in a crackling orange glow. His mouth hung open in a perpetual hiss, eyes raw balls of fire in his skull. The demon's hair and beard were stiff and standing on end with the electric aura of magick surrounding him.

Worst of all, Camazotz's wounds were gone, and though they were still vestigial and worthless for actual flying, his wings seemed more whole now, less withered. They moved slowly on his back as if in rhythm with his breathing. The dark god moved with reptilian grace and swiftness, swaying in anticipation as he stalked across the deck of the *Quintana Roo*. His footfalls seemed to shake the ship.

In her peripheral vision, Buffy saw the others begin to move, to race toward Camazotz to aid her.

"Stop!" she snapped.

They all paused.

"Buffy, you need our help," Giles insisted.

Camazotz laughed at that, the sound like the slithering of cobras.

"I need you alive," Buffy told him, deadly earnest.

"Are we back to that again?" he asked.

"No," she replied, as calmly as she was able. "But there are still times you all have to stand aside. Back off, right now."

There was a moment's pause in which Camazotz slowly moved toward her, watching them all with dark curiosity.

"The only thing you can do for them now, Slayer, is die first," the demon told her.

Buffy held the sword out to one side and ran at him. Long before she would have reached the demon-god, she leaped high into an aerial somersault that took her a dozen feet off the deck of the ship. Without a weapon of gold there was always the chance he might return for her, but she could still destroy him. The sword whipped around and she slashed the blade down toward Camazotz's skull. Had it connected, it would have split his head in two.

Like a serpent, Camazotz dodged to one side. His arms shot up and snatched Buffy from the air. One hand clutched her throat and the other wrapped around her right arm at the bicep. The Slayer jittered with the dark, draining surge of demonic power that shot through her when Camazotz touched her. Her teeth clamped together and pain lanced through her body, making her arms and legs shake. Buffy dangled upside down far above the deck of the ship. She snatched the sword from her right hand and used her left arm to hack down at the god of bats again.

The blade bit deep into Camazotz's shoulder and only stopped when it hit bone.

With a cry of rage, the demon-god let go of her throat and knocked the blade from her hand. Still clutching her by the arm, he lifted her up, arms and legs splayed, and then slammed Buffy against the deck over and over as easily as if she were a rag doll. Something cracked in her teeth and she bit the inside of her mouth. Blood spilled across her lips, tasting of wet copper.

She could hear Giles and Willow screaming.

Her vision began to dim as she saw Xander rushing toward Camazotz with a sword upraised. She wanted to call to him to stay back but then she crashed to the deck again and her voice failed her. Camazotz swatted him away effortlessly and Xander rolled across the deck.

At last the demon-god simply hurled Buffy away. She struck her head as she landed. For several heartbeats, she blacked out. A second later, her vision cleared and Willow was kneeling above her, stake in hand. Even as Buffy began to sit up, her best friend began to intone a spell in French. Buffy made out the words for gold and fire, but that was all.

Then Willow started back as if someone had slapped her and the stake fell to the deck with a metallic clank.

It was made of gold.

"That was ... I did ... did you see that?" Willow asked excitedly.

Buffy lifted the heavy, pointed shaft of gold and shook herself to clear her head. She shot a sidelong glance at Willow.

"Thanks. Just what the Slayer ordered."

"But ... how?" Willow asked.

Buffy grinned as she advanced toward Camazotz. "I think you're going to be amazed at what you're capable of."

She left the young witch standing there staring after her. Power still crackled in a sheath of lightning that emanated from Camazotz's body. Buffy ached down to her bones, her head felt like her skull was splintered in pieces and there were bloody scrapes all across her face.

All it did was piss her off.

Again, Camazotz darted his head back and forth as she moved in toward him. Buffy held the stake down along one leg, careful not to let the demon-god see it. She stepped even closer, but what she truly wanted was to draw him out; she was not about to make the first move again. Buffy closed in, watching, waiting for him to strike this time.

"You face me unarmed?" Camazotz asked. "You rush to your death."

"Why not?" Buffy asked. "Time to put an end to this thing."

With a hiss of fetid breath and a flutter of bony wings, he swayed to the left and then darted in at her from that side.

Buffy barely sidestepped; his talons slashed her side. She grabbed his arm with her left hand and hauled him closer, pulled him down to her level. Her right hand flashed up and she buried the heavy gold spike in one of those burning orange eyes. There was a popping noise as she pulled the stake out.

Camazotz screamed and clapped his clawed hands across his face.

The Slayer sprang at him, wrapped her legs around his torso and rode him backward. With both hands, she stabbed the sharp length of gold through his chest and pierced his demonic heart.

When she landed on the deck on top of Camazotz, he was already dead.

EPILOGUE

Knees weak, Buffy nearly buckled as she climbed to her feet. She took a long breath to steady herself and stared down at the corpse of the prince of the Mayan underworld.

His eyes were sunken pits now, one of them cored out by the golden stake. The energy that had burned like an inferno within him was gone now, dissipated into the ether or drawn back into whatever nether realm spawned him. But Camazotz was dead, and if the scribblings of a vampire despot who would now never exist were to be believed, the god of bats was destroyed once and for all.

The dead thing had already begun to wither.

Buffy turned her back on Camazotz to see Xander retrieving her compound bow and Oz picking up pieces of a shattered crossbow. Giles, Anya and Willow stood watching Buffy as she walked toward them.

As she approached, a bruised and bloodied Giles

smiled tiredly at her. Buffy went to him and hugged him tightly.

"Ow!" he said sharply. "Cracked rib, I think. If not before, then certainly now."

The man shifted awkwardly, perhaps a little uncomfortable with such an obvious show of affection from her. Buffy did not care. A thousand things went through her mind, feelings she wanted to convey about what he meant to her and how it had tormented her to see him so horribly transformed in that dark future.

Instead she just smiled up at him. "We make a good team," she said. "All of us."

When she stepped back Giles swayed a bit as though he might need her to lean on, but then he straightened up again. "I confess I feared the worst earlier tonight," he said. "In the harbor master's office, I mean. You ought to have run, you know. Left me behind. He'd likely have left me alive as a negotiating tool. The first rule of slaying is—"

"Don't die," Buffy finished for him. "I know. But sometimes you have to break the rules."

"Excuse me!" Xander said loudly as he and Oz strode over, both of their arms laden with weapons. "Not that I want to interrupt the hey-look-we're-alive mushy moment, but how 'bout some rousing applause instead? 'Cause I'm thinkin' we were a well-oiled machine. We opened the industrial-size can of vampire whup-ass tonight, and it was a double-header! We were spectacular."

"Songs will be sung of it," Oz observed solemnly.

"We were the magnificent six!" Xander added.

Oz raised an eyebrow. "Weren't there seven?"

Xander was indignant. "Not tonight."

"Ah." Oz nodded sagely.

Buffy smiled. This was how it was supposed to be. Xander alive and laughing, Anya at his side. Oz with eyes wise and kind instead of wild. Giles, Willow, all of them together. Buffy thought that soon she might have to make a call down to Los Angeles, just to hear Angel's voice. She might not speak, might just hang up, but she would know he was there.

"We *were* pretty amazing," she agreed. "Thanks, you guys. Really. You all really came through."

Anya piped up brightly. "I was nearly killed many times and even helped save Xander's life. I was an asset. I still feel strangely exhilarated by our triumph."

"You were great," Buffy assured her. "You all were. And Willow gets the MVP for pulling off the magick trick Giles didn't believe existed."

Giles blinked and began to protest.

"Ah, it was nothing," Willow said with a broad grin. Then her expression faltered. "Hang on."

As they all watched, she went to the decaying corpse of the ancient demon-god. With both hands, Willow tugged the golden stake free of his chest cavity. She flinched as though he might come back to life but Camazotz was truly dead. Willow went to the far side of the deck and dropped the heavy gold spike overboard. They all heard the splash as it hit the water and sank immediately to the bottom.

"All right, now who's acting like a crazy person?"

Xander protested. "Will, what the heck was that? Do you have any idea how much that thing is probably worth?"

"That's the rule," Willow replied, eyes ticking toward Buffy and then back to Xander. "Alchemy only works if you have no thought of personal gain."

"Well, that sucks," Xander said. "Who made that rule?"

Buffy shivered, the words familiar, an echo of a future that would never be. Her gaze lingered on Xander and Anya then as they stood with their arms around one another and a lightness that was nearly giddy swept through her.

It was an echo, but that was all. That future was gone forever now, impossible. Anna and August might never become Slayers. It existed only in her memories. The memories had begun to dim, but they did not leave her. Buffy would not let herself forget, for she never wanted to take what she had for granted again. For a short time she had thought that in order to achieve contentment and still fulfill her duties, she had to split herself in two, separate Buffy Summers from the Slayer. But she knew now that without all the things that made Buffy Summers unique, and all the people who cared about her, the Slayer could not survive.

Together, leaning on one another for strength, carrying weapons which now seemed so much heavier than before, they left the *Quintana Roo* and trudged along the wharf back to where they had parked. Buffy lagged behind, not because she was more tired than they were, but because she was watching them.

Willow noticed and dropped back to walk beside her.

"You have an awful lot of explaining to do, you know," the young witch said.

Buffy smiled. "I'm sorry I've been cryptic. If it's okay with you, though, I don't really want to go into it too much. Let's just say I had a vision . . . a kind of prophecy, I guess. That's how I knew what I knew."

"How much of it came true?" Willow asked.

The others had gotten even farther ahead. Buffy cast a sidelong glance at her, studied Willow closely. It was a long moment before she replied.

"Only the good parts," Buffy replied. "You know, you're quite the witch."

Willow linked her arm with Buffy's. "You're not so bad yourself. But—and not that I'm knocking it—when did you become Positive-Outlook-Girl?"

Buffy laughed softly. "We're alive, Will. That could change at any time, but right now? We're alive. If we're careful, and we plan ahead, and we back each other up, I think we can stay that way."

They walked on in silence then and rejoined the others in front of Oz's van. It occurred to Buffy that the life she had just described to Willow—a life of constant war, with the ever-present threat of attack from the forces of darkness—was hardly the brightest she could imagine.

But it would do.

After what she had seen, it would do just fine.

THE END

About the Author

CHRISTOPHER GOLDEN is the award-winning, *L.A. Times* bestselling author of such novels as *The Ferryman, Strangewood, The Gathering Dark, Of Saints and Shadows, Prowlers,* and the Body of Evidence series of teen thrillers, several of which have been listed among the Best Books for Young Readers by the American Library Association and the New York Public Library.

Golden has also written or co-written a great many books and comic books related to the TV series Buffy the Vampire Slayer and Angel, as well as the script for the Buffy the Vampire Slayer video game for Microsoft Xbox, which he co-wrote with frequent collaborator Tom Sniegoski. His other comic book work includes stories featuring such characters as Batman, Wolverine, Spider-Man, The Crow, and Hellboy, among many others.

As a pop-culture journalist, he was the editor of the Bram Stoker Award-winning book of criticism, *CUT!: Horror Writers on Horror Film,* and co-author of both *Buffy the Vampire Slayer: The Watcher's Guide* and *The Stephen King Universe.*

Golden was born and raised in Massachusetts, where he still lives with his family. He graduated from Tufts University. There are more than six million copies of his books in print. At present he is at work on *The Boys Are Back in Town,* a new novel for Bantam Books. Please visit him at www.christophergolden.com.

Buffy the Vampire Slayer™

IT'S BACK!

She slays, she sings, she kicks demon butt – and now Buffy's mag is back for round two!

Buffy the Vampire Slayer magazine takes you on a joyride through the streets of Sunnydale and right up to the doorsteps of your favorite *Buffy* and *Angel* characters.

Including:

- Exclusive interviews with the cast and crew
- Behind-the-scenes set reports and photography
- Latest news in front of and behind the cameras
- Reviews of all the latest *Buff*-stuff!

To subscribe, E-mail: **buffysubs@titanemail.com**

or call: **847-330-5549**

AVAILABLE NOW AT NEWSSTANDS AND BOOKSTORES

Buffy the Vampire Slayer™

Giles (to Buffy): "What did you sing about?"

Buffy: "I, uh . . . don't remember. But it seemed perfectly normal."

Xander: "But disturbing. And not the natural order of things and do you think it'll happen again? 'Cause I'm for the natural order of things."

Only in Sunnydale could a breakaway pop hit be a portent of doom. When someone magically summons a musical demon named Sweet, the Scoobies are involuntarily singing and dancing to the tune of their innermost secrets. The truths that are uncovered are raw and painful, prompting the question, "where do we go from here?"

Now, in one complete volume, find the final shooting script of the acclaimed musical episode "Once More, With Feeling." Complete with color photos, production notes, and sheet music!

The Script Book: Once More, With Feeling

Available now from Simon Pulse
Published by Simon & Schuster

Everyone's got his demons....

ANGEL™

If it takes an eternity, he will make amends.

Original stories based
on the TV show
Created by Joss Whedon
& David Greenwalt

Available from Simon Pulse
Published by Simon & Schuster

ROSWELL™

ALIENATION DOESN'T END WITH GRADUATION

Everything changed the day Liz Parker died. Max Evans healed her, revealing his alien identity. But Max wasn't the only "Czechoslovakian" to crash down in Roswell. Before long Liz, her best friend Maria, and her ex-boyfriend Kyle are drawn into Max, his sister Isabel, and their friend Michael's life-threatening destiny.

Now high school is over, and the group has decided to leave Roswell to turn that destiny around. The six friends know they have changed history by leaving their home.

What they don't know is what lies in store…

Look for a new title every other month from Simon Pulse—the only place for *all-new* Roswell adventures!

SIMON PULSE
Published by Simon & Schuster

BODY OF EVIDENCE
Thrillers starring Jenna Blake

"The first day at college, my professor dropped dead. The second day, I assisted at his autopsy. Let's hope I don't have to go through four years of this...."

When Jenna Blake starts her freshman year at Somerset University, it's an exciting time, filled with new faces and new challenges, not to mention parties and guys and... a job interview with the medical examiner that takes place in the middle of an autopsy! As Jenna starts her new job, she is drawn into a web of dangerous politics and deadly disease... a web that will bring her face-to-face with a pair of killers: one medical, and one all too human.

Body Bags
Thief of Hearts
Soul Survivor
Meets the Eye
Head Games
(with Rick Hautala)
Skin Deep
Burning Bones
Brain Trust

BY CHRISTOPHER GOLDEN
Bestselling coauthor of
Buffy the Vampire Slayer™: The Watcher's Guide

Published by Simon & Schuster

Aaron Corbet isn't a bad kid—he's just a little different.

On the eve of his eighteenth birthday, Aaron is dreaming of a darkly violent and landscape. He can hear the sounds of weapons clanging, the screams of the stricken, and another sound that he cannot quite decipher. But as he gazes upward to the sky, he suddenly understands. It is the sound of great wings beating the air unmercifully as hundreds of armored warriors descend on the battlefield.

The flapping of angels' wings.

Orphaned since birth, Aaron is suddenly discovering newfound—and sometimes supernatural—talents. But not until he is approached by two men does he learn the truth about his destiny—and his own role as a liason between angels, mortals, and Powers both good and evil—some of whom are bent on his own destruction....

the fallen

a new series by Thomas E. Sniegoski

Book One available March 2003

From Simon Pulse

Published by Simon & Schuster

Once upon a time

is timely once again as fresh, quirky heroines breathe life into classic and much-loved characters.

Reknowned heroines master newfound destinies, uncovering a unique and original happily ever after. . . .

Historical romance and magic unite in modern retellings of well-loved tales.

THE STORYTELLER'S DAUGHTER
by Cameron Dokey

BEAUTY SLEEP
by Cameron Dokey

SNOW
by Tracy Lynn

They're real,
and they're here...

When Jack Dwyer's best friend
Artie is murdered, he is devastated.
But his world is turned upside down
when Artie emerges from the ghostlands
to bring him a warning.

With his dead friend's guidance,
Jack learns of the Prowlers. They
move from city to city, preying on
humans until they are close to being
exposed, then they move on.

Jack wants revenge. But even as he
hunts the Prowlers, he marks himself—
and all of his loved ones—as prey.

Don't miss the exciting
new series from
BESTSELLING AUTHOR
CHRISTOPHER GOLDEN!

PROWLERS

AVAILABLE FROM SIMON PULSE
PUBLISHED BY SIMON ≡ SCHUSTER   3083-01